ADVANCE PRAISE FOR LANDFALL

"A deeply soulful novel set during the chaos of Hurricane Katrina and the long, moody ebb of its aftermath, *Landfall* recalls Zora Neale Hurston's *Their Eyes Were Watching God* for the strength of the women in its pages, and their resilience despite immeasurable loss. Urbani knows it's only love that truly overcomes catastrophe, that even as we search for the answer to that most elusive question—*Why?*—everything in our lives can always change in an instant, sometimes even for the better."

— Tony D'Souza, author of *Mule: A Novel of Moving Weight*

"From the first sentence, I was drawn into the intricately wrought emotional lives of Urbani's nuanced characters and didn't put the book down until I'd found my way to the end. This novel is as delightful and compelling as it is necessary, broadening the cultural conversation around community, love, loss, and inequity. It's about making human connections, particularly during times of grief. *Landfall*, like the best literature, delivers an expansive, rich sense of humanity."

— Monica Drake, author of *The Stud Book*

"Reading Ellen Urbani's writing is like reading a painting, or a song. It's that colorful and alive. Urbani sweeps you up into her world and carries you through this gripping story about two young women affected by similar tragedies."

— Kerry Cohen, author of *Loose Girl: A Memoir of Promiscuity*

"Urbani has crafted a powerful novel that will resonate in your soul long after you have turned the final page. Outstanding!"

— Garth Stein, author of *The Art of Racing in the Rain*

"I absolutely loved it and rank it as one of the best books I have read in years."

— Mark Suchomel, President, Client Services, The Perseus Books Group

"Ellen Urbani's story of Katrina and its aftermath is an important part of America's modern mythology, a chronicle of one of our greatest national trials. But Urbani's characters reach beyond mythology: two rich and complex young women, two troubled and heartbreaking older women, whose separate journeys and literal collision are unique yet timeless. *Landfall* is a mirror in the floodwaters, showing us our own distorted faces in the murk and mayhem of our recent past."

– Samuel Snoek-Brown, author of *Hagridden*

"Urbani's lyrical voice tells a story that reminds us to look for hope when we're in the midst of tragedy, for connection when we feel lost. And when we do, life just might surprise us. Powerfully told, this story will stay with you long after you've read the final page."

– Ali McCart, PNBA events coordinator

"This is one of the best mother-daughter books ever. ... This book could have fallen into maudlin territory but Urbani never lets that happen. I grew to love all the characters and she does an unflinching job of bringing the chaos, terror, and sadness of Katrina to life in a way so primal and so removed from what we saw on the news. She is a seriously good writer."

– Cindy Heidemann, field sales, Legato Publishers Group

PRAISE FOR WHEN I WAS ELENA (THE PERMANENT PRESS, 2006)

"The writing is gorgeous. While [Ellen's] own story is riveting and bursting with observation, illustration, color, action, and life, the stories of the local women are extraordinary gifts of insight and caring that can make a difference in the way these women, and women like them, are seen. Perhaps understood. It is a book that one stays with, because [Ellen has] not backed away from the razor's edge—which is the truth of [her] own experience."

– Alice Walker, author of *The Color Purple*

"I loved this book. The writing is smart and gorgeous. The storytelling is equal parts sad, funny, insightful, and surprising. I was inspired by this book and also riveted."

– Cheryl Strayed, author of *Wild*

"She records events with unflinching precision, leavened with an amiable sense of the absurd—as when a crone blithely steals [Urbani's] mattress, which is imbued with new value by a white woman's touch. Even the kindness extended to her is riddled with poignant irony, as a neighbor slaughters her chickens to feed the author's ailing dog. "

– *Publishers Weekly*

"She possesses a magical empathy."

– Francisco Goldman, author of *Say Her Name*

"She is an honest observer and her voice is convincing. Her mixed feelings of love and anger at the country are clearly conveyed."

– Kathleen Isaacs, *School Library Journal*

"This is a very rich and disturbing tapestry that I hope will make you think about life outside of our privileged bailiwick where most of the planet's citizens live."

– John Nichols, author of *The Milagro Beanfield War*

"Rich in detail and character, this memoir will have great appeal for anyone interested in Guatemala or in volunteer work."

– David Pitt, *Booklist*

"I had to wipe the tears from my eyes after finishing this wonderful story of war and peace, mostly 'Elena's' peace, told beautifully by her and her female friends."

– Pam White, Skyland Books

"Women's stories so need to be shared, particularly women's hero stories, and that is what *When I Was Elena* is. We need authors who give us our wings; Ellen, as Elena, gives women the notion to take flight. She is a brave and gifted writer with a grand story to tell."

– Susan Chernak McElroy, author of *All My Relations*

LANDFALL

LANDFALL

a novel

ELLEN URBANI

FOREST AVENUE PRESS
Portland, Oregon

Publisher's Cataloging-in-Publication Data
Urbani, Ellen, 1969–
   Landfall : a novel / Ellen Urbani.–1st ed.
     p. cm.
   ISBN 978-0-9882657-7-6
   1. Hurricane Katrina, 2005—Fiction. 2. Louisiana—Fiction. 3. New Orleans (La.)—Fiction. 4. New Orleans (La.)—Race relations—Fiction. 5. Hurricane Katrina, 2005—Social aspects—Fiction. I. Title.
PS3621.R365 L36 2015
813.6—dc23

                                                  2014950267

First Edition

1 2 3 4 5 6 7 8 9

Library of Congress Control Number: 2014950267

Distributed by Legato Publishers Group

Printed in the United States of America
by Forest Avenue Press LLC
Portland, Oregon

Cover design: Gigi Little
Author photo: Gabrielle Urbani
Interior design: Laura Stanfill

Forest Avenue Press LLC
6327 SW Capitol Highway, Suite C
PMB 218
Portland, OR 97239
forestavenuepress.com

Along with virtually every other good thing in my life, this book is a gift from and for my mother, whom I adore.

And with her, my father, who each day gives everything he has for his family.

We are caught in an inescapable network of mutuality,
tied in a single garment of destiny …
We shall hew out of the mountain of despair, a stone of hope.

– Martin Luther King Jr.

I. ROSE AIKENS

"My feet're cold."

FOR NEARLY NINETEEN YEARS, Rose lived with a woman she barely knew. They engaged in all the parallel activities of a shared life
one might expect: Rose did the laundry using detergent Gertrude
bought with the Sunday-clipped coupon at Wal-Mart. Gertrude
laid the heel end of every used-up bread loaf on a chipped sau-
cer beside the sink; Rose gathered the stale remnants and tossed
them to the birds. Rose chatted frequently with the postal carrier
(for whom she left festive bags of boiled peanuts and praline pecans in the locked mailbox at Christmas) and carried in the daily mail; Gertrude opened it. "You won a million dollars, *again*,"
Rose would say as she dropped the stack of letters on the kitchen
table, the Prize Patrol package positioned conspicuously on top,
to which Gertrude would reply: "Sure as the world, I don't know
how these people keep getting my name. Just chunk it; it's junk
mail." Not until late at night—after she'd washed up and indulged
her sole vanity by plucking any encroaching grays from her ash-
blond hair, after she'd paused to listen for Rose's snores from the
second bedroom—would Gertrude fish the Prize Patrol form from

the trash, fill it in according to the directions she read twice, and slide it into her purse to post from the office the next day.

They ate together most nights, always at the table. Gertrude cooked; Rose cleaned up and put away. They used placemats. Both understood and respected the other's food preferences, so that neither anchovies nor blue cheese ever entered the apartment, and either could place the Sunday-night pizza order from Alabama Al's without needing to inquire as to topping preferences. Though the accoutrements never varied, Rose and Gertrude had recently agreed to switch from deep dish to thin crust in a collective effort to mind their figures.

They shared a bathroom. At times a razor.

Neither woman entered or exited the premises without acknowledging the other. As often as not, "Goodbye" was accompanied by "I love you," and they traded kisses every night before bed. Neighbors oozed envy; they pined for such affection in their own relations.

"Now ain't that just the sweetest damn thing you done ever seen," the woman across the way would remark when she peered through her blinds and spied Gertrude offering Rose a taste of the buttery grits simmering away on the stove, or Rose tucking a blanket over Gertrude's exposed feet while Leno light stippled the living-room wall. *I be wanting that life!* she would think as she broke up the day's third fight between her youngest two and bumped bare asses with her husband in their dual rush to pull from the sock drawer her hose and his woolens. She imagined love to be a serene thing and saw it in the purposeful way Gertrude smoothed her hand across Rose's hair as they descended the staircase to the driveway together, and in the languid way Rose leaned across the car seat to unlock Gertrude's door.

Squinting through the venetians while plaiting her little girl's hair, what the jealous woman couldn't see is the *why* behind her neighbors' gentility. They neither fought loudly nor crashed together because such interactions called for an intimacy they didn't share. True, come evening, they curled together on the same sofa, but at opposite ends: Gertrude with an ear to *Entertainment Tonight*, eyes skimming the pages of a Harlequin; Rose's nose buried in Neruda or Nabokov. They had individual dressers in separate rooms; they shared neither clothes nor dreams. They read the same paper, but different sections, and their conversations resembled the headlines: straight facts, condensed, without commentary. They never saw each other naked.

Not anymore.

There had, of course, been a time when Rose was nude before Gertrude with daily regularity and Gertrude, too, had slipped off her clothes with no inhibition. In fact, the very first time she tried to bathe her daughter, when Rose was only a few days old, Gertrude had been unsure how to juggle the soap and the washrag and the baby with no one there to help her, no extra hand to slip beneath Rose's head to be sure the infant didn't slide underwater while she lathered her skin. So she simply climbed into the tub with Rose and cradled the child on her thighs while humming lullabies and washing their bodies together. They bathed that way every night for years, churning up the water with their feet, splashing each other, rocking together in the folds of the white towels. But it didn't last. Eventually the towels got cinched tightly around their bareness, and then bathrobes appeared on the door hooks. Showers on the run replaced the leisurely evening bath. Doors closed.

Though Rose had long since forgotten the contours of Gertrude's body, she maintained, as many eighteen-year-old daughters do, that she knew everything else there was to know about her mother. "You're *so* predictable!" she sneered when annoyed, faulting Gertrude most for her immutability. Rose saw her mother at thirty-seven in loafers, driving a sedan, looking forward to the Friday night meatloaf special at Luby's, and mistakenly assumed that as a teen she'd done those very same things. Acquainted only with Gertrude post-child, unmindful of the fact that she'd arrived tardy on the scene of her mother's life, Rose couldn't imagine a day when "carefree" wasn't a misnomer, couldn't see Gertrude as someone who had ever chewed her hair or walked with a skip in her step.

Gertrude hid her young self well. With Rose still in diapers, she'd torched her yearbooks, hocked her class ring, and took the job at Kinko's because it was the first place to say yes and it paid the rent with some to spare. By the time Rose could walk Gertrude moved slowly and smelled old. An odd mix of chemicals and moldering flowers hovered always about her, thanks to a daily spritz of Beautiful onto wrists infused with carbon toner. But she didn't care; she didn't even notice. Her attention had long since shifted away from herself.

On those rare occasions when her past intruded—when five-year-old Rose drifted past the foot of the bed wearing a yellowing bridal veil ferreted from a shoebox in the back of the closet or when a recipe for something called *canya*, penned in a stranger's hand and language, unwedged itself from page 207 of *The Joy of Cooking* and fluttered to the floor—even then, Gertrude refused to indulge any recollection of her youth. Instead she looked ahead, imagining a teenaged Rose at her homecoming festival, crowned the queen, or a grown-up Rose arm-in-arm with her husband-to-be, a Capstone man, or a senator. She not only expected Rose to do well; she expected her daughter to live out her own abandoned dreams.

So every night while they brushed their teeth together over the single sink, frothing in unison, spitting in turns, they stared at each other in the spotless mirror and saw distorted images of each other reflected back.

What now could change? With Gertrude dead at such an early juncture, Rose's misperceptions wouldn't be easily altered, and Gertrude's would be left to fester in her grave.

THE EULOGIES FAILED TO resonate with Rose. For one thing, she couldn't even identify the first speaker; only afterward did the stranger introduce herself as Gertrude's first cousin on her father's side, in from Atlanta for the affair. That's what she called it—an affair—as if it were less a wake and more an exhibition.

"It's been a bitty bit since your mama and I last talked at each other," the woman said to the side of Rose's head, which didn't turn to acknowledge her. Rose's eyes had settled on the coffin's edge the moment she entered the building and had yet to uncommit themselves. Their deep blue was the sole colorspot preventing her nude skin and austere blond ponytail from disappearing entirely into the matronly black dress that swallowed her body. She hated wearing dresses; didn't own any; had salvaged this one from her mother's closet. It was two sizes too large. The shoulder seams sagged over her ramrod form, which didn't move at all in response to the woman who'd settled into the pew beside her. Not even a wan smile or a purse of her chapped lips.

"Well, okay, you might could say it's been more'n just a month of Sundays since I last bent Gertrude's ear," the woman added, as if Rose had asked for clarification.

The words were echoed by five quick snaps of the second knuckles of Rose's right hand.

From the moment she sat down alone in the front row, and proceeding uninterrupted through the entire service, Rose had cracked and re-cracked her knuckles, first bending her fingers into her palms to pop the big joints, then stretching each finger sideways to snap the second knuckles, then twisting the tips back and forth to flex the connection just below the nail beds. Each digit popped three times, loudly, before she began the whole process anew. Her obsession crafted the illusion of automatic gunfire ricocheting off the coffin and into the apse; it made the mourners flinch.

"Lord have mercy!" the woman snapped, snuffing Rose's hands with her own. "If I'm to tell the God's honest truth it's been about twenty years since Gertrude last rung me up, but—good heavens, honey, you're driving me batty here! It's like trying to pray in a popcorn factory!" She lowered her voice: "You're gonna wreck your hands if you don't stop with that. They'll turn *ugly*. And besides that it's so *trashy*! I mean your mother'd just *die* if she—*Auh-ooh!* Oh, honey, I'm sorry about that. What I meant to say is that if she were still alive it'd just *kill her* to see you—Goddammit!" The stranger abruptly pulled away from Rose, slapped her hand over her own mouth, and stood up. "I'll be praying for you," she whispered as she skittered away for good.

Rose paid her no mind. She did her best thinking while cracking her knuckles. She could go at them for more than an hour if caught up in a real mindbender, and would move on to her toes when the fluid in her finger joints finally petered out. Every major decision Rose ever made, every creative thought, hitchhiked into her mind on a contorting appendage. Gertrude always hated the habit.

"It isn't polite (... ladylike ... in good taste)!"

"You'll give yourself the arthritis (... the osteoporosis ... the bone cancer)!"

"People'll think you're a heathen (... a pervert ... an imbecile)!"

Before they were even fully cooked, Rose's best ideas wound up brewing in a stew of her mother's admonishments.

In the days following Gertrude's death, Rose could hear her mother's reproachments just as loudly while she cracked and cracked, considering how to eulogize her. She cracked for so long that her hands ached when she finally dialed the priest and asked him to please just organize the service on her behalf. Would she be speaking? "No." Did she want to pick the readings, the music? "No. No." What about the—"Really," she interrupted, "I'm much obliged to you for handling it all."

With no other option, he placed all the calls, made all the arrangements, and modeled Christian tolerance of Rose's abeyance. "She's plumb tore up," he murmured in defense of her detachment as people filed past the coffin the daughter didn't stand beside.

In truth, she hadn't the foggiest idea what to say. One couldn't fill a eulogy with a reiteration of a day—rise, eat, work, sleep—and so she found herself short on content. After all, her mother hadn't ever done anything noteworthy, and Rose had no intention of standing before everyone and prevaricating. The assistant manager of Kinko's, Gertrude's underling, had that covered. Gertrude had never liked her assistant. In fact, not a week before her death, she'd come home one night seething at the woman's incompetence. "I swear on all that's holy," she said, "that woman's dumber than a box of hair! She went and made me so mad today that if her head hadda caught on fire I wouldn't even of stopped to pee on it!"

Now here stood the assistant, a woman who'd never crossed Gertrude's threshold, who couldn't name her favorite color or cite her birth date or begin to fathom how she took her eggs, saying things like: "On behalf of all y'all ... profound loss ... so deeply touched my life ... remembered forever." When she snuffled into her hankie the action lent credence to her words, as if in the course of the week between Gertrude's death and funeral they'd morphed into intimates and she authentically grieved.

Death disguised many mundane interactions as intimacies.

They were all there. All the people whose lives merely brushed up against Gertrude's, all the people who, in the course of a workweek, had become accustomed to looking up from their taskmaking into her familiar face with her familiar smile and her familiar dress. In the course of years that drifted into decades, these people had come to recognize her stance, her steady gait, her neutral sartorial palate—everything pressed, loose ends neatly tucked in, sensible shoes polished—so that even if only glimpsed from behind, someone could confidently call out, "Hey there, Gertrude!" and never question that it was she who would turn around.

Her pharmacist sat in the third row, with his white beard neatly trimmed and combed. Every Monday morning Gertrude had wished him "Pleasant week!" when she stopped in for the latest *People* magazine. He could have afforded not to work, she was certain of that, having sold the store his grandfather built, where his father apprenticed, to that Rite Aid conglomerate six years back. But he was still there every day, and that made him an honorable, hard-working man.

Her hairdresser sat behind the pharmacist, the only person in pink, her feet squeezed into open-toed, scratched heels a size too small, but a good bargain. Every six weeks for eight years the pink lady had scissored Gertrude's hair into her customary style:

close-cropped, straight, requiring no product or tools to maintain. "Let's try something a little different," Gertrude would say every third visit or so, but as Pink clipped, with Gertrude directing ("a little shorter on the top ... a few more layers in the back ...") they ended up shaping her hair into nothing more dramatic than a slightly shorter version of the style she'd walked in with. "I'ma *really* liking this," Pink would say as she worked. "You looks just as cute as a bug's nose!" To which Gertrude would reply, staring into the mirror from varying angles: "Yes, yes, I like this. The change is refreshing."

To Pink's far right, along the church aisle, sat Gertrude's co-workers, mostly young kids looking lost, unfamiliar with Catholic funeral decorum, judging whether they should sit or stand by the movements of the crowd, but getting a rush out of being there. One girl with black-rimmed eyes even cried big streaky mascara tears that dripped onto her dog-collar necklace, and when she bent with embarrassment to brush away the evidence her spiked hair poked the head of the elderly woman in front of her, Gertrude's physician's receptionist, who let out a startled screech just as the Responsorial Psalm began.

All these people thought they knew Gertrude, and she them, mistaking their parallel lives for shared existence. Yet she didn't know that the pharmacist's wife had cheated on him four times in the course of their thirty-eight-year marriage, each dalliance lasting a minimum of a year; she didn't know he threatened to leave each time but never did because he had no recollection of an unmarried day and he couldn't cook and he didn't know why or how to sort his laundry. She didn't know Pink had had three abortions and voted a straight Democratic ticket in order to protect her right to have another, but marched in the annual Pro-Life rally and threw eggs at the very clinic she frequented because to do so assuaged her guilt. She didn't even know the physician's receptionist's name. So it goes in small but not-small-enough towns.

And if her mourners were honest, they could speak to nothing more than these facts: Gertrude kept up-to-date on celebrity news, tipped a dollar-fifty for a thirteen-dollar haircut, and scheduled her annual Pap smear on the first working day after the New Year. Still, that gave them more of a connection to the proceedings than the strangers who hovered, gawking, imagining themselves to be familiar with the accident and its participants because the story unfolded inside their houses via the nightly news. Gertrude and Rose had flitted across the townsfolk's television screens every day for a week, after all, at dinnertime and then again at bedtime—while viewers disrobed, made the requisite inquiries as to the nature of each other's day, and fondled their spouses absently beneath the covers. So when the day of the funeral came, the entire community dressed in black and sat behind the daughter, bless her heart, mourning with her, barely suppressing the urge to reach out and smooth her hair in the mother's absence.

In the end, though, Rose walked home alone. There was no mail to carry in. No flower deliveries waiting on the stoop. The answering machine message light did not blink. On the day of her mother's funeral, no one called. That dead light cemented it. Years later, though the idea had first come to her while she sat cracking her knuckles at her mother's funeral, she would always picture that empty answering machine in her mind's eye whenever someone asked her what possessed her to do what she did.

"She was all I had left," Rose would whisper.

So it is that her search for the identity of the girl her mother killed started with a light that refused to blink.

BARE FEET. THAT WHOLE wretched day—the whole pernicious turn of events that ended two lives and sent others into an irreversible free-fall—Rose concatenated with this one simple act: she slipped off her shoes and settled her bare feet on the sun-warmed dashboard.

Then Gertrude sealed their fate.

"Get your feet off the dash," she said. Not a question. Not:

"Could you please put your feet down? I find it so distracting to drive with your little toe prints on the windshield." No, just a dictate: "Get your feet off the dash." And that made all the difference.

The day's errand had taken nearly the whole week to prepare for, and had seemed like a good idea at first. Every day Gertrude had gone rummaging through their bureaus, their storage shed, their pantry, in anticipation of the excursion. She had boxed up all their canned goods and loaded them into the trunk of the car on Tuesday, but was waiting to go through everything, to have a full load before making the delivery, for she prided herself on being well organized. "No sense in going round your backside to get to your elbow," she said frequently, with verve.

By Friday, old dresses plucked from the closet, still on hangers to preserve their shape, lay across the backseat. Suave shampoo and conditioner bottles, on sale for half price as a matched set and, therefore, bought in bulk, lined the floorboards. Atop them sat the unused set of holly-rimmed red hand towels from the office Christmas gift exchange, which were themselves topped by a toilet plunger. Gertrude thought that plunger might be particularly useful, what with all those waterlogged toilets and sinks, and something no one else would think to donate in their rush to flood New Orleans with potable water and diapers in the wake of Hurricane Katrina.

Come Saturday, the car was chock full of miscellany and they were set to make the delivery. Settling into the driver's seat, Gertrude reached an arm toward the back of the passenger seat, looking over her shoulder to reverse out of the parking space. In so doing, she smoothed her hand across Rose's blond hair, relieved to have a day off after a week and a half, happy to spend it good-deed-doing with her daughter.

"*Coats?*" Rose asked as she shifted a pile of old parkas off the passenger seat and onto the floor in order to make more room for herself.

The simple question speared Gertrude—as if Rose had said, "Coats, *you idiot?*"—especially when she followed it with: "Coats.

There's a brilliant idea. People are dying of heatstroke in the Superdome, and you're sending them *coats.*"

Even as it came out of her mouth, Rose wished she could have scaled back her tone, said it without the sarcasm. She understood the effort that had gone into her mother's donation-gathering, and was genuinely excited to help. She'd even augmented their contribution at the last minute. To the box of reading material her mother had amassed, she'd added a few paperback classics culled from her own bookshelves—a bit of Scout and Boo Radley, some George and Lennie, the indomitable Celie and Shug Avery—to balance out the bare-chested swashbucklers and loinclothed Turks populating her mother's books. But the minute she saw the coats and opened her mouth she oozed venom, then blamed her mother for inciting her fury—all because Gertrude had fingered her hair. For the love of God, they were about to have a nice time together—but no!—Gertrude couldn't so much as get into the car without tugging on her ponytail to remind Rose of her shortcomings.

For over a year Gertrude had been riding Rose to cut her hair. "It's getting so stringy," she'd say, eyeing the daily ponytail with dissatisfaction. Not only might a short style give her some bounce, Gertrude noted, it might also do for Rose what Jennifer Aniston's post-wedding haircut did for her: minimize her nose.

Rose liked her nose. She liked the ease of her ponytail lifestyle. She thought Jennifer Aniston looked like shit with short hair. Rose said *"Coats?"* as she slammed shut the car door because her mother's fingertips, in smoothing her hair, had said, in effect, "You're neither pretty enough nor obedient enough."

And now that she'd belittled her mother, she was mad at Gertrude not only for the hair-smoothing gesture, but also for compelling her to speak so hatefully. *I could've been nice,* she thought. *I could've had a nice day, if she hadn't ruined it by touching me like that.*

From there, it nearly came to licks.

They argued first about the coats themselves, with Rose refusing to cede Gertrude's point that colder temperatures would eventually befall Louisiana and its destitute residents.

Next they argued about where, precisely, they were headed with the much-maligned coats and other household staples. Rose insisted the Tuscaloosa headquarters of the American Red Cross was off the parkway, by the mall, but Gertrude held that they should take Bryant Drive past DCH Regional Medical Center and turn in by the Alabama Credit Union. "I give blood twice a year! I'm a giving woman! Don't you go telling me I don't know how to find the Red Cross building!" Gertrude fumed.

"That's the blood drive center!"

"There's a flag with a red cross on it flying right out front!"

"A flag isn't an invitation to deposit coats on their doorstep!"

Gertrude snapped. "Quit talking to me like I'm some field hand who just fell off the turnip truck! Does my skin look black to you?"

Rose gasped and, unable to up and walk away, deliberately turned to stare out the passenger-side window, as far from her mother as she could get. A shunning. In a tone exuding a preternatural calm, she said, "Racist," slowly, as they rolled in the direction of the Black Warrior Bridge.

"Racist?" Gertrude spit, leaning forward and to her right, trying to catch Rose's eye, taking the steering wheel with her. "You're calling *me* a racist? So that Connie West fellow can parade his sassy self on that national telethon and say 'George Bush hates black people' and claim nobody's helping none of those people in New Orleans cuz most of them are black, and here I am driving round trying to give them what all I can and you're calling *me* a racist?" The car slipped back and forth across the double yellow line as Gertrude fought to get Rose's attention.

Rose pointed angrily at the road, her gesture doing the shouting for her—*Get back in your own lane!*—and faced her mother. "It's Kanye."

"What?"

"It's pronounced KAHN-yea. *Kanye* West. Not Connie." Then she reached down and switched off the air conditioner. "My feet're cold."

"Turn that back on, it's almost ninety degrees out," Gertrude said, reaching to turn it on herself, which meant that, as they approached the shoals of the Black Warrior River, they had to argue, finally, about whether or not ninety degrees was truly hot for the first September Saturday in Alabama.

Shoes off. Feet up.

"Get your feet off the dash."

Toes pressed harder against the windshield.

A reach, a swat, to knock them down.

THE POLICE REPORT CONTAINS none of that. It notes that for "reasons unknown" the navy sedan driven by Mrs. Gertrude Aikens, traveling south, veered off the right side of State Highway 69 sometime in the early evening, striking a pedestrian at the foot of the Black Warrior Bridge, before "catapalting [*sic*] down the ravine" alongside the river. The investigating officer surmised that there were no witnesses to the crash, despite this being a well-traveled throughway, due to the fact that "every God-fearing body and his brother's either at the Bama game, or home watching it on ESPN."

It was not, therefore, until 9:45 p.m., after Rose Aikens was found unconscious alongside the highway by three middle-aged men returning from Bryant-Denny Stadium, subsequently arrested on drunk driving charges, that officers were called to the scene and discovered the car and the bodies of the driver and one Jane Doe.

The last notation on the officer's pad reads: "The Tide whupped Middle Tennessee, 26-7."

ROSE REGAINED CONSCIOUSNESS UNDER a crimson sky. Deeper hues of aubergine freckled the vista, until her eyes adjusted and her mind slowly began to process the scene and one of the freckles dripped, proving to be blood on the shattered windshield. Gertrude gurgled her last three breaths and died, seated beside her, while Rose frittered away the first important seconds considering how it came to be sunset already.

She turned then—the gurgling noise, maybe, calling to her—and saw her mother. She looked at her only once, swiftly, before averting her eyes, and would never see Gertrude again, buried as she was in a closed casket that Rose wouldn't agree to peer into. All it took, though, was the one glance to stain her memory. Eighteen years' worth of images of her mother were supplanted by the young and dainty Southern Longleaf Pine, the state tree with the wispy needles, impaled through the windshield, through the driver's seat. It split Gertrude in half with its tapering trunk, a pinecone still dangling from the twig pressed to kiss her ruptured lips.

Rose drew herself into a tight ball on the passenger seat, nose to knees, heels to crotch, arms around shins, and in so doing realized, finally, that she was still in the car, there was a tree in the car, the car was not on the road, her mother was .... Yet Rose—sheltered as she'd been by the airbag—felt oddly okay. Achy and dizzy, but she could move. The blood pooling, cooling everywhere: not hers.

Her feet hurt more than anything else. Deep, deep throbs and pins on the surface. A perfect triangle of glass stuck through the sole of her right foot, protruding up and out between her second and third toes. She pulled her foot toward her face with her right hand, took the edge of her shirt in her left palm and, using it for traction, gripped the shard and wrenched it free. She needed shoes. Where the hell were they? They weren't on the floor beneath her where they had been ... when? ... just a moment ago. Just a moment ago she'd slipped off her shoes and put her feet on the dashboard. Maybe they slipped over toward the ... no! She couldn't look to the left for them. Couldn't look left because ... because! She had to get out of the car. She couldn't stay in the car with ... she had to get out of the car! The dash: red. The seat: red. The roof: red and dripping. *Jesus, fuck, there's blood everywhere! Get out of the car!* The door handle slipping and slick and slopping out of her grip because it's locked but the little lock down in the door frame is wet and red and her hands are so slimy she can't grip it to pull it up and the automatic lock release is on the driver's side across … across … *fuck it!* She jumped up on the seat and threw her shoulder against the cracked window glass in the passenger door till the whole plate buckled. Then she put her bare foot on the window frame and leapt from the vehicle.

She landed lopsided atop the other body on the ground beneath her. On the other body's legs.

That's when she screamed.

She'd borne silent witness to all the other noises of death and descent—the gravel spitting and her mother's gurgling and the roar of trees cracking, axles snapping, and metal crunching—but when she lost her balance and crashed down onto a stranger's cracked, exposed shinbones, she screamed to be standing on legs that weren't her own. Even as she fell she began to backpedal, kicking herself away on all fours from the car and her mother and that dead person's legs. Her wounds filled with blood-made mud. About four feet out, spent, she fainted.

THE EASIEST WAY TO escape the accident scene would have been to follow the riverbed. Instead, they found her on the road.

Call it instinct. Call it the effects of a concussion. Call it crazy. Or just say the road was the known path home. Regardless, when she came to, instead of sliding downhill through the weeds to walk along the sandy riverbank, where she might have encountered a fisherman or a boater from whom to solicit help, Rose tackled the steep bank of the ravine. She tried, for almost an hour, to avoid going back for shoes. To the glass in her feet and the mud in the open wounds were added pebbles and thorns and pieces of small twigs, which she would sit down to pick out before trying, over and over again, always in vain, to clamber away from the wreck. She kept her back to it, facing forward, facing up.

When, finally, she capitulated and went back for shoes, for the only pair she had seen and could easily put her hands on, she did so with eyes averted.

She spent the whole ascent trying, trying, not to think about where the shoes had come from.

II. ROSEBUD HOWARD

"Mama, seriously, I think we hafta get outta here."

THE SHOES ORIGINATED IN New Orleans.

To say Cilla Howard moved to New Orleans would be to imply she had a choice, as if the central Alabama weather didn't suit her and she wanted to be closer to the shoreline, or she preferred the exoticism New Orleans exuded to Tuscaloosa's aura of intellectualism. But no. Poor, black, pregnant, unmarried: nuance had nothing to do with her decision.

There just wasn't anyone left in Alabama for her. Being on her own there had been doable, but a baby added complications she couldn't sort out. Her coworkers among the kitchen staff would have helped her, as they were able, being like an adopted family to her, but an infant smuggled daily into the sorority house would have eventually been discovered. Oh, the coeds would have thought it cute, at first—a baby in the kitchen!—and maybe they'd have offered to hold her a few times, during that first week, while she slept. Patting her with their manicured hands, bouncing her around on their monogrammed hips. They might even have snuggled her close, but when the brown baby woke and pursed

its hungry lips to suckle on the sparkling white Greek letters emblazoned across their breasts, those girls would toss her back, dis-
gusted, and that would be that. Maybe a few would make a larger
effort, would come around to the back door, sneak through the
servants' entrance when no one was looking, with a gift: a silver
rattle, an embroidered blankie, a pair of fleece booties with the tag
still attached. Bright-eyed, their good breeding and good manners
would dictate the charade, and they'd say something like: "I can't
wait to have a family of my own; you're so lucky!" or "I left the tag
on in case you got a dozen of these already at your showers and
wanna exchange it" or "Babies are truly a gift from God! Your life
must feel so complete now!" But no sooner would the words escape their mouths than their eyes would notice the flour on Cilla's
dress, her drooping hem, the scouring pad in her hand, the charred
industrial pan at the sink and—poof!—goodbye pretense. She was
too much someone they were happy not to be.

Even those sweet ones would have complained, eventually,
when the baby cried. Babies always cry. Then they'd voice their
dainty discomfiture to the housemother, or, worse, their parents,
and Cilla would be barred one morning at five o'clock when she
arrived to mix the pancake batter. Told to go, never to return, like
had happened to Ada May when that pretty blond cheerleader
found a coarse black hair in her drinking water and pointed out to
her daddy that just the day before Ada May had been seen polish-
ing the silver place settings without a hairnet on.

Better to leave because you choose to than to be forced out. So
after her man killed himself, buried in a grave no one knew to tell
Cilla the location of, she left in search of the only family she still
had, her sister in Louisiana.

She arrived in New Orleans desperate.

Hard to believe, but nearly twenty years later her daughter
left New Orleans even more so. Classified runaways—Cilla in
1986, Rosebud in 2005—neither was ever officially found. Neither
was ever officially searched for. Just two more missing black girls
in a South that's full of them. In truth, however, neither ran away

from anything; neither had anything left behind to run from. Both ran *toward*.

Cilla's daughter, Rosebud, almost made it, too.

Before Gertrude stopped her, before Gertrude killed her, Rosebud had covered nearly six hundred miles in less than seventy-two hours and oozed gratitude every minute for the presence of mind that had compelled her to grab her sneakers as she fled.

ROSEBUD PREFERRED TO GO barefoot. Except in the coldest of months, she and her mother both opted to pad around the Lower Ninth Ward shoeless, hands clasped as they walked and talked their way through their daily post-dinner stroll. Cilla initiated the routine shortly after her daughter's birth, as a means of grounding them in their new neighborhood while filling her empty evening hours. Everyone stops to coo over a swaddled baby. The matriarchal gray-haired marraines dispensed advice on hiccup cures and sleep schedules, while her twenty-something peers—many already trailing a whole passel of fatherless babes—suggested Boudreaux's Butt Paste for diaper rash and vinegar/alcohol drops to prevent ear infections. But it was the corner grocer whose words reverberated forever in their lives. "Babies're the kinda blessing what'll make your life downright rosy," he said in passing.

"That right. You my Rosy girl," Cilla cooed against her baby's warm cheek as she sauntered past the store that night, and Rosy is the nickname that stuck.

As Rosy grew up, those nightly walks became their sacred ritual—a chance to swap stories of their separate days, tease out secrets, spy on strangers. They thrilled to peer through the back-lit windows of the clapboard houses crowding the street; enjoyed catching someone high-stepping to a radio's funky groove, or judging a cook's proficiency by the number of times she upended the Tabasco over her frying pan.

Anyone similarly observing Cilla and Rosy might have pegged them as sisters, the way they leaned together and giggled.

Beautiful ebony-hued sisters. Cilla, a petite and disheveled version of *American Idol* winner Fantasia Barrino, all sass and booming voice; Rosy, her fairer and more statuesque twin. At five-foot-five, Rosy had a couple of inches and a cup size on her mama, and though she lacked Cilla's dreads and beignet belly they were an otherwise matched set: sinuous of limb and light on their feet; round faces sporting even rounder eyes (nearly black but streaked with gold, like lightning eruptions in a midnight sky); cocoa lips plumped in perpetual pout, naturally glossy. At rest, every feature fought for attention. But when they smiled their high cheekbones took over, rouge balls bouncing above mouths wide open in laughter, heads thrown back, nothing hidden. Such geniality inspired people to josh along with them. Catching strangers' eyes Cilla or Rosy would sing out a friendly "Where y'at?" from the banquette, and Fats Domino himself once called out "A'right" and waved back at them from his pink Cadillac as they crossed St. Claude on their way toward the levee.

Rosy cherished that sense of community even among strangers. "Makes me feel like we're not so alone in the world," she'd often say as the sound of cheering fans wafted over from Holy Cross's sporting fields or a steamboat's calliope greeted them at the bank of the Mississippi.

"Rosy girl," Cilla would assure her as they turned toward home, the night heavy with the scent of pomade and vetivert, "this here the heart and soul of poor black Louisiana. These're our kinda people. You ain't never got no cause to go feeling lonely round these parts!"

But Rosy knew what a neighborhood would and wouldn't tolerate; she knew it was really just the two of them the minute they crossed their threshold.

Before the water's levee-rush obliterated their shotgun house, that threshold was distinguished by two pink plastic milk crates pilfered from the street one day when they bounced off a delivery truck and into the yard. They stood stacked, one atop the other, to the left of the doorway. Open ends facing out, the makeshift cubbies sheltered the shoes that never made it into the house: a single pair each of flip-flops, sandals, sneakers, and scuffed black heels. Something for every occasion. All were seven-and-a-halves to accommodate both Rosy's size-seven feet and Cilla's size eight. Given that neither favored footwear, and since they rarely donned it at the same time, Cilla tolerated her pinched toes and Rosy her slipping heels in exchange for the money they saved by sharing shoes.

Cilla developed the shoeless habit early on, when she began cleaning other people's houses. She learned straightaway not to track anything in, given that it would only complicate her workload. That, at least, is how she justified it. Easier on the ego than the truth: the gentrified society she served preferred servants who knew their place. Shoes at the back entry. Hair in a net. Starched white uniforms. These things made her days easier, brought a relaxed smile to the pale faces she served. Shod, they watched her warily, pointing out spots she missed and scooping their loose change into clasped wallets. Unshod, they offered her a glass of water, asked after her daughter. There was something about a barefooted black woman in their homes that filled the Garden District residents with an inherited, atavistic comfort.

Which is why she came, over the years, to reject shoes almost entirely.

Old man Silas, who owned and managed the corner superette—the same man who'd inspired her daughter's nickname—rode her about it every day for years.

"Evening Silas," Cilla would say when she stopped by the store at the end of each workday, shucked shoes in hand, trolling for dinner. "Catfish will ya?"

As he leaned into the meat counter, weighing in his hand the prescribed amount for two, Silas would reply, "Evening Cilla. Shoes will ya?"

Another day, by way of greeting, her "Where you hiding that mac 'n' cheese, Silas?" would be met by his "Where you hiding your shoes, Cilla?"

Her "I see you still ain't ordered what ice cream flavor I done asked you for" inspired his "And I see you still ain't done nothing about your bare-ass feet."

If she came in and headed directly down the aisle, hidden behind the cereals and candies on her way to the seasonings, Silas could gauge her mood and modify his scoldings based on the heft of her footfalls. The months of lighthearted padding allowed for some flirtatious banter; at her most playful, she'd hoist a foot up onto the counter as she paid, toes painted in rainbow hues, a different color on each digit, and he could act the part of a fifty-years-younger man by exclaiming, "Cilla, you hussy you! Go on now and get yourself outta here with those Jezebel feet of yours." She'd laugh and ignore him, inhale her sweet tobacco fumes, blow them over his head. The months of heavy footsteps, her dark days, left him begging without any response whatsoever from her: "Come on now, Cilla. Mind the rules, why ain'tcha? Put some shoes on them there feet, girl."

For years it went on that way, as inviolate a wrap-up ritual at the end of her days as were the early-morning routines that initiated them. Eight o'clock on the nose: drop Rosy across the street with dear old Maya who, from the moment of Rosy's birth, had cared for her as any good nannain would. Eight-twelve a.m.: stake out the street corner and stare down the causeway in search of the bus. Eight-fourteen a.m.: let the *clink clink clink* of the coins carry her away.

Every day began and ended in precisely the same way.

Which is why, had Silas been someone who paid attention to such matters, he'd have known something was different simply by noting the clock. On the day the banter ended, Cilla strode into his store before the morning milk delivery. In the 98-degree heat she wore six layers of clothing, with a coat over the top, and more makeup than a French Quarter whore. She'd tottered over to Maya's house first, unsteady in the black heels, and if Maya hadn't been more concerned about separating Rosy from her mother, in shielding the child from the scene, she would have chased Cilla down the street and accosted her as she headed, ranting, away from the bus stop and toward Silas's store. As it was, Maya kept watch over her from the open window, and when she turned into the superette Maya dialed Silas's number thinking to tell him to corral her, calm her down, give her a cup of coffee—could she be drunk?—but the line only rang and rang.

Blame age-addled vision, blame the Saints who lost the night before with a last-minute fumble that Silas was still replaying in his mind, blame the phone that started ringing the minute Cilla entered the store and drowned out the unaccustomed click of her heels on the floor. Whatever the reason, habit or distraction, Silas saw her and called out, "Shoes, Cilla!" before he registered any of the irregularities, and by the time he did a double-take the black pump was already off her foot and spinning through the air in his direction. He turned back toward her just in time for it to strike him dead-center in the forehead, snapping his head back against the shelf edge, which is how he came to fracture his skull and land, unconscious, on the floor behind the register.

It took some doing for the neighbors to talk Silas out of pressing charges, though by the time he left the hospital Cilla'd already been involuntarily committed for observation and treatment by judge's order, and the rampant gossip regarding her insanity made his humiliation easier to bear. Maya's insistence that the child must be their larger concern gradually swung his sentiments. He liked the child. Liked how she called him 'Ilas. Credited her love, instead of her lisp, for the pet name.

He couldn't be responsible for jailing the only parent that sweet little six-year-old had ever known.

⋙—

THAT FIRST TIME, MAYA managed to shield Rosy from the sight of her mother being straitjacketed, cinched to the gurney, and hauled away. But in the subsequent twelve years of her life, Rosy witnessed the scene too often. On occasion, she initiated it herself. Placed the call. Led the authorities inside. Every time, every damn time, she'd awaken in the pitch dark of night, her mind having replayed the nightmare of the men manhandling her mother while Cilla screamed and cried and begged not to be taken, and when she sat up in the bed it would be soaked with urine. Six or sixteen, no matter, she wet the bed on the nights they dragged her mother away.

Sometimes, whole years passed between episodes. Whole normal years. Days morphed into weeks and then months of breakfasts together on the red vinyl chairs, Cilla on the ripped one so it wouldn't scratch Rosy's thighs when she balanced her toes on her mother's knees under the Formica tabletop. Months marked by celebrations—jazz festivals or fais do-do or krewe balls—that they would sneak into if possible or listen in on from the curb if not, sandwiches in one hand, doubloons in the other, crowds jostling past them. Cilla would spin stories about what went on inside those events barred to them so that Rosy—with eyes squeezed shut and imagination wide open—could picture raffish women twirling in feathered headdresses as saxophones riffed, and thereby imagine herself more a participant in the joy and less a bystander to it. Easy, as a youngster, to lean into her mother and feel secure amid New Orleans's raucous traffic of tourists and hawkers and showmen; even easier to become so habituated to the security that Cilla's subtle changes passed unnoticed. For young Rosy, the switch from spreading impromptu curbside picnics *under* trees to scaling their branches and picnicking *inside* trees seemed more cause for alacrity than alarm.

In truth, before she knew enough to know better, she experienced Cilla's manic phases as pure fun. Though everyone's mother sometimes skips in parks and dips toes into fountains, only *her* mother could be counted on to skip down the highway neutral ground and dive headfirst into fountains. Before she reached the age of reason, before the onset of inhibitions and the contemplation of consequences, those traits seemed to Rosy to make her mother special. Mania as lagniappe.

All that ended at the gates of Disney World.

Rosy would have been almost eleven, Cilla thirty. The trip started by moonlight.

"Quit playing possum!" Cilla said, jumping on the bed they shared, hands planted on either side of Rosy's cheeks, wild smile full of glistening teeth and ruby lips that reeked of tobacco.

When medicated, Cilla always quit smoking. Couldn't afford the habit. When manic, she smoked. And smoked and smoked. Once, Rosy knew it was time to place the call when she came home to find Cilla sitting Indian-style on the floor in the kitchen, a carton of Lucky Strikes emptied into a pile before her, eating cigarettes. When Rosy walked into the room and set her algebra books on the kitchen table, Cilla glanced up, extended her hand toward Rosy, a smoke balanced on her palm, and stopped chewing momentarily to inquire: "Hungry?"

"Thanks," Rosy said, feigning indifference, "but I just ate."

"Hmm…'s good," Cilla replied, biting the offering in half. "You lemme know if you go changing your mind!"

That day, as had become her habit at these times, Rosy left the kitchen in search of dirty laundry. Laundry always needed washing on days like this, for Cilla customarily emptied the communal dresser, stained every shirt collar they owned with lipstick, and spilled hair dye on the towels and bathmat. Red, this time. But beyond hygiene, the dirty laundry gave her an excuse to get out of the house without sounding any alarms, and it also kept her occupied long enough to miss the debacle at home. She paged Officer Hamilton from the payphone at the washateria.

Years ago she'd memorized his number on just such an occasion. He was always kind enough to send a policeman directly to the washateria with the judge's emergency order so Cilla wouldn't see her review it. Before she began slipping out of the house and hiding out around the corner, the first time she was old enough to initiate the proceedings herself and did so from the home phone, the paramedics made the mistake of handing her a clipboard in front of her mother. She hadn't done anything more than reach for it before Cilla bit a hole in her arm that required seven stitches.

Rosy rode to the hospital in the front of the ambulance, beside the driver who kept laughing, gesturing toward her mother tied up in the back, and saying, "I can't believe she bit you! She really bit you! Got you good, huh?"

As the doctor held Rosy's right hand, elevated, needle poised to pierce her mocha skin, Officer Hamilton pressed his business card into her intact left hand and said, "If it happens again—"

"*When* it happens again," she corrected him.

"When it happens again," the officer agreed, "you go and get yourself someplace safe before you ring us up. No sense in the both of y'all getting carried to the hospital next time. You tell me where you're at, and I'ma have somebody pass by to take care of things for you."

Officer Hamilton was true to his word and also, without fail, instructed the ambulance to approach the house with lights and sirens quieted, a kindness Rosy much appreciated given that it drew a smaller crowd. Mother and daughter suffered embarrassment enough on those days without attracting undue audience. Even Rosy herself couldn't bear witness to it; she sat out the time at the washateria, rereading the detergent labels until terms such as "anionic surfactant" were as familiar to her as her own name. In a place alive with static, it was the shame that clung to her. Even with every empty dryer spinning, as many machines as she could scavenge quarters to activate, her mother's howls still echoed through the neighborhood, cutting through the racket, rending Rosy all over again.

The howls reminded her, every time, of Disney World, of the hysteria at the gates that marked the moment she left her childhood behind to become her mother's keeper.

"Quit playing possum!" Cilla said. "I wanna get up! I can't sleep!" She bounced on hands and knees, straddling her child, rattling Rosy's body in an effort to rouse her. Bounce … bounce … flip—Cilla pirouetted in the air and landed with a resounding *boiiing* on the mattress, face up, staring at the ceiling. "I got us an idea!" she shouted, kicking her feet and clapping her hands. "Come on!

Wake up!" The clock read 11:42 p.m. in glowing red that cast a sinister haze over the wild-haired woman who lifted the deep-sleeping child into her arms and stormed outside. The door hung wide open all night, house exposed, radio blasting, every lamp lit, keys and wallet forgotten on the kitchen counter next to a melting Dilly Bar and eight bags of Popeyes fried chicken, still warm.

Cilla carried nothing with her into the chill dark but her woozy pajama-clad child and a single drumstick.

By the time Rosy awoke in the morning they were on the Florida Turnpike, heading south, about an hour outside of Orlando. For the past eight hours Cilla had talked without cease to the long-hauler who picked them up at the truck stop on I-10 just outside the city at about one o'clock in the morning. After his initial "Where y'all headed?" he hadn't spoken another full sentence to her, and within two hours had stopped even bothering with "hmms" and "uh-huhs." Not necessary. Cilla's commentary carried them across three states with Rosy's body nestled on the seat between them, head pillowed on Cilla's thigh, hair slick with palm oil from six hundred miles of her mother's perseverative stroking. The trucker never asked why they traveled by night, never made mention of their bedclothes, never tried to quiet Cilla's ravings. He'd watched the same silent road for many long nights; her mania proved welcome refreshment. With a wistful goodbye, he dropped them at the gates of the amusement park shortly after it opened.

Rosy did everything she could to stay in the semi. She'd waited her whole life for such a trip, begged her mother every summer to bring her, sulked at her excuses of no time, no money, no way. Yet finally here, she now balked; there are rules of decorum at Disney World, evident even to a ten-year-old. Rosy clung to the door handle, crying "Mama, stop it! You embarrassing me! We wearing pajamas!" even as Cilla wrapped both arms around her waist and wrenched her loose. Cilla pushed their way through the lines, dragging Rosy by the wrist, free arm extended ahead of her to shove people aside, shouting, "'Scuse me, 'scuse me!" as she tore to the front.

Rosy fought her all the way, knocking over a little boy as she jerked loose of Cilla, only to be knocked to the ground herself by the toddler's teenaged brother who leaned into her face and growled "Nigger!" as he picked up his crying sibling and stepped over her. Butt on the ground, face buried in her knees, Rosy felt invisible, wonderfully invisible, and stayed put. Hands over head, curled in a ball, toes rolled under her haunches, she made herself tiny and unnoticed, hidden. The crowd, in fact, folded her in. The line parted around her but came together again on the other side, kept moving forward, each person looking around as if for the others who might step forward to save the child-lump in their midst. A few shrugged at each other: *What to do?* One woman reached toward her, thought better, pulled away. Kept moving forward.

Cilla by then had reached the gate. "Two tickets!" she shouted, only then realizing she had no money, vowing to send a check later. Already perturbed by Rosy's behavior—not even noticing she was gone from her—Cilla's mood ratcheted from belligerent to livid when denied access to the park.

"But ma'am—" the token-taker started out, only to be interrupted by Cilla's rage.

"But ma'am—" the young girl kept interjecting when Cilla took a breath, never getting past those two words.

"But ma'am—" the sweet collegian finally said, with round frightened eyes, after Cilla called her "bitch" and "cunt" and "redneck slut" and paused, for a moment, searching for a better insult "—there's a dress code!"

"You gotta problem with the way I dressed? You not liking my clothes, you white honky ho? This better?" she asked, cackling, as she ripped her nightshirt over her head and stood stark naked at the gates of Disney World, whipping the employee about the face with the sweaty cloth.

Prompted by screams and curses from the crowd, Rosy finally looked up and glimpsed her naked mother through the pivoting legs in the queue as parents spun to bury their children's faces against their bellies. Rosy died. Something died. Her first thought was not to move, to stay hidden, to stay as far away from her mother as possible. She even looked behind her to see if in the confusion she might be able to crawl away unnoticed.

But when a security guard—dodging Cilla's spit, unable to grab her, clawed on his cheek—beat her to the ground with a baton blow to her clavicle, Cilla's howl recalled Rosy's attention.

"Stop it! Stop it!" Rosy screamed, leaping up off the ground and racing toward Cilla. "Stop it! She my mama! Stop it!" she threatened. Not crying, not cowering. Authoritative. The guard actually took a step backward. Rosy laid her body, prostrate, over her mother's, shielding her. From eyes. From batons. Without moving far enough to expose Cilla's body again, she reached for and grabbed the nightshirt, pulling it over her mother's head, smoothing it down over her breasts and crotch. Then she folded Cilla into her arms, where her mother continued to howl in pain, but at a lower pitch. "She my mama," she said, looking up at the guard. Staring him down. "My *mama*. She sick. Call an ambulance."

There it was: their tipping point. Cilla the child. Rosy the adult.

⁂

ROSY FAST DEVELOPED INTO a lay psychometrist and pharmacologist, diligently monitoring her mother's moods and meds, modulating as best she could exterior circumstances to balance Cilla's interior variances. It was tricky work. Took constant care, and vigilance, and calm.

Storms never ended well, literally or figuratively.

Which is why she'd hoped it wouldn't come to this. Had hoped it would blow over. Hated to have to say what she did.

"Mama, seriously, I think we hafta get outta here."

Rain fell in bursts, driven against the windows when the wind gusted, smacking straight down onto the drenched street when it subsided. The house still had electricity.

"It's a Category Five now. Landfall tomorrow. With 175-mile-per-hour winds." She spoke in measured tones, even about a hurricane; around Cilla, anxiety could foment hysteria.

Cilla poked her head out of the bathroom, mascara wand in hand, a black spear pointed in Rosy's direction. "Y'all feeling that 175-mile-per-hour wind? Oh, oh, I feels it coming!" she teased, hanging onto the doorframe, swinging her upper body out into the hallway. "Catch me, Rosy girl, catch me! Else I'ma get blown right on outta here!" At that she laughed and ducked back into the bathroom. She held her tongue for just a moment, mouth wide open, lips wrapped over teeth in a taut O while she applied the second layer of mascara to her left lashes, then her right. Blink. Blink. Blink blink to transfer the makeup to the lower lids. "Girl, you better be putting on your go-to-meeting clothes if you coming with me. The service is for 10:30 and you know Reverend Armour ain't holding up his preaching for nobody." Quick pause, then: "Not even that Katrina of yours!" and she bust herself up all over again.

Rosy slid off the ottoman onto her knees before the TV, listening closely over Cilla's hoots, hands touching the screen, pressing hard on the set, divining portent from the newscaster's coloring. He appeared pallid. Sleepless. It made her nervous. She lifted her right thumbnail to her front teeth, bit it to the quick, and chewed the edge off. Then she turned her thumb over and gnawed on the frayed nail bed while listening to him. She held his eyes with hers, willing him: *Tell me, really, what should we do?*

She trusted MSNBC's Brian Williams more than New Orleans's mayor. The white folks listened to Mayor Nagin, of course, but they ran scared from everything untoward in the city. They started queuing their SUVs in orderly gas lines last night when he dutifully encouraged everyone to evacuate. This next morning, about forty minutes ago, he'd shown up on TV again, looking more frantic, issuing a mandatory evacuation of the city, as if there was any hope of enforcing that. "The storm surge most likely will topple our levee system," he said.

What did *he* know?

But Brian Williams … Brian knew. Look at that suit. It cost money. A man with money like that surely knows what he's talking about.

Suddenly the newscaster raised his right hand to his ear and his left hand in the air, extended toward the camera. Brian had been talking on a live feed to someone from the Weather Forecast Office up in Slidell, Louisiana, regarding their "urgent weather message" when he suddenly had to cut the forecaster off. "I'm sorry to interrupt," Brian said, oh-so-politely, "but this is just in: I have before me a report from Robert Ricks, meteorologist with the New Orleans/Baton Rouge National Weather Service office, issued just a moment ago at 10:11 a.m. Central Daylight Time. I'm going to read this in its entirety."

Devastating damage expected from Hurricane Katrina, a most powerful hurricane with unprecedented strength, rivaling the intensity of Hurricane Camille of 1969.

Most of the area will be uninhabitable for weeks, perhaps longer. At least one half of well-constructed homes will have roof and wall failure. All gabled roofs will fail, leaving those homes severely damaged or destroyed.

The majority of industrial buildings will become nonfunctional. Partial to complete wall and roof failure is expected. All wood framed low-rising apartment buildings will be destroyed. Concrete block low-rise apartments will sustain major damage, including some wall and roof failure.

High-rise office and apartment buildings will sway dangerously, a few to the point of total collapse. All windows will blow out.

Airborne debris will be widespread, and may include heavy items such as household appliances and even light vehicles. Sport utility vehicles and light trucks will be moved. The blown debris will create additional destruction. Persons, pets, and livestock exposed to the wind will face certain death if struck.

Power outages will last for weeks, as most
power poles will be down and transformers
destroyed. Water shortages will make human
suffering incredible by modern standards.

The vast majority of native trees will be
snapped or uprooted. Only the heartiest will
remain standing, but be totally defoliated. Few
crops will remain. Livestock left exposed to the
wind will be killed.

An inland hurricane wind warning is issued
when sustained winds near hurricane force, or
frequent gusts at or above hurricane force, are certain within the next twelve to twenty-four hours.

Once tropical storm and hurricane force
winds onset, do not venture outside!

Fucking hurricane, Rosy thought. Six months before, notified
that she'd won a full scholarship to Tulane, a classmate had asked
if she was going to accept it. "Are you *kidding* me?" she'd asked.
"It'd take an act of God to keep me from going!"

Act of God, indeed. So much for matriculating in the morning.

She pushed herself to her feet to go tell Cilla to begin packing
so they could catch one of the redeployed city buses that would be
coming to the neighborhood at noon to start removing residents to
a "shelter of last resort." But there stood Cilla, directly behind her,
hands on hips, smiling.

"Now that some bogus shit," Cilla crooned as she sauntered
out the door on her way to church. Over her shoulder she shouted,
"They nuts if they think I'ma leave my house on account of some
wind!" right before a gust slammed the door shut behind her, cutting her off.

Rosy packed in her absence. She triple-bagged the brown
paper grocery sacks they saved under the kitchen sink for trash,
and filled the four Schwegmann's (two per woman, one for each
hand) with all the practical necessities. She figured two days at
most away from the house, but packed for four just in case. She

sealed Cilla's prescription bottle of lithium in a Ziploc, for added security, and then, on second thought, safety-pinned the Ziploc to a deeply-packed sweatshirt, to anchor it if they wound up being jostled in a crowd. Under no circumstances could they afford to lose the meds. Around the clothing she tucked a flashlight, a Hershey's bar, a nail file, and a pair of earplugs she found in the junk drawer while rooting for batteries—who knew where they'd wind up sleeping tonight? Finally, on top, she nestled her mother's jewelry box. Then she lined up all four sacks by the front door and sat back down in front of the TV.

By dusk, when Cilla returned, eight hours later than expected, carrying a hotpot full of shrimp and roux, trailing company, yelling out, "We gonna have us a hurricane party!" they had missed the last bus and were trapped, prey of disaster, in the Lower Ninth Ward.

III. Rose

"Everyone belongs to someone. Everyone belongs somewhere."

It was Monday, September 12. Two days after Gertrude's funeral. Nine days since the accident. Fourteen days since Katrina's landfall inspired Gertrude to riffle through their closets and sling some threadbare coats across the passenger seat in her car. Rose's feet felt better but her hands felt worse. For over a week she'd been cracking her overwrought knuckles ceaselessly as she worked her plans over in her mind, and she began cracking again in anticipation as she sat still and alone, swallowed by a wooden interrogation chair in the patrol room of the Tuscaloosa Police Department. Everything she intended to do hinged on the results of the next hour. She had to win the detective over, get what she needed from him, and had willingly falsified her nature to sway things in her favor.

She felt like one of those X-rated tramps off the cover of her mother's ridiculous romance novels, despite the fact that her best efforts at dolling up achieved nothing more bawdy than a PG-13 version, a somewhat genteel Dulcinea. Regardless, she willed herself not to care as long as playing the sex card worked.

She'd devised the act because she didn't imagine her authentic self would get her very far with a civil servant; clearly she wasn't going to succeed in seducing the detective with a witty conversation about shared interests. He likely collected guns or some such violent paraphernalia, whereas she collected hardcover editions of Pulitzer Prize and National Book Award winners going back to 1987, the year of her birth, and was halfway through her fourth rereading of the set. Nor did she believe they'd find common ground in taste or style. He probably cultivated a drinking habit at NASCAR rallies, whereas her fascination with Latin American writers' magical realism had prodded her into making an informal study of the visual artists Tooker and Wyeth, which then segued into a fixation on American folk art in general.

She knew that even if he initiated the typical small-talk blather about pop-culture phenomena she wouldn't be able to keep up, as she preferred Sunday's *New York Times Book Review* to television programs, NPR's political commentary to WTXT's Top 20 country, and she couldn't begin to remember the last time she saw a movie. Today was the one and only time when she thought that emulating her mother's false connection to the world—forged through talk shows, Hollywood gossip magazines, and blockbuster reviews— might have served her well. Policemen probably went to movies to relax. If only she had some idea what was playing.

Rose raised her right hand to her mouth and bit into a fingernail, but that quick flinched and spit the hand back out, repulsed and startled by the taste of nail polish. The acrid flavor of the acetate made her gag. Without turning all the way around, she cut her eyes right, left: had anyone noticed? *Relax*, she coached herself: *be cool*. She needed something to do with her hands to keep from biting her fingernails. She put her hands in her lap, smoothed her dress over her thighs, tapped her fingers on her kneecaps. Gripped the edge of the seat, poked old gum dried on the bottom, reached for her hair.

Growing up without a father—he'd left her mother before she was born—and never having had a boyfriend, Rose had minimal interactions with men. In fact, no man besides a super had ever so much as entered their apartment, and then, only twice: once to unclog an overflowing garbage disposal, once to change a sparking heat coil in an electric grate. Deliverymen received a warm welcome at the doorstep but were just as warmly waved away; schoolmates were restricted to relationships at school; neighbors went mostly nameless and unnoticed. Yet all around her, Rose saw women manipulate men daily to their purposes: The lady at the drugstore, staring woefully into her wallet, leaning forward onto the counter in her low-cut blouse and tracing her cleavage with her fingertips as she whispered, "I seems to be a wee bit short today," only to be offered her full purchase and a smile. The cheerleader who balanced her short skirt and bare thigh on the edge of the history teacher's desk and said, "My mama was feeling sick again last night so I hadda cook dinner for my family and then get the little ones into bed ..." while caressing a curly lock, which earned her an A for the missing homework assignment.

Rose had taken their sultry tutelage to heart. She'd called ahead and checked the detective's schedule, then arrived early, twenty minutes before he was due in, to give herself time to get collected. She'd felt farcical traipsing from her apartment out to the street and then again up the public stairs to the stationhouse. Thank God for the early hour and the anonymity of the cab; no one recognized her en route. Her tight dress, over-exposed skin, and free-flowing hair affronted her feminist principles, and her cheeks raged red enough from embarrassment that she'd been able to avoid blush altogether after laying the other artificial colors onto her face. But as she sat alone beside the detective's desk, awaiting his arrival, having found something productive to do with her hands, she relaxed. Felt emboldened. *It'll all be worth it,* she thought as she adjusted her décolleté, *if I can get him to open the dead girl's file for me.*

Detective McAffrey arrived at the station fifteen minutes early that morning, as he often did, to study his schedule in peace before the raucous change-of-shift. "Hey Mac!" the desk clerk greeted him in the anteroom. "You got one fine-looking chick waiting inside!" The man leaned over the far side of his cubby to peer with Mac through the doorway at the young woman sitting with her back to them at the far side of the room. McAffrey eyed the woman's blond hair trickling around the zipper of her pink floral sundress. The girl twirled one loose lock over and over again around a freshly manicured fingertip.

"Ain't you got nothing better to do?" McAffrey asked, landing a jocular blow to his colleague's shoulder that bounced the fellow back behind the reception desk as he strode into the patrol room. As he walked, McAffrey smoothed his uniform over his barrel chest and sucked in the beer belly he'd lately accumulated. Gotta admit, the woman sure was a sight, but it was her scent that did him in. From five feet away, he could smell her. She smelled like Easter. Or vanilla. No, a lemon cake. She smelled like something he might want to lick. The thought startled and aggravated him. He wasn't that kind of man, not anymore. He was better than that. *Jesus Christ*, he admonished himself, *get a grip!*

It had been a long time. As a younger officer, he'd had a reputation among the local cops as quite the playful rogue, a serial bed-hopper, never one to leave a party or bar without a trophy on his arm. But by his mid-thirties he began to feel emptier after each successive one-night stand, and by forty he judged his conquests as desperate and himself more so. So by the middle of that decade he'd resigned himself to singledom and wedded himself to other passions. He fished, he home-brewed a lager with a devil's kick, and when he made detective he took up the cause of child abuse with a vengeance. He had the best track record in all of Alabama for putting pedophiles behind bars, and had reopened—and subsequently closed—more cold cases involving murdered children than anyone else in a five-state radius. Kids were his special cause.

Still, the silhouette of such a well-scented woman aroused in him the sensations of that twenty-years-younger man.

Rose had spent almost an hour meandering around the make-up counters at Parisian's the night before, choosing a perfume, hunting for something with a touch of cinnamon, vanilla, lavender, and frankincense, the bouquet deemed "most likely to invite intrigue." For some reason, that information had lodged itself in her memory one long-ago evening despite her efforts to ignore her mother's habit of reading aloud one smarmy article tidbit after another from the women's magazines she bought weekly at Rite Aid. Those rags were, to Rose's mind, a profligate waste of resources outdone only by those blasted Prize Patrol packages. "Every dime you spend on those is a direct contribution to the dumbing-down of American women!" she would huff.

"Oh yeah, Little Miss Nose-So-High-in-the-Air-You'd-Drown-in-a-Rainstorm?" Gertrude once responded. "Well then tell me this: can *you* name the four scents most likely to invite intrigue?"

Rose had sniffed so many perfumes while wandering through the department store last night she'd awakened with a headache this morning. In the end, she went with a fragrance that reminded her of sipping lemonade in a garden with a cookie in her pocket. "My boyfriend likes that one a *lot*," the salesgirl said with a wink. "Now you know where to put it, right, to get them boys really going?"

Rose had no idea. She didn't date, didn't go to the university, didn't get her hair styled. She wore sunscreen and a ponytail and planned to double up on classes at the community college before transferring to the university in order to get her undergraduate work over with quickly; she already had her heart set on an MFA residency at the Writers' Workshop in Iowa. Her best friends were her books and a cozy pair of sweats. She smelled like soap. "Gimme your wrist," the girl instructed, spritzing perfume there and behind her ears and into the air over Rose's head so the misty beads settled into her hair. When Rose mentioned she also needed a dress, the salesgirl pointed into the mall and said, "The sexiest selection is in that store cross the way."

Detective McAffrey's initial response when he circled around in front of her and extended a hand in greeting made her think it had all worked. He actually gasped. She took his proffered hand in hers and squeezed it intimately between her two palms while he stared at her. He had a powerful handshake but a gentle face—more round and jolly than chiseled—and advancing age had added jowls and laugh lines that softened his imposing stature. When she flashed her lipsticked smile at him and asked to see the dead girl's personal effects his hand went clammy, but he never asked What? or Why? or even scanned the room to see if anyone noticed his impropriety. He just retracted his hand from hers, reached into his desk, and handed the documents to her as if he regularly passed out crime victims' possessions in response to sincere inquiries, as if it were ethical. "This is … um … all she had on her. When we, uh"—and here he cleared his throat like a nervous boy, and dropped his gaze, sorry to have to say it—"pulled her body away from the car." He paused, waiting to see if Rose would react. But she kept looking at him. Steady. Supplicant. So he continued. "I mean, she had no other ID on her. No money other than a few coins. Nothing besides this business card, this page from the phonebook, and this receipt from City Cafe."

The sensual jolt that had surged through him on his approach, his eyes on her back, dissipated the second he circled his desk, faced her, and recognized Rose as the girl from the accident scene. No honorable man can shelter a girl in his arms—neither a swaddled infant of one's own, nor a young one scooped up, bloody and pliant, from the roadside gravel on a late summer's night—and ever think of her as anything but a daughter again. That instantaneous change in perspective—from sexual to fatherly—so flabbergasted him that he didn't think, just reacted, when she asked to see the dead girl's things.

He'd had a chance, once, to be a father. Didn't know it till a year after the woman aborted, when she casually mentioned it while rising from the hotel bed they'd made a habit of sharing annually at the national law enforcement conference. He couldn't blame her, really, but neither did he ever speak to her again, and he shocked and humiliated himself by sobbing in the shower after she left. He swore after that he wouldn't think about it again, and hadn't for many years, never equating the fervor with which he worked the missing-children cases with any longing to recoup the child he himself had lost. But the older he got, and the more resigned he became to his aloneness, the harder he had to work to stifle his regrets.

And then he discovered Rose's body on the side of the road. When he'd lifted her into his arms and whispered, "Hold on, sweetheart, help's coming," it struck him that she could have been his daughter, that if the baby had lived it would have been this girl's age, and he held her as if she were in fact his, warm against his chest, stubbly cheek shielding bruised face, guaranteeing her safety in his well-muscled arms. He hugged her in a way he'd never embraced a female, all his familiar urges supplanted by the same startling surge of protective, paternal emotion that had humbled him in that hotel bathroom two decades earlier.

It disoriented and upset him now to see the girl flip her hair around, coaxing her curls toward her cleavage with too-bright fingernails as she spoke to him.

"I saw the news, that first night in the hospital," she said. "They called her 'a Jane Doe runaway.' But how do you know she's a runaway? What tells you she's not from round here?"

More than anything, he felt sorry for her. She was a week behind on her news and he couldn't imagine how she'd managed to cloister herself enough to avoid updates on the biggest story in the city that week: herself. *God*, he thought, *this girl must be so lonely*. It worried him. Made her suddenly seem like a child in need of sheltering. She was, after all, still just a teenager. He reached out his hand to comfort her, but recoiled when she leaned her shoulder seductively into his outstretched palm. "Please stop," he said. She lurched from him, and flushed a deep red from her cheeks to her chest, but he went on, gently: "I wanna help you. I wanna help you because you *deserve* to be helped. That's all."

Then he lifted a navy sweatshirt, standard-issue, from the back of his chair and handed it to her. "They always crank the

AC way too low in here if you ask me," he said. "You gotta be chilly in just that dress. Why don't you go ahead and put this on?"

Rose obeyed. She set the small pile of evidence on McAffrey's desk while she pulled his sweatshirt over her head and loosed her hair from under the collar. Before rolling the cuffs up to liberate her hands, she scooped the paperwork back into her lap and leaned over it covetously. But he had no intention of taking it away from her. He merely sipped his coffee, allowing her time to look it over.

A stranger's business card and a local restaurant receipt fluttered into her lap from within the folds of the ragged-edged phonebook page when she lifted it and uncreased it. She flipped the White Page back and forth, checking to see if there were any markings, any names circled, any clues. Nothing. She had just begun to refold the paper, shifting her attention away from the anonymous list of alphabetized names, when she realized, with a start, which one of the hundreds of phonebook pages she held. She dropped the paper as if it had scorched her skin, but just as quickly grabbed it from the air as it fluttered toward the floor. It was a sign. She knew it. She didn't need a sign, but it was a sign.

She scanned the list with her right forefinger, and there it was. There *she* was. G. & R. Aikens..........(205) 348-9223. Gertrude and Rose. A single listing among thousands. She brought the paper closer to her face, let it speak to her. She heard it, loud and clear: "You're meant to find me."

McAffrey watched her carefully, taking another long sip from his thermos, recomposing himself. *Her bruises are healing well,* he thought. *Black eyes almost gone. She's actually pretty in daylight, cleaned up, in spite of all that makeup she's piled on.* But the longer he observed her odd behavior—the way she dropped the paper, grabbed it back, plastered her nose against it—the more he wondered about the long-term effects of concussion.

"I *did* find you," he said.

Rose looked up at him as if his voice startled her. "Pardon me?"

"I did find you," he said. She furled her brow and glowered at him as if he were insane. "Well, okay, actually it was the Burns brothers and that Justice kid what found you, but I was first on the scene. Called you an ambulance. You don't remember?"

"What're you talking about? Why're you telling me this?" she asked.

He shook his head. Frustrated, he replied, "You're the one just said, 'You're meant to find me,' and I'm just saying I did."

"Oh. Oh, right." Rose hadn't realized she'd spoken aloud. How embarrassing. "I'm sorry. Of course, Officer." She was scared she'd pissed him off even more now—first the silly sexy subterfuge, then that damn tone of hers—and had screwed everything up. Her face crumpled. She'd ruined too much already this week to ruin this, too.

Her look killed him. He felt a swell of pity for the girl—injured, orphaned, obviously confused. "Okay. How about we just start over," he said kindly, stepping closer and leaning on the edge of his desk nearest her. "Why're you here, darling? Why do you care so much about that girl?"

His sincerity startled her. Where at first she had shied from him, embarrassed by his ability to see through her behavior so quickly, his subsequent frankness, coupled with his gentle manner, won her back. She decided just to be herself. To trust him with her truth. She'd been so overwhelmed by the need to know the girl's identity, by her contrivances to find out, that she hadn't consciously addressed the why, though when he asked, she knew that she knew. So: act over. She tenderly folded the phonebook page around the business card and the receipt, snugged them between her palms, cupped it all under her chin, and reflexively sniffed at the paperwork, inhaling deeply, eyes closed. Breathing her in. "Because she belonged to someone."

She looked directly at him and tacitly pleaded: *Can you follow me? Will you understand?*

"She belonged to someone, right?" she asked. When he didn't move, she answered herself in a whisper, "Everyone belongs to someone. Everyone belongs somewhere."

The officer narrowed his gaze, intent. He was really listening, really trying to understand.

"But what if they never know what happened to her?" she continued. "Do you know what it's like, never to know? To have whole pieces of what and who you're supposed to belong to missing?"

Yeah, I do, he thought to himself.

Rose lowered her gaze to her lap, fingered the girl's insubstantial possessions, sighed. Then she leaned back in the gargantuan chair, drawing her knees up, heels caught for balance on the edge of the seat, instinctively pulling on the hem of her dress and cinching it around her ankles, for propriety's sake. "On the news every night starting the minute Katrina hit, they began showing the survivors down in New Orleans holding up pictures, pleading, 'Have you seen this person?'"

She looked back at the detective, still balanced on the edge of his desk. "Do you remember that same thing happening after September 11?" She paused, then added, "It was four years ago yesterday," as if a cop needed reminding.

"I saw the towers fall, like everybody else, but there was something so surreal about it," she said. "I might could've imagined it hadn't really happened. But those walls with the faces taped to them, and the way their family members held pictures up to the camera and said, 'This is my son who worked on the 57th floor,' or 'My wife's a broker at Cantor Fitzgerald—have you seen her?' God, that killed me. Every time I saw a face, I'd set to crying. The newscasters would say, 'Three thousand people unaccounted for,' and it meant *nothing* to me, like they were talking about a lost shipment of … pencils, or something … but then a woman would run over with a photograph of a man in a baseball cap, his arm round a friend, with a kinda lopsided smile and big dimples, and she'd point at the image and say, 'My husband …' and I could hardly breathe!

"I can't stop thinking about those people's photo albums— about the pictures they tore out to hold up to the cameras. Imagine the rest of the album. Nothing but blank pages following after.

"You know how they keep saying, with Katrina, that we may never know the tally, or exactly who was lost, or how? What will *those* families' albums look like? No pictures, no answers, no nothing."

She tugged her hands through her hair, pulling it back from her face until she held it all tightly bound behind her in one fist, a makeshift ponytail, and then leaned her cheek into the crook of her bent elbow and stared off across the room.

"Empty pages are haunting," she murmured. "I can't be the cause of somebody's empty page."

They stared at each other for a moment.

"Okay," McAffrey said. "Come with me."

HE TOLD HER EVERYTHING he knew, walked her through it in chronological order as they strolled down the road a piece to Krispy Kreme, where the hot-light turned red on the half hour marking the moment the glazed doughnuts plopped soft and steaming off the conveyor. At every corner, as they turned, he put a hand on her back and gently guided her away from the curb, moving her away from the sidewalk's edge, resuming his place streetside. Twice he bent to lift litter into a nearby trashcan, but didn't let it interrupt his storytelling.

They put a mortuary photograph on the local newscast the day after the accident. Felt bad about having to do it, since they preferred to notify next-of-kin in person, but they all had a sense from the beginning that the girl wasn't from here, so they ran her picture. Her body showed evidence of having been treated at a hospital within a few days of her death, but nobody working the ER at either of the DCH medical centers in Tuscaloosa or Northport recognized her. Couldn't find nobody to identify her in the Birmingham- or Montgomery-area hospitals, either. No hits on fingerprints. Doc Cabbott, the coroner, did a right nice job on her, fixed up her face so she didn't look quite so bad. Wasn't such a scary picture as it could have been.

Lady called in two days later, Tuesday morning. Said she hadn't been able to get the girl's picture out of her head, looked a lot like a girl she found asleep on the steps over at First Baptist, off Greensboro, when she went in to the church office to get caught up on some filing last Saturday morning, September 3, about ten o'clock.

"Sermons."

"Pardon?" Rose demurred.

"Sermons," McAffrey said. "The lady was sorting sermons." It pleased him to remember that detail.

"Oh. Sermons. I see. And the girl?"

"Rosy."

"Actually, I prefer Rose."

"No," he said gently as he pushed open the Krispy Kreme door and stepped aside, allowing her to enter ahead of him. The sweet scent of plumped yeast and melted sugar greeted them. "Rosy's the name of the other girl." He gave it a moment to sink in, steering her toward a cafe table in the back corner. Only after he'd pulled out her chair for her, then sat down himself, did he resume. "Rosy's the name she gave to the woman at the church. Kinda strange, huh?"

She came in on the Greyhound on Friday night, September 2. Didn't know a soul, didn't have a dime. Camped on the church steps overnight and that's where the secretary found her come Saturday morning. Said she'd lost everything in Katrina and had come to town hoping to find some relatives to help her and her mother out. Secretary thought maybe the pastor could help her track them down, but he was off at a revival all day, so she let Rosy sleep in the office for a while. Then she gave her a loan from petty cash and dropped her off at City Cafe so she could get a meal. Girl said she'd walk back to meet the pastor later that evening and that's when …

"That's when we killed her," Rose said.

"That's when she died," McAffrey replied.

The hot-light flashed red, illuminating the words HOT NOW. Rows and rows of original glazed doughnuts toppled out of the oil vat, skittered along the conveyor belt, and landed on trays that the aproned workers slid into the front case. McAffrey was on his feet and headed in that direction before the first doughnut cleared the cooling tunnel.

Left alone at the table, Rose rested her chin in her hand, only then noticing that she still clutched the paperwork—the phonebook page, the receipt, and the business card—in a tightly rolled bundle in her fist. She'd released it only once, momentarily, setting it on the countertop in the restroom at the stationhouse while she'd washed her face before they set out for Krispy Kreme. She'd splashed cold water onto her skin, rubbing aggressively with wads of toilet paper until the tissue turned purple and blue and black as a bruise. She'd kept at it until the face in the mirror reminded her of herself again. Then she pulled the officer's sweatshirt off and tied it around her shoulders, a makeshift shawl; too hot to wear outdoors, this way it still preserved her modesty. Finally, she'd pilfered a rubber band from the clerk's desk on her way past and pulled her hair into its customary ponytail before rejoining McAffrey outside, where he'd been waiting patiently for her under the blazing sun.

Now his change ploinked noisily against the bottom of the glass tip jar as he turned and walked back toward her, offering up a steaming doughnut and a glass of orange juice. To be polite, she took a small bite before pushing the food aside and asking, "So what about these things?" as she unfurled the phonebook page onto the tabletop. "What does this tell you?"

In one bite he devoured half a doughnut, then swallowed quickly. "Don't tell us nothing. There ain't no markings. No nothing. We know the girl's full name is Rosebud Howard—found that out just a few days ago—but the page she was carrying is a page of *As*. So's not like we know who she was looking for based on last names—hers doesn't match none listed there."

As Rose lifted the page, the receipt and business card slid off it.

"As for that receipt from City Cafe … well, that's useless," he continued. "Alls it tells us is she paid cash for three sides and a meat with sweet tea. Like everybody else in there that day." After taking a swig of coffee, he said, "Least she had a decent last meal.

Hell if those cheese grits and biscuits they serve up over there ain't the best damn thing I ever tasted!"

Rose frequented City Cafe for the sweet tea. More tea than you could drink, a never-empty glass. Filled her down to her toes. Suddenly she saw the black girl, under the car, sweet tea leaking out of her body through her bloody legs. Sweet tea blood splashing up onto her own body when she leapt from the car and landed on the girl's legs. She felt herself about to retch. Hadn't eaten much of anything in almost nine days, so sick was she of having it all come back up after it went down. She smelled that sweet tea blood again and her mouth bubbled with saliva that boded an attack of the dry heaves. She closed her eyes, hand to forehead, steadying, calming herself.

When she looked back up at McAffrey there were six deep furrows spanning his forehead, between his brows. Softer than frown lines. Pure concern. "I'm okay," she assured him. "Really." She pushed the doughnut farther away. "Keep going. What about the business card? That's something specific."

He had to raise his voice. The shop was filling quickly now with other customers, people drawn in by the glow of the hot-light, the lure of fresh glazed. "Business card's no use to us right now. Can't get through to the number. Must be a land line, and phone lines are still out down round New Orleans on account of the hurricane. Whole place is a sorry mess. Not enough police in those parts to deal with the looters and the snipers, let alone help us out cuz we found a business card we wanna track down."

As he spoke, another uniform strode across the shop toward them. The cop stopped behind Rose, sniffed the air, smiled as he stared down at her. His grin grew, Joker-esque, pinched with presumption at the edges as he turned to McAffrey and nodded. "Hey Mac!" he joshed as he reached between them to pluck a doughnut off Mac's tray. "You're not stepping out on me now, are you?"

McAffrey shook his head. He introduced Rose to his partner as the girl from the accident scene they'd worked last weekend and explained to him why she'd come by.

"Hi," Rose said offhandedly, then refocused on McAffrey. "Okay, so the phones aren't working and the police down there can't help. So have you sent somebody to interview the woman from the business card?"

The absurdity of her question shocked McAffrey, though he contained his surprise, betrayed only by the slight widening of his eyes, because he'd held this girl's body in his arms just a week ago. He had cradled her head against his chest and loosened a dried, caked strand of hair from her cheek. Spurred by that intimacy, augmented by his growing affection for her today, he forgave her earnestness. But his partner laughed out loud.

"Are you kidding me?" the cop asked. Rose spun to face him as McAffrey jumped quickly from his chair, one hand on her shoulder, the other raised, palm open, fingers splayed, as if to hold back his partner. "Is she kidding me?" the cop repeated, stepping back, looking at his partner but pointing at Rose.

"Come on, man ... " McAffrey urged.

The cop didn't listen. "We already wasted—what?—four days last week tracking down bus passengers, only to discover we had nothing more than another black hitchhiker on our hands, and now you—" here he glared at Rose "—want us to ditch our work and drive down into that shithole to find out—what?—huh?—that our dead girl swiped a business card along with God knows what else when she broke into this lady's store with a band of looters? Something like that?"

"Lay off," McAffrey insisted, stepping between his partner and Rose. "Look, I'ma carry her home. Why don't you polish off these doughnuts for me and I'll meet you back at the station in half an hour." It wasn't a question; it was a command. His voice was pacifying, paternal, paced. That cadence and tone had earned him the nickname Father; fellow officers referred to the interrogation room as his confessional. His verbal oeuvre had the cumulative effect of making folks want to sit up straighter, do better, provide the right answer. Calm down.

His partner sank into his vacated seat as McAffrey offered Rose a hand to help her from her chair and ushered her back outside. They both squinted into the light as he ministered to her, soothed her. Sentence by sentence, he lulled them back to task.

"So we ran a background check on that lady, the one from the business card"—he took it from her, confirmed the name—"Jennifer Goldberg. She's not related to our victim. She's a thirty-five-year-old white woman from the Midwest, just moved to Gretna, outside New Orleans. Owns some kinda flower business. Who knows where this girl got the card or why she had it … coulda bought flowers, any number of things."

He figured looting, too, but didn't say it. Talked instead about distributing missing person bulletins throughout the South, focusing on the three states they knew she'd traveled through: Alabama, Mississippi, Louisiana. DMV had no records matching her name and age range, which Doc was dead-on in estimating to be between sixteen and twenty-one. Turns out she was eighteen. Even tried lots of unusual spellings of her name. Rosebud Howard seems pretty straightforward, but some folks spell the simplest names in the strangest of ways. Got her full name by tracing the passengers on the Greyhound bus. The church secretary had been sure her name was Rosy, but since there wasn't anyone by that name, or anything close to it, on the bus, they wound up having to contact each passenger individually to ask if anybody recognized, or went by, the nickname Rosy. Took him and his partner four days. Next-to-last passenger, before they figured it out. An ER nurse in Natchez, Mississippi, used her own name to buy the girl a ticket, which is what caused the confusion.

McAffrey pulled a notebook from his back pocket as they crossed the street, flipping through it to check his facts. "Amanda Worthington. That's her name. The nurse. We had an alphabetized passenger manifest from Greyhound," he said, rolling his eyes at the time he'd wasted calling every damn name clear through to the Ws. "She works the midnight-to-noon shift at Natchez Community Hospital."

Ticket cost sixty-eight dollars. Amanda charged it to her own credit card. The vic had been a patient of hers, and at the end of her shift, around noon, she dropped her off at the bus station. Bus left there at 2:40 in the afternoon, last Friday, September 2. The nurse hadn't heard a thing from her after that.

McAffrey left Rose standing on the sidewalk in front of the stationhouse while he jogged into the lot for his patrol car to drive her home. He retrieved his keys, then tucked the notebook into his freshly emptied pocket. There wasn't much that needed reviewing. He remembered the sound of Amanda's cry when he'd introduced himself on the phone and said he was trying to track down a young woman by the name of Rosy who arrived in Tuscaloosa last week on the Greyhound.

"Oh, no," she'd said, immediately. "Look, I know they request the passenger's name when you buy the ticket, but she didn't have any ID or any money and I was just trying to do her a favor. Is that a crime in Alabama? To do that? I mean, I know they've gotten so particular about that stuff on airplanes ever since 9/11, but is it really the law on buses too now? I didn't mean to—"

He'd assured her she'd committed no crime. Wondered what all she knew of the girl, which amounted to nothing more than what was in the hospital record, which she wouldn't disclose due to hospital regulations. In answer to her questions as to why he was calling then—"Am I liable for something? Has the girl done something wrong?"—he told her that she had no responsibility for anything. He was just searching for information because the girl had died. Hit by a car. Which made the nurse gasp, then cough. He'd thought she was coughing, something stuck in her throat, but then he'd realized: she sobbed. Racking sobs. "Ma'am," he'd said, over and over, "ma'am, ma'am, are you gonna be all right?" In answer, so softly he hadn't heard the click, she hung up the phone.

He didn't say any of that to Rose when she climbed into the patrol car. He didn't say anything at all for most of the ten-minute drive, just watched in silence as gnats assaulted the windshield. When she finally leaned toward him and nudged, "Officer?" he resumed his liturgy. Told her they accessed the girl's full name,

Rosebud Howard, from the hospital records. There wasn't much else in there. She had no insurance, listed no address, walked out on the bill. Gave the same story there as here: lost everything in the hurricane; trying to get to Tuscaloosa to track down relatives. But after a week of TV coverage, and printing her full name, when they finally got it, in the paper, nobody other than the church secretary came forward claiming to know her.

Rose sighed. "So she got hurt in the hurricane? That's why she was in the hospital?"

"I don't know about all that."

"What do you mean you don't know?"

"I don't know if she got hurt in the hurricane."

"How can you not know? You've seen her hospital records."

At her direction, he stopped the car in front of her apartment building, then looked away nervously. "Doc Cabbott—the coroner—he's got all that info. It got sent right over to the morgue."

"But you've seen it."

He put his head in his hands. Closed his eyes.

Then it hit her: it wasn't just the hurricane.

"What happened to her?"

McAffrey was a police officer, but also a Southerner. A gentleman at heart. "It's got nothing to do with you, or with what all happened in that car accident." He jumped out of the car and strode around to open her door, but she was already out and waiting for him when he came around the hood.

"What *happened* to her?"

"Don't do this to yourself, darling," he whispered. Pleaded. "You don't wanna know."

IV. ROSY

*"This is gonna be worse than anything
we've ever seen, Mama."*

WHENEVER ROSY HURT HERSELF, whenever she got scared, whenever as a child she kicked off her shoes and ran inside to huddle in her mother's lap, gnawing her fingernails to nubs, Cilla sang to her. From the folds of her memory, Cilla harvested hundreds of songs: tunes she'd heard as a youngster, or practiced in the church choir, or picked up randomly as they wafted to her from a radio in an anonymous house with an open window beneath which she'd pause on the street, listening intently, learning. She was never much of a reader—no *Goodnight Moon* or Dr. Seuss for her daughter—but she could match a song to any occasion and, as such, anchored Rosy's childhood in well-worn melodies, waking her every day with the sweet comfort of Mahalia Jackson's "Move on Up a Little Higher" crooned against her cheek, soft words of a morning when burdens would be lifted and cares forgotten.

Similarly, no "London Bridge" or "Rock-a-Bye Baby" for Rosy; nothing so generic. Whenever she sobbed over a booboo, Cilla soothed her with a take on Aretha Franklin's "Mary Don't You Weep," which, until she was a teenager and did an online search at the library, Rosy believed was titled "Rosy Don't You Weep, Don't You Mourn." Where Aretha would croon about the Pharaoh's army getting drowned, Cilla substituted lyrics about Rosy's toe getting stubbed or scab falling off or tooth coming loose.

But then Rosy grew up, and lost her faith in Cilla's voice.

In the darkening hours post hurricane-party, their kitchen now rang with song—Kurt Carr's "Surely God Is Able"—punctuated by the sound of water running, pots clanging against each other when set to dry, the increasing tenor of the storm outside. Of the revelers, only Maya remained—dear old Maya, who, beginning on the day of Rosy's birth, had segued from neighbor to nanny to virtual kin. Maya's second soprano answered Cilla's first as they scrubbed and sang about the Lord's ability to soothe storms, to chase off the gathering dark clouds and provide hope for tomorrow.

Yeah right, hope for tomorrow. As if. Though Cilla had noted the gathering clouds, she warbled away as if the electricity hadn't died an hour ago, shortly after the phone. She and Maya washed the dinner dishes by candlelight, though the wind had kicked up and screamed through the cracked window pane; the candles couldn't burn much longer.

"Rosy girl," Maya called into the other room, "it be getting too airish for a body in here. Be a heart and come on in and raise that window down, why don't you?"

Rosy walked into the kitchen, hit a puddle of water on the linoleum, and crashed flat onto her back in the middle of the room. She just lay there, spread-eagled, immobile on the floor, not knowing whether to laugh at the insanity of their predicament, kick her mother's legs out from under her, or indulge her fear by hiding in the broom closet as she used to do when she was still small enough to fit in there and count the bristles on the broom. She never managed to count them all, but by the time she emerged, whatever had scared her had by then dissipated.

Not so now.

"The roof's leaking," Rosy said, almost calmly, but then repeated herself with fear and anger and frustration creeping in, "The roof. Is leaking." No one paid her any mind until she shouted. "The roof's leaking! We can't stay—"

"Good God, girl, you make like doomsday herself with your 'roof's leaking!' Ain't no roof leaking!" Cilla said, laughing. "Maya just done spilled some water outta that pot she fixing to dry. Now get yourself up offa that floor and pull yourself together!"

Rosy sat up but didn't stand. She leaned back on one hand that was placed, almost precisely, over a handprint she had first traced onto a square tile on her eighth birthday. Old man Silas had given her a set of markers as a present that year—permanent-ink Sharpies instead of water-soluble Crayolas—and by the time Cilla found her, she'd irreparably traced both hands onto the kitchen floor and was in the process of adding a different shade to the edge of each finger. "Look, Mama! My hands're like yours!" she said when she noticed Cilla in the doorway. Because she was almost finished, Cilla let her polish off the last two digits before repossessing the markers. But the next year, Cilla broke out an indelible marker again, and had doled one out first thing in the morning on each of Rosy's subsequent birthdays. Eleven increasingly larger hand-tracings now dotted the whole of the kitchen floor.

Rosy stared up at Cilla and Maya, who were trying to reconnect with the tune they'd been singing when her fall interrupted them. Maya hummed in C minor, heading back toward the refrain, when Cilla said she had a song better suited for the moment.

"Maybe a funeral dirge?" Rosy asked.

Cilla looked down at her, fuming on the floor, and rolled her eyes. "Actually, I'ma thinking of one about that boy done cried 'Wolf!' Or a party pooper. Whatcha prefer, Maya?"

"Heart, get on up outta there," Maya urged. "You acting nervous as a long-tailed cat in a room full of rocking chairs. You know we gets ourselves one of these every few years; it just coming a cloud today like it do every now and again. Hell, last year they was yelling 'Hurricane! Hurricane!' and calling it … what they done called it?"

"Ivan the Terrible," Rosy reminded her.

"There you go! Ivan the Terrible. And they about got the whole city camped out on I-10 and Airline Highway. Just sitting there on that road in them cars. Old people was out there dying from all that sitting in traffic! And what about us? We home eating some shrimp, playing some cards, having us a fine time while old Ivan the Terrible headed off down the coast."

"Weren't so terrible to me," Cilla said.

"Ivan was just a Category Four," Rosy said, standing, taking the dishtowel out of Maya's arthritic hands. "Sit down, Maya, I'll dry." She pulled a chair over toward the sink, and asked, "You want a chair for your feet too?"

"That'd be good, heart."

"Ivan was a Four, and it turned at the last minute," Rosy resumed. Maya lowered her tired body into the chair—one hand on the seat back, the other on the counter, slowly easing her bottom down. Cilla handed Rosy a dripping slotted spoon. "Katrina's a Five." She paused to let that fact settle on them. "And you know what they say—it's not just the storm, it's what would happen if the levees broke. A direct hit on the city—"

"There ain't gonna be no direct hit on the city," Cilla interrupted.

"So now you're a meteorologist, Mama? What's that make you? A house cleaner with a side business in fortune telling and weather predicting?"

"Aww, Rosy, listen to yourself, will ya?" Maya cut in. Rosy and Cilla knew too easily how to provoke each other. Neither could stand it; both did it; Maya quelled it. Neighbor as referee. "Come August, every year going on damn near forty years, they been saying the big one's a coming," Maya continued. "They been preaching doom for decades, but them storms always turn away. We got us too much good gris-gris hanging over this city! Twixt the Catholics and the Baptists and that Caraïbe mumbo jumbo … hell, we got every possible angle to God covered!"

Cilla pulled the drain plug, and the water swirled from the sink. Rosy hopped up onto the counter and slid the pot Cilla passed her onto an overhead shelf. Her legs dangled from the countertop and Maya cradled one of her feet as if it were a kitten snuggled in her lap. Just as Rosy said, "I have a bad feeling. I think we shoulda left this time," a gust of wind snuffed out the candlelight.

Cilla snatched the book of matches off the stovetop in the dark. Their faces lit up again.

"How you reckon we gonna get outta here?" Cilla asked. "We ain't got us no car, and I ain't see no city bus outside offering me a fare-free ride to Houston."

"Not anymore," Rosy hissed, glaring at her mother.

"Oh Lordy. Enough about missing them buses this afternoon! Where'd they take them people anyways? Some 'shelter of last resort' as our *fine* mayor's been putting it? What his idea of a 'shelter of last resort' for us Five-fours? Betcha it ain't no place *he'd* go! Those Red Cross shelters—I seen them on TV—they look bad enough, everybody crammed into some gymnasium. But least they giving out food and cots and blankets. Hell, I even seen them passing out art supplies to the kids, and teddy bears, after that tornado over in Alabama. But ain't no Red Cross shelters round here. Oh, no. They don't come to New Orleans. They everywhere else, but not New Orleans! So where you reckon we oughta go?"

"The Convention Center," Rosy said. "The Superdome."

"The Superdome? Shut your mouth! Now you talking like you ain't got the good sense God gave a goose. I ain't gonna get caught dead hiding out in no Superdome! You remember in '98 after Hurricane Georges, those niggers tore that place up. How many folks they done stuffed up in there?"

"Fourteen thousand."

"There you go! Fourteen thousand folks crammed up in there, hungry and angry enough to make you wanna start slapping your own mama. They stole shit. They ripped stuff to shreds. They..." she thought better of going on, and instead waved her hand in the air dismissively. "That there's the devil's breeding ground! What I wanna get crammed up in there with fourteen thousand throwed-off niggers for? That's messed up."

Maya intervened again. "Listen, heart. No need to get yourself so scared of this dark. We all lost electricity in Georges, too. Ain't hurt us none."

"We in a house in a city in the United States of America!" Cilla yelled. "We protected!"

"Protected by what, exactly?" Rosy snarled. "The ten thousand body bags they've got waiting in the FEMA office downtown?"

Maya bored her eyes deep into Cilla's, as if to warn her to quit fueling Rosy's fire. Cilla, for once, heeded.

"Please listen," Rosy said, composing herself. "This is gonna be worse than anything we've ever seen, Mama. And you, Maya, you watch. This is gonna be worse than Betsy even."

"My house survived Betsy, no real problem," Maya insisted, indignant.

"You said there was seven feet of water in there after Betsy! You tell stories about—"

"Yeah, well, it dried!" Maya cut in. "And in the forty years since, not one drop of water from one single storm has ever gotten inside my house!"

"Georges was a Category Two. Ivan was a Category Four. Betsy a Three. Katrina's a *Five*. That's an enormous difference."

"Well, ain't nothing to do about none of it now," Cilla said, ending the discussion. "So I taking myself to bed."

Together they walked Maya to the door and held it open for her against the storm. Too old to run, she let the rain soak into her and, at the sidewalk, turned around to face them. Then she threw back her head, mouth open, capturing enough rainwater to spit in a wind-twisted arc back toward Rosy and Cilla, huddled together in the doorway. It had the effect she'd hoped: they both laughed. Then she raised her hands to the black sky, waved her arms over her head as if to prove the sky had not fallen far enough to intimidate her, and screamed, "Rosy, you see those horsemen a-coming, you run on over to old Maya's place! It's solid brick, and you know the story—not nothing gonna blow it down! Me and that house gonna withstand Armageddon!"

A clap of thunder swallowed everyone's laughter as she hiked up her skirt and splashed her way home across the empty street.

ROSY COULDN'T SLEEP. EVERY few hours, after intermittently tossing and dozing, she'd get up and tiptoe to the front door to check the weather. Rain. Wind increasing. Things banging against the outside of the house. On her third or fourth pass from the bedroom to the entry, the wind whipped the screen door from her hand as she tried to shut it, and mashed it against the outside wall of the house so violently that it drove the doorknob partway into the exterior shingles. She had to brace her foot on the wall in order to pry it loose, while rain pummeled her with hypodermic force.

Too damp to go back to bed, she fished the flashlight from one of the grocery sacks she'd packed and shone the light around the inside of the house. It surprised her, happily: no obvious leaks. Bored, she made shadow puppets on the wall until she exhausted her repertoire, then sank to the floor and lifted Cilla's jewelry box from the bag nearest her. Her mother owned no jewelry; the box was more a sort of hope chest, sheltering tokens of her youth: A key from the first house Cilla lived in. The filter from the first cigarette she smoked. A crayoned picture, all squiggles, signed "Rosy, age 5" in her mother's hand. A photograph of a younger Cilla standing in a kitchen, surrounded by other cooks and housecleaners; an elderly woman with a crazy afro spilling through a hairnet had her arms wrapped around Cilla's shoulders and an inscription on the back read "Ada May and gang, Kappa Alpha Theta house, 1985." Some stickers. A mood ring. A petrified dragonfly. A list of requisite spices to blacken catfish, penned in palsied scrawl. A mass card for someone named Bubba Brown, who drowned at age fifteen. A cardboard valentine, signed in a youthful script by BB, whom Rosy took to be

Bubba, with the question: "Will you be mine?" Dried rosebuds. Eleven of them.

Rosy's father's obituary.

She unfolded the yellowed newsprint and read it for the umpteenth time. It didn't mention her, didn't mention her mother. Her parents weren't married, which meant that Cilla and her unborn child didn't count as his survivors. Rosy stared at the photo and tried to see herself. More than anything, she thought, she had his ears. In all other ways she was her mother's child, but her ears were his. Big, detached lobes, a funny indentation on the edge of the right ear, almost a divot, which she fingered every time she looked at his picture. Staring at him, she expected his face should stir some latent knowing in her, a familiarity. Every time she unfolded the paper she felt an anticipatory extra heartbeat jumpstart her pulse, but today, like every other: nothing. Just another dead man's picture in a newspaper. She felt nothing but the divot, and that she felt with her fingertip, not her heart.

The obituary didn't state the precise details of his death, for suicides weren't spoken of so directly back then. It said "a fall on campus." Cilla, on the other hand, felt no compunction to curtail a saucy story and had provided Rosy with every detail she knew about any person or event that affected their lives. They had come, of late, to refer to this trait as compulsive honesty.

"Compulsively honest," Rosy had answered a year back when Cilla had asked her daughter to describe her in three words or less. Rosy had just returned from the library with a printout of the latest *Survivor* application and was penning in her answers at the kitchen table. Cilla watched *Survivor* religiously, all nine seasons to date, and talking Rosy into applying was her latest scheme to elevate them out of poverty.

"If you could hold any political office, what would it be and why?" Rosy read aloud from the questionnaire. "Everyone's gonna say president," she considered, "so I think I'll say mayor. Give your friend Ray Nagin a run for his money!"

Cilla growled at the mention of Nagin's name. Then she cried out, "I got it! I'ma be ambassador. To the Bahamas!" Though she wasn't applying, herself, she had no intention of being left out of the fun of contemplating her own answers.

Rosy laughed. "Ambassador's not a political office; it's a political appointment made by the president."

"Then you better be putting 'president' for your answer, girly! Next question!"

Limited to a three-word description of herself, Rosy chose "resourceful," "fearless," and "curious."

"For me, I says 'joyful,' 'sexy,' and 'a damn good cook!'" Cilla said.

Rosy smiled at her mother. "Too many words."

"That's cuz I too much woman for such a limiting question! Wouldn't you say?"

"I'd say 'compulsively honest.'"

"Those're just two words."

Rosy smiled again. "They're the only two necessary."

The first time Rosy asked how her father died she couldn't have been more than six. "He done jumped offa Denny Chimes," Cilla said. For some weeks, Rosy eyed the wind chimes on the front porch suspiciously, until she thought to ask for clarification and learned that Denny Chimes is an old bell tower anchoring the central quad at the University of Alabama.

"But *how'd* he die?" the little girl asked.

"He died when he done landed."

Still perplexed: "So then why'd he jump?"

"You got me there, Rosy girl. You got me there. Ain't nobody got no damn good enough reason to go jumping offa no towers. You remember that! Just ain't no call for such a thing never."

Other details came out more slowly.

One time, mired in a depressive valley, Cilla cried for days about "bloody football players." Got herself so worked up she finally hyperventilated in the shower, passed out, and spent a few days in the hospital after they stitched up the gash on her forehead while they readjusted her meds.

When she got home, she couldn't remember a thing about the "bloody football players" but, after a few days' rest, Rosy found her waiting on the front steps of the middle school when the bell rang at the end of the day. "I got it," she said. "Did I mention 1961?"

Yes, Rosy remembered Cilla ranting about that year.

"Billy Neighbors, All-American, 1961, and Pat Tramell, Most Outstanding Player. They share a slab in the Walk of Fame."

"Who?" Rosy asked. "What?"

They turned the corner, hand in hand, and headed home.

"The Crimson Tide football captains all got they names in concrete slabs, long with their hand and footprints, back in Tuscaloosa. Tradition they got going on since sometime in the '40s or '50s. All them names of football captains round the base of Denny Chimes. Billy Neighbors and Pat Tramell share a slab on the corner by the street where your daddy done landed. Landed right on they handprints. Goddamn, there was so much blood on them football players! They cleaned it up best they could, but still, every time I walks down the street after that I tell you I could feel those bloody hands of Billy Neighbors and Pat Tramell fixing to reach out and grab me by the ankles. Finally took to going the long way round, just to avoid them. Never did walk past that way again."

If Cilla didn't hesitate to reveal the details of her lover's death, neither did she hold back the details of his life. The ones she knew, at least. They'd had only three-and-a-half months together. Eleven dates in three-and-a-half months. He worked in the same sorority house where she did, but they were an altogether different class of folk. He was a student who worked a few jobs for extra money; being a houseboy secured him not only free food in return for serving meals to the collegians, but something even better: an invitation to all the girls' parties. Whereas Cilla was just hired help going nowhere, which lent an air of the clandestine to their couplings. It started as nothing more than exchanged glances as they passed in the kitchen, but they were glances she could *feel*. Then, quite by accident, they met up at the folk art fair over in Northport one autumn Saturday. She'd gone to see Nora Ezell's Martin Luther King quilt that everyone was talking about and recognized him as he crouched over a whittled statue of a wolf, examining the smooth contours of its haunches. The first words she ever spoke to him— "I didn't take you for no wolf man"—made them both laugh at the double entendre. Within five minutes he confessed to her his secret passion for woodcarving, and the next day, when she slid her hand into the pocket of her sweater on the walk home from work, she discovered a hand-carved wooden talisman tucked inside. That was it. They were on.

The older Rosy got, the more expansive the descriptions became.

"And the sex—mmm hmmm—it was *good*." By the time Rosy was in her late teens, Cilla would stop at this point in the story and say: "Just eleven times. Eleven times, and look what I wound up with!" Here she smiled and pinched Rosy's cheek. Then she stopped smiling and pointed her finger in Rosy's face. "You using the birth control? I don't want no babies and none of that AIDS round here!"

"Mama, leave me be!" Rosy always countered.

"Well, you just remember—"

"I know, I know. All I hafta do is ask."

For her seventeenth birthday, Cilla gave Rosy a pocketbook. With a box of condoms inside. "Just in case something happens you ain't expecting!" she laughed.

Rosy just rolled her eyes. The things her mother didn't know. By the time she turned seventeen, she no longer had any need for condoms.

Rosy'd had sex for the first time when she was fourteen, shortly after sunset on the base of the shoot-da-chute at Bonart playground. It was a hasty rut she succumbed to when the school's top dawg spoke to her for the first time ever—"What's happening, girl? Who you be with?"—and culled her from the street corner where she'd been loitering with her homegirls, eating snowballs from their favorite stand. She wasn't the prettiest, or by any means popular enough, but she was the only one who'd merely shrugged her shoulders when he asked, "What time your mom and them expecting yous?" Beyond that, she smiled at his jokes and said, "Yeah, you right," as if she got the punch lines that she didn't while shuffling her toe in a nervous circle on the sidewalk. That clinched it. He wanted to get laid bad and didn't have time to coerce the more confident, the more deserving. This one's thrall would get him what he wanted. Easy choice. Sure thing.

He hit it three more times in the next two weeks, which she knew for sure meant he liked her. Soon after, when he didn't even bother to acknowledge her presence when she bumped into him while making groceries at Silas's, she figured he was just distracted, surrounded by his crew and busy deciding on the Slim Jim or the jerky. She could sense his eyes on her, though, as she turned her back on him and paid for her purchases. Silas himself stared past her with a menacing moue, her bills untouched on the counter.

"What's wrong, Silas?" she asked.

"I ain't like the way them sorry boys be looking at you," he said, scrutinizing them.

Rosy glanced over her shoulder at them. Three broke into big grins. One raised a hand along with his eyebrows and nodded a 'What's happening!' in her direction. She flushed and turned a joyful smile back on Silas. "For true!" she said. "They're my friends."

Silas looked at her like she'd grown a horn. "Girl, them boys ain't nobody's 'friend.' They slicker than snot on a door knob." Then he raised his voice loud enough to carry over to the smoked meat display. "Nobody gonna be pooning round in my store lest they wanting to get they asses tumped!"

"Oh, Silas," she murmured, patting his hand. Old man; he didn't understand. She knew better. They liked her.

Bonart Slide's main homie was her second lay, two weeks into her freshman year. "All y'all oughta pass by Monte's party come Saturday night," he said as he sauntered past her lunch table, bumping her with his elbow as he hitched his jeans up to mid-thigh. But for all her anticipation, the party started out pretty lonely. She spent the first two hours leaning against the living room wall, ignored by the dancers and druggies alike. But when Saggy Pants finally arrived, he homed in on her, swapping her well-nursed go-cup of punch for a beer, then another, then a Crown Royal. Once she was good and sloshed he corralled her into a bedroom and locked the door. When she murmured "What …?" he replied that he and his homeboys were practically brothers; they shared everything.

She went through twelve more of them in the next two years.

She didn't mind the sex. It was fine, usually fun. But it was the before and the right after that she lived for. A boy's smile from the far side of a crowd, his practiced movements as he circled toward her—picking up a beer here, filching a quick toke there—her own self his end goal. She loved the rush that came with knowing that, despite all the pretty girls in the room, she'd been targeted: *He wants me!* Most didn't even have to walk the last ten feet to her. Feeling lucky, she'd up and go to them. Then she'd bang them to get to the next part: their arms still around her right before they rolled off, man's arms, weighty and strong. A well-muscled shield surrounding her at her most vulnerable, a few addictive seconds of relaxation—of feeling cared *for* set against her daily reality with her mother, which required her to be on constant guard to take care *of*.

Fourteen boys in twenty-four months to indulge her lust for those fleeting moments of safety in the embrace of someone stronger than she.

Soon she was part of the herd, absorbed into the boozing and partying crowd, where everybody slept with everybody else. One great big fucking family. Everything Rosy always thought she wanted. Until a story made the rounds by the end of homeroom on the first day of her junior year about some girl who'd fucked three brothers in one night, two of them at the same time under a blanket on the staircase at the end-of-summer bash out at the Vieux Carré Towers apartment complex. Which was not how it had been, exactly; she'd only screwed two guys that night, one doggie style in the backseat of his Olds on the way there—a quick pit stop on a deserted side street while her friend paced around outside, smoking a cigarette, yelling, "Ain't y'all fucking done yet?"—and the other on the hood of a parked car in the lot while the party raged on inside. Sure, at one point she'd been huddled under a blanket on the colorfully-tagged stairwell with two guys, one fondling her nipple through her shirt, the other more direct, his hand down her pants, pushing a finger inside her. But she hadn't had sex in public for God's sake! In fact, for appearance's sake, she'd kept her body still under the crocheted throw while people climbed the stairs around them, feigning normal, only a shrug here or there to keep the boys' concealed hands in separate regions, not wanting either of them to be aware of what the other was doing but also not wanting to push either one of them away, wanting to be wanted by each. When Nipple Boy went for a beer she'd walked off toward the parking lot with the one who already had her scent on him. He was the star running back, after all, the other just a wide receiver. Later that night, recollecting the thrill of their mutual affections, she lauded herself on having kept them unaware of how close they came to bumping knuckles in their tandem grope.

But then she went to school and realized they'd known all along.

Nipple Boy and Star Running Back were loving this story, having discovered and added Backseat Boy into the fray, bragging about a "gang bang." Thank God they'd withheld her name. By noon, everyone in school knew the tale and had started speculating about who the girl was. Rosy actually had to sit at the lunch table with her friends calling the anonymous girl a crunk ho, scared to death she'd be found out, sick with shame when even the real whores insisted, "I'da never! That bitch ain't got *no* class!" And there, one table down, sat her under-blanket fondlers, listening in on the whole conversation, smiling their sly proud smiles. They hadn't kept her identity to themselves to protect her, she realized. Instead, by not naming her, they kept all the attention focused on themselves. They didn't give a shit about her at all.

She left school early that day, went home to Tylenol, tissues, and an *Oprah* show that spoke directly to her, wouldn't let her hide: guests bemoaning the plague of promiscuity among father-less girls. She perched on the edge of her seat and listened, trans-fixed, as psychologists described not just the stats—increased teen pregnancy, rampant STDs—affecting such girls, but also their low self-esteem, the lack of confidence she'd always known her end run at popularity had merely whitewashed. She wept as if at her own wake, staring compassionately into the hole she dug for her-self. Then someone named Dr. Sellers turned and stared straight at her, the camera zooming in so he practically put his face in hers as he spoke. "You might think a mother's love would be sufficient. But we're witnessing a plague of young girls who are spurning the love that's available to them in favor of fruitlessly hunting for the father's love that should have been theirs but isn't. And in their desperation, they'll substitute any man's affection for the love they're missing."

Rosy drew in her breath, wiped her eyes, and blinked back at the TV screen. She saw her own image reflected in the glass, lean-ing forward on the couch, as if she were one of the now-strong, now-secure guests speaking with authority about a past she'd overcome. Then Oprah leaned right toward Rosy, as if reaching out to grasp her hand, and spoke the words that truly motivat-ed the change, insisting she must love herself and let that love be enough. "Only then," Rosy repeated after Oprah, saying the words aloud, a vow to herself, "will you be able to stop searching for love in someone else."

And that was it. By the time Cilla pushed the box of condoms on her for her seventeenth birthday, Rosy'd forsworn sex for social status or any other reason. She'd had a taste of mainstream pop-ular, and it didn't suit her. It left her sitting at a table, calling her-self a cunt, with people who agreed and thought it funny. Enough of that shit. So, while the rest partied on, she biked to the library, honed a love of research, did all the extra-credit projects, prepped for AP classes, graduated top of her class. She also took up the habit of listening to books on tape, a recorder always tucked into her back pocket, reciting the words with the reader and practicing perfect diction, aiming to lose the Ninth Ward accent that otherwise might hold her back. By the time she started applying for scholarships she believed she could, with focus, sound like your average all-American girl from anywhere-USA. Her efforts won her a free ride to Tulane, tuition and room and board and all expenses paid. She accepted the scholarship gratefully while declining the room and board in favor of an annual cash stipend to live at home, where she could take care of her mother while completing her degree. The money would pay the rent and then some. Cilla wouldn't have to work nearly as hard or as much; Rosy could carry her own weight for the first time.

Come morning, sans Katrina, she'd have stepped into a Tulane classroom and embarked on a whole new life. Instead, sitting on the floor of their dark hallway while Cilla slept, the storm fast making landfall upon the city, Rosy shone the flashlight on her father's obituary and read it again: "… the President's List during each collegiate semester … early-acceptance to the School of Medicine at the University of Alabama at Birmingham … nominated to Who's Who in American High Schools as well as Who's Who in American Colleges and Universities …" Having striven so hard to live up to his academic splendor, she couldn't imagine what possessed him to forsake it all by killing himself. *Why in the world?* she wondered yet again.

But for all the unsolicited courtship details that Cilla had foisted on her, Rosy never got the answers about her father that she craved. Not to that question, nor any others: Who were his people? What did they do? Cilla religiously waved away such inquiries. "I don't know, Rosy girl, we never got to all that." Then she'd re-launch the litany they both knew by heart: "He's from Tuscaloosa. He had brown eyes that turned a little bit green when he laughed or when he started to sweat. Which means his eyes were mostly green round me!" She smiled wickedly and arched one eyebrow with a sigh at the memory. "He could sit still and fish for hours on end, no need to say nothing, out offa the edge of the dam, and when he focused like that I used to rub the knots outta his shoulders. He was thin, but all muscle. Liked to tell me stories about pitching for the Jaguars over at Northridge High School, how he done shut out ..."

Something suddenly shattered outside and Rosy instinctively ducked. A neighbor's window pulverized by the whipping wind? A tree through a windshield? The worst of the weather was upon them, and she was scared. Cowering on the floor as thunder roared outside, she closed her eyes and tried to calm herself by imagining her father celebrating that baseball shut-out with his first beer, twirling a leather keychain his father gave him on his sixteenth birthday around his pinkie finger. She saw his lips, blue from a cold swim, as he leaned to kiss her mother. These are the stories Cilla lulled her to sleep with as they lay curled beside each other in bed.

But she imagined other things too, details Cilla hadn't meant for her to be privy to, secrets her mother spoke aloud only after she believed her child had fallen fast asleep: The way he fumbled with the buttons on her shirt the first day, ripping one off in his haste, grinding it into the grass so that it smelled of clover when she sewed it back on that night. The way his callused thumb rubbed her nipple and made her come against the pressure of his hand. Rosy knew so well what he did with the eleven rosebuds now sheltered in the jewelry box that she could almost smell their long-lost fragrance as she lifted them, one by one, from the velvet-lined case and cradled them in her hands while the hurricane raged outside.

Her father had, at one time, dipped those rosebuds into her mother's palm, circling the tender skin of her hand and the inside of her wrist with the petals before he circled other places, other flowers, with the rosy corollas. Eleven rosebuds. Eleven dates.

Weekly for almost twenty years, Cilla spoke aloud of this to keep him alive in the bedroom with her, in her heart, while their child breathed steadily beside her, feigning slumber. Thus, Rosy learned the allure of her father as she kept watch over her mother, knowing herself to be named for the rosebuds that had been her parents' foreplay.

MORNING DAWNED DARK ON August 29, 2005. The sky, still gray, still weeping, did not register the changing hours. Rosy lay in bed, not entirely asleep but not awake either, when she heard a boom. Not a crashing—nothing that loud nor obviously threatening—yet ominous. As if the boom came through the earth itself, up between the floorboards and into her bones. Not an earthquake. Not that jolting. The ground speaking. She lay perfectly still, and then it came again. A booming vibration. She climbed out of bed, still fully clothed from the evening before.

"You feel that?" Cilla asked, alert, from her side of the bed. She'd rolled away from the wall and faced her daughter.

"Yeah. What is it?" Rosy asked, alarmed that it roused her mother also; Cilla could sleep through anything.

"I don't know," she said, but slid out of the bedclothes and into a pair of slacks, tucking her nightshirt in as she followed Rosy out of the bedroom and toward the front door.

Each step was their last in that room, on that inch of flooring. They would never return.

There were others, a smattering of residents throughout the Ninth Ward, also pulling on clothes behind their flimsy drywall, sensing a change, turning to each other and asking, "You hear that? What was that noise?" They couldn't place the sound, deathly ignorant as they were of what was barreling toward them. But in the weeks after the disaster, as survivors began to speak of the boom that roused them that morning, they speculated that barges had ripped loose of their moorings in the Industrial Canal bordering the neighborhood, sending forth the final warning anyone there would get: an alarming *boom boom boom* as they rammed the levees. As they breached the walls.

The hall clock read 7:45 a.m. Rosy stepped over the jewelry box she'd left sitting on the floor as she reached for the door handle. Cilla, behind her, bent and picked it up. Which is why it was in Cilla's hands, the only possession she salvaged from her home, when Rosy screamed and they took off running.

THEY BEAT THE FLOODWATERS to Maya's house, but only because she lived directly across the street. The levee water barreling toward the women paused for a moment a block away, when a roof swirling on its crest wedged itself between two cars. The wave quickly flung the obstacles aside, but the delay bought them enough time to smash through Maya's door, sprint up the stairs, and hoist each other high enough to grab the rope and pull down the attic ladder. They pushed the old woman ahead of them as the water swallowed up the stairwell. In concert, Cilla shut the trapdoor, Rosy pulled a trunk over it, and the three women threw their bodies atop it as if the flood were a giant they could barricade into another room. They sat wordlessly, stunned. From a long way away, someone screamed, a scream that wouldn't end, a child-ripped-from-the-arms kind of wail. Below them, something metallic bent with a groan. Thunder clapped around them, again and again, but on the third or fourth stroke they realized it wasn't thunder. It was houses. Every wooden house caught in the upsurge plowed into Maya's brick facade and dissolved around them. Her mortared walls shook, but held. Maya looked at Rosy. Rosy looked at Cilla. Cilla, the last of the three to ascend the ladder, had a watermark on her pants halfway up her shins. Looking down, examining her wet legs, she noticed the current starting to spit in around the hinges of the trapdoor in the floor. Rosy, too, noticed the staining of the rafters as the insulation soaked through. But before either woman could remark on the encroaching waters, Maya slipped one arm over Rosy's shoulders, the other over Cilla's, and broke their silence.

"What y'all done brought over, heart?" she asked, as if inquiring after a forgotten hostess gift still nestled in the giver's grasp.

Only then did Cilla realize she held the jewelry box in her hands, while Rosy clutched their shared pair of sneakers in her fist by the knotted-together laces. Rosy had tied them that way on her way home from the library the other day. The library required shoes but she preferred to pedal barefoot so she knotted the laces, tossed the sneakers over the handlebars, then slung them atop the milk crate beside the front door as she entered the house. The crates were long gone, blown away in the early hours of the storm, the other shoes carried off by the winds. But the knotted laces of the sneakers snagged on an overhead hook and hit her in the face as she leapt off the porch; she grabbed at them as she raced ahead of the rushing water toward Maya's house.

Despite the crashing and shattering outside, with the waters of the Mississippi and Lake Pontchartrain swelling beneath them, trapped in a neighbor's attic, it wasn't until Rosy tied the shoes onto her feet that she felt a surge of real terror. Focused on what she'd carried from the house, she suddenly realized the sacks she'd packed—the ones sheltering Cilla's medicine bottle, which she'd ziplocked for added security and pinned to a sweatshirt for safekeeping—had been left behind and were now surely submerged in the flood.

With all that raged around her, nothing frightened her more than the loss of her mother's lithium.

V. ROSE

"La mandra és la mare de tots els vicis."

ROSE COULDN'T ESCAPE THE bizarre sense of betrayal she felt, the sense of bringing a stranger home to the apartment while leaving her mother behind. She could have shucked the shoes—pilfered off the dead girl's feet—outside, bedded beside the doormat, but she didn't. She thought about it, mind you. She thought about little else as the nurse wheeled her from her hospital bed to the waiting taxi at the entry. "I can walk," she'd said, but the nurse insisted the wheelchair was hospital policy, which was probably a good thing since the shoes gripped her like cement blocks and she needed time to practice lifting her feet in them, which she did while being wheeled through the corridors.

She signed her own hospital discharge form early on the morning of Monday, September 5—thirty-six hours after Officer McAffrey whispered to her on the side of the road, "Hold on, sweetheart, help's coming," before lifting her into the ambulance and riding along with her to DCH. He watched over her until they began to cut the bloody clothes from her body. He exited, eyes averted, as an ER nurse slid the shoes off Rose's feet directly into a plastic bag that she sealed, stickered, and placed in holding.

The bag reappeared on Monday morning. "I brung you some things to wear home, darling," the nurse said, taking the liberty of untying Rose's hospital gown and holding a shirt in the air for her to slide her arms into. The nurse had talked with the social worker during shift-change about what to send the girl home in. Typically, family members brought fresh clothes for patients, but no one had come with anything for this girl. No one came at all. *Why was there no one close enough to visit the orphaned girl?* they wondered. *Who would support her in her recovery and grief? Would she be alone in the house when she got back there? How would that affect her mental health? Might she be at risk for*—

"Disposable scrubs."

The nurse and the social worker turned to find the male intern standing behind them.

"Send her home in disposable scrubs," he said, "and gimme the chart. I've gotta sign off before rounds and I'm already late." He scrawled his name, said, "Come on, ladies, get her outta here. We need the bed," and tossed the chart back to the social worker.

So the question of Rose's welfare evaporated, unanswered, when the nurse left to get the scrubs from the utility closet and the social worker turned her attention to the unit's twenty-four other patients' more solvable dilemmas of pain management and long-term care placements.

"I know these're a little big, but I'ma cinch the waist and it'll do you till you get home," the nurse said, chatty in the awkward way some women adopt to disguise sadness. "Lots of people actually find scrubs to be downright comfortable. Fact is, we used to have a problem with them getting stolen all the time. Then they come up with this disposable kind, which the docs say ain't as nice as the cotton ones, but they sure do cut down on laundry and they lots cheaper to replace if folks walk off in them! Toss them in the trash when you get home; no need to worry about returning them. We got your own shoes for you, though!"

"They're not my shoes," Rose said as the nurse ripped open the bag and lifted the dead girl's sneakers out.

"Oh yeah they are, honey," she said as she handed Rose the labeled bag then wrangled the mud- and blood-splattered shoes onto her feet.

Rose meant to protest, to insist the shoes weren't hers despite the official label, but before she could think of a reasonable way to explain how she came to be wearing them when she arrived at the hospital, she got caught up thinking: *Why did I take my own shoes off in the first place?* She remembered punting them to the floor-board of the car—the red ballerina flats she loved because they were sort of kicky but still ultra-comfortable—then pressing her bare toes against the windshield. She remembered, too, being intent on making new toe prints instead of overlapping the ones that were already there, because toe prints on the windshield pissed her mother off and she wanted badly to piss her mother off. *What for?* Rose wondered. *What were we arguing about?*

But then a vision of trees flying toward her overwhelmed her, and in slow-motion horror she saw anew the branches angling toward the car, her own body straining against the seatbelt, instinctively trying to dive into her mother's arms, the way she used to do as a small child whenever dogs ran toward her after she got bit by the Chow in the playground. Gertrude never failed to scoop her up, high above the danger, turning it into a game, letting loose with a giddy "Whee!" as she tossed little Rose into the air. Her mother's arms had always saved her back then, and so at eighteen she lunged for them again at her most desperate moment, after many years spent trying to evade their reach. But Gertrude rejected her before their bodies came together. The fingernails of her mother's right hand bit into the fabric of her shirt, and saved her life by pushing her away, pinning her, immobile, against the passenger seatback. The last word that passed between them was Gertrude's voice screaming "Rooooose!"

The memory made her gasp. She must have looked stricken because the nurse looked up and asked, "Did I tie them too tight?"

And there were the stranger's shoes, already back on her feet, and Rose realized that is exactly where they belonged.

She might never get them off. They were hers now. To leave such cathectic possessions outside, beside the doormat, would have felt like leaving her own feet behind as she entered the apartment, truly alone for the first time in her life.

SEVEN INTERMINABLE DAYS STRETCHED between Gertrude's death, on Saturday, and her funeral a week later. For three days after coming home, Rose didn't open a blind or even turn on a light. During those times when enough sunlight leaked in past the slats to make reading possible, she tackled Andrew Hurley's translation of *Collected Fictions* by Jorge Luis Borges, but by the second day realized that, in her haze, she simply kept rereading the same four chapters of *A Universal History of Iniquity* over and over again and tossed it to the floor. Mostly she slept. In her mother's bed, face buried in the overstuffed goose down pillow, one of Gertrude's few indulgences. Her body needed time to recover from the concussion and the bruising, and her spirit craved darkness.

On Thursday, when she arose from the womb of her mother's bedroom, she looked around with altered eyes. First thing, she lifted a carton of orange juice from the fridge, tilted the spout to her mouth, and began gulping. She'd never done such a thing before; decorum ruled their household. But the household was no longer *theirs*. She carried the carton through the rooms with her, tearing at curtains while she drank, emptying the quart while simultaneously flooding the space with sunlight.

It all came back up later, an acrid wash, when she tore the bedclothes from the bed to launder them and tripped over the shoes, laces meticulously retied, placed with care in sentinel fashion at the foot of Gertrude's bed. She regurgitated, too, the memory of the stranger's broken body in that same position, sprawled on the ground, feet tangled in the footwear. She might never have risen from the floor were it not for all the things she had to do. Memory couldn't be allowed to interfere with her obsession to purge. She tossed the bedclothes into the washing machine, the wrinkled scrubs into the trash, and her own naked, bruised body into the tub.

Almost immediately, though, she raised herself up out of the bathwater and went back for the shoes. She clutched them tightly under one arm, rehydrating the dried dirt, smearing mud onto the side of her left breast. She cradled them along with the phone, which she also grabbed in her nude dash through the rooms. As she dialed information she mentally quantified the hoarded grocery sacks beneath the kitchen sink and the rubbish bags stored in the shed, guesstimating they'd accumulated enough to house all of Gertrude's garments, so she scheduled an early-evening pick-up with the United Way volunteer. Before pacing the full sodden path from tub to shoes and back again, before resettling herself into the water beside the sneakers that now balanced on the tub edge while she soaked, she'd formulated a plan that would get her through to nightfall. As long as she kept occupied, she felt certain she could hold herself together.

Laziness is the mother of all vices, she thought, but heard the echo of her mother's voice, putting it another way: *"La mandra és la mare de tots els vicis."* Gertrude used Catalan—the language of her long-deceased mother—to chide Rose for her indolence whenever she lazed about the apartment lamenting the lack of something interesting to do. Gertrude hadn't used the phrase to honor her Catalan roots, but only out of habit, given that she'd never heard the words spoken any other way.

Gertrude's father, an army grunt in his youth, served for a time near Barcelona. He returned stateside, to the Anniston Army Depot where he worked as a mechanic, with a pregnant Spanish wife. He only ever mentioned the wife part of that clause to his daughter; Gertrude had figured out the pregnant part on her own, as a curious teen, counting backward from her birth date. She let her father go to his grave, dead of a massive heart attack six weeks after his granddaughter Rose's birth, without ever cluing him in to her knowledge of their indiscretion.

The story of her parents' first meeting peppered Gertrude's childhood, oft-told with joy by her father. Him: in uniform, in search of Spanish sweets. Her: behind the counter, baking bread in the *panadería*, with flour on her nose. She'd turned to take his order but sneezed instead, raining puffs of white powder onto his starched dress-greens. Startled by her touch when she reached to dust him off, and stumbling over the foreign phrases, he mistakenly apologized to her when he meant to forgive her, which left him sputtering insensibly.

When he finally quieted, she'd said in studied English, "But it is I who must yet ask forgiveness of you."

"And don't I wish we'd hadda whole lifetime to keep asking for and offering each other forgiveness," he would say to his daughter every time he finished recounting the story.

They'd had no longer than a single gestational period. Gertrude's mother, dead in childbirth, transmitted nothing more than her DNA to her daughter; it was the father who brought the mother to life while rearing the child she'd left him. He made it his life's work to retell their courtship stories: detailed accounts of first dates spent bread-baking in the dark hours of morning, motorcycle-touring on country roads tourists never noticed, puddle-jumping at midnight through cobblestone streets. There came a moment, as an adult, when Gertrude realized with shock that courtship was all her parents ever really had, and that, over the years, she'd vicariously witnessed their whole life together while seated on her father's lap listening to his stories. She knew the color of the earrings her mother wore at their wedding; the shape of her fingernails; the precise placement of each piece of furniture—and how and from where it was acquired—in their first (their only) home, on the base in Anniston. And she knew that just before her mother died, she'd reached out and touched her baby on the left cheek with her right index finger and with her last smile said, "*Ets maca.*"

"You *are* beautiful. And when she said so you smiled right back!" her father always said at that point, which ended every storytelling session about her mother. "Don't you pay no mind to what they say about babies not being able to smile till they're two months old! I was there. I was holding you, Gertie. And you smiled right back at your mama. Last thing she saw in this world was your smile.

"Now go on," he'd say, shooing her off his lap. "Your mama'd tan my hide if she could see us lazing round like this, telling stories. She always said, '*La mandra és la mare de tots els vicis.*'"

So it is that the Catalan phrase got passed from an Alabaman laborer to his daughter and then on to his granddaughter—Rose's only Mediterranean inheritance, for talk of her grandmother ended the day her grandfather died. Gertrude prided herself on living in the present, not the past. Whatever hurt, she erased from memory. Only this phrase slipped through the generations, iterated with a Dixie drawl that virtually negated its Barcelona roots.

On the morning of September 11, 2001, however, the words took on a new association, becoming forever linked in Rose's mind with the crumbling of the World Trade Center towers.

Gertrude's shift at Kinko's started that late-summer morning at eight, so she was fully dressed and made-up, eyebrows tweezed and ironed skirt on, eating her toast and rinsing her coffee cup, absently letting the *Today* show keep her company, when she heard Matt Lauer announce a breaking news story. Breaking news stories intrigued her, as did fire engines and tornado sirens. Rose regularly had to admonish her not to chase after ambulances entering the apartment complex. ("For God's sake, Mother, you're the worst kind of Nosy Nellie!") Though Gertrude hated to think of anyone hurt, she couldn't help rushing to the scene in hopes of having a story to tell at work the next day. Notably mute on the disasters that defined her own life—her mother's premature death, her husband's untimely departure—she effectively filled the void with talk of others' misfortunes.

So she checked her watch, 7:52 a.m., and sat down on the edge of the sofa, waiting through the commercial break, thinking she might have time to get the story before leaving for work. Realizing all of her coworkers were likely already en route to the store, she savored the idea of swooping in with a scoop. Secretly she hoped for a tragedy, something big—on the scale of a school shooting. She bit her lip in anticipation.

There it was, finally. Good heavens! The World Trade Center on fire! Matt said a small commuter plane crashed into the North Tower, but Gertrude didn't credit that. How could someone accidentally fly into something so huge? And a small plane wouldn't do all that damage. She assayed the video imagery so intently she didn't think to check her watch again until 8:02 a.m. Already late and still with a five-minute drive ahead of her, she reached to turn off the television and was, therefore, nose-to-nose with the South Tower when it exploded inside her television.

She sank to her knees on the floor and put her hand on the screen, smacking Katie Couric in the face, cursing at her to get off the screen. She wanted to see the replay footage.

There, finally. A better shot from a different camera angle. It was a jet. With her disaster preoccupation, Gertrude understood instinctively what was happening.

"Rose!" she screamed, as an eyewitness—some producer linked in via phone—wondered aloud if there could be air traffic control problems.

"Rose! Get up! We're under attack!"

As Rose crashed bleary-eyed out of the bedroom, she heard her mother scream, "The United States is being attacked!"

They sat together on the floor, holding hands without realizing it, until 9:30 a.m. when Katie Couric and Matt Lauer moved to the anchor desk with Tom Brokaw. Then Gertrude and Rose moved to the sofa. At noon, when Tom began his special report, "Attack on America," Rose came back from a trip to the bathroom carrying a box of Cheerios, which they held between them and ate dry, straight from the box, respectful of each other's hands going in and out, not bumping. Right before Katie and Matt's special report began at 4 p.m., realizing they had sat silently transfixed for over eight hours, Gertrude still in heels, Rose still in pajamas, Rose tried to lighten the macabre mood a touch by saying, "*La mandra és la mare de tots els vicis.*"

To which Gertrude replied: "*I, com a mare, cal respectar-la.*"

Rose looked at her mother quizzically, having never heard this Catalan response.

"If laziness is the mother of all vices," Gertrude translated, "then, as a mother, we must respect her." Then she settled her arm around her daughter, which Rose indulged, and they watched the coverage until they fell asleep safely, body beside body, while Tom continued to narrate their dreams of terror, and of atrocities, and of carnage outside their door.

Every September 11 thereafter, without prearrangement, they would reclaim their spots on the sofa shortly after 7 a.m. and honor the dead together. Rose, clad in pajamas—an immoderation Gertrude would have disallowed on any other day—would bring a box of Cheerios and say, "*La mandra és la mare de tots els vicis.*"

Gertrude would take her daughter's hand, which Rose let her grasp for those few hours annually, and reply, "*I, com a mare, cal respectar-la.*"

They mourned not just those unknown to them in New York City and Washington, D.C. and a Pennsylvania field, but also those much missed but never spoken of in their own lives. Rose paid particular attention to the children holding up pictures of missing fathers; Gertrude noted grown women searching for vanished parents, departed spouses.

They sat together. They stared together. They mourned separately in communion with ghosts too personal.

THE NEIGHBOR THOUGHT MAYBE Rose had lost her mind. In the accident, you know. Bless her heart, there could be no other explanation.

She'd been watching the apartment for days, having accumulated the ingredients for succotash in anticipation of the young girl's return from the hospital. It was no easy trick to keep her spouse and three kids from nibbling on the fixings. Twice she caught her man about to slice into a tomato and had to swat it out of his dark, calloused hands. "You put that down! Ain't for you! It's for that poor girl cross the way with the dead mama!"

"You don't even know that girl," he whined.

"She our neighbor!"

"Ain't matter none to you before."

"Before she ain't had no dead mama!"

"How's her mama being dead mean I can't eat the food in my own house?"

At that, the woman put both hands on her hips, planted her right foot hard into the linoleum ahead of her and, while holding the rest of her body ramrod stiff, whipped her head back with an avian circuitousness that made it look as if she might peck a hole in his carotid. He knew to retreat before she really unloaded.

"Then least get her food on outta my kitchen!" he said, to save face. "If the food be in my house, I got me a right to be eating it!"

"I can't!" the woman answered. "She ain't home yet!" She thrumped across the apartment to the sliding glass door and stole another peek through her blinds at the still apartment across the way. Didn't want to come off as meddlesome.

The local newscaster said the sole survivor of the car crash had been released from DCH on Monday but she didn't spot any signs of life all week until early Thursday when, on her umpteenth pass to peer through the glass, she finally spied the whole place lit up like a marquee. At that, she tied a do-rag over her cornrows, cinched an apron around her expansive waist, and began whipping together ingredients. By the time she crossed the parking lot with her food offering, making a beeline for the girl's front door, she had to walk a gauntlet of bags brimming with blouses and pumps and gray wool skirts.

"Lordy, gal," she said aloud to herself as she ascended the stairway from the drive, "that child gone and got herself possessed! Who done ever heard of tossing your mama out in the trash on day one? That there's one crazy-ass thing to do!"

She knocked with trepidation.

The pale and bleary-eyed girl who opened the door wore a black silk slip on her head, the waistband pinching her forehead, the fabric enveloping her hair like a wig. She waved a knife in the air as she said, "Hey! Come on in!" but the succotash was by then already spiraling toward the ground, and the casserole dish rained a thousand shards of porcelain on the WELCOME mat between their feet.

The black woman stutter-stepped, tripping on her own toes, uncertain which inclination to indulge: habit, which bid her stay and clean up, or instinct, which bid her run. When the girl swapped the knife for a trash bag and bent to scoop up the squashed food and ceramic shards, oozing apologies for having startled her, she warily crouched alongside to assist. Slivers of serving dish *ping ping pinged* off each other in the plastic sack in a lulling chorus, but she couldn't concentrate on the mess what with that strange get-up distracting her. It took a minute to work up the courage, but she finally asked, "What you wearing?"

The girl looked down at her shorts, her T-shirt, confused.

"Not on your body. On your head. Girl, you got yourself a slip on your head!"

"Oh!" The girl pulled the slip off of her hair, stood suddenly, and burst out laughing. "Oh, God! How embarrassing! I forgot I had that on!"

The neighbor stood, too, somewhat off-balance as she backed away.

"I used to ..." Rose tried to explain, but laughter overtook her. She doubled over, hysterical. She spat out, "When I was little ..." before she choked again on the laughter, which made the word 'little' erupt from her as if from a banshee. Bent in half on the doorstep, she laughed and laughed until she couldn't breathe, laughed so hard she started to cry, laughed and cried so hard she began sucking in air, big desperate gulps between sobs as she pressed the slip to her face. The neighbor thought she should comfort the girl, thought *someone* should comfort the girl, but opted instead— in a split-second decision that took in the earlier consideration of

Rose's potential possession as well as the otherness of her skin tone, the fact of the underwear on her head, and the question of where that knife went—to race home and lock her door behind her. Hidden safely behind the blinds again, feeling terrible about it but unable to summon the courage to act otherwise, she watched the crazy girl hug her own self and sob on the doorstep for another twenty minutes, the casserole a steamy mush at her feet.

Rose had meant to tell her neighbor that she used to wear the slip on her head when she was a child. In it, she'd felt transported and imagined a secret life for herself as a princess inside one of the castles sealed within the massive collection of snow globes atop her mother's dresser. The slip transformed her into the silken-haired, much-adored, sultan's choice.

Tearing through her mother's lingerie drawer, mindlessly pitching belongings into sacks, Rose found the slip again, this decade later. It paused her ravenous efforts. With the silky fabric pressed against her cheek, she recalled the illicit pleasure aroused when Gertrude acquiesced to her youthful pleas to rummage among the womanly accoutrements, legs sliding into pantyhose, bejeweled necklaces dug out of a box stored in her mother's underwear drawer and slipped over her neck. She remembered pushing bangle bracelets up her arms to ring her biceps, like an imperial heir. And always the slip for hair. Standing before her mother's ravaged dresser, she meant to toss the slip into the donation pile but couldn't do it. Instead, she pulled it down over her head again, until once more it encased her hair in a sensuous facsimile of royalty.

Clad in savage mementos—dead mother's underwear on her head, dead girl's sneakers on her feet—Rose had wandered into the living room and pulled a photo album off a low shelf. From the kitchen she gathered an apple and knife, with which to quarter it, then settled into a chair at the kitchen table and perused the album until the neighbor's knock interrupted her.

On the third page, she found the picture she'd gone looking for. Her six-, maybe seven-year-old self, in Gertrude's blue cotton nightgown with lace-capped sleeves that draped on her more diminutive frame to bridal-train effect. Silk hair in place, held taut against her scalp by a gold necklace harboring a fake jewel that she had positioned in the center of her forehead, bindi-style. The child smiled a gap-toothed smile and held a flowerpot aloft, mid-rub, as if expecting a genie to pop out. The sight of her homespun version of Aladdin's Jasmine made Rose giggle.

She licked apple juice off her fingers. Two pages later, she came upon her favorite photo. Her mother and her, age eleven, in the first car of the Georgia Cyclone at Six Flags, snapped by remote camera as they crested the initial peak and began the long dive down the coaster's crazy-steep hill. Though it wasn't a flattering shot—they looked like their eyes were fixing to pop out of their heads—Gertrude had bought the picture along with some cotton candy, a Looney Tunes toy, and two hotdogs. Hadn't packed a lunch to save money, hadn't said "you don't need it" or "you won't use it" or "you can do without it." She just said yes all day long. Yes to every snack and yes to second and third rides on the same amusement and yes to staying until the very last moment when the security guard finally cornered them and said, "The park is closed, ladies! Y'all have to go now!" Then Gertrude ran—her mother *ran!*—hand in hand with Rose to the car in the parking lot, where she whirled her in a circle in the air (for the last time ever), and said, "Wasn't that the most fun we ever had?"

It was the most fun they ever had, which is why Rose loved the picture. For just that one day, all day, her mother didn't remind her at all of her mother and, as such, she thought the bug-eyed shot at the top of the Cyclone was the most beautiful picture Gertrude had ever inhabited.

There had been others, other beautiful pictures, but Gertrude had torn them out of the album before Rose grew anywhere near wise enough to go looking for them.

⋇

THEY CALL IT NESTING, that instinct to prearrange the environs in anticipation of a baby's birth.

Absent the resources to nest in any grand fashion, Gertrude acted out her pregnant urge by sifting through a shoebox full of photographs and starting an album for her unborn baby. She backed up two years to track the baby's path to conception. Began with her junior prom picture, Roger in a royal blue bowtie under his white tux, to match her royal blue dress: their first official date. Beside it she pasted her senior prom picture and then one from her high school graduation: she in white cap and gown, Roger in a Roll Tide red shirt with his arms snug around her. Two years her senior, Roger was already heading into his junior year at the university she had been destined her whole life to attend.

When her mother died, Gertrude's father left both Anniston and the Army behind for a job in Tuscaloosa, servicing the groundskeeping vehicles for the University of Alabama. He groomed the machines that groomed the prodigious athletic fields while simultaneously grooming his daughter to expect, someday, to cheer on the hallowed turf in Bryant-Denny Stadium where she took her first steps. He labored at a job that meant nothing to him, married to his work first and his daughter second, in order to ensure her a free pass to the college education he never had.

The fourth picture she pasted into the album documented the death of that dream.

Gertrude's three closest girlfriends huddled together, beaming in their pledge shirts on the patio of the coveted Chi Omega house. Those three achieved what all four friends had always talked about doing, together. It wasn't a well-focused picture; it betrayed Gertrude's trembling hand on the shutter and, as she lined it up on the page, she struggled, again, to prevent the tears that wanted to come as she witnessed her longed-for future slide away. The bump in the next picture explained why: the swelling belly beneath the waistband of her white 50-percent-off formalwear gown from Parisian—not a real wedding dress: no time for all that. Her baby would arrive in March, on the heels of the spring-break exodus to Daytona Beach that she'd never realize.

She only added two other photographs to the album before

halting the project: one of Roger's folks and her dad flanking them at TGI Friday's restaurant after the curt marriage ceremony at city hall; the other of her and Roger, her three girlfriends, their boyfriends, all smiles and laughter against a backdrop of the City Cafe decked out for Christmas in plastic holly and metallic tinsel. Her belly really showed in this one, but no one looked as if they minded there in the back booth where the four girls and their series of beaux had lunched every Saturday afternoon for four years.

In the moment before the phone rang, that picture stood for everything she loved most about her life. Her husband, her friends, her youth. She only turned her gaze from the image for a few seconds—thirty, tops!—one hand pressing the taped corners onto the page while reaching with the other for the ringing phone, but when she looked back it had already morphed into a visual testament to a closed chapter. They'd never all be together again.

Roger abandoned her without so much as a formal goodbye. Gertrude got nothing more than the phone call, informing her he wouldn't be coming home—not that day, not any day after. She put the phone down without remembering to disconnect the line, stunned more than anything. At first she didn't even cry. Just rested her head on the table, left cheek pressing down on a pile of loose pictures that would never make it into the album, hands stroking her belly, then encircling it, as if holding the baby in, listening to the *beep beep beep beep* of the phone as it fought with her to let it go.

The album sat untouched on the kitchen table as the season passed from winter to spring, just two pages complete, scissors half-open as if in mid-snip, while the rest of her world crumbled. She birthed her baby alone. One morning, not long after, when she ran to him, hoping to ply him for advice on this single parenting mess, she found her father dead in his bed. Mere days later, Roger's family moved away without leaving a forwarding address, and never contacted her again. No surprise, really. They obviously blamed her pregnancy for derailing their golden boy's future. Even her girlfriends fell away quickly, unsure of what to say or do, preoccupied with the life Gertrude no longer shared with them. In less than three months, every single person she'd relied upon disappeared, every load-bearing wall in the house of her life succumbed to gravity as the roof caved in.

And the infant cried. Day after day after day she cried. No nap. No break. Wouldn't settle. Hardly ate, because her fucking mouth wouldn't close around the nipple, the formula gurgling out each time the rebellious fucking tongue poked out to beg, beg, beg, all shriveled skin and squawking that wouldn't stop, no off button, no volume control. Crying crying crying whether swaddled or held up or put down or jiggled or rocked or patted or swung around or squeezed. That damn baby cried when locked in the bedroom, over the sound of the blasting stereo, blanket stuffed under the door. Hands over ears, stomping on the floor, kicking the wall—no escape. Over the bathwater running, over her own sobs, baby screams kept coming. Inside her *bones* Gertrude could hear the crying.

But not underwater. It came to her as she sat in the tub trying to hold the screaming, writhing infant and wash her and think— just think! That's all she wanted to do, just take one quiet minute to think of what to do to muffle the sound. *Water does that,* she realized. *It mutes things.* So she just let go, and Rose bobbed under the surface and it worked, for a second. For just a second, quiet! Until Rose flailed and her face buoyed up and the shattering screams came again and Gertrude pressed her index finger against the baby's forehead, not hard even, and under she went. With eyes closed in quiet detachment, Gertrude held Rose under the water and took one full deep breath, legs astride the baby in the warm water and head lolled back to savor the silence. She might have sat there all night, just breathing, but for the little hand that, in its desperation, encircled her finger. Reached out for, clung on to, called back its mother.

Gertrude catapulted from the tub so quickly that a wave of water crested the side, soaking the mat on which she laid the baby's limp body. She rubbed Rose's chest vigorously, flipping her over to whack her back, like they'd taught in childbirth class to do when a baby chokes. She begged, "Cry! Cry!" And then Rose did. Kneeling, naked, over Rose's gasping form, Gertrude offered up her own life as penance. Bait and switch. She'd sacrifice herself for her daughter's salvation.

When she arose from the bathroom floor, every moment that had come before was dead to her. Forgotten. What mattered now would be the child. Only the child.

Twenty minutes later, while Rose slept in a towel on the bathroom floor, Gertrude tore the two finished pages from the photo album, gathered up all the loose photographs, set a match to a Duraflame log in the fireplace, and began feeding every paper testament of her past to the flames. Amped, she moved on to Roger's belongings, ravenously hurling his books into the fire. His clothing, too voluminous to burn, she carried in four loads to the dumpster in the parking lot. Then she started eliminating herself and her family, dumping her father's toolbox, her varsity pom-pons, and a few cartons of accumulated memorabilia onto the sidewalk. Emblazoned with a big FREE sign, it would all be gone by daybreak.

At two in the morning, she took up the pair of scissors and hacked off her hair to chin length, then sliced through every item of her clothing but that which she wore. Last thing, she rearranged the furniture. It felt good. Divested of her past, she could think her way clear to her future.

Spent, she slept on the bathmat, curled around Rose.

She woke with a solid sense of what they both now needed. The baby: attachment, unthreatened union with her mother. Her: independence—of movement, of spirit—while mothering. It took her half of a post-dawn hour to arrange a makeshift sling from an ultra-absorbent gym towel, one with some give but not so much as to overstretch and loosen the knots that held in the baby. Rose rebelled at first, as she did at everything, flailing and screaming. Still, Gertrude persisted, ceaselessly pacing the apartment, rhythmically patting Rose's rump through the fabric.

And then the baby settled. Nuzzled in and went to sleep. It had worked! Gertrude offered a prayer of thanksgiving to the world at large and smiled for the first time in months. Raising her face to the sun at the window, she sensed communion with the long history of parents—her own father included—who had patched a way through to some semblance of success with their infants. But her relief fractured when she noticed a neighbor outside waddling away with the last item from the discard pile on the sidewalk, the boxful of snow globes. Suddenly she felt as if someone was strolling away with the key to her future, her crystal balls.

Cradling the sling so as not to jiggle the baby awake, she raced outside and immediately intercepted the woman, begging for the return of the globes.

"But you done throwed them out!" the neighbor insisted. "They was a sign there saying FREE."

"I know, but I changed my mind."

The snow globes were pretty. "Little late for that," the woman said, holding tightly to the box.

"But, but ..." And then she did it. Told her story for the last time in her life. "You don't understand. My father gave those to me. He gave me one every Christmas to remind me of my mother. She died when I was born."

Nothing. No spark of empathy. She pressed on, "My mother was from Catalonia. You know, in Spain?"

The woman stared blankly.

"Catalonia is where my mother was born, where my parents met. The name means 'land of castles.' My father bought me a snow globe with a castle in it every Christmas, so I'd remember her. Every year I'd find one in the toe of my stocking, and my father'd say the same thing when I pulled it out: 'Never forget, sweetum, that your daddy may be poor Alabama farm stock, but your mama done come from kings!'

"Please gimme my castles back," Gertrude pleaded.

"What you doing putting them out here if—"

"I've been crazy lately. My father just died, my husband's gone, and I'm on my own with this baby. Just please lemme have them back."

That was the first of only two actions from the night before that Gertrude ever reversed. The other involved the group picture from the City Cafe, which she discovered among the firebox ashes. Seared edges, discolored by smoke, but all the friends' faces still intact. She felt bound to honor providence's dictates and preserve for her daughter this single image of Rose's father.

She opened the album to the new first page, which abutted the ragged edges of the torn-out sheets, and taped the picture back in. But then she waffled. Took it out. Didn't want to remind herself, looking at the album, of what she'd once had, lest she dwell on it. But still, if it were meant to burn, it would have burned. She taped it back down again.

She needn't have struggled so with the decision. Turns out, when she set her mind to something, she possessed terrific capacity to accomplish it fully.

The first time Rose flipped through the album as a little girl, she asked who all these strangers were, forcing Gertrude to point out her own younger self to her daughter. More than once in Rose's later sojourns through the album she'd call out: "Mother, what one's you again?" The image struck Rose as so unfamiliar that she didn't even recognize the background as being that of the City Cafe even though the furnishings remained the same and the wait-staff unchanged when, after a few years' hiatus, Gertrude started taking Rose there for the mac 'n' cheese.

The hostess didn't recognize Gertrude either.

The woman who entered the restaurant anew, clinging to the hand of her daughter, wore re-polished loafers and carried a clutch with a gold-plated closure. She scanned the clientele critically for smokers, loud-talkers, and out-of-control toddlers to steer clear of, and inspected the spoons for crusted food and the glasses for lipstick residue. She bore no resemblance to the giddy girl in flouncy Laura Ashley hair bows who had lunched there weekly throughout her teenage years, surrounded always by a gaggle of friends. She was not the woman anyone might have imagined Gertie Chiles would grow up to be.

Instead, Gertie Chiles grew up to be Gertrude Aikens, a woman who flipped through photo albums from the back, beginning with the present, never delving far enough toward the front to reach the past.

VI. ROSY

"Stop, please! Equalize with the city!
Draw this water down!"

INSIDE CILLA'S JEWELRY BOX, safely centered on the back of a chifforobe floating face-down in the pool that had once been Maya's attic, nestled a snapshot of Rosy with her foot bound in gauze. It documented one of Cilla's maternal triumphs: pulling a nail out of her five-year-old daughter's foot with her teeth.

For as long as Cilla could remember, the bottom stairboard leading up to their front porch had been loose. It shifted with each footfall and made a gentle *crkkn*, as if to imply the house were welcoming home its occupants after a long day of separation. She'd liked the sound; it spoke of homecoming and rest-to-come, until the day Rosy caught the corner in her haste to halt the ice-cream truck, split the board in half, splintered the edge, and somehow landed standing in the grass with a nail driven straight up through the bottom of her left foot.

From inside, Cilla heard the crash. She waited for Rosy's squeal of shock or a cry that might mean she'd suffered a scrape or, at worst, a deep cut. But no: a mewling moan spilled from her child, unlike anything she'd ever heard, and it sent her charging, terrified, toward the porch.

For a moment, seeing Rosy standing upright on the lawn, relief flooded her. But then she followed her daughter's gaze and saw the nail sprouting two inches through the top of her foot.

Cilla had the forethought to get exact change for the bus and Rosy's favorite toy and a juice box before rushing from the house with her child held tightly against her chest, wrapped in a blanket. She moved quickly, but without panicking, and kept Rosy soothed by singing softly into her ear during the four-and-a-half-mile bus ride to Charity Hospital downtown.

She never once put Rosy down, even during the second hour when she rechecked with the ER clerk to be sure they were still in the queue. She continued rocking and crooning to Rosy until the third hour when her voice tired and she despaired that they'd ever be seen. In the fourth hour, their care preempted by gang members and drug pushers and all manner of hoodlums who left bloody wheel marks in their wake, she decided her daughter didn't belong in such a place anyway. No one in that whole hospital—not the doctors with their fancy degrees or the nurses with their experience and know-how—cared about her child as much as she did.

Rosy had been such a good little thing, too. Exactly the kind of child you'd think someone should care about. She hadn't fussed or cried, just settled into Cilla's arms uncomplaining, waiting out the ordeal. Had the good manners not even to bleed, the nail staunching the flow. So when she turned her face to her mother's and muttered her first words in five hours, "I wanna go home," Cilla decided to oblige her. She walked up to the clerk's desk, gathered a wad of tissue, lifted Rosy's foot from the blanket, clenched her teeth around the nail head, and yanked. Then she spit the nail onto the waiting room floor and stormed out the automatic doors that parted before her. Hard to say if anybody even noticed. Back home, she filled the hole with a poultice, wrapped the wound in bandages that she changed twice daily, kept it peroxided and clean, cadged a tetanus shot and a penicillin prescription off one of the physicians she cleaned house for, and had Rosy toddling around again in just over two days.

Despite the fact that she couldn't always control her own demons, Cilla trusted herself to keep her head and save the day during other people's crises.

She waded the short length of Maya's attic slowly now, running her hands over the roof boards, pausing here and there to rap her knuckles against the wood, listening for a hollow reply. She stopped and balanced on a reinforced joist, waist-deep in water.

"Here."

"Here, what?" Rosy asked.

"Here's where I aim to bust out," she said. "Sounds less solid in this spot, like maybe it's more rotted out over here. Best chance to break through."

"How're we gonna do that?"

Cilla swept one arm in a wide arc in front of her, indicating the rising water. "How're we *not* gonna do that?"

Maya and Rosy could see Cilla moving, shadow-like, some fifteen feet away from them, but the darkness prevented them from accurately interpreting her motions. The two windows, at either end of the attic, were by now halfway blacked out by the rising water, and the cloud-laden skies outside sifted little illumination through the glass. Twenty-seven hours into their confinement, their eyes had adjusted as much as possible to the lack of light, but if someone had said it was ten o'clock they couldn't have accurately guessed whether it was a.m. or p.m.

Cilla continued navigating by touch. She punched at the roof boards with the heel of her hand; they failed to yield. "Our only way out is up, so by God, we going up. I done got us through too much in this lifetime to watch my daughter drown in ... in ... in this cesspool trying to pass for a house!" She lowered her voice, conspiratorially: "Cuz y'all know this only half storm water we in right now. Other half's pee from all the folks done pissed they pants when they saw that wall-a-water barreling down on us!" She laughed at herself and winked at Maya and Rosy huddled together on the chifforobe, another lost gesture. "I might done gone and lost everything else, but long as I got breath in me, I aim to hang onto my sense of humor," she insisted.

"Well ain't this a fine mess?" Maya piped up, breaking the silence she'd kept since the chifforobe started floating, which likely occurred sometime early the previous evening.

The first day divided itself neatly into two distinct sections: before the chifforobe started floating, and after. Early on in the ordeal—as the three sat on the trunk for hours after ascending the ladder and slamming shut the hatch—there'd been an otherworldliness to their plight. They actually played word games, actively ignoring the rising water. Rosy had started it. Noticing the water starting to seep through the attic floorboards, suffering the horror of having left Cilla's lithium behind, noting that defenestration might be their only way out of the attic, sensing the onslaught of hunger and thirst, Rosy realized she could panic, pray, or practice patience. She opted for the last, preferring to believe that if they could somehow keep their wits, if they could treat the day like any other fraught by weather too threatening to venture out in, it might all turn out to be just that normal. Why not? So she turned to Maya, sitting beside her, and said: "Butterfly McQueen."

"Marian Anderson," Maya replied good-naturedly, using the first letter of McQueen's last name as the first letter of the first name of the next famous person.

Cilla quickly chimed in with "Alvin Ailey," a double-letter name, which sent the play back in the direction from which it came. Maya then pulled a coup by turning it back on Cilla, reversing the turns again with "Arthur Ashe."

Cilla: "Armstrong Williams!"

Rosy: "Whitney Houston!"

Maya, less swift than the other two, thought a moment. "Hurricane Carter!" she exclaimed, and they all laughed. Nervously.

The hurricane reference threw Cilla off, and she said "Kirk

Franklin!" which Rosy had to remind her began with a *K*, not a *C*, so she switched her response to Coretta Scott King.

"Kirk Franklin!" Rosy yelled, and they laughed again, this time with real pleasure.

Cilla hummed a Kirk Franklin tune while they played, hours on end. Played until they ran out of famous black folk. Played until they ran out of famous white folk. Played while their stomachs rumbled and until they had to pull their feet up and wrap their arms around their knees to keep out the chill and the wet. Played until Cilla said, "Rosy girl, gimme a hand," and they tipped the chifforobe forward to crash face-down with a tremendous splash, drowning out Maya's furious cries that it belonged to her grandmother!, it was an antique!, it was the only thing she had left from that side of the family!

"Look round here, Maya," Cilla said as she squatted and relieved herself in the murky water that, by then, covered the floor to a depth of about two feet. "None of us got nothing left from nobody no more."

With that, Maya stopped speaking. Not a word, not even when she slipped while clambering onto the flat back of the chifforobe, sinking her right leg up to the thigh through the flimsy ceiling boards into the space that had once been her bedroom below. Not so much as a whimper when they pulled her out, bleeding, and nested together dead-center on the piece of furniture that had housed her grandmother's wedding quilt and her mother's communion dress, the bedclothes Maya had been born on and the blanket she swaddled the infant Rosy in. Once a week, for the sixty-plus years it had resided in her bedroom, Maya had dusted the piece she now huddled on. More than 3,100 times, her hands had caressed the wood with a dry rag, not a wet one; wet is not good for wood, it must be kept dry.

The chifforobe bobbed in the floodwaters.

The attic was supposed to have been a safe place for it and the things interred inside. Maya had coaxed Cilla and Rosy and Silas into hoisting it upstairs a few years back, relieved to have it out of public view. No more putting out a hand to stop a distracted man from slamming it shut too hard after fumbling for a spare blanket, no more needing to step between it and a child careening toward its well-preserved finish with a bike or a marble or a loosely swung bat. In the attic it would be hidden and her valuables would be secure even if some thief broke in, which could easily happen, what with the way the young people on that crack cocaine nowadays ransacked neighbors' houses and took everything within eyesight to swap out for more drugs.

Below them, in the belly of the chifforobe, her tarnishing silver tinkled as the water lapped at it, bumping the forks and the knives up against the just-shattered china—those plates and saucers her grandmother had put aside a nickel a week to buy, piece by piece, over the course of twenty-two years. Now all was lost, and it paralyzed her. She kept thinking how it would be different were she young: there would be restorative years ahead. But not so when all that is lost is all one will ever have time to collect.

Haunted by the sound of tinkling that punctuated Maya's sorrow and by the sounds of others' losses that came to them in isolated bursts of screams or wails or bumps beyond their walls, they waited. Silently. Waited without sleeping; too unsettled for sleep. Waited to see if the heirloom would float beneath the weight of all three of them, listening for creaks that might presage their demise, terrified that if they closed their eyes they might never awaken should the chifforobe sink beneath the waters that would not cease rising.

TWENTY-SEVEN HOURS AFTER THEY sealed themselves in the attic, somewhere in the area of ten o'clock on the morning of Tuesday, August 30, the silence and the waiting broke when Cilla jumped off the floating furniture into water that broached her waist, and crept hand-over-hand into the darkness, to divine a way out of their tomb.

Her splash roused them all from their morbid stupor.

"Well ain't this a fine mess?" Maya asked, breaking her silence of the day before.

From the darkness, Cilla's voice answered lightly, "Well, if this ain't the mess, it'll sure as hell do till the mess gets here."

Rosy held her tongue. She'd been holding her tongue since the episode in the kitchen on Sunday. No time for personal recriminations. Didn't much matter now how it got to this; "I told you so" wouldn't reverse their circumstances. Were she to point out that everyone from herself to the president had predicted the possibility of this "mess" beginning a few days back, when their participation in the "mess," or at least this degree of "mess," could have been mitigated, it would have been a bit like Noah leaning off the edge of the ark and shouting down to the drowning townsfolk, "Did y'all notice it's raining?" Valid but cocky. Earned, but cruel.

Instead, she ignored the banter, recognizing with each *thud* of the heel of Cilla's hand on the rafters that it would take more than a punch from a bare fist to get them through to the roof. "How're we gonna bust through?" she asked.

Cilla didn't answer; just kept punching. In the face of her recalcitrance, Rosy ventured that perhaps Cilla could use her sneaker like a boxing glove, at least add some padding. When finally Cilla spoke up she admitted it would take the boxer himself to break through the roof boards. They wondered next about breaking the ornamental facing off the chifforobe to use as a battering ram, or balancing back-to-back and kicking through the roof, or, failing that, smashing through the upper glass pane of the window and diving out, hoping for a nearby piece of flotsam to cling to. But none of them could swim; they would most likely drown trying. It was a last resort.

Intrigued by their creative musings, Maya listened for a bit before suggesting, "Why don't y'all just chop through the roof with the ax?"

Unable to see each other clearly in the darkness, Cilla and Rosy nonetheless managed to coordinate their responses. "What ax?"

"The ax in the trunk," Maya said.

"What trunk?" Rosy asked.

"The one we done sat on all morning," Maya answered.

A pause.

Incredulous, Rosy actually giggled. Cilla remained silent. Stunned.

"There's an ax in the trunk?" Rosy confirmed.

"Course there is," Maya said, indignant.

"Maya, whatcha mean 'Course there is'? What in the world is an old woman like you doing with an ax in a trunk in her attic?"

"Been up here since '65."

"And you use it for ..."

"Nothing. Still got the tag on it. Ain't never needed it!"

"So why'd you buy an ax you've never used?" Rosy asked. "String of ax murders, or something, back in '65? You figured you'd beat them at their own game should they come climbing in through your window?"

"No, Smarty Pants. I got it cuz they said to."

"*They* said to ..." Rosy let the sentence trail off, a question.

"They said to after Billion-Dollar Betsy. Levees breached, flooded a buncha folks out. I done told you, I had me some water in my kitchen. Last time water ever got into this house!" This she said straightforwardly, as if she hadn't noticed that she made this pronouncement while floating on an upended piece of furniture in her attic. "After that hurricane, they said every soul oughta keep an ax in they attic. And I'm nothing if not obedient."

Oblivious as Maya might have been, the irony did not escape Rosy. "Were you obedient, you'd be high and dry in Texas by now," she mumbled.

"Well, okay then. I be prudent."

Cilla finally spoke: "And you didn't mention this before cuz ..." Like Rosy, she left the obvious unstated, letting the silence become the question.

Maya exploded: "I wasn't gonna have nobody chopping at my house for the fun of it!"

"Well, that makes sense to me," Cilla murmured into the

darkness. "Cuz I don't know about all y'all, but I'm having myself a fucking ball over here."

✦

THERE WERE HINTS. TAKE the hapless way she dove off the chifforobe, despite the fact that a single misstep could have sunk her through the attic floor into the watery tomb of Maya's house. Also, her wielding of the ax in darkness? Nuts. Make no mistake: it saved their lives. But still. It signaled a changing tide. It wasn't just cavalier. It was the edge of insanity.

By nightfall on Tuesday, Cilla stood balanced on the ridgeline of the roof, head thrown back to the heavens, singing her soul out beneath the still-cloudy sky, clutching her jewelry box to her belly. In the late afternoon, when Rosy had reached for her mother and urged her down to a safer perch on the shingles—scared, angry, sick of the goddamn singing—Cilla smacked away her outstretched hand and screamed, "Don't touch me!"

Rosy looked around her and thought, *Now we're talking mess.*

Any other day, from the roof, she would have had a glorious view. The lake behind them, the canals to the left, the city to the right, all her regular places, the places that made this home: school, library, washateria, Silas's superette, the playground two blocks over with her favorite red swing. All gone. The whole Lower Ninth Ward reduced to some treetops, scattered roofs, maybe the top edge of the shoot-da-chute at Bonart playground? Church spires, mostly. And floating things in black water: pillows, cups, cats and dogs (dead), a chicken (dead), a bike missing its front tire, the hood of a car, a banister with rails still attached, a bouquet of waterlogged lilies cinched together with yellow polka-dotted ribbon. A framed family photograph—the big wall-hanging kind, someone's beloved living room centerpiece—with an enormous gash down the center, splitting the family in half. Rosy imagined somebody running with the portrait pressed against her breast, ahead of the floodwaters, when something sharp came up out of nowhere to slash the image sheer through.

It had gone still but for Cilla's singing. The howling of the dogs had stopped by the second day. No more sounds of other people, either. Just the three of them on the roof, and six bodies in the water. All still flowing toward the city, New Orleans proper ever the draw. None of the bodies was decent, each of them overexposed in one manner or another. An old man, clothed, face up, eyes open and glowing, bloated corpse bursting buttons, those naked eyes worse even than the naked bodies. A child, a little girl, with pristine plaits and a black Mary Jane on her left foot, her brown buttocks bobbing up and down in sensual aquatic dance. Rosy didn't want to see, let alone stare, but she couldn't remove her eyes. *What kind of force leaves the plaits and one shoe,* she wondered, *but takes everything else?*

They smelled. All of them: the dead and the living, too. The floaters oozed gas, bubbles percolating between and beside their legs, remnants of last meals yet moving in bodies long stilled. The stench of innards leaking out: stale lung air, blood, uric acid, stomach juices flowing in yellow rivulets down dark cheeks. Compost untended. A crow rode one corpse like a sea-bound vessel, screeching hale and hearty with a *caw caw caw*, plucking offal from the host's nose. In the hair of both the dead and the living clung the scent of fires that burned in places where the houses still stood on soggy foundations but the stoves, displaced, gorged their energy on the higher-up wood that had been spared the water. Could have been a crematorium somewhere out there, a burn bin for medical refuse, a pile of diseased organs set to flame, so said the winds.

Quelled in the dead, unique to the living: sweat, adrenaline stench, the mephitic reek of fear.

The water kept coming. Almost level now with their hole in the roof, whereas it had been just over the gutters when they had clambered through the escape hatch Cilla wrenched open for them. Given this rate of rise, by the next day Cilla's wicked-crazy perch on the ridgeline would be their only refuge. Rosy stood, faced north, and scanned the horizon. She couldn't see far, couldn't see any signs of change. She bit three fingernails to the quick before despairing aloud to Lake Pontchartrain: "Stop, please! Equalize with the city! Draw this water down!"

"No use praying now, heart," Maya mumbled.

Rosy turned to argue that she wasn't praying, but something in Maya's carriage stopped her. Maya sat differently. Not just that she sat on a roof, surrounded by water, above the tree line. She sat *old*.

She slouched.

As much as some people despise drunk drivers and Enron executives, gum-poppers, loud-talkers, and the home-grown demons Gilbert Gauthe and John Allen Muhammad, Maya hated slouchers. For years, if she caught Rosy hunched over a book or her homework with curved spine, she made her march the full length of the house five times with a broomstick across her upper back, hooked under her elbows in a manner that shot her shoulders to the sky. Even at her advanced age, Maya's posture had always modeled unwavering perfection. "I'ma be sitting tall on my deathbed!" she frequently joked.

To see her slouching, then, equated to staring down a ghost: the shell of a woman already half-crossed to the other side.

And she should have been praying. Maya prayed, always. Prayed for any gamut of things, from good weather to good health, from world peace to neighborhood peace. ("Hey there, God: Please can't you kill that yappy dog next door? Quickly, though—I ain't cruel!") She took God for an intimate and wasn't beneath making recommendations to him. Regularly allowed (though she'd never admit it) that if sinners had to exist, maybe they could be put to good use and assassinate President Bush. And Vice President Cheney. That Condie Rice and Colin Powell could be spared.

She made a habit, when shopping, of pausing outside the store and praying that the item she coveted would be on clearance. Never disappointed in God, if she paid full price she simply vowed to pray better next time.

For Maya not to pray implied a hopelessness Rosy could not tolerate.

"What're you talking about, Maya? 'No use praying'?" She couldn't even get Maya to look in her direction. Her gaze took in only water.

"Come on, Maya, pray with me," she implored.

Rosy never prayed. Not that she didn't believe in a God, or the possibility of one, but she didn't think rote recitations effected anything other than a meditative trance in the beseecher. A good feeling, perhaps, but not the result of divine intervention. Once, shortly after September 11, she spent the night asleep in a chair at the kitchen table as punishment for refusing to join her mother and Maya in a pre-meal prayer that planes would never again be taken hostage by terrorists. (Her logic was lost on them: "If the terrorists are praying to be granted access, and we're praying to deny it, our prayers nullify each other! Or otherwise you have to figure they're praying to the right God and we're praying to the wrong one, since it's their prayers that were answered. Don't y'all see that this kinda praying makes no sense?") Neither Cilla nor Maya spoke to her for three days.

She went and rested her head on the stooped shoulder of the old woman who had raised her during her mother's absences and cupped Maya's ruddy, wattled hands between her palms. Cilla crooned in the background.

"Come on, Maya, pray with me."

"No, heart. Just hold my hand."

"Please, Maya, pray with me."

"I done praying, heart. But you go on if you wanna. I'ma just sit here and listen."

That's when she realized Maya wasn't going to make it.

❖

THERE WAS THE DAY in the attic followed by the day on the roof. The next day, the man died. That was also the day they got saved, Cilla and Rosy, something not easy to eclipse: survival. Only death can do that.

The three women huddled together on the roof as they slept,

fitfully, Tuesday creeping toward Wednesday. Not that temperatures in the low seventies could ever be considered cold enough to necessitate huddling, though it was a sufficient change from the daytime nineties, amid all that damp, to induce a shiver or two. And two-and-a-half days without food or water made their bodies susceptible to chills. But no: they huddled to feel someone else breathe, to not be the only living creature adrift in this haphazard sea.

It didn't rain on them, and in the morning some sun shone. They could see farther. They could see him drifting toward them.

Maya saw him first. She'd been sitting when Cilla and Rosy fell asleep and was sitting still when she nudged them awake, one arm extended straight in front of her, index finger parallel to the horizon, reaper-style.

"G'morning," Maya called out softly, splaying her fingers and waving gently.

He smiled and called back, "G'morning, ladies! How y'all doing?"

"Been better," Maya replied. "Been worse."

"Now ain't that the truth!"

"Reckon you'd like to join us?" Maya asked.

"I'd be much obliged," he replied. Just like that: a normal exchange. As if he'd been invited to set a spell on the stoop and share a pitcher of lemonade. As if he weren't holding with one hand onto the garish red handle of the plastic cooler he straddled, the other arm waving wildly in the air as he strove to keep his balance. The softly swaying current carried him ever closer.

"Name's Willie," he said, bobbing toward them, thirty or so feet away.

"Pleasure to meet you, Willie," Maya replied, introducing herself and Cilla and Rosy. "Welcome to my home."

"Right sturdy home you got there, too! I sure hope you ladies don't mind an old man barging in on y'all like this."

"Old" could have meant any age from forty-five to seventy-five; hard to say: no one looked like who they had been three days ago.

Cilla was already humming, but she paused a moment and observed of Willie's perch: "That don't seem all that safe."

"Sure is safer'n what some folks is hanging onto!" he retorted. "Trust me. I done took a tour of these here parts, and I can't say I been much impressed with the accommodations." All four laughed. His outburst was foreshortened, though, for when he laughed the cooler began rocking wildly from side to side.

He'd clearly adapted well to his mount: he rode the agitated container like a champion bull rider, squeezing with his thighs, kicking with his feet, swinging his free arm in high arcs to compensate for the vagaries of his steed. Fortunately, the lurching drove him in the right direction, toward safety.

Twenty feet out from the roof, he steadied himself.

Cilla placed her jewelry box in Maya's lap. Maya and Rosy kept their eyes pinned to the man.

"Nice save!" Rosy hollered.

"Willie, you a steady man," Maya teased. "Steady's good. Steady's my kinda folk!"

"Aw now, y'all gonna make an old man blush!" He smiled, enormously, but did not laugh. More careful. Almost there.

Cilla saw something the rest didn't.

"So tell me, sir," Rosy said to keep the banter going, to do what she could to help reel him in, "what line of work are you in to have developed such terrific balance? After all, it takes some talent to be able to surf these waves on a cooler!"

Maya reached out and patted Rosy's shoulder, pleased. Perfect tone: conversational, witty.

Cilla stood, and began to stride, backward, up the crest of the roof.

"You sure wouldn't believe it none looking at me now, but in my day I was a dancer."

"Really!" That impressed Rosy. "Professional?"

"Yup."

"What kinda dance? Ballet, mod—"

Gone! The log that had been closing in from behind caught

their visitor unawares, knocked the cooler out from under him, and upended Willie into the water.

Cilla crouched down and assumed a sprinter's pose at the apex of the roof, as if waiting for the *pop!* of a gun to initiate her race. Willie bobbed up, sputtering, kicking, hand still clamped around the handle of the cooler. With his free hand, he smacked at the water, spraying them all. His eyes verged on rabid, pupils constricted and whites glowing, all horrified wonder, but his voice maintained a practiced calm.

"I gotta learn to swim," he said. That smile again.

"Don't we all?" Rosy replied brightly, trying hard to replicate his levity. Still seated, she braced her feet at the waterline, and stretched as far forward on the declivitous slope as she dared in order to reach a hand out to him. "Keep kicking. You're almost here."

His panicked paddling propelled him about ten more feet. He couldn't have been but another kick or two from connecting with Rosy when Cilla's footsteps thundered downhill and she screamed, "Don't worry, I'ma save you!" as she leapt off the roof and disappeared beneath the water.

"Mama!" Rosy leapt to her feet, scanning furiously, arms outstretched to balance on the pitched shingles.

"Cilla! Cilla!" Maya screamed. To Rosy: "Where's your mama? Can you see her?"

"Mama!"

Maya tried to leap up, too, but the whole world spun around her—what with no food, no water, blood sugar spiraling wildly—and she fell flat onto her back, then slid down the pitched roof, smashing into the roadblock of Rosy's body. The imbroglio broke Maya's fall; stopped her just above the water. Took out Rosy's legs, though, and drove her down into the murky depths.

One safe; three drowning.

Rosy landed on her back on the submerged lower half of the roof. Solid something beneath her, she twisted toward it as she floated upward, so that she was facing Maya when her head broke the surface of the water. They locked eyes. She flailed for a shingle,

a handhold, but nothing: all water. Triangulation thwarted her—
her body straight up and down, the roof angling away beyond her
reach. She heard Maya scream her name as she sank under and
heard Maya's muffled cries, "Kick! Kick!" even as the water closed
over her head, so she did as she was told, she kicked, and the toe
of her sneaker connected with a low point on the roof with enough
force to volley her upward and break the surface, time to catch a
breath, before sinking back below.

"—ick! Kick! Kic—"

Maya's voice urged her on as she kicked, caught an edge,
popped up for a breath, went back under.

"—ick! Kick! Kic—"

She cupped her hands and dug at the water, plowed desperately through it, which helped move her closer, leap by leap, to
the place where the roof jutted up into the air. Each kick came
more swiftly, with less distance between the surface and the
kickpoint below, until finally her fingers caught a set of shingles and she pulled herself prone against the building, head out,
body submerged.

"Maya, help me!" she cried out.

Maya tried. Truly, she tried. Got a hand over Rosy's. But three
days without nutrition wreaks special havoc on the elderly. She
couldn't close her fingers, couldn't grip, couldn't pull Rosy out.

"Grab onto me, heart!" Maya urged, but Rosy realized she'd
just pull Maya in. She was on her own.

"Where's my mama?"

"Grab onto me, heart!"

"Maya, I'm fine! Where's my mama? Can you see her?"

Rosy craned her neck as far to the right as she could, face
turned toward where Cilla had disappeared, and resumed screaming, "Mama! Mama!"

"Cilla!" Maya yelled.

"Mama!"

"Some bubbles!" Maya said. Rosy looked where she was pointing. "I seen some bubbles right over there! Cilla!"

Right hand leading, searching out new grips then releasing with the left, Rosy dragged herself down the waterline toward the bubbles, her right leg extended as far out as she could stretch it, hoping Cilla had her eyes open and would see it and grab on.

She did. In fact, Cilla latched onto her daughter with such ferocity that she ripped Rosy off the roof and plunged her right back underwater.

Drowning is part accident, part murder-suicide. The accident of falling in, followed by an internecine desperation that compels the victim to attack the rescuer so fiercely as to potentially sink them both. Cilla clawed her way up Rosy's body and pushed off her chest, using her child as a stair-step in a frantic air-grab at the surface. Underwater, her mother's feet pummeling her head, Rosy somehow kept her wits. She spun toward the submerged roof again, planted the rubber soles of her sneakers against it, and ran in slow, waterlogged motion up the incline toward the surface. Before she could get there, Cilla slipped back under, grabbed Rosy by an ear, pushed against her face to propel her own self up, and snatched another breath while her daughter languished underwater. The third time, they fought. Cilla, in her hypoxia, perceived Rosy as ballast; Rosy, fast drowning again herself, perceived Cilla as blockade. So when next Cilla grabbed her arm, Rosy bit into her mother's hand as hard as she could, and kicked herself up to gulp some air as Cilla recoiled. They struggled loudly: choking, coughing, water flying, making waves, Cilla wrenching on Rosy's shirt, driving her daughter down, her own self up, Rosy going for the eyes. Aggressive turn-taking ventilation. Finally, a blow to Rosy's sternum drove her *smash!* against the roof, three feet east of where she'd been previously, and that made all the difference.

What saved them, for the second time, was the attic hole Cilla chopped open that now sat level—this day and a half later—with the surface of the water. Rosy put a foot on the edge of the opening, grasped some exposed plywood, and pulled herself fully up and out of the water before reaching back for her mother who, disoriented by her ongoing oxygen gluttony, scratched four fingernail-width ridges the whole length of Rosy's left cheek and dragged her right back down.

They'd have died, had Rosy not done it: grabbed hold of the edge of the hole with her right hand, grabbed a fistful of Cilla's hair with her left, and, with a tremendous burst of energy born of frustration and fear, raised them both up out of the water to smash Cilla's skull against a wooden beam projecting out of the attic.

Dehydrated, starved, exhausted, it didn't take much to induce unconsciousness.

But Rosy bashed her mother's head one more time, for good measure, lest she come to and kill them both.

※

IN THE LATE MORNING hours of Wednesday, August 31, two men in a skiff helped Rosy lift her still-unconscious mother off the roof and rowed the two of them to safety.

Maya refused to budge. "I'm not leaving my house. It's mine. It's all I got."

"This isn't a house no more, Maya," Rosy whispered. "It's an island."

"I ain't going."

Rosy had no more fight left in her. "I've gotta take care of my mama," she said: part apology, part resignation, all truth.

"That's right," Maya said. "You take care of your mama. She need you."

"I'll come back for you," Rosy promised as they floated away. "I'll get help and come back. I will. I won't leave you here."

She kept an eye on Maya for as long as possible, pretending she would see her again, refusing to believe this might be the last image of her guardian/confidante/friend: alone on a desecrated roof, clutching a bloody cooler, waving valiantly but unable to smile.

They'd used the cooler as a buoy, to hoist Cilla's body out of the water. Maya shimmied down the roof to them and did what she could to help. The cooler was her idea. With one foot on the edge of the attic hole, the other foot in the cooler, Rosy straddled Cilla's body precariously but earned enough leverage to inch her up *thrump* by *thrump* by *thrump* until at least the top half of her body was on solid ground. It would do. Her legs could float.

Rosy collapsed above her mother, hand wound into the collar of Cilla's shirt so that any movement might rouse her should Cilla's body succumb to inertia and begin to slide away. She laid her head down behind Maya's back, deliberately. She didn't want to have to look at her yet.

She was almost asleep when Maya said, "We do what we gotta do."

So she'd seen.

Without disrupting their private boundaries, Maya repositioned her body a smidge. Repositioned herself so she could stroke Rosy's hair, as she used to do to coax the child to nap, and Rosy fell into such a deep sleep that she never even heard Maya calling the oarsmen to their rescue.

The men did not speak to Rosy as they rowed, each person observing the destruction around them from a cocoon of silence. The men looked without; Rosy looked within. Stroked Cilla's jewelry box, cradled in her lap. There were some memories to hold onto, others to erase. To eviscerate.

She focused on forgetting one detail. Every time it came to her, she banished it from her mind's eye. Never-occurred. Instead, she imagined Willie reaching for the roof, never securing a grip, his hands slipping off because of the damp, the mold, the slippery slick on his skin. If his survivors found her one day and asked, she would speak of those last moments when he slid peacefully below the waters, spent on the effort of saving himself, and the way he'd looked so accepting, almost smiling, as he vanished. Or maybe she'd say he died saving her mother. That's it! He died saving her mother, who fell in, and he jumped in after her because she couldn't swim. Heroic. Memorable. A privilege to witness.

His eyes, big saucers of hope, superimposed themselves over

those thoughts, and she squeezed shut her own eyelids—clamped a hand over them—to lock him out.

Go away, memory! Go away!

I erase you.

It really could have been that way; he could have reached for the roof. Instead, drowning himself, not a swimmer, he had stayed in the water with them. Tugged Rosy up, at least once, after Cilla knocked her underwater, gifting her a breath. Even extended the cooler to her, hoping she would grab on.

Let go, memory! Let go!

I erase you.

His voice, deep and resonant, guided her. Cutting through the guttural scrabbling and the hasty loud intakes of air and the wild water splashing, his voice: a life ring. "Grab hold of that hole in the roof!" he coached her. "You can reach it! Right behind you! Grab on!"

Shut up, memory! Shut up!

I erase you.

He was strong. That grip, tightening around her wrist, all hopeful eyes and the smile, always the smile. Rosy finally up out of the water, reaching back for her mother, him latching onto her extended hand, that close to safe, but her mother still floundering just beyond him.

Get out of the way, memory! Get out of the way!

I erase you.

She couldn't save two. It wasn't a thought; not a cognitive process she had time to consider in the moment. Just a reaction. She couldn't save two.

So when Rosy reached for her mother and he grabbed onto her instead, she kicked him square in the face and never saw him again.

I erase you.

VII. Rose

"The misunderstandings end here. The questions,
the hauntings, they end with me."

ON MONDAY AFTERNOON, SEPTEMBER 12, Rose returned home
from her meeting with Officer McAffrey and placed a number of
phone calls in quick succession. The first—to the insurance company—he'd instructed her to make; the second—to the coroner—he
facilitated against his better judgment; the others were entirely of
her own doing.

The automobile insurance rep informed her that they would
assign an investigator to settle all payments and handle the disposal of the wrecked vehicle. He then walked her through her
entitlements: funeral cost coverage; rental car benefits; vehicle
replacement settlement; potential accidental death pay-out to the
insured's heirs; and monetary settlement to victims, should fault
be determined to lie with the insured.

"The girl's death was definitely our fault," Rose said.

"Not necessarily," the man corrected. "There will be an investigation to determine that."

"We drove off the road into a pedestrian. Who else's fault would it be?"

"An investigation will determine that," he reiterated.

"Um hmm. How does the victim get her money if she's dead?"

"If fault is, in fact, determined to lie with the insured, and the victim cannot file a claim herself, then it can be filed by the victim's next of kin."

"But what if we can't find a next of kin?"

"Well, if there's no next of kin, then there's no one to file a claim."

"So she dies, and nothing happens. Her life is worth nothing?"

The insurance rep insisted, in an increasingly pedantic tone, "As I *said*, there will be an investigation to determine …"

She'd heard enough. It was a bit freaky, actually, the way everything pointed her in the same direction. Proof upon proof upon proof. What began as an inchoate thought at the funeral had solidified into a definitive plan of action. She knew what she was meant to do.

What she meant to do was entirely uncharacteristic.

Rose and Gertrude had lived the better portion of their lives autonomously. Two women, nose to the ground, making their way, refusing to need or rely on anyone. Such was the mantle Gertrude assumed young and laid upon her daughter; the soundtrack of Rose's youth resounded with "You can do it yourself." Oh, she cried sometimes and skulked often in response, but, in the end, she could dress herself fully by the time she was three, prepare her own school lunches by second grade, and had paid enough attention from the passenger seat to audit driver's ed her sophomore year and progress straight to a license.

Gertrude measured her love by Rose's precocity, marveling at the persistence of her stubby fingers manipulating the laces, wowed by the thousands of highlighted words she'd looked up in her dictionary, in awe of the fierce determination with which she paddled her way across the deep end of the pool her first time in. Planted on the sidelines of her daughter's life, Gertrude cheered with joy and fierce pride, shouting, "Do it yourself!" in affectionate tones, while Rose, tossed into waters over her head, choking, clawing furiously for a handhold and a sense of security, saw her mother clapping and smiling and thought, *I'm drowning, and it makes her happy.*

What Gertrude proffered as a legacy of self-reliance, Rose assumed as a lonely inheritance.

Never before had the loneliness been this palpable. It hit her full force—or, better stated, she finally allowed it to visit her—the day after her mother's funeral. At 7:15 a.m. on Sunday, September 11, remote in hand, Cheerios box beside her, she turned the TV on for the first time in over a week. The official tribute wouldn't begin until 7:46 a.m., the anniversary moment memorializing the first crash, but as filler the station had spliced together a harrowing retrospective of newsreel footage. It broadsided her.

Had she given it any thought, she shouldn't have been so surprised. But she wasn't thinking; just acting out of habit. Honoring a ritual of commemorating death without weighing the implications of a week when the dead had taken up residence too near her.

She turned on the TV because that's what she did every year on this day, at this time. Instinctively, she opened her mouth. "*La mandra*—" escaped, but she swiftly silenced herself. No one to hear, no one to respond. The couch swallowed her, too enormous for just one body. And then the screen filled with a picture of a girl her age, her complexion, clutching a photo against her breast while murmuring, "My mother ..." and it finally hit her full-on: *My mother's dead!*

She leapt off the couch in a panic, horrified by what she'd done over the past few days. *My mother's gone!* Cold sweat, bile rising, escalating pulse throbbing in her throat. It took effort not to release her bowels. She threw open the door of her mother's room. Too neat: bed freshly made, bedclothes laundered. Where could she be? Rose pulled the pillow out of the case and pressed it hard enough against her face to suffocate herself, suckling for Gertrude's essence, hoping to root out a trace of her scent. Any residue of Estée Laudered cheek sunk into the fabric, or Suave-scented hair matted against the ticking, had been subsumed by Tide with bleach, everything spring-fresh, as anonymous as if still shrink-wrapped on a store shelf with other feather downs that belonged to no one.

Rose wrenched open every drawer until they all hung from the dresser in an empty, sagging stack. She'd been too thorough; she'd missed nothing! The closet, too: bare. Years' worth of dry cleaners' hangers clung to bare white rods, shelves devoid of everything but dust, light from the bare bulb ricocheting off walls no longer cluttered by the trappings of a life that Rose had jettisoned in her effort to expunge the memory of what had happened.

She'd meant just to start fresh. To start over. To do what had to be done and do it quickly. Do it strong, without breaking down, without feeling, like her mother taught her. To keep her mind and her hands occupied by task, to get through the day.

Rose raced from the cavernous closet toward the bathroom, hope rising. Surely, somewhere, she'd forgotten something. Medicine cabinet open, shelves ransacked. One toothbrush. One razor. One hairbrush. No makeup, no perfume—only a stained ring where her mother's beveled flacon had sat, leaking fragrant oil through the years. Head in the cabinet, all she picked up now were whiffs of Dial and mint floss and the rubbery remnants of Band-Aids long-aged. Everything unique to Gertrude had disappeared two days ago, into a plastic sack, into the dumpster. Rose balled her hands into fists and pressed them against her forehead: Think! She beat her head once; twice. Which day is it? Fists to forehead, she pounded once more, harder. Sunday. Oh, shit. Sunday. The trashman came on Friday, likely mere hours after she'd let the dumpster lid slam shut and scurried away—the blush brush Gertrude cradled in her palm every morning crushed between aluminum cans full of moldering soup concentrate and tomato paste, the powder she dusted over her alabaster skin commingled with gritty coffee filters and tacky popsicle sticks. Before sundown on Friday, while the priest prepared Gertrude's eulogy for the next morning's service, her appurtenances had been dispatched to the landfill, churned back into the earth even before her body was lowered into the ground.

Stunned by her own stupidity, Rose shivered and realized, *I've erased her.*

She slowly closed the mirrored cabinet door, but then re-opened it and lifted out the toothpaste. She couldn't remember brushing her teeth recently. Gertrude may have been the last to squeeze this tube, the gel inside connecting with the bristles that caressed her teeth. Rose unscrewed the cap and, while doing so, eyed the mouthwash. With her free hand she reached for the cup inverted over the bottle cap into which Gertrude decanted the astringent each morning before slugging it back. Hungrily, she licked the edge of the cup, then put her tongue to the toothpaste, wheedling the tip into the opening, greedily sucking the gel from the tube. Eyes closed, she assessed the flavor, searching for something that might remind her of Gertrude's breath, or hint at her lips pursed in kiss, but Rose's mouth only stung. It tasted like Crest, like Listerine; nothing more. Not at all like her mother.

She scanned the rest of the apartment. *Is there nothing else here?*

The TV came to her rescue. A woman's South Bronx voice wafted into the Alabama living room, speaking about her firefighter husband, last heard from over his walkie-talkie four years ago when he checked in from the 82nd floor on his ascent up the north stairwell, taking the steps two at a time despite hauling oxygen tanks and metal tools and weighty gear. What caught Rose's attention was the catch in the woman's voice when she described for the interviewer the process of collecting his belongings from the stationhouse: "He'd laugh at me if he knew how much importance I've assigned to his stuff—crazy things that probably meant nothing to him, but they mean the world to me because they were some of the last things he touched. His wallet, his keys, but some really odd stuff, too: a wadded-up gum wrapper, a *Sports Illustrated*, a Homer Simpson bobble-head—and he wasn't even a fan of the Simpsons! But they all went into this box when I emptied his locker, and once I got home I couldn't bear to throw any of it out. Sometimes I bring the box up out of the basement"—and here is where her voice caught—"and I just sit it beside me on the couch while I watch TV, and it sort of feels like he's still here, keeping me company ..."

Rose flung the front door wide open in her mad dash down the stairs, across the parking lot, to snatch the box back off her neighbor's stoop—the box she left there as a gift for the neighbor who'd come to check on her, the box of her mother's snow globes with a note taped on top: "For Your Children."

The assortment of snow globes atop Gertrude's dresser always intrigued Rose as a child, more so, perhaps, because her mother never let her touch them. Gertrude guarded her collection as if they were precious heirlooms instead of plastic nothings that she herself never shook or wound up; the snow crystals had, over the years, coalesced into gummy lumps in the bases. Once, costumed as Jasmine, needing a castle, Rose filched one and shook it while crouched behind an armchair. Gertrude caught her, wrenched it from her grip, and raced to replace it in the bedroom, threatening to "whup your backside!" should Rose touch it again. That was the only time she'd ever witnessed a snow globe in either of their hands.

She would've hated to disappoint the neighbor's children by reclaiming the gift, but fortunately, no one had yet retrieved it off their doorstep, allowing her to repossess the snow globes surreptitiously and without guilt.

One stride back into her apartment, one half turn to shut the front door; Rose made it no further before she slid to the floor in the entryway, sobbing, her face pressed to the box sheltering her mother's collection. Sobs of relief, yes, but then of so much more. Using her body as ballast, forcing shut the door and sliding down it, she sank into the spirit of her mother and it opened her eyes. With everything in her, she knew Gertrude had done this. Knew it for sure.

Until that moment, Rose thought sobbing against the front door had been her private history. She'd made a scene, daily, in first

grade, hurling herself against the door from the outside, screaming and sobbing to be allowed back in when Gertrude shoved her
forth at the start of the day and locked her out.

At age six, replete with new shoes and sharpened pencils
and the promise of friends to come, Rose had initially looked
forward to school. But the first day, when no one offered her
a seat on the bus and the driver finally had to force one of the
older boys to let her sit down beside him, the boy said loudly, "I
thought roses were supposed to smell good, but this one here"—
sniffing loudly, waving a hand over her head as if to dissipate
a noxious odor—"she stinks!" For the rest of her life, whenever
Rose heard group laughter, she experienced a quick stab to the
gut, momentarily reliving her daily punishment on the school
bus. It escalated past snubbing to insults to shoving before the
bus driver finally reserved the seat directly behind hers for Rose
and the equally harassed boy with Down syndrome; still, it took
another month or so before she quit waking with diarrhea, and
even longer before she realized no amount of sobbing and rail-
ing on the front door each morning would ever earn her refuge
with her mother.

Until she sank to the floor with the snow globes, it had never
occurred to her that Gertrude was not a party to her torment.

Now, as bagpipes moaned from the television behind the
names of the dead read aloud in a steady cadence of sorrow,
Gertrude's loneliness rose up in concert through the floorboards
to saturate Rose's skin and infuse her for a moment with her mother's perspective. She intuited, finally, that on the opposite side of
the locked doors of her youth there lingered a woman suffering
just as fiercely, crying for Rose as Rose cried for her.

For all the unnecessary isolation, she wept.

Her tears could not touch the depth of the recriminations
Gertrude felt, more than a decade earlier, sobbing against the interior doorframe, listening to the wails of her child on the outside: a
child forever denied a sibling's hand to hold, who would have to
learn to do things alone—who would require that mentality to be

forced into her by her own mother, mortared over a tenderness that would not do. Once, sitting alone on a bench at the playground, overseeing Rose's play, Gertrude had eavesdropped on some other mothers' conversation. They spoke of their fears for their children. One talked about not gaining admittance to a particular school, another spoke of her husband's gruff demeanor around her son, but the third said, "It's not those typical things that scare me. What I'm afraid of is that my child might someday be lonely."

My child was born lonely, Gertrude realized, a torment hammered home by Rose's early-morning flailings against the front door. While her child's cries rent her, she pressed herself up against the door from the inside, hands splayed beside wet cheek pressed to wood, whispering over and over, "I'm here, I'm right here," but refusing to open the door despite every better instinct, wracked with sobs at the effort to keep herself from disengaging the lock and scooping up her child. How else would Rose learn to fend for herself? Either strangers would pound the lesson into her, cruelly, or Gertrude could do it lovingly, from right there on the other side of the door, *so close!*, so Rose could learn safely, at home.

Some mornings Gertrude had to sit on or bite her own hands, to keep from unlatching the door lock, an act that killed a fresh piece of her every day, but she did it. She did it for the benefit of her daughter.

Rose would never know that, naturally, but with her back against the door, face pressed to the cardboard box of snow globes, something impenetrable between them finally burst ajar, and she sensed within her the communion of their sadness.

To the firefighter's widow, to the anonymous girl holding a photo of a missing parent up to a TV camera, to the memory of herself and her mother crying in unison but without connection, she made a spontaneous, irrevocable promise: The misunderstandings end here. The questions, the hauntings, they end with me.

There was one daughter's mother Rose owed answers to. One estrangement she could prevent. She would find the identity of the dead girl; she would lead her home.

ROSE EXPECTED WORSE OF the morgue. The smell, for one, surprised her. She anticipated formaldehyde and rot but encountered only a citrus odor that alluded to cleansers used liberally on
hands and all solid surfaces. Mostly, it smelled like an office: a
paper—not a body—repository. It *was* an office, replete with smiling receptionist, cubicles, desks adorned with family photos and
pencils upended in mugs lauding "World's Best Dad." A port-
ly woman escorted her through brightly lit corridors, hung with
colorful amateur vacation photos, to a windowless room awash
in fluorescent light and fresh white paint. She'd imagined rows
of cold-storage cases in a darkened storeroom, at best, but had
prepared herself for a worst-case scenario of body bags in an endless hall of shadows, tagged toes peeking out. The incongruity
between the bleak descriptions of morgues she'd read about and
the bright, pleasant surroundings here unsettled her, the dispar-
ity compounded when a man who was more frat boy than Grim
Reaper glided through the door and gave her a hearty handshake.
Young, casual, in a golf shirt and khaki slacks, a slightly matured
SAE boy with straight white teeth behind a crooked, jaunty smile.

"Hey," he said, "I'm Doc Cabbott. Officer McAffrey said you'd
be swinging by."

Both eyebrows raised, a laugh barely suppressed, Rose exclaimed, "*You're* the coroner?"

"Yup," he said. "You were expecting someone more morose,
somebody older, weren't you?"

"Yeah, I guess so."

"Nah. Old Quincy's got a few years on me still."

"Who?"

"Come on ..." he coaxed. "You know: *Quincy, M.E.*"

She shook her head: no idea.

"Ah, he's before your time," the doctor said, waving his hand
in the air, proving it didn't matter. "Actually, he's before my time,
too, but I'm hooked on the reruns on cable. It's not a bad show! But

come on, coroners are getting younger and hipper every day—just look at Jill Hennessy on *Crossing Jordan*."

"I don't really watch TV," Rose admitted.

"Well, I guess that works in my favor," he said. "In everyone else's opinion, I can't help but pale in comparison to *CSI*'s prosthetic-legged, rock 'n' roll coroner. Still, I get the job done."

"Officer McAffrey said you're really good. He said you helped the girl"—and here she spoke her name for the first time—"Rosy. He said you helped her look okay, look better, when they needed to take her picture for the news."

He shrugged. "Mac's biased. He has to say nice things about me so I keep letting him kick my a—. Pardon me. Beat me at golf."

Rose pursed her lips and nodded softly, saying nothing. She tugged on the edge of her T-shirt, planted the toe of one shoe on the floor and rolled her foot around, impatient. She had come to stare into the face of a dead person, not chat about golf. "Will you let me see her?" she asked.

He took a deep breath, creased his brow. "Are you really sure you want to?"

"Mmm hmm." She stared straight at him as she murmured. A dare. No backing down.

"Okay then," he acquiesced. "But let's keep it kinda hush-hush, okay? It's a bit unorthodox, but Mac said it's important to you." He took another pass at light and chipper: "Now here's where you're reaping the benefits of bumping into a young guy! If I were one of those old fogeys, I might not bend the rules, even for a friend."

Rose didn't bite. Just smiled and said softly, "Much obliged."

"Sure," he said. "You've been through a lot. I'm happy to help."

HE BROUGHT THE BODY to her, in a tiny white room, covered by a sheet, which draped the corpse in a way that seemed indecent: nipples erect, breast contours straining against the fabric, triangular mons discernible between the hillocks of her thighs.

Rose approached the gurney. She reached out, instinctively,

with both hands, then retracted her arms and cupped her palms together against her chest. "Can I ...?" She reached a second time toward the body, her left hand extended, wanting to uncover the girl but lacking the nerve to do it. "Will you ...?" With the slightest back and forth motion of her fingers, she mimed the turning down of a sheet.

The coroner folded back the fabric, exposing Rosy's face and the tips of her shoulders. Rose bent toward the body and stared with the wide-open gaze common to mothers crouched over the forms of their sleeping newborns. She thought she'd be scared, but she wasn't.

She cocked her head further and slowly pondered the girl before her, looking past the overt injuries to see the person beneath them, letting her eyes make Rosy's acquaintance by taking in each of her facial features: close-cropped whorls of pitch black hair; detached, pierced earlobes—the right one distinguished by a small divot; a wide, prominent nose; the thickest, longest eyelashes she'd ever seen; and the kind of full lips movie stars pay money to manufacture. She leaned closer and smiled. Freckles—harder to see on Rosy's dark skin, but freckles nonetheless—dotted the crest of her cheekbones in the same pattern that danced across Rose's own pale face.

The coroner, behind her, noted her close observation of the victim's right cheekbone. "Those lacerations on the supraorbital ridge and zygomatic arch are from a crush injury."

"Oh my God!" Rose exclaimed, reaching out her palm as if to protectively shield Rosy's right eye and cheek, still not quite touching, but so much closer now that the long edge of one stitch scratched the tip of her pinkie. "We ..." She looked at the wound and stumbled, but recomposed herself. "We hit her *face?*"

"Oh! No! Oh, God, no!" he stammered, realizing that she'd interpreted his words to mean they'd crushed her, literally. "What I meant to say is that you *didn't* do that. The insult from the MVA resulted in supracondylar femoral shaft fractures, a Type IIIC open tibial fracture, multiple fractures of the pelvic rami with massive internal hemorrhage—"

"You're not speaking English."

"Sorry. The MVA ... that would be the car accident. Its effects were limited almost exclusively to high velocity trauma in the region of the lower extremities—"

She cleared her throat.

"Oh. Sorry." He paused. "Let's just say, the car accident resulted in injuries confined primarily to the lower part of her body. You didn't hurt her face. There are some abrasions, from the drop, down the ... you know, from the fall, when y'all went over the edge, after the collision. But the damage to her face isn't primarily from the car accident. What you see was already there, before you hit her. She's got three distinct sets of injuries from three separate incidents."

As Rose turned to face him, her right hand settled compassionately onto the shrouded shoulder of the young girl behind her. The cool of the dead flesh radiating from beneath the sheet smarted against her warm skin—a shock, a shiver—but she held on, bracing them both. "Oh my God," she repeated. "What in the world happened to her?"

She looked so stricken, he tried again to dissuade her. "You don't need to hear all this. Really. What can it help? What's it going to change?"

She steeled herself. Jaw set, spine rigid, tears blinked back. "I wanna know. Really, I do. I *need* to know."

Bending back over Rosy's body, resting an elbow on the gurney, she cupped her own chin in one hand and, with the other, maternally smoothed the girl's matted whorls of curls as she said, "Tell me. Start at the beginning, and tell me what happened to her." If Rosy had borne it, Rose felt the least she could do was stand gentle witness and keep the lost girl company through the recounting.

"See those four lines on her left cheek?" Doc Cabbott asked, backing up to lean on the countertop behind Rose's back, affording the girls their privacy. "She got scratched, pretty badly. Somebody gouged her cheek. The scabbed-over scratches indicate they were inflicted anywhere from maybe a couple days to a week or so before she died. Contusions clustered mostly round her shoulders and chest likely stem from the same incident. One or two on her face, too, but the most notable one's centered on her sternum. Size and shape hints at a foot, like she got kicked. Combine that with the scratches … maybe a fight? But there's no way to know for sure, especially since the coloration of the bruising—greenish-yellow, hard to see with the naked eye on her brown skin—dates those injuries to coincide with the hurricane. Woulda been all sorts of things flying round, and all manner of ways to get injured. No way to know for sure what happened."

He kept his tone professional; his cadence, even. She slid her hand down from Rosy's hair, over her temple. "Can I …"

"You can touch her face."

She stroked the skin around the cinched-shut wounds on the swollen cheek, the purple-black eye.

Resolved to hear it all, she said, "And these …"

Two days before Rosy died, she was raped. She had extensive, typical injuries, but also severe lacerations on her right cheek and above her right eye.

"You called them 'crush injuries'?"

"Crush injury is a term that refers to trauma caused by any significant, direct impact—could be a fist, a rock, the pavement in a fall. It's differentiated from incised wounds—cuts caused by knives or glass penetrating a body. Both types of injuries can split the skin, but the injuries on this victim have notably ragged edges, indicating a crushing force. She wasn't slashed. She has defensive wounds, too, all over her hands and forearms. She fought back. Hard."

Rose stayed with Rosy's body even after there was nothing left to be said. She raised the sheet up over her face, billowing the fabric a bit in the process so it wouldn't continue to hug the rest of her body so tightly. Finally, she felt beneath the sheet for Rosy's right hand and held it for a moment between her palms, lending her warmth to the girl's cold flesh, rubbing briskly as if to spark something. The hand weighed heavier upon her than she imagined a hand would. As Rose slid her own hands out from under the sheet

Rosy's hand shifted, too, and her whole arm started to slide off the side of the gurney. Rose reached for it as if to catch a fluttering leaf set adrift by a breeze. As she lifted it, intent on tucking Rosy's body back in under the sheet more carefully, their arms pressed together—forearm supporting forearm, fingers reentwined—and that is how Rose discovered it: this most magical of things. The outline of a dragonfly flitted across the fatty pad at the base of Rosy's thumb. Rose murmured a soft sigh of delight.

"Great tattoo, isn't it?" Doc Cabbott responded from behind her. "Unusual place to put it, though. You don't see much work done on palms. The skin regenerates too quickly; tattoos there tend to fade."

"Maybe it wasn't meant to last forever," Rose said after a moment's consideration. "Dragonflies are temporary beings. They morph, into light, toward joy."

The coroner didn't respond. As if his silence were a question, Rose tucked the girl's battered arm back under the sheet and said: "My mother. She loved dragonflies. I was weaned on their symbolism." Only then did she lift her eyes from the body and turn to thank him for the privilege of the visit. But, startled, she looked up into the face not of Doc Cabbott, reclined as he was against the countertop, but of Officer McAffrey, standing silent sentinel behind her. They smiled at each other.

"I didn't hear you come in," she said.

She scrunched her brows as if to inquire, but before she could speak aloud he explained himself.

"I couldn't have answered to myself if I'da let you go through this alone," he whispered, extending a hand to her, which she grasped between both of hers, with gratitude.

✳

As Rose buckled herself into the squad car for the ride home, the detective slid a manila envelope across the seat toward her. Inside were photocopies of the business card and receipt taken from Rosy's body after the accident, as well as the original phonebook page found folded in her pocket.

"Don't you need this?" she asked, holding up the White Page full of names.

"I kept a photocopy for the records," McAffrey answered. "Thought you'd want the original."

She looked at the paper in her lap, then stole a sideways glance at the officer.

"I know what you're thinking," he said. "I know what you're doing. You really think I didn't notice your name's listed on that page? G. & R. Aikens, halfway down on the back side?"

Rose pursed her lips as if to say, *So?*

He took his eyes off the road and turned to her. "It don't mean nothing. There're hundreds—hundreds!—of names listed on that page."

"Including mine."

"But that doesn't mean whatever you're assuming it means … that you've got some responsibility to her just cuz your name's on some paper she had in her pocket, or that she's calling out to you or trying to reach you …"

Rose quit listening. She'd held Rosy's hand in hers, she'd been with her when she died, she'd walked around in her shoes for a week now. She wouldn't let go of her, couldn't do it, no matter what.

"You know," he continued, "if my name didn't start with that Irish Mc, I'd be listed on that page, too, and it wouldn't mean she was calling out to me. It wouldn't make it my job to find her!"

Rose laughed aloud. "First off, you're *not* on the list. Second, it *is* your job to find her. More yours than mine."

He adopted her style: "First, she's as 'found' as she's gonna get. I don't know what else you think you're gonna discover. And second—and more important—you know what I mean. If my name were Affrey or Ainsworth or any other *A* name I'd be listed there right along with you Aikens folk. You *belong* on that particular page in the phonebook. Only coincidence is that the vic happened to die with that page in her pocket. You can't go interpreting coincidences as signs."

"The victim has a name. Rosy. And I can interpret things any way I want."

They sat in silence but for the air conditioner's hum and the thrum of his fingers on the steering wheel.

"Besides, what would you have me do, Officer?" she asked. "You think I'd be better off being eaten alive by questions?"

He exhaled loudly and cocked his head toward her. "Seems like it's about time you started calling me Mac, like everybody else does."

She paused; collected herself; continued more calmly. "Okay then, Mac. Listen to me, please. The last place you tracked her to was Natchez—where that nurse bought her a bus ticket to Tuscaloosa. I just wanna go there. I just … what can it hurt? Maybe I'll learn nothing, but at least I'll be able to sleep at night for having tried."

He stopped thrumming on the steering wheel and paused. "Goddammit. I don't believe this." Another pause. "'Scuse my language. Okay. Listen, I'm not encouraging you, but if you're hell-bent on doing it, I'll try to help you. What do you need?"

"Remind me of the name of the hospital, and the nurse."

He pulled into her apartment complex and stopped the car. "Christ." He imagined how he'd feel if a daughter of his were exposed to all this. "Your father'd probably kill me for supporting this cockamamie plan of yours."

"Not unless you're in the mood to open a new case and track him down, too. He's been missing since before I was born."

She stepped out of the car, but reopened the door before it latched and leaned back in. "There. Now you really do know. See? Rosy's the only one left I've got any connection to.

"Do you still judge me as wrong for trying to find her?"

🪰

As for those other calls Rose made that last day in town: she scheduled a cab for the morning, bought a bus ticket, and took an indefinite leave from her college classes. Only two weeks into the semester, with a death in the family, they would hold her tuition and make accommodations when she returned. She didn't expect to be gone more than a few days, but still. Easier that way. Then she took all the perishables out of the refrigerator and poured them down the sink, emptied all the trashcans, packed a bag.

She met the cab at the curb at daybreak. En route, she made the driver pull over before the bridge, where she got out and stared down upon the scene: the flattened trees, the skid marks cut into the hill, the place her mother last breathed, the spot where they'd driven Rosy's body into the dirt.

She closed her eyes and, without speaking, spoke. Half prayer, half promise. *Rosy, I'm coming for you.*

Then she got back into the cab and crossed the river, passing the First Baptist Church and the Red Cross office as they cruised the quiet streets, on schedule to catch the 8:55 a.m. Greyhound bound for Natchez, Mississippi. She'd get a rental car when she arrived but felt obliged to start her journey the way Rosy had ended hers.

Retracing the dead girl's steps backward, she chased a life.

VIII. ROSY

"They're all about change. About transformation. The belief
that what's to come can be better than what's been."

SUPERSTITION, AS INDIGENOUS TO Louisiana as gators and
Tabasco, holds that the spirits of the dead avenge any disruption
of their bodies, which makes one wonder at the rancor released
on the 1957 day when fifty-five white families re-interred their
beloved in Hope Mausoleum after the Rt. Rev. Girault M. Jones,
Bishop of Louisiana, deconsecrated the Girod Street Cemetery,
condemning every last African American bone to anonymity in a
mass grave in Providence Memorial Park. From that pogrom grew
the Superdome. Thirteen acres of structural steel framing stretch
up 273 feet from the unholy ground, a towering testament to the
American propensity to cheer black men into end zones and desert
them entirely six points later.

Ghosts do not so easily forsake their heirs. It is said the
Superdome was cursed from the start.

Take as evidence the quadrupled construction costs and de-
lays; the Saints' dismal record; the roof, meant to withstand

200-mile-per-hour winds, which peeled back in response to Katrina's 145-mile-per-hour gusts. To say nothing of the six dead bodies left behind when the refugees finally escaped her walls. Which is why it cannot be said that Cilla and Rosy sought shelter at the Superdome. By the time they arrived there, shelter had long since ceased to be offered.

Their rowboat sluiced easily through the downtown streets, waterlogged to a depth of three feet, enabling the makeshift gondoliers to deliver mother and daughter directly to the raised walkway surrounding the stadium in the late afternoon hours of Wednesday, August 31. Cilla stumbled from the boat, holding her head, crying. She moved as if the sludge surrounding them had settled in her soles, though Rosy expected the mania to envelop her anew when the headache passed. She needed to get them inside and isolated, way up in the nosebleed section where no one might notice them, before it happened.

Thirty thousand people stood in their way.

An elderly woman in a housedress, clutching a gold lamé pocketbook and wearing only one shoe, grabbed Rosy's shoulder for balance as she slid off the back of a Humvee whose wake upended the rowboat moments after Cilla and Rosy disembarked. Beside the Humvee, a pickup labeled "Louisiana Wildlife Enforcement" backed up and disgorged from its bed a young woman with four children, one a babe in arms who wailed so fervently that the driver had to ask the woman to repeat her question three times before she shouted loudly enough for him to hear:

"Whatcha expecting me to do with these children?"

"Take them inside!" he shouted back, waving in the direction of the arena.

"But they ain't mine!" she replied, pointing at the two unattached to her, maybe five, maybe six years old, clutching each other while she stood separate, protecting her own two, one pressed to knee, one pressed to breast.

"Who they belong to?" he asked, staring at the two mute boys, white knuckled in their efforts to hold tightly together.

"Why you asking me? They was already in the tree when I grabbed on there, and you the one lifted them out!"

"Well, take them inside anyways," he said, then jumped from the cab roof through the driver's side window to confront a freshly stalled engine and water lapping at the door. His job: to collect, not to consider. Certainly not to reunite.

As the wildlife specialist flooded his engine, the oarsmen up-righted their boat, soaking the crowd with backwash, and a national guardsman stormed past, gesticulating wildly. He bumped into Rosy, then the elderly woman with the pocketbook, then the mother of two/four, making no apologies.

"Whatcha mean, there's *one* bus?" he shouted into his walkie-talkie. "We got folks stacked up and screaming like white trash at a goddamn tent meeting, fixing to stampede offa the end of the loading dock and drown they stupid selves like a buncha fucking lemmings, and y'all saying we got one bus on the way? *One* bus? Get me General Lupin on the line! I'll see what he has to say about ..." The guardsman's voice trailed off as he pushed his way through the disordered cacophony of parents urging children to "Get back in this line!" and singles asking perfect strangers "You seen my husband?" and militants shouting "This ain't no fucking 'sanctuary'!" and over-eager newscasters inquiring "What's the most meaningful possession you had to leave behind?" Their noise only accentuated the deafening silence of all the people who had already ceased to speak, absorbed by hunger or thirst or regret, who shuffled forward, propelled by equal parts resignation and peer pressure every time the person in front of them inched closer to the distant doorway opening into this shelter of last resort.

Rosy corralled Cilla in the direction of the undulating mass, pulling away from the hand of the one-shoed woman, who mumbled, "What do I do? What do I do?" and ignoring the overburdened mother plighted with two orphaned boys. She had no attention to spare, no time for special cases.

All thirty thousand were lost to the mayhem in one way or another.

Within four hours, it would swallow Cilla whole.

IT TOOK NEARLY ALL that time to make it inside the doors and onto the sideline of the FieldTurf playing surface. Stanchions and armed guardsmen herded the line of refugees toward the security checkpoint at midfield, with a demeanor that had begun on Sunday as polite and empathic but had withered by Wednesday to exhausted, plain and simple.

It had been easier on everyone in the beginning: security checkpoint outside—in the fresh air, more manageable—until the rains hit and shivering babies soothed by old folks wrapped in soggy blankets made shelter a human-rights issue and they hauled the metal detectors inside under the fixed dome and set them up on the fifty-yard line. The wait had been excessive from the beginning, but at least on Day One there had been charitable food distributions and enough bedding to go around, and the streams of people had not so much fled their homes as made a deliberate choice to temporarily relocate. Which is to say, they came prepared, whereas the tens of thousands of victims tripling the occupancy on Day Four were an entirely different beast: terrified people plucked from rooftops without food or water; no clothing; no medical necessities. They entered a building without electricity, thick with condensation from storms and sweaty bodies, and met a locked-down population whose cigarette lighters and flasks had been frisked from them four days back. The tormented squeezed in among the viceless and agitated. Pure insanity.

Cilla almost fit in; might actually have fit in better had her mania been on parade, for the guardsmen ignored the agitators for the most part. Here and there twenty-something-year-old men, hobbled by low-riding pants and 'roid rage, pumped branded fists in the air, and a smattering of rancorous women cursed at anyone in uniform—whether military, social service, or medical—and at anyone else otherwise engaged in charitable behavior that did not meet their most immediate personal needs.

"Whatcha mean you ain't got no Motrin? Looks to me like he be getting what he wants!" a woman shouted at a physician from the New Orleans Health Department. The physician had been tracking the weather for two weeks, and had evacuated his own family to his in-laws' three days ahead of the eye, but voluntarily stayed behind and made his way to the Superdome with a well-stocked first aid kit as soon as he heard the doors had opened. In the subsequent four days, he'd ingested only three bottles of water and six granola bars. It made him slow; reminded him of his residency days. Hard to keep track of the IV rotations, so he wrote himself very specific notes about timing and contents on the generic bags with a black Sharpie he brought from home. His wife used the pen to mark bags of chicken she stored in the freezer. *God,* he realized, *the house must stink.* Four days without electricity; all that rotting defrosted poultry ... so it went: his mind wandering. He reread what he'd written on the IV bag: two parts H2O to two parts—

"Did you hear me?! I said how you ain't got no Motrin for me but you giving him what *he* wants?" The woman would not be ignored. She shouted down at the doctor from the wall above the end zone, where the wheelchair-bound were stacked five deep, one man's IV held aloft by a stadium seating sign, others rigged to the goal post.

"For God's sake," the physician shouted back at her, "he's got jaundice!"

"And I got the cramps!" the heckler retorted.

The physician's assistant sidled up and whispered, "Let it go, man," while patting his colleague's shoulder. "Hang in there. I hear they got a bus coming to evacuate out some of these dialysis patients."

In time, the woman fell back in amongst the set jaws and puffed-out chests pacing the upper concourses, pounding on the rails, raising a ruckus but nothing more. Amid a crowd more interested in acquiring diapers than apologies, such private soapboxes tended not to result in full-scale uprisings, so the docs and the guards and the good-deed-doers turned a deaf ear for the most part and the rogues soon enough raged themselves hoarse and irrelevant.

Cilla entered the Superdome that way and might not have faltered, standing silently in line while waiting to be searched, rocking gently back and forth beside her daughter as they inched forward through the line of still-unprocessed refugees. Listening to the woman scream at the doctor, Rosy thought, *That could be my mother.* Then she wondered, *Why isn't it?* Cilla's normality had her worried; perhaps the uncharacteristic calm was a side effect of injury. Rosy put a hand to her mother's cheek. Cilla let her. Bad sign. A manic Cilla would not tolerate touch; a hurt Cilla might. Her skin felt clammy. Her pupils were fixed. Guilt rising, Rosy wondered if the action she'd taken to save her mother's life—slamming Cilla's head on the roof beam to ensure her compliance—had fractured her skull. Could she be brain damaged? Sweat rolled in rivulets from her hairline and pooled in her ears, dripped from the edge of her nose. Rosy wondered if Cilla had spiked a fever until a droplet from her own nose landed on her outstretched forearm. Everyone oozed sweat, close-pressed together, the AC dead these four days. Even the stadium bricks leaked pent-up fluid inside this sealed Southern summer swamp, the result of weather- and body-borne humidity germinating over half a week. Christ, it stank. Stank so much it made Rosy retch. She had to stop thinking about it, stop noticing the smell, turn off her senses. Maybe that's what accounted for Cilla's fixed pupils and everyone else's. The solution: just look ahead, don't think, do as you're told. Otherwise, unbearable.

Unfortunately, when Cilla turned and looked at Rosy doubled over with dry heaves beside her, she began retching too. A nearby guardsman broke the cordon and directed them toward the restroom, promising to hold their place in line until their return, so close were they to reaching the security check-point at midfield.

It was the worst thing he could possibly have done.

Thirty thousand people, four days, dozens of untended toilet stalls. Every single one stuffed full and overflowing; the toilet seats peppered with menstrual blood and feces; the floors an insalubrious mix of urine and coagulated paper—the toilet paper used up on Sunday, the paper towels run through by Monday, the flyers and book pages people resorted to wiping with on Tuesday. Come Wednesday, folks were squatting in corners; it was cleaner. Not wiping; nothing left to use. By the time the Superdome was emptied at the end of the week, more than four thousand tons of trash and human debris would be hauled away on the backs of the guardsmen left behind. It would take an additional thirteen months and $193 million to fully repair and refurbish the structure picked to pieces by the hordes that ravaged the doors, ripped seats from the tiers and relocated them outside, and smashed the bathroom mirrors into shards that they used to etch their names into the concrete causeways.

Rosy and Cilla skirted the shattered glass of the mirrors littering the floor around the sinks but didn't make it five feet further into the restroom before the stench drove them out, both of them sinking to the floor against the wall on the lower concourse, retching up nothing, not even bile after half a week without food. Uncontrolled stomach spasms moved through Cilla's body, and her legs began to tremble. Rosy pressed down on them with her hands, to keep Cilla from toppling out of her seated position. "Hold it together," she whispered, to herself and Cilla both, knowing they couldn't get to the doctors out on the field yet, not until they'd gotten back in that blasted line and been cleared through the metal detectors. When Cilla nodded her head, complicit, and smiled with gratitude instead of raging with fury, this frightened Rosy even more. She mistook her mother's weariness for failing consciousness, erroneously believing her mania—which had always been the strongest force within her—should have trumped starvation, dehydration, and injury. Unless the injury was too severe. So after years of wishing the mania away, under these most desperate of circumstances, Rosy wished it back.

Mania beat a head injury any day.

In that moment, terrified her mother had some sort of brain bleed, Rosy wrapped Cilla's arm around her own neck, hefted her aloft, and half pulled, half dragged her back toward the crowd. *To hell with it,* Rosy thought. Circumventing the requisite security line, she stormed toward the medical personnel out on the playing field, calling for help.

The guardsman who'd ushered them toward the restroom now stepped in front of them. "Whoa, ladies! Y'all need to get back in line."

"My mother's ill!" Rosy insisted. "She needs medical attention. *Now.*"

"She don't look no worse than nobody else," he said, peering at Cilla.

"I'm fine," Cilla said. She pulled herself away from Rosy and repeated, "I'm fine. I'm fine. I'm fine." Rosy's fluster had raised Cilla's alarm. She nodded her head up-down-up-down. Big smile. "I'm fine!" She was coming back to her demented self.

"See. She fine," the guardsman said, and pointed again toward the metal detectors where people stood, arms overhead, up to ten minutes apiece, being felt up, patted down, grocery sacks and plastic bags full of salvaged clothing and foodstuffs upended in a search for weapons and contraband. With only Cilla's jewelry box in tow, they'd have made it through quickly.

Cilla began to laugh her high-pitched cackle, and the familiar sound comforted Rosy until she realized this hint of returning psychosis did not necessarily preclude a skull fracture. "She's got a closed head injury," Rosy said with authority. "A brain bleed! She needs immediate medical attention!"

"She'll be getting medical attention once she been cleared through security," the guardsman said. "She can walk, she can talk, she can pass by that line. For God's sake, you been waiting now for what? Almost four hours? Calm the hell on down. You almost there!"

Rosy likely would have acquiesced, except that just then a physician walked off the field near them, headed outside in search of fresh air, and she turned toward him to ask him to take a quick look at Cilla. But as she spun, she moved into the path of a policeman, deep in conversation with a military officer about how best to evacuate the dialysis patients. Emphasizing his point that the barricades should be shifted toward midfield with a straight-armed thrust to his blind side, he walloped Rosy mid-sternum with the bony back of his hand.

She'd have screamed no matter what, caught by surprise and knocked windless. But misfortune had directed his hand to the precise place where Cilla's foot had earlier that day landed a desperate underwater kick, bruising Rosy's breastbone and displacing a sliver of rib cartilage. So Rosy not only screamed but also fell to her knees, clutching her chest as if assaulted. Which brought her mother fully back to life.

Made her crazy, in fact.

In the ensuing skirmish, Cilla broke the cop's jaw, toppled two National Guardsmen, and had a firm grip on the startled policeman's unholstered Glock, its semiautomatic barrel aimed at her own foot, of all things, before she was tasered into submission. Too many potential felonies to count, including assault on a police officer, on military personnel. Oh, they did not treat her kindly. Used her hair as a grip to drag her, handcuffed, to the temporary jail constructed of chain-link cages at the Union Passenger Terminal a few blocks southwest of the Superdome. She bucked with a fury that would put a rodeo bronc to shame, roiling with full body spasms that tossed waves up into the faces of her wading captors, showering them with equal parts sputum and splash.

Rosy plowed along behind the furious security contingent, struggling to keep up as the knee-deep water on Liberty and Girod, working as suction, impeded her pursuit of the well-hydrated, well-fed men. The swells her mother raised up made it that much harder for her. She sobbed and begged the men for mercy, getting handcuffed herself when she caught one cop by the sleeve, clinging to him as she tripped headfirst into the dark water, coming up still sputtering the phrase she'd been breathing when she went under: "But you don't understand! She's not a criminal! She's sick!"

They released Rosy at the makeshift jail but processed Cilla alongside two thugs arrested in the Superdome on sexual assault charges and an evacuee who shot a National Guardsman in the Convention Center, as well as some of the interstate snipers and thieves, a passel of looters, and the scavengers who snatched suitcases from tourists chased from the flooded downtown hotels.

Rosy pressed herself against the chain-link until nightfall, re-soaking her damp clothes with urine because she wouldn't leave Cilla for a single moment, holding her mother's hand through the metal fencing while Cilla wailed. But after dark, the prison staff withered to just one broad-shouldered corrections officer on loan from Angola, who raised a baton over Rosy's head and threatened, "If you don't get the fuck outta here I'm gonna break your goddamn arm and then toss you in there with her. And look round: ain't nobody here to stop me."

Realizing they'd both be lost if she were arrested, too—understanding the best thing she could do for her mother was to get away, to get help—Rosy pried Cilla's fingers from her hand and ran from her mother.

"Don't leave me! Don't leave me!" Cilla begged, sobbing with fear that quickly transmuted to fury. "You ungrateful bitch! You left Maya to die, and now you killing me, too! Murderer!"

Those words that she slung at Rosy's retreating form—slurs motivated by a mania that suffused them with hate, with desperation—would be the last words Cilla ever spoke to her daughter. Her forever goodbye to her beloved child: "I hate you, you fucking coward cunt!"

꘏

CILLA AND ROSY HAD always been an affectionate pair. They burrowed unabashedly together beneath blankets, knocked hips as they strolled their neighborhood together each night, and never shied from a hug or a kiss. But they preferred handholding.

It's not just that Rosy grabbed on, as a babe, to cross a street or access the stairs safely: it's that she never let go. They slept beside each other, hand-in-hand between the threadbare bedclothes, and awoke with fingers still intertwined. And whenever her child retreated, frightened, into the broom closet during the daytime, Cilla would wedge her hand inside the door, nothing more, and Rosy would grip it, secure, fears forgotten. They held hands so often in Rosy's early childhood that she grew to be ambidextrous: she could print her name or play or eat with either hand, whichever wasn't cocooned in her mother's.

Moreover, from such an early age that Rosy had no recollection of the tradition's inception, they silently communicated their love via their hands, taking turns initiating the devotion with three squeezes of the other's palm in quick succession, one compression per word: "I-love-you."

"Me (squeeze), too (squeeze)," the respondent concluded and, at that, they always turned and smiled upon each other, pleased with their voiceless communiqué.

Even as adults they held hands regularly, Rosy on the floor at Cilla's feet, fingers commingled from seven to eight o'clock every Thursday night, the pressure of their clasp documenting the pace of action on *Survivor*. Michael Skupin falling into the fire pit: almost a broken digit; Rob Mariano proposing to Amber Brkich: double-fisted entreaty of joy. It bothered some strangers, people married to a particular standard that dictated who should and should not have a right to touch publicly, to see two grown women holding hands as they sashayed down the city streets. But such small-minded folks couldn't diminish their mother-daughter bond. Rosy had inured herself to the stares and remarks of meddlers, whereas Cilla just plumb never cared. Besides, whenever she closed her hand around her daughter's she got so caught up in the visceral memory of their first touch that everyone around them virtually melted away. She still relished the way Rosy's right hand had reached out from inside her body before any of the rest of her baby was born. It is the first part of her child that she ever touched.

The birth wasn't complete; no baby yet to hold. But Cilla felt something that compelled her to roll a bit to the right, knees bent, body propped up between the toilet and the wall and, while still pushing, she stretched her left arm over her belly and felt between her legs, where she encountered Rosy's right hand. The slippery baby fingers, plump with an instinctive, undeniable wisdom, wrapped themselves immediately around the mother's pinkie.

"Move that hand!" Maya said. "I can't see what I need be doing."

Maya had burst through the door moments before. For the past few weeks, she'd noticed the young pregnant girl going in and out of the formerly vacant house across the street, looking like she could drop that baby any minute. Though their paths hadn't previously crossed, Cilla's screams changed all that.

Cilla had tried to be quiet. Figured women give birth all the time, nothing to it. She'd stockpiled towels in the bathroom and planned to get it all over with there at home without raising anyone's attention. But Lord Almighty! The pain kept getting worse and worse till she forgot about not raising a ruckus and instead clung to the toilet seat, kicked a hole in the wall, slung back her head, and screamed like a banshee. Pitch that high carries, and Maya recognized the sound: either a woman making a baby, or a man with a testicle caught in a vise clamp. Without giving it a second thought, she wiped her flour-crusted hands on her apron, turned down the flame on her stove, dumped the skillet of catfish in the sink, and took off running to help the stranger across the way.

Rosy knew the story of her birth forward and backward, as it was oft-repeated with verve by both Cilla and Maya, each staking proprietary claim to the process. Cilla insisted she birthed her daughter alone, having caught hold of Rosy's hand the minute it breached and never letting go, pushing and pulling the newborn from her body in equal measure. Maya insisted she deserved credit for coaxing Rosy free: "Had old Maya not arrived, sure enough your mama'd still be hanging out in that there lavatory, banging on the toilet with one hand and caressing your fingers with the other!" They rehashed every detail with pride and in jest on regular occasion. Hard, therefore, for Rosy to believe anything could have been left out.

Still, some secrets take decades to reveal themselves.

Rosy always insisted that on her eighteenth birthday she would get a tattoo. Cilla opposed tattoos, and also piercings, acrylic nails, and, most specifically, "those dumbass fraternity boys branding theyselves like it's 1800 and they slaves all over again! Think what their granddaddies would say about fighting to be free just so they's ungrateful grandbabies could turn that damn iron on theyselves!" The way she figured it, no sense messing with what God gave you; the body's a temple and all. But, at eighteen, Rosy wouldn't need a parent's permission to get a tattoo, and by then she'd talked about it for so long that Cilla'd become reluctantly accustomed to the idea. Which is how they came to choose the tattoo together at the kitchen table on the eve of her birthday.

Rosy held the final four design options against her chest, waiting to reveal them. She'd spent much time seeking out the images, line-drawings all, intent on a simple figure, outlined in black; nothing showy or colorful; nothing to diminish the symbolism. Each design related to the others—each one contributed something to what she wanted to say—but only one would be the perfect prayer.

She struggled to find the best way to explain her choices to Cilla without burdening her, for they related to Cilla, of course, to the havoc of late. The doctors could not pinpoint whether too many medicated years had dulled her response to the lithium, or whether the advent of early menopause had skewed its effect, or whether things were just getting worse, as they are apt to do with bipolar disorder, but the episodes had become more tormenting, the onset more rapid, the peaceful lulls less enduring. There had been hospitalization upon hospitalization, police involvement beyond just commitment, Cilla's name in the paper, debt accrued for damages incurred. Embarrassment extended beyond the confines of their street, beyond the boundaries of neighbors inclined to forgiveness.

Rosy looked at her mother, roughly shorn, bald and eyebrow-free, scarred where the straight razor she'd wielded had dug into her convex pate, an indigo hue still slightly discernible at the edge of her scabs despite repeated scrubbings to remove the spray paint she'd gotten all over herself in the process of tagging cars up and down North Claiborne.

"They're all about change," Rosy said softly, referring to her tattoo design options. "About transformation. The belief that what's to come can be better than what's been." Cilla met her gaze, sadly. Rosy jumped in: "But that's not to say—"

"Shhh ..." Cilla whispered. "I know, Rosy girl. We could use us some better times. Better'd be good." She touched her head contritely, as if in apology. "Lemme see whatcha got."

Rosy laid a drawing of a hummingbird on the table. Cilla lifted it up and examined it while Rosy explained its meaning: A joyful messenger. One who appears during a time of sorrow and pain as a harbinger of healing to follow.

Then she handed Cilla the next drawing. "The phoenix. You know the story—about rising gloriously from the ashes and all."

"That might could work, but don't it strike you as being chug full of drama?"

Feeling mischievous, Rosy pursed her lips and directed her gaze to the stubble just starting to sprout from Cilla's dyed skull. Just shy of laughing, she broke into a full smile and shrugged her shoulders as if to say, *You said so.*

"Yeah, you right," Cilla said. "But still, the phoenix ain't my favorite."

Rosy handed over the third option. "The butterfly. Classic symbol of change, rebirth and renewal, but it's *super* popular. I sorta worry it might come off as unoriginal."

"Not for you, then," Cilla insisted. "You nothing if not original."

"Okay. Now this last one's similar to the butterfly," Rosy explained, delaying the reveal and thereby implicating her preference, "but it's more a symbol of the sense of self that comes with maturity. Native Americans believe it represents emotional and passionate early years balanced by the mental clarity and control of age."

"Lemme see it." Cilla took the paper and turned it over to reveal a delicate dragonfly, the wings crafted of simple swirls, like ripples in a pond; the tail a sinuous line ending in stars. Water to air, inhabitant of dual realms, pain to joy. Cilla gasped, knocking over her chair in her haste to dart from the room. "Don't move!" she shouted. "I be right back!"

She returned bearing her jewelry box. She set it on the table between them, rested her right hand atop it, and stroked the velveteen cover with the edge of her thumb as she had done almost daily as an adolescent. The fabric had not held up well under her deluge of love: the cover of the box had been rubbed clear down to the bare wood, with nary a trace left of the lustrous red pile that now clung only to the outer edges and sides of the oversized box.

Even new, it had never been much of a jewelry box: too big, too red, too tacky. Who knows what it began as? An expansive cigar box, perhaps, or an underdeveloped toolbox? No mind: Cilla's grandmother never concerned herself with what objects were meant for, focusing instead on their potential. A Depression-era bride, she cut curtains into dresses and dresses into curtains, and fed her children on the darning she took in and accomplished by moonlight while her husband snored off the benders he bought with their milk money. She breathed new life into anything with a needle and thread, once coercing a single pair of pants into accommodating three youthful owners—her eldest boy to younger girl to knee baby—fire-engine patches sewed over flowers that had, themselves, been appliquéd over fire engines. Her mantra: If it existed, then by God, it existed to be re-covered. Ain't no damn thing in all of life that can't be made more beautiful if you work hard enough to hide what it started out as.

Works with people, works with household objects, works with food, too.

Cilla arrived on her grandmother's doorstep clutching nothing but a baby bottle full of Coke with peanuts floating around inside and awoke every morning calling out with equal fervor for her mother and potato chips. Truth is, the toddler lost her memory of her mother before she lost her taste for the chips. For that first year or so, Cilla's grandmother had to trick her into ingesting anything nutritious by stirring raw eggs into milkshakes, lacing cupcakes with applesauce, enriching cookies with oats and nuts. But by the time the Louisiana Department of Children & Family Services took the budding adolescent from her grandmother eight years later, the picky eater had evolved into both a gourmand and an accomplished cook. She notably experimented with Zatarain's filé powder till she had a blackened catfish like no other and earned a reputation for her roux—a savory blond for crawfish étouffée, or a butter-based dark that required an hour of whisking but resulted in a gumbo the color of bittersweet chocolate. Even something as simple as her pot liquor could bring grown men to licks. Her culinary skills made her a coveted foster child; made her valuable; made it improbable anyone would have ever guessed she'd once been a food-averse child.

But no one ever bothered to wonder about Cilla's childhood; her history became obsolete the day she heaved her grandmother down the stairs.

Her maw-maw never blamed her for what happened. "I fell," she told the paramedics who secured her fractured hips to the backboard. "I fell," she repeated, staring hard at her granddaughter through her tears, feeding Cilla the lie she expected her to propagate. She knew Cilla didn't mean it. Really, it had been an accident. That's what she kept saying all the way to the hospital, over the sound of the wailing sirens, both to convince Cilla and to ensure the paramedics would put it on their form. She knew the social workers might alert the police if it read otherwise. "Is it on there?" she probed. "Does it say I fell down the stairs?" She didn't stop asking until finally the EMT showed her his clipboard where, under 'Cause of Injury,' he'd noted 'Fall Down Stairs.'

"Yeah," she said. "That's right. I fell."

For at least a year, ever since she'd noticed the first changes in her granddaughter, she'd harbored a fear that something would happen to result in Cilla being taken from her.

Puberty had been the old woman's first thought when the moodiness started. Puberty can make a girl crazy. Can even affect her sleep, which is how she explained the first few nights when the radio woke her around three o'clock in the morning, full volume, and she found Cilla singing along with the Jackson 5 and shimmying to "Serpentine Fire." But then came the night when Cilla wasn't dancing in the house, but outdoors, her naked skin alive with more sweat than a whore sported in church. Under the moonlight, arms spread, head back, she belted out a spot-on Roberta Flack impersonation about moaning and touching and feelings that show as she twirled in slow circles in the vacant street.

"Good Lordy God," Maw-maw hissed as she slung a blanket around Cilla and dragged her toward the house. "What you doing?"

To which Cilla—this little girl she tucked in every night with a kiss; this child she held during thunderstorms to staunch her fears; this young'un who still dunked her cookies in milk—replied by leveling her grandmother with the disdainful stare of a street-walker and shouting, "I feel like making love!"

Maw-maw about fainted right there in the street. Likely would have if she hadn't been so anxious to get Cilla inside, away from the sleep-crusted eyes she could sense peeking out from behind drawn curtains up and down the block. She realized now that something dangerous was happening to her grandchild and realized also her responsibility: keep it quiet, keep it controlled. The state takes uncontrollable black children away.

The self-locking door bolt she installed on the exterior of Cilla's bedroom door bought them a few months of inscrutability during the unpredictable ebbs and flows of the blossoming disease. Kept them safe and together right up till the day Cilla announced she could fly and Maw-maw stepped between her and the uppermost riser of the staircase, exclaiming, "We people, not birds, darling! People ain't meant to fly."

To which Cilla gleefully answered, "Course we are!" and heaved her grandmother backward down the stairs to prove it.

"I UNDERSTAND IT WAS an accident. No one's saying it wasn't," the social worker repeated for the sixth time after explaining the physician's orders for up to three months of rehab in a skilled nursing facility. "But accident or no, you're not going home, and since there's no other family member available to take care of your granddaughter, we have no option but to place her in foster care."

Cilla slept in the chair beside her grandmother's hospital bed. She'd been asleep there for three days; every time she awoke, Maw-maw slipped her one of the pain pills she pretended to swallow in front of the nurse but secreted inside her pillowcase in order to sedate her granddaughter. Cilla behaved herself, eating the food from the hospital tray, then ingesting the pill upon Maw-maw's order, cowed by the circumstances and woozy from the narcotics.

The old woman sobbed softly, so as not to disturb Cilla's sleep. "Ain't no other way?" she asked the social worker.

No words: just a shake of the head.

"Then might could I oblige you for a favor?" Maw-maw asked.

Though she wasn't supposed to involve herself in the personal affairs of her patients, the young woman nonetheless accepted the proffered house key and the directions, for she felt sorry for this old lady and this child. She realized neither of them was likely ever to see their home again, so she felt compelled to honor the request for a few belongings: a wooden box off a closet shelf, a sewing basket, a gold chain hidden in an Arm & Hammer box at the back of the freezer. She never did find the child's doll, and the clothes she gathered for her from the closet were those that were clean, not the favorites in the bottom of the laundry hamper, which meant that Cilla lost everything she most cherished. That is why the gift—crafted by Maw-maw from her hospital bed while Cilla slept and strangers in offices plotted their separation—assumed such status and became so beloved. It was all she'd ever have of home.

Cilla stayed sedated right up until the end, when her grandmother roused her and pressed the gift upon her in lieu of saying goodbye, while a child protective services worker paced the hospital corridor, eager to depart. "Take this, and go with that lady. She gonna see to you for a little while," Maw-maw said, nothing more.

Despite nine foster home placements in the subsequent seven

years, Cilla never stopped believing in the temporary nature of "a little while," always trusting her grandmother would find her again and bring her home. Emancipated from the system when she ran off at seventeen, determined to get the hell out of Louisiana unless she had a good reason to stay, the first thing Cilla did was hitch her way back to the hospital and sweet-talk a records clerk into disclosing which nursing home her grandmother had been transferred to all those years ago. Shortly thereafter, a sympathetic administrator at the home confirmed she'd died of pneumonia five-and-a-half weeks after her arrival.

Still, Cilla never stopped searching for her, doing a double take through diner windows if a stocky woman of similar height cocked her head to the right, as Maw-maw did when contemplating the flavor of a dish before reaching for more cayenne, and she listened in on conversations among the grandmotherly crowd, searching for her voice. Fact is, she took the job at the Theta house in Tuscaloosa for no other reason than that Ada May, the head cook, said "darling" with the same cadence and lilt and frequency Cilla had grown up loving. But it wasn't until she met Maya that her grandmother came fully back to life for her. Same mannerisms, same attitude, same drive—she could see and sense it the minute Maya first ran through her bathroom door, distracted though she was by the pain of childbirth. The shock took her breath away, which made Rosy's birth slightly easier because it slowed and helped regulate her breathing. While reaching between her legs to pull on her birthing daughter's hand, she looked up at Maya and decided God was in the process of delivering her grandmother back to her at the same time He delivered her baby.

"Move that hand!" Maya said with gentle authority. "I can't see what I need be doing."

With that phrase, a whole decade folded back upon itself, so that ten-year-old Cilla stood once again in the hospital room, the sound of someone's heels *click click clicking* impatiently in the corridor beyond, as Maw-maw wriggled her wedding band off her ring finger. Despite her drug-induced torpor, Cilla recognized the import of the moment. Many had been the time, playing dress-up or snuggling together, when she'd asked if she could try on her grandmother's wedding ring. "Can't allow it," Maw-maw always replied. "Can't take it off. I done made a promise once, 'Till death do we part,' and I intends to die with this ring on my finger."

Despite all those days in the hospital, it wasn't until her grandmother took the ring off that Cilla grew frightened. By the time Maw-maw had threaded the chain through the ring and reached over to latch it behind Cilla's neck, Cilla had begun to cry. Embarrassed, she raised her hand to swipe at the tears.

"Move that hand!" Maw-maw said with gentle authority. "I can't see what I need be doing."

Then she pressed the makeshift jewelry box, freshly covered in rich red velvet, into Cilla's hands and said, "Take this, and go with that lady. She gonna see to you for a little while."

The stranger then clicked into the room from the hall, took Cilla by the hand, and ushered her swiftly toward the doorway.

"But wait!" Cilla said, turning back toward her grandmother. "Your ring!"

"For you, darling," she said, fighting back her own tears. "You guard it for me. Till we back together again."

Cilla didn't remove it until the day after Rosy's birth, when she slid it off the chain and onto Maya's finger.

"I can't," Maya said.

"Shhh. You can," she replied, with a soft kiss to the hand that cradled her baby's head. "Trust me: it was always supposed to be yours."

In the jewelry box full of collected memorabilia, Cilla safe-guarded the barren gold chain among the rosebuds and recipes and ticket stubs that made up the history of her displaced youth. Rosy scavenged through the box once or twice a year throughout her childhood and adolescence, intrigued by her mother's souve-nirs, but Cilla rarely opened the box herself anymore. She had a child's life to focus on now. Truth be told, until Rosy handed her the design for the dragonfly tattoo, it had been years since she'd even thought about the box or its contents. Now she rummaged inside it, having resettled herself at the kitchen table. "I knew it. I knew it!" she murmured.

"Look at this," she said, lifting from the box and placing before Rosy a wooden dragonfly about as wide in diameter as a Susan B. Anthony dollar. It was carved in relief, so the insect's image appeared to be embossed onto the piece of softwood. She laid the paper embellished with Rosy's tattoo design beside the woodcut: they were exact facsimiles.

"Oh my word," Rosy said. "How strange. I haven't looked in that box in forever. I mean ..."

The two women met each other's gaze across the table. Their skin erupted in goose bumps. Cilla's eyes welled with tears, and she brushed her fingertips along the edge of Rosy's jawline before picking up the woodcut. "Did I ever tell you the story of this dragonfly?"

"It's the one Dad made you. The one you found in your pocket after you spent that first afternoon with him at the craft fair."

"Mmm hmm. But did I tell you the rest of the story?"

Rosy shook her head.

"I held it, all through your birth," Cilla said. "I thought I could do it alone, but when it got harder, I got scared. And I sure missed your daddy that day." She set her right hand upon her abdomen, tracing her fingertips over the place where Rosy had once grown. "I went and got this dragonfly, when the pain got bad, to have a little piece of him near me, so as how I might feel less alone. I musta held onto it something fierce cuz later that day I noticed the picture of it was still there, right here below my thumb." She opened the hand that had been clutching the woodcarving tightly while she spoke, and Rosy glimpsed the image etched into her palm. "See. It was just like it is right now. But here's the thing: it stayed there for hours that day. Just wouldn't get gone. I took to thinking it might never go away, but come the next day, when I woke up, my hand were back to normal. I tell you, I squeezed on that dragonfly every day, for near on a week or so, trying to get your daddy's design to stay on my body, but it didn't work. Always faded away, 'cept on the day I made you, when he stayed on my body all day long.

"Lord have mercy, I miss him."

Rosy reached out and grabbed her mother's left hand, still splayed between them on the table. She held the tattoo design up beside it. "Right here," she said, pointing to the fleshy place below Cilla's thumb, where the impression had once lived. "And right here," she said, pointing to the same place on her own palm as she pressed her hand into her mother's, entwining their fingers, grasping tightly, squeezing three times: "I-love-you."

Which is how they came to get matching tattoos on their palms on Rosy's eighteenth birthday.

They held hands through the process—of the tattooing, and all the rest of life.

Hands clasped is how Rosy and Cilla began together; it's how Rosy came into Cilla's world, and also how she left it. Those palm-borne dragonflies, a prayer for joy, were the last part of their bodies ever to touch, their hands united desperately through the chain-link cage behind the Superdome until Rosy wrenched hers free and ran off into the night, racing toward her death in the hope of saving them both.

IX. Rose

"A pocketed phone number is a connection, an ally.
It means you're that much less alone."

AMAZING, THE THINGS PEOPLE will tell you if you ask with a smile and act as if you know what you're talking about.

"Hey!" Rose exclaimed as she bounced up on the raised desk surrounding the nursing station in the restricted-access area within the emergency room at Natchez Community Hospital. She propped the whole upper half of her body on the laminate desk surface, chest pressed against forearms, leaning in collegially as if she'd just popped down from another floor and needed a quick favor before getting back to work. Without introducing herself, she asked, "Is Amanda in at midnight again tonight, or did she pull an earlier shift?" Rose hoped the nurse who was frantically posting orders online would think she should've recognized her and assume her requisite nametag must be caught up between her arms and her shirt. When the nurse paused before answering her question, Rose pressured her by rapping her knuckles *boom boom boom boom boom* on the countertop as if to imply, *Come on, come on, we've got work to do! I don't have all day!*

The nurse humphed and rolled her eyes but switched quickly to a different computer screen. "Yep. Amanda'll be in at midnight."

"Thanks!" Rose said, all bright teeth and crinkled eyes, winking with a promise to repay the favor someday. Then she darted back out the way she came in, through the automatic doors, into the lobby, leaving the confused woman to turn to the charge nurse behind her and inquire, "Was that the new respiratory tech from Cardiac they were in-servicing? What's her name again?"

"Found her," Rose said into her cell phone as the ER doors swooshed shut behind her and she stepped back into the hospital's main lobby. The phone had been nestled in her back pocket, line connected, caller silent but listening, during the charade. Mac had bought her the phone before she left Alabama and made her promise to check in throughout her trip; now he waited for confirmation that she had tracked down the nurse who treated Rosy and bought her the bus ticket from Natchez to Tuscaloosa.

"Good girl. Now get yourself some rest," he said. "Oh! Wait. There's this place over there you just gotta see. Called Mammy's Cupboard—follow Highway 61 a little further south and you can't miss it. That place is older'n water, but by God, they got the best damn lemon icebox pie you ever tasted. And a whole wall full of jellies and jam—"

"Mac," Rose interrupted with obvious amusement, "is it *always* about food for you?"

"A body can't forget to eat! 'Specially at times like this!"

"Yes, Dad," Rose said sarcastically, hanging up the phone to the sound of his laughter.

It had been Mac who'd walked her through the casing of the ER, told her to take a seat in the lobby with a magazine and watch where people went in and out, insisting she locate the nursing station (behind the double doors) as differentiated from the public reception desk (out front).

"I can't go back there," she'd informed him from her perch in the waiting room between a guy holding an icepack to his head and a teenager who looked to have a broken arm. "There's a sign on the door that says STAFF ONLY."

"Do you always believe everything you read?" he'd asked, reminding her that signs are only signs, not locks. He swore that if she strode in as if she belonged there, no one would stop her. "You gotta get to the nurses," he said, "cuz they're usually less suspicious than the receptionists at the check-in desks out front might be." Then he coached her through the demeanor and phrasing to use. She practiced her script for more than half an hour before summoning the courage to pull off what ended up taking fifteen seconds, tops, which was good since her cool had a shelf-life that expired the minute the ER doors sealed shut behind her. Having successfully met her objective, she beelined her way to the public restroom adjacent to the hospital lobby, where she vomited up half a bag of Cheetos and a warm Diet Coke into a toilet. She hated hospitals; hated strangers. *What in the name of God am I doing here?* she wondered.

Just then, a voice behind her called out: "'Scuse me, ma'am."

The voice, high-pitched and nasally, startled her. (*They've caught me!* Rose thought. *With my head in a toilet!*) In her haste to lift her face out of the bowl and spin around to answer for her deception, Rose conked her temple on the oversized tissue dispenser and fell to one knee on the floor where she came face-to-face with a little girl. The child crouched on all fours, peeking up at Rose from beneath the stall door. "'Scuse me, ma'am," she repeated. "But is you drinking the toilet water?"

Bam! Bam! Bam! A fist pounded hard and fast on the divider between the stalls, and a woman's voice called out over a urine stream, "Rebecca Sue! Mind your own bee's wax!"

The cowed child made to retreat but, under cover of the flushing water from the next stall, coaxed Rose to bend toward her with a come-hither crook of her index finger and whispered, "Don't make no sense to me, but Mama says that toilet water ain't the same as sink water, and if you's thirsty you should just—" With that, the child's body was wrenched backward by a strong hand grasped on her ankles, and all Rose could see were her chubby hands hanging onto the bottom of the stall door as she yelled "—ask for a glass!" before vanishing into the public domain of the restroom.

Rose's laughter covered up the words of reprimand as the embarrassed mother scooted her daughter away.

Rose had done the exact same thing once, as a child: squatted to peer up at a stranger beneath the half-wall partition between toilet stalls. At a hospital, in fact. Gertrude had brought her to the ER at age eight when she claimed to have swallowed the button eye off her stuffed bunny. Truth is, she'd pulled the eye off and dropped it down the air vent in the floor in her bedroom. She had often wondered how far down the vent went (maybe to China?) and had hatched a plot over the preceding week or so to craft a shrinking potion, like Alice did, to facilitate an exciting Asian excursion. She just needed to confirm that the vent went all the way through the earth without obstruction and could still recall her profound disappointment when the button eye sang out *plink ploink plonk* as it bounced off the metal surround of the heating duct and rolled to a stop just far enough under the floorboards to be irretrievable.

Later that evening, with the rabbit perched in its usual spot in the chair directly across the dinner table from her, Gertrude paused while placing the customary single leaf of iceberg lettuce on its plate, then turned and leveled Rose with a hard stare.

"Where's Bunny's eye, Rose?" Gertrude asked.

Rose doted effusively on her stuffed animals. Though she thought nothing of speckling chicken pox all over her Barbie dolls with a Magic Marker, or blithely abandoning her two-wheeler to rust in the rain, each animal was honored with a precisely-appointed position in her bed, which she painstakingly rearranged every morning before attending to her personal needs. Ever the tedious caretaker, she took care to keep the wolf far from the sheep ("He could eat her, you know!" she once screeched at Gertrude when her mother'd had the audacity to position them beside each other after changing the bedclothes) and religiously separated the noise-making animals (who chirped or barked when their bellies were squeezed) from the bat and the bears, who needed quiet, after all, to facilitate their hibernation. The only time she awoke in the night anymore was if one of her precious animals fell from the bed onto the floor, which she immediately perceived with an extrasensory nocturnal aching that dissipated only after Gertrude rushed in and returned the lost creature to the fold. Had Bunny's eye accidentally fallen off, Rose would have gone racing to her mother in tears begging for her to reattach it post-haste. So Gertrude knew this business of staring nonchalantly across the table at a one-eyed rabbit meant Rose had deliberately sabotaged Bunny's vision for an important—and surely subversive—cause.

"Rose?" Gertrude repeated into the silence. "The eye?"

Given that Gertrude had growled, only the day before, "Don't you dare even think about it!" when she caught Rose staring suspiciously through the vent grate, Rose knew the truth would result in trouble. With a natural preference for coddling over a reprimand, she put a hand on her belly, turned her best sick face to her mother, and said instead, "I swallowed it."

The tactic worked well enough, with much fawning attention from Gertrude as they sat in the ER lobby awaiting the X-ray, but the joy fractured when Rose went to the bathroom to pee and, intrigued by the sound of a boisterous fart from the adjoining stall, stuck her head under the divider to see who had made such a noise. The result: a bloody lip that required three stitches to close when the gaseous retiree in the next stall, mortified to be caught ungirdled in mid-wipe by a laughing child, bopped her in the face with a cane and screamed, "Get outta here, you nosy varmint!"

It took two hospital administrators to soothe the old woman, who screeched about privacy laws, unsupervised children, and the modern generation's failure of both manners and morals while Rose hid under a sheet on the gurney, bleeding blood and embarrassment into the fabric. For the rest of the evening, Gertrude apologized profusely to anyone who would listen, including, two hours later, the newly clocked-in intern who arrived too late to witness the scene but just in time to sew shut Rose's wound.

"I'm very sorry," Gertrude said.

"No worries," the intern replied as he injected painkiller into Rose's lip.

"She was only outta my sight for a minute."

"That's all it takes," the intern replied, poking her skin with the needle to test for numbness.

"She knows better."

"I'm sure she does," he said as he moved to pierce Rose's skin.

"I'da cut her tail, too, had I been that woman," Gertrude said.

Rose's face flushed red, and her unnumb lip trembled.

"Look, I don't know—and it doesn't matter to me—what happened," the intern said, turning to Gertrude. "But if you wanna come over here and hold her while I sew her up, it might make it easier on her."

"Easier don't teach nobody any lessons," Gertrude said, crossing her arms and leaning back against the wall by the door. For the five minutes it took the doctor to repair Rose's injury, mother and daughter glared at each other across the room, both sets of eyes brimming with tears, neither allowing a single drop to fall.

Just the thought of that day, so many years past, raised on Rose's face the mottled red flush of renewed humiliation. She bent low over the sink in the public restroom at Natchez Community Hospital, splashed cold water on her skin to combat the color, and gurgled to purge the taste of vomit from her mouth.

Reaching up for a paper towel, Rose spied the stall she'd recently vacated reflected back at her in the restroom mirror and surprised herself by smiling. She imagined the little girl crouched there, watching in awe as a grown woman lowered her head into the toilet bowl and made a curious noise. Lapping up the toilet water? Indulging in a drink? She laughed aloud, and it took the edge off her melodrama. The more she laughed, the more relieved she felt.

Walking toward the exit, still giggling, she reached for the door and that is when it hit her, this very simple thought: that little girl was mighty cute.

Cute. Cute! Not abhorrent. Not even all that inappropriate! A child peering under a toilet stall door is funny! Natural! It is not something to be met with a cane to the head or an expectation of apologies. Kids will be kids, no? Re-visioning the child under the stall door ("'Scuse me, ma'am, but is you drinking the toilet water?"), it occurred to Rose for the first time that perhaps her behavior had been characteristic, not crude, and that it was that nasty old woman, not her, who'd been wrong.

So why didn't my mother stand up for me? Rose wondered.

This question—not security staff, not nursing personnel, not some irate hospital administrator—stalked her out of the hospital and nearly rear-ended her as she turned the rental car out of the parking lot into the city streets. Every red light a blushing cheek, a burst of blazing fury: *Why didn't my mother stand up for me?*

A police car raced past on her left and, in the siren's shriek, she heard her mother's voice impeaching her: "Easier don't teach nobody any lessons!"

A garbage truck caught a curb and, in the metallic smash of ricocheting trash, she heard her mother's denunciation: "If you hadn't caused so much trouble, we wouldn't be in this predicament!"

An engine revved: "What have you done this time?"

A trunk slammed shut: "I'm so ashamed of you!"

Horns reverberated with the unuttered refrain she'd heard with each indictment, the imagined tagline for which she held Gertrude accountable: "I'd be better off without you." Again, a horn: "I'd be better off without you." Again: "I'd be better off without you." That obnoxious horn screamed at her, over and over, until finally she looked up and saw a vehicle heading straight at her and pulled swiftly into a driveway, ceding right-of-way to the irate driver, who flashed her the finger as he stormed past on the one-way street Rose had heedlessly turned down in the wrong direction.

Her whole body began to shake. She bent her forehead to the

steering wheel, letting the engine rock her, and cried. Like some tired ditty she couldn't keep from humming anew, Rose reheard every word that over the years had made her wince. Fresh incisions over old wounds. She sat and sobbed until she lost the energy to continue, at which point she finally sensed her audience. An old man bent to her window.

"You okay, honey?" he asked.

"Oh, yes." She quickly wiped her eyes and struggled to catch her breath. "I'm fine, really." She turned and pointed behind her toward the one-way street. "I accidentally headed in the wrong direction."

The gentleman nodded. "Happens sometimes to everybody. No cause to get so worked up about it. You know, all you gotta do is turn yourself round."

She smiled at the simple advice. The man reached through the open window and patted her hand.

Rose turned herself around. Reversed the car out of the driveway and headed in the appropriate direction, feeling unexpectedly fortified.

She waved goodbye to the old man, who waved back.

Nearby, a garbage man upended a can into his truck. This time, only the trash rumbled; no voices echoed alongside it. From the line of parked cars, a door slammed, but now it was just a door. The light changed to red because that is what lights do.

As she pulled through the intersection, Rose glanced at the passenger seat beside her. Empty. She touched her hand to the upholstery for confirmation.

Her mother no longer occupied the car.

✜

AIMING SOUTH ON HIGHWAY 61, she figured she'd pull into a service station and ask for directions to Mammy's Cupboard if need be. But she soon realized that Mac's "You can't miss it" meant, literally, "There's no way in hell you're gonna be able to drive past that building without stopping."

"Good Lord, Mac!" she exclaimed into her cell phone as she stepped out of the car, leaned back on the engine hood, and stared up at the thirty-foot-tall black woman-cum-building looming over the parking lot. "Only in Mississippi!"

"She's something, huh?" he replied. "I heard a rumor they went all PC on us over there, though, and done painted her lily white. How's she look to you?"

Rose continued to ogle Mammy's busty body, replete with kerchief and gaudy gold earrings, service tray in hand as if to pass up vittles to the man on the moon, her trunk balanced atop a red hoop skirt with door and windows cut into it, inviting guests to settle in for a snack in the most indiscreet of domains.

"She looks like the love child of Aunt Jemima and Paul Bunyan," Rose finally said.

"But is she *black*?" he asked.

"I think I'd call her mocha-colored."

"What the hell's 'mocha'?"

"Tan."

"Goddammit! I knew it! She used to be black! Why're people suddenly inclined to go tiptoeing round the truth? If she's wearing a head scarf and serving food to white people in the South, she's black whether you paint her tan or not!"

"Mac!"

"Rose!" He paused for a moment and said, "Okay, you're standing there looking up at her. Now imagine she's yellow. Golden yellow. Are you now thinking our Mammy's some Asian transplant, or are you still thinking she's a black woman that some color-blind liberal went and painted the wrong color?"

Rose sighed. "Mammy's definitely a black woman."

"That's all I'm saying."

Only the structure itself had succumbed to the revisionist's art history: the smaller, one-dimensional wooden Mammy in the parking lot, advertising "Open Tues-Sat, Lunch Only," still sported coal-black skin.

Hanging up the phone, Rose stepped toward the front window

and peered between the curtains, parted to let in the cool from the sill-mounted air conditioner that rattled away. Snuggled in the muggy twilight under Mammy's petticoat were three tables and a set of shelves housing Mac's wall-of-jams along with an eclectic assortment of miniature mammies personifying every possible stereotype—the nurturing nanny molded into a full-bellied cookie jar, the sensible protectress with slotted lips sized for quarters, the cook crocheted onto potholders, the disciplinarian etched into a wooden spoon handle, the ceramic mediator sized to stand sentinel on a mantle or a nightstand. Rose half-expected to see Sambo come sauntering through the door to the adjoining dining room. *But no,* she thought. *Sambo's banished nowadays. It's only the black* women *who are still available to the highest bidder.*

When the window fabric billowed behind the leaded glass, as if a mammy leapt to life to draw the curtains on the intruder, Rose startled backward. But as the sheers continued to sway, she realized it was pestering from the air conditioner, not the ghost of Hattie McDaniel, that moved them. Someone—some real live person—was still inside somewhere, trying to stay cool.

Rose glanced at her watch: 8:15 p.m. The Greyhound had dropped her in Natchez, Mississippi, at 4:05 p.m., ten minutes ahead of schedule after the seven-hour bus ride from Tuscaloosa. It took a bit more time than usual to secure the rental car, given that the manager had to verify through local authorities Mac's legal override granting her permission to sign for the car despite the fact that she was only eighteen, still many years away from being able to rent a car under her own authority. Then she located the hospital, confirmed Amanda's schedule, found a room for the night ... another four hours gone. Though her stomach grumbled to no avail—she'd not be getting any food at this restaurant tonight, what with no dinner service—she couldn't bring herself to leave just yet. Besides, she had the whole rest of the night to kill; no need to hurry. Although Amanda's shift started at midnight, Mac had advised Rose to wait and approach her mid-shift, about 6 a.m. tomorrow, when she'd be due for a break anyway. So Rose slowly circled the building, running her hand along Mammy's skirt-wall as she stepped over the weeds and discarded cigarette butts on the ground.

Ever since a tenth-grade art class that focused on modern American techniques, Rose had cultivated an affinity for folk art—especially the faux naïve style of Afro- or Southern-oriented female artists such as Faith Ringgold and Grandma Moses. All year long, she anticipated the autumn folk-art fair in Northport and spent hour after hour appraising the handicrafts before selecting one to adopt. Buying art was like building family; her purchasing decisions had little to do with talent and everything to do with heart. One year she fell for a four-dollar elf fashioned from tree limbs, with a nail for a nose, hammered out by an anonymous blind man. Another year she became so enamored of a miniature wolf—meticulously carved by an artist of such renown as to preclude purchase—that she spent an entire dinner hour raving about the creature, and the emotions it evoked in her, to Gertrude. Come morning, she awoke beneath the wolf's gaze; he balanced on the windowsill above her bed.

By Rose's estimation, that was just about the kindest thing her mother ever did for her, second only to securing them tickets to the opening reception for the Birmingham Museum of Art's "Alabama Folk Art" exhibit last winter. There were cocktails and canapés and chorales, and the governor himself gave the opening remarks, but all that paled before the quilts. Seventy bold, geometric, fabric-as-story masterpieces from the Bend. No Log Cabin or Nine Patch here; nothing so well-mannered. These were resistance pieces, the spirit of Harriet Powers turned indignant; six generations of women from the Black Belt counties of Alabama who turned the utilitarian into an art form and, by banding together in the '60s, saved their families from ruin when every last man lost his job after registering to vote at the behest of Martin Luther King Jr.

Rose stared in awe at the exhibit's crown jewel. Gertrude wrinkled her nose.

"You like these?" Gertrude asked. Rose nodded her head so hard the loose edge of her ponytail whipped her chin.

"Don't you think they look kinda, well ... *used?*" Gertrude whispered.

"Of course they're used! This is a museum, not a retail store!" Rose laughed. All joy, no sass. "Do you really not know anything about the Gee's Bend quilts?"

Gertrude shook her head.

"Okay, do you see the way they're stretched out, off-canter?" Rose extended her hands as high as possible toward the wall-hung quilt before them, spreading her arms wide, as if to smooth it out and prove its corners off-square. "People *used* these! Not just to pile on their beds to stay warm, but they stretched them over windows in wintertime and nailed them to walls to keep out drafts. They spread them on the ground for picnics. *Real* people used these as part of their *real* lives. For over a century women made these cuz they had to in order to survive! Art critics say these quilts're some of the most miraculous works of modern art that America has produced, yet, until recently, none of the quilters thought of herself as an artist! I remember reading a quote from one of the women, who said, 'If my husband had seen me painting instead of working, he woulda knocked me clear into the backyard.' Don't you think that's just amazing?"

Gertrude cocked her head bemusedly. "You think it's amazing her husband woulda knocked her into the backyard?"

"No, not that!" Rose said, eyes alight, rushing on. "The idea that at any given moment any one of us could be engaged in something that someone might one day consider miraculous, and we don't even know it! We're just doing what we need to do to get to the end of the day, or to keep a baby warm, or to ride out a storm, and someday someone will write a book about it, or hang the product on the wall of a museum, and the whole world will look at it and be inspired! *That* is what I think is amazing! *That* is why I love these quilts."

Though not converted, Gertrude couldn't help but respond

to Rose's enthusiasm. "Which one is your favorite?" she asked.

"I love them all, but for different reasons. Look at this one. Can you tell what this is?"

Gertrude leaned in close, but shook her head, no.

"Somebody's denim work pants! See these shiny worn spots? Those woulda been the knees! This is quintessential vernacular art."

"What's that?" Gertrude asked, delighted when her question aroused a smile, not scorn.

"It's something more than folk art," Rose said, thinking aloud. "How can I ...? Okay, well, vernacular refers to the manner of speaking in a particular place—like, for instance, Creole in New Orleans. So vernacular art is a way of visually depicting the culture of, say, a specific group of people—like African Americans—or a specific place—like Gee's Bend."

Turning her gaze to an anteroom, Rose gasped. "Come and look at this!" she said, grabbing her mother's hand and wending their way around a gaggle of Mountain Brook soccer moms sipping champagne and standing with their backs to Nora Ezell's "A Tribute to Civil Righters of Alabama," which dominated a small side hall.

"*This* is my favorite quilt of all time! I didn't realize it'd be here!" she gushed. "It's like a book come to life. Look, here in the center is the Sixteenth Street Baptist Church—"

Gertrude shook her head again, unfamiliar. Rose was taken aback.

"—right here in Birmingham! Where those four little black girls were killed at the height of the civil rights struggle."

"Oh. Of course," Gertrude said.

"And Rosa Parks's bus is over here." Rose paused and glanced at her mother.

"I know about that," Gertrude said.

"And this is the Edmund Pettus Bridge." Rose looked at Gertrude again. This time she shrugged her shoulders, confused.

"You're kidding me," Rose said.

"No. What?"

"The Selma-to-Montgomery march for voting rights? 'Bloody Sunday'?"

Gertrude's look said, *Go ahead and crucify me, but I still don't know.*

Rose rolled her eyes but checked her tone, as if the quilt might reproach her for telling its story with attitude. "In March of 1965, about six hundred civil rights marchers started out from Selma, but they only got about six blocks—to the Edmund Pettus Bridge—before they were attacked by police and driven back into town. Two days later, MLK led a symbolic march back to the bridge, but it wasn't until later in the month that they won protection from the federal court to complete the full march. By the time they reached Montgomery, there were over twenty-five thousand marchers! Just a couple of months later, President Johnson signed the Voting Rights Act of 1965, giving blacks the right to vote."

"What were they doing?" Gertrude asked.

"What do you mean? What was *who* doing?"

"The marchers. What'd they do that caused the police to get involved?"

"Nothing," Rose said, drawing out each syllable for emphasis. "That's the point. They weren't doing anything 'cept walking cross a bridge."

"Go on," Gertrude prodded. "You know they had to be doing something wrong. Police don't go interfering with people for no reason."

Rose sucked in a deep breath, cemented her arms across her chest, and snapped, "Not people who look like you and me."

Gertrude realized her logic threatened to unravel their connection and began backpedaling. "Well shut my mouth!" she said with uncharacteristic vim. Then she smiled at the quilt as if it had led the rally right across that bridge and she planned on offering up to it a congratulatory high-five. "Ain't that the berries!" she added, stealing a glance at Rose. "It's because of marches like that that such stuff just don't happen to people nowadays! Right?"

Rose took a step away from her mother, as if wrenching up

a provisional drawbridge, her spirit hunkering anew behind its stone wall. At such moments, Gertrude customarily retreated. But not tonight. Tonight, she sprang with derring-do across the space looming between them, tethered her arms around her daughter's shoulders, and said, "I'm buying you that quilt!"

Stunned by the embrace, by the insane comment, Rose wondered if her teetotaling mother had sneaked a drink. Sensing her daughter's confusion, Gertrude said, "Well, of course I'm not *actually* buying it for you. As if I could afford that! But come on. Pretend I'm gonna buy it for you—cuz if that don't get your fire started, then your wood's all wet. Now what're you gonna do with it?"

"It belongs in the Smithsonian," Rose said icily. But Gertrude would not release her, even when the moment went on too long and turned awkward; she clung to her daughter as to a buoy, and her desperation melted Rose's resolve. "Fine!" Rose said, shaking free. "You can buy it for me, but only if you let go of me!"

Gertrude smiled and dropped her arms. "Done."

Rose rolled her eyes and humphed, but still said, "Okay then, I'll keep the quilt for a week or so—sleep with it wrapped round me! After *that* I'll donate it to the Smithsonian."

"That would be selfless."

"Though I might prefer to see it hang in the Museum of the Confederacy," she said, smirking.

Gertrude shook her head and matched Rose's expression. "Slightly less selfless."

"Ah, yes. But infinitely more gratifying."

They both laughed. Connection re-secured. "Okay," Rose said. "My turn to ask a question. So what's the most selfless thing you've ever done? And what's the most gratifying?"

"Those're two questions!"

"What's that you always say to me, Mother? 'Get mad, get glad, or scratch your ass. It don't make no difference to me.' Answer the questions!"

Gertrude laughed aloud at the unaccustomed mimicry. "Fair enough," she said, and so went the rest of their evening. They strolled through the halls, oblivious to the crowd, taking turns, prying, actually listening, learning each other. Some of their questions had nothing to do with the art; other times the exhibits inspired them. An hour or so into it, standing beneath a rose bower made of tin scraps, Rose asked, "Why'd you name me Rose?"

"It was my favorite flower, once." Gertrude stared off into the distance and blushed. "It was your father's favorite flower, too."

Gertrude never spoke of Rose's missing father. Aside from acknowledging the single preserved image of him pasted into her photo album, this was the first time in eighteen years she had mentioned him to her daughter. The comment begged for follow-up but, instead, the lights flickered and a docent appeared to usher them out into the night. In the general jostling of the crowd, the retrieving of coats, and the trawling of the lot for their briefly-lost car, the cloak of their intimacy slipped from them as if caught in the doorjamb upon their exit, and they proceeded into the winter air without it. By the time Rose settled into the passenger seat, removed her shoes, and rested her feet upon the dashboard, Gertrude's disclosure had already drifted beyond Rose's consciousness, her mind absent a secure place in which to store information doled out nearly two decades too late.

Only now, in the wake of her mother's death, running her hand along the red brick wall of a strange little restaurant in a strange town, replaying a short-lived connection in a short-lived life, did Rose even recollect her mother's comment. "It was your father's favorite flower, too."

He had a favorite flower. The rose.

During her mother's lifetime, Rose rarely considered her father. He was not a broachable subject, so he did not exist to her. He was nothing more than a glossy image on a three-by-five piece of paper, not a person with preferences and a personality. Rose hadn't missed what had never been real to her; she'd had her mother. But now, with Gertrude dead, this recollection that her father had a favorite flower made him something more than an anonymous face in a fading photograph. She raised both hands to her chest and pressed the palm of her right hand hard against the bent fingers of her left. *Pop!* the knuckle of her thumb cracked.

Whereas, before, his absence only made him an asshole, she suddenly realized: his absence now made her an orphan.

Pop! the joint of her index finger snapped.

What more might I have learned, she wondered, *had we not been interrupted by the closing of the museum?*

"We closed," a woman's voice boomed from behind Rose's back and, in her surprise, she squeezed her hands together so fiercely that the last three digits popped in clamorous union.

"You shan't be doing that," the woman said, shaking her head as she thwacked her flour-crusted hands upon her apron. Her heft filled the entire kitchen doorway, hips wedged against the jamb on either side, one foot kicked forward to hold the screen ajar. She wiped the sweat off her brow with the back of her right hand, leaving a pasty white smear across her dark forehead, and said, "You be giving yourself the arthritis, you keep on like that."

"That's what my mother always said," Rose replied.

The woman slowly disengaged herself from the doorway, pushing the screen door fully open with her left hand, an inviting gesture that shifted the air just enough to waft the comforting aroma of fresh-baked pie in Rose's direction. Cinnamon, peach, coconut and meringue tumbled together into the yard. "You ought be minding your mama, then," the woman reprimanded.

"My mother's dead," Rose said.

The woman did what any compassionate person might do: she bent to comfort the suffering girl, who crumpled to the ground in tears, folding Rose into the cocoon of her lap. Rose had no recollection of ever being held in that way, nestled in arms that indulged her sadness as opposed to pushing it—and her—away. Seduced by such succor, she succumbed to the atavistic tendency young white girls have long indulged in the embrace of grandmotherly black women: she told her story, beginning to end. The coats that never reached Katrina's victims. The shoes unlaced from dead feet, now bound to her own. The funeral. The morgue. Her quest, its next step, its unknowns.

In the end, she left with the woman's phone number, but not her name. She never thought to ask it.

"In case you be needing something," the kind woman said, tucking the piece of paper with her number on it into Rose's pocket as they walked hand in hand from the kitchen to the car. Rose knew she'd never use it, but still: it made a difference. A pocketed phone number's a connection, an ally. It made her feel that much less alone.

She also left fully sated, with a bonus "for the road" pie: the lemon icebox with the towering meringue, boxed and secured with trussing twine.

"Like I done said," the woman repeated, "ain't no kinda sorrow can't be softened by some sugar."

She had said this, the first time, as she lifted Rose up off the ground after her tale ended and guided her into the kitchen, where she dispensed sugar with abandon, cutting the virgin slice from each of the evening's labors: Mississippi mud pie, coconut meringue, Italian crème cake, grilled peach pie, plantation peanut butter, and, of course, the unforgettable lemon icebox pie that inspired Mac to recommend Mammy's Cupboard to Rose in the first place.

Perched on the edge of the butcher-block island, Rose ate it all up—not just the desserts, which she savored until nothing but crust crumbs remained, but also the maternal caress for which she'd been starving. Behind her, as she devoured the pies, Rose's Mammy stood sentinel. Finished for today with the crimping and fluting of dough, her hands sluiced instead through Rose's silky hair, plaiting the strands. Length by length, she made art of the mundane, turning tragedy's witness into a thing of unexpected beauty.

∗

AFTER LISTENING TO THE nurse greet the barista at the kiosk in the hospital lobby, Rose introduced herself by commenting, "You're not from round here." It seemed a less intrusive opener than "Excuse me, there's a dead girl I wanna grill you about," and it required no measure of creativity. Amanda's word choice, to say nothing of her accent, betrayed her heritage: not a Dixie girl. Had she been from the South, she'd have pronounced "hey" as "hay" and certainly never would have uttered a full and uptight "hello." Still, Amanda wasn't aloof, so not from the North either. Rose fell into line behind her when she strolled to the coffee counter during her mid-shift break at 6 a.m., and by the time they each paid for their morning's first lattes and scones, Rose knew Amanda's college roommate had answered a recruiting ad that landed Amanda a $6,000 signing bonus and her friend a $2,500 referral fee that more than paid for the cost of the move from Sacramento. Nurses are in high demand.

"There's actually something more I was hoping to ask you," Rose said as Amanda turned back down the corridor toward the ER.

"Me?" Amanda paused, uncertain what a visitor might want of her beyond directions to the restroom or the maternity ward.

"Mmm hmm," Rose nodded, falling in step beside her. "You treated a patient a few weeks ago—"

Amanda stopped abruptly. "I can't discuss a patient's care with you."

"I know. I didn't come to ask you about a patient's care … exactly …"

It made no sense to do anything other than tell the full truth, but it's no easy thing to admit to being involved in killing a person, however accidentally. The look of condemnation that Amanda leveled upon her in response felt unfair. It pissed her off. For the first time in the week-and-a-half since the accident, anger swelled larger in her than guilt. The set of her jaw said, *Fuck you; I lost something here, too.*

So there they stood, face-to-face, posturing in the corridor, two sets of hands encircling cardboard coffee cups pressed to chests—heart-guards, modern-day shields. Neither woman spoke as passersby detoured around their stand-off; they just stared at each other, still awash in their emotions, but responsive as well to a sparking sympathy. In the hush between them came these logical recognitions: The nurse actually cared. The girl meant to atone. Neither was entirely virtuous nor entirely fallible.

"Look," Rose said, finally, "I don't want or need medical information. I've talked to the medical examiner; I saw Rosy's body. I know more than I probably need to know. Certainly more than I wish I knew. I'm just trying to figure out where she came from. Do you have any clues, at all, that might help me get her home?"

Amanda breathed deeply, looked surreptitiously up and down the hall, toyed with her coffee until the corridor cleared of personnel. Then she gestured for Rose to join her and, as they walked toward the ER, she leaned into Rose's ear and whispered, "She said she came out of New Orleans after Katrina hit and needed to get to Tuscaloosa. Her father's family's there." Amanda thought a moment. "Shit, I can't remember her last name."

"It's okay, I already know," Rose said. "It's Howard."

"That's right." The back entry to the ER loomed ahead. Amanda slowed her pace. "She had gone to Alexandria, I think it was, and was hitchhiking to Tuscaloosa, when—"

Rose interrupted. "Do you know what she was doing in Alexandria?"

"No. I don't know."

"Did she stay there with somebody? Somebody she knows?"

"I don't know. I didn't ask any further. I just asked where it happened, where she got ... injured. It was for the medical report. And she said she'd hitched a ride from Alexandria. That's all I know."

"How'd she get to Alexandria from New Orleans?"

Amanda raised both hands, palms up, one cradling her coffee cup. "I have no idea. None whatsoever. I don't know anything else. I wish I did. I wish I could help you." She pulled her hands back into her chest and looked at the floor. "She was such a sweet girl. So alone." She raised her gaze to meet Rose's. "You know, like everybody else, when I heard the news coming out of New Orleans I figured I'd make a donation. Then I met her and paying her bus fare seemed like a more personal way to do something good." She hid her eyes behind her free hand. "But I've wondered a thousand times since that officer called, might she be alive if I hadn't bought her that ticket?"

Rose wrapped her hand gently around Amanda's wrist. "*You* had nothing to do with it. You were only being kind, and kindness never killed anyone. She'd be alive today if only *we* hadn't hit her."

Amanda slid her hand down from her eyes to cover her mouth, but only for a moment. She lifted it quickly and placed it on Rose's shoulder. "Thank you."

Rose nodded. "I appreciate your help." Then the women parted ways: Rose back down the corridor the way she came; Amanda through the security doors into the ER.

"WAIT!" AMANDA TORE DOWN the hall, yelling. "Wait!" Rose was four steps from the exit when she heard her and turned around.

"Thank God I caught you," Amanda said after catching her breath. "I just realized there's somebody else who might be able to help you. There was a housekeeper who spent some time with Rosy that night. She worked last night; I think she gets off at eight this morning." She handed Rose a twenty-dollar bill. "Consider this an extension of my original donation. There's a Shoney's within walking distance. It'll be a good place for the two of you to sit and talk."

Rose waited in the parking lot for the housekeeper, who exited the ER with four other night-shift staffers at 8:15 a.m. Rose knew whom to single out, for Amanda had described her well: "Forty-something, black, singing."

"Singing?"

"Singing," Amanda repeated with a chuckle. "You'll see."

Fortunately, because housekeepers—unlike nurses—do not travel far for work, the woman was a Southerner through and through, meaning she happily accepted even a stranger's invitation to breakfast. As they walked, Rose told her story. With only periodic pauses for an "mmm hmm" or an "aw, Lordy" or a "you poor baby" and a pat to Rose's back, the housekeeper hummed. When Rose finished talking, the woman nodded her head, contemplatively, and added the words back to the tune she'd been humming, singing aloud. When the song ended, she turned to Rose. "So how can I be of some service to you?"

Rose could have kissed her. First, though, she opted to satisfy her curiosity. "Are you always singing?"

"Oh, yes'm. I ain't never stop no more. When I first come to know the Lord, I thought and thought on how's best to share His Word. And I said to myself, 'Latonya, the Lord done filled you with a gift. You owes it to Him to sing His praises!' And that's what I been doing ever since!

"But still," she said, extending her index finger for emphasis, "there's times I tries to be a touch more quiet about it than others. Sometimes I just hum, especially at work, cuz I understand there be some folks might not be wanting to hear the praise of the Lord. But they others that really like it. Fact is, I got me more customer service stars than any other body works in that whole dang hospital," she said, pointing to the stickers encircling the name on her nametag. "They even wrote an article about my singing in the newspaper. Truth be told, that's how I come to meet Rosy. She done asked me to sing for her."

Beaten and left for dead, Rosy had been delivered to the hospital by a good Samaritan. Alone and injured, awaiting care in the ER, she called out to the housekeeper, whose feet she could see beneath the curtain drawn around her; in the adjacent exam area, Latonya sang a gospel tune as she swabbed up a puddle of blood. "Please," Rosy called out, shyly, "might you come sit with me for just a few minutes and sing that song again?"

Leaning on her mop, swaying gently beside Rosy's gurney, the housekeeper performed a private rendition of Mahalia Jackson's "Move on Up a Little Higher." When she finished, Rosy's face streamed with tears.

"Your singing reminds me of my mama," she sighed.

At Rosy's request, Latonya stayed with her through the entire four-hour ordeal. Together they sang while the nurse plucked twenty hairs from Rosy's scalp and dragged a nit comb through her pubic hair for possible DNA comparison between her strands and the assailant's. They crooned about a day when burdens could be laid down while a phlebotomist drew Rosy's blood, six unsuccessful sticks before a viable vein finally gave up enough to test for HIV and hepatitis. Their musical prayer covered the sound of a CNA scraping skin and fibers out from under Rosy's fingernails and from inside her wounds. They sang about meeting in the morning as the bulb flashed and captured photos of Rosy's face, of her breasts, of her bleeding crotch. They sang about meeting on an altar while the nurse swabbed every orifice for semen. They sang about meeting when angels call the roll while the doctor stitched her back together again.

Away from the scene, weeks out from the incident, Latonya finally faltered in her recounting of the experience for Rose. She did not sing this time; she did not hum; she openly wept. "We was like a broken record. Every time we finished one round we'd just start on up again. Sang that same song for four hours. Was only one second when Rosy stopped singing in all that time." She covered her face with both hands at the memory. "Poor thing, the way she screamed for her mama when they pried her legs open and put them in those metal stirrups!" She took a deep breath and composed herself. "But I kept on with the singing and she caught back up with me and we just held hands and sang and cried together the whole time."

Having reached the front step of Shoney's, Latonya turned and looked at Rose, who'd been listening in silence throughout the walk. "I has to tell you, I tried not to look, I surely did! But I feel like I done witnessed that girl's violation all over again." Latonya reached for the restaurant door with one hand, dried her eyes with the other. "It's a good thing whatcha be doing, trying to make sure she ain't forgotten."

They stepped inside to a bustling breakfast crowd. In the locating of a table, the scanning of the menu, the placing of orders, they paid unwitting obeisance to Rosy's suffering. A moment of silence before the other inquiries began.

"I'm stuck at Alexandria," Rose explained. "I know as much as I care to know about what happened between Alexandria and Natchez, and I know how she got from Natchez to Tuscaloosa, but I can't figure out what Rosy was doing in Alexandria or how she got there."

"She went to Alexandria cuz her aunt lives there," the housekeeper said, matter-of-factly.

Rose stopped and looked up, the spoonful of grits halfway between the plate and her mouth, dripping butter. "You know the rest of her story?"

"I know what she done told me. She went to Alexandria to see if her aunt could help her get her mama released—"

"What do you mean, 'released'?"

"They was at the Superdome when her mama got arrested—"

"For what?"

"Well now, she ain't said exactly. Said it were a mistake, that she weren't no criminal, that she were sick. Anyways, she went to see her aunt in Alexandria to see if she could help her out somehow."

"And?"

"And her aunt told her—I'll never forget this!—'You wanna go springing somebody outta jail, you either gotta be white or you gotta be rich, and I ain't neither of those two things.' Now ain't that the truth?" Latonya chuckled momentarily, but then got serious again. "Rosy said she don't have no other family, so she fixing to try and track down her daddy's folks, in Tuscaloosa, to see if they might could help her a spell."

To the rest of Rose's questions—"Do you know the aunt's name? Do you know anything about her father? Do you know which part of New Orleans she lived in?"—the housekeeper answered no.

"Only other thing I know—and it probably ain't all that helpful since I can't remember her mentioning a name—is that Rosy said the lady what carried her from New Orleans to Alexandria was one of the kindest people she done ever met. Saved her at exactly the moment she needed a savior, that how she put it."

Just like that, Rose stopped breathing; she kept still in order to capture the hint of an idea that flitted near her consciousness, elusive, a subtle sense of knowing that remained unformed until the housekeeper said, "That lady done saved her offa the bridge what cross into Gretna." And then there it was! The memory of the pie-baker's hand sliding a piece of paper with a phone number on it into her pocket the night before "in case you be needing something." *It's what kind people do!* Rose thought. *They share their numbers, just in case. A pocketed phone number is a connection, an ally. It means you're that much less alone.*

She remembered Mac's hand nudging the business card across his desk toward her that first day. "This is all she had on her when we pulled her body out from under the car," he'd said. "No ID, no money other than a few coins; no nothing besides this business card, this page from the phonebook, and this receipt from City Cafe."

Rose raised her hip up off the seat and retrieved the phonebook page from her back pocket. Uncreasing it, she extracted the photocopied business card from the florist in Gretna, Louisiana.

"Is this the woman?" Rose asked, pointing at the name.

"Jennifer Goldberg! That's her, all right! That's what lady Rosy said done saved her offa the bridge into Gretna."

Rose sighed with relief. She'd discovered the next link, the next step, but her joy was momentarily trumped by curiosity. "What do you think Rosy meant by 'saved'? She wasn't—"

Latonya interrupted her. "Is you saying you somehow ain't heard what done happened on the Crescent City Connection?"

"Well, of course I heard about the Gretna police attacking evacuees on the bridge," she said. "But you don't think Rosy could've been—" She stopped speaking in response to Latonya's nod.

"I suwannee," Latonya said softly. "Rosy was there, bless her heart. Don't seem fair, now does it? One soul, so much suffering. But she was there. Fact is, far as I know, she the only one done made it safely cross once they locked it down."

X. Birmingham News

Special Edition: Katrina, One Year Later
August 2006

Who's the Bad Apple Now?
Op-Ed
By ROSE AIKENS

Ethylene kills.

It preys in particular on the aged, the injured, the weak. Rots them from the inside out. Its power to infect and destroy everything around it is a well-documented scientific fact. Though in small doses its effect is relatively benign, prolonged exposure to high concentrations can result in complete annihilation of the species.

In the immediate aftermath of Hurricane Katrina, conditions were ripe for the biosynthesis of ethylene: flooding, drought, chilling, wounding. Therefore, were ethylene transmitted via human hosts, one might excuse New Orleans's neighbors for fearing an outbreak. It might explain why authorities east of the city, in St. Bernard

Parish, stacked cars in roadways to seal off their communities from escaping flood victims. It might explain why a white West Bank officer aimed a shotgun at a band of African Americans—primarily women, children and the elderly—who were walking across the only navigable span over the Mississippi River and exploded his weapon over their heads, roaring "Get the f--- off of my bridge!" It might excuse Ronnie C. Harris, the mayor of nearby Gretna, Louisiana, for disputing charges of racism and inhumanity by asking, "What were people expecting us to do?" after his police chief—with full support of the city council—elected to barricade the only passable interstate highway out of the Crescent City to foot traffic, trapping survivors in the floodplain even while waters continued to rise.

But ethylene is a plant hormone. In its gaseous form, ethylene is the invisible factor behind the "bad apple" theory—whereby one rotten fruit destroys the entire bushel. Abetted by the 90-degree temperatures during that first week of September 2005, ethylene blackened bananas and bruised apples citywide, turning starches to sugars and moldering the produce counters inside every one of New Orleans's padlocked and abandoned groceries.

People manipulate ethylene for many obscure purposes, synthesizing the hydrocarbon into trash-bag liners, cable sheaths, cardboard veneer. We ingest it in soft drinks, wash our hands in its soapy suds, wear it. We wrap our fragile packages in it and insulate our homes with it. We can extrude it in many forms, but we do not exude it. People are not apples. One rotten individual does not irrevocably taint the group.

Try telling that to the residents of Gretna, who overwhelmingly backed Police Chief Arthur S. Lawson Jr.'s decision to shut down the Crescent City Connection bridge and insulate them from the influx of fleeing

New Orleanians. "It makes you feel safe to live in a city like that," Paul Ribaul told *The Los Angeles Times.* Interviewed on NPR's *Morning Edition,* Judy Burchette gushed, "We were ecstatic. [In New Orleans] they were looting and they were shooting and we didn't want that over here. I had my two small children and we were scared to death and thank God for the city of Gretna because they took care of us."

To be fair, New Orleans is notorious for its propagation of bad apples. Perennial favorite in the race for murder capital of the United States, it was on track to capture the title again in 2005—202 murders had taken place by the time Katrina made landfall on Aug. 29—with computer models predicting another 107 before year's end had not the criminals been displaced along with everyone else. Infamous for the corruption of its politicians, it is a city further hobbled by the corruption of its judiciary: of all the lawbreakers arrested between 2003 and 2004, only seven percent were eventually sentenced to prison. And its police force had become a rogue laughingstock, a reputation further bolstered when up to a third of the officers deserted the city in anticipation of Katrina's chaos—many in their department-owned patrol cars, and some in vehicles stolen from the local Cadillac dealership. As for the committed officers who did stay behind, a tourist reported approaching one to request help after the onset of the storm. "Go to hell," he was reportedly told. "It's every man for himself."

It didn't start that way.

In the beginning, compassion ruled the day. Neighbors shared attics and rooftops. Men leapt into floodwaters to help drowning girls even when they themselves could not swim. Volunteers abandoned their own families to pluck victims from trees; women sheltered rescued orphans as their own. And the people of New Orleans listened and obeyed when their mayor told them there would be food

and water and buses waiting to take them to Texas, if
only they would walk across the Crescent City Connection
bridge to claim it.

So on Wednesday, Aug. 31, thousands of evacuees trudged
their high expectations across the 3,000-foot-long cantile-
vered bridge spanning U.S. Highway 90 and followed the
first exit off onto the west bank of the Mississippi. They
stopped at the intersection of Whitney Avenue and the
West Bank Expressway, near a blown-out high-rise hotel
and the Conquering Road Christian Academy, in the mid-
dle-class suburb of Gretna, population 17,500.

And Gretna, ultimately vilified as the epitome of the bad
neighbor, did something no one took much notice of in the
shadow of her subsequent actions. On the morning when
they first appeared, Gretna welcomed the refugees. This,
despite the fact that no official of New Orleans had ever
contacted Jefferson Parish authorities to ask for their help,
or had even alerted them to the fact that refugees were
being sent in their direction. This, despite the fact that
about 5,000 of Gretna's own citizens remained trapped in a
town bereft of power, potable water, or sustenance; a town
whose own damaged levee threatened to burst; where water
rising from the south mixed with diesel fuel that spilled
from a tanker into her streets.

On the morning of the third day post-hurricane, repeatedly
denied assistance by the state of Louisiana and the Federal
Emergency Management Agency for his own citizens, Chief
Lawson looked toward the bridge and witnessed an influx that doubled his human responsibilities in a matter
of hours. And still, he did what he could. He ordered an
underling who moonlighted as a school bus driver to begin ferrying evacuees to a staging area outside of Gretna.
Shortly thereafter, other officers commandeered two buses
from a depot and joined the rescue operation. In a period
of less than 24 hours, it is estimated that Gretna's police

force caravanned over 6,000 New Orleanians to Metairie, some 16 miles away, where a food and water distribution center had been hastily set up.

But the people kept coming. For every one bused to safety, three more appeared, begging for help. "We had never planned on evacuating anybody," said Lawson and, as increasingly desperate survivors amassed on Gretna's shore, "I realized we couldn't continue, manpower-wise, fuel-wise."

Still, they came. But now: angry. Hungry, thirsty, frustrated, they spied too few buses for too many people and realized the guarantees they'd been given were false. "They had been told in New Orleans—they were looked in the face and told!—'There's something over there for you,'" Lawson said. "Then they got mad at us when they got here and realized there wasn't. It was promised as a land of plenty, but it wasn't. We were in disarray." The crowd, increasingly unruly, swarmed the buses, and an African American officer fired the first shot, into the air, in an effort to enforce calm. At that, fights erupted as men in the crowd brandished weapons and the mob surged around and into nearby Oakwood Mall. Tempers flared, windows shattered, and the building erupted in flames. Redirected from rescue efforts to crowd control, cops moved to confiscate weapons and chase suspected looters from the retail shops. "It was a very tense situation," Lawson demurred. Gretna Mayor Harris, on the other hand, called in the state police. "I said: 'There will be bloodshed on the West Bank if this continues! This is not Gretna. I am not going to give up our community!'"

It is as if Wednesday's setting sun sucked the release valve off a pressure cooker set to explode and, by Thursday, Sept. 1, New Orleans and its environs had devolved into a banana republic. Early in the day, New Orleans Mayor Nagin issued "a desperate SOS," on CNN, and it wasn't just for food or water. It was for help in quelling a population raging out of control. FEMA Director Michael Brown added, "[We are working] under conditions of urban warfare."

Looters, armed gunmen, and gangs of miscreants roamed the streets with seeming impunity. Air-assisted hospital evacuations halted, trapping hundreds of patients and healthcare workers inside decimated medical facilities. "At every one of them," according to Coast Guard Lieutenant Commander Cheri Ben-Iesan, "there are reports that as the helicopters come in people are shooting at them." Among those fired upon by rogue civilian snipers included a professor from Tulane Medical School, a physician, and local ambulance employees who attempted to ferry food by boat across the street from Tulane Medical Center to Charity Hospital in an effort to feed the 200 patients who had been trapped for four days with only a few cans of vegetables and some graham crackers. In response, police posted their own snipers on the roof of the precinct and issued body armor and assault rifles to those charged with keeping order in the French Quarter and other parts of downtown.

Meanwhile, the shelters deteriorated into frontline trenches. From inside the Superdome, speaking via cell phone, displaced resident Raymond Cooper stunned an international television audience with his eyewitness account: "They have quite a few people running around here with guns. You got these young teenage boys running around up here raping these girls. You got two old ladies that just passed, just had died, people dragging the bodies into little corners." New Orleans Police Chief Eddie Compass confirmed, "We have individuals who are getting raped, we have individuals who are getting beaten. Tourists are walking in that direction and they are getting preyed upon."

And yet, 88 officers dispatched to restore order at the Superdome were driven back by a swarming, angry mob. In a city where the citizenry never trusted police, where police spied criminals lurking in every civilian's shadow, when hell descended they turned upon each other. Gordon Russell, a reporter for *The Times-Picayune*, described "a near riot situation. The city is not safe for anyone."

"It's every man for himself!" the police officer shouted at the tourist. Where the tourist heard callousness, plain and simple, it may be that the officer meant only to speak the plain and simple truth.

Every man for himself: news reporter Gordon Russell, hiding out in his home with photojournalist Marko Georgiev of *The New York Times*, after the two witnessed a shootout between police and civilians that left one person dead. "[We] plan to flee the city tonight," Russell posted on his paper's blog. "There is a totally different feeling here than there was yesterday. I'm scared. I'm not afraid to admit it. I'm getting out of here."

Every man for himself: Texas Governor Rick Perry's communication director, Eric Bearse, emailing the state's homeland security director on Thursday, Sept. 1, after watching televised images of Superdome marauders being loaded onto buses bound for Houston. "Question between you and I: At what point do we go from being compassionate to being taken advantage of (meaning, are they sending us folks we don't want)?"

Every man for himself: a Jefferson Parish sheriff's deputy, armed with a shotgun and fortified with an attack dog, standing proudly as part of the human barricade that prohibited New Orleanians from escaping over the Mississippi into Gretna. "The West Bank is not going to become New Orleans," he said. "There will be no Superdomes in our city."

Four months later, while media accounts of the violence were being amended, while civil service responses were being questioned, while the crime rate in Houston was sky-rocketing, Ed Bradley took a *60 Minutes* crew to Gretna in an effort to understand what happened on that bridge. Or, more importantly, why.

Police Chief Lawson, implicated in several federal civil lawsuits as well as a criminal probe stemming from his decision to close the bridge, had by then ceased giving interviews. But Mayor Harris spoke to Ed Bradley. He said he sealed off the city because he wanted to protect the lives of Gretna's residents. "You had to be there to understand and witness total chaos, total mayhem, the lack of information," he said. "This environment of police officers being shot, citizens lying dead in the street, images of looting going on in the city of New Orleans made me realize that our community was in a crisis of far greater proportion than just of the hurricane."

Still, Ed Bradley asked, did he feel it necessary to condemn everyone because there might be some bad apples in the group?

"Absolutely not!" the mayor said.

But, the newsman pointed out, that is exactly what he did. They turned everyone around—even the elderly and children—because there might be some bad apples among them.

"I'm sure that there were very good people," the mayor retorted. "There were scared people. There were desperate people. And, unfortunately, contained within that crowd was a criminal element. That criminal element burned, looted, stole, threatened, and terrorized."

The bad seed spoiled the bushel. The whole harvest: branded rotten. This full year later, the world at large is still endeavoring to distinguish the one from the other.

XI. ROSY

"Dad, it's me, Rosy."

ROSY RAN SCARED AS clocks tolled the witching hour between Wednesday's August night and Thursday's September morning. Having just abandoned her mother in the outdoor holding pen by the Amtrak station, she launched into the night, seeking help. Instead, she found herself disoriented. None of the streets made sense anymore, what with everything underwater and all the landmarks down. Puzzling even in daylight, they were that much worse in the dark, with unlit ground melting into blackened sky and barely a sliver of the moon's last quarter still visible as it waned toward its new phase.

Adrenaline had carried her far—into an attic, onto a roof, out of the Superdome—but four days without sustenance thwarted her now. She might not have made it back to the shelter—might have lost consciousness at the lock-down—had not the day guards earlier passed her a small bottle of water from the stash of prisoner privileges the masses lacked. The water gave her the energy, later, to run from the night guard's threats and respond to the impulse, *I hafta get help,* but it wasn't sufficient hydration to allow that motive to stay fixed in her mind.

She started out okay, angling toward the imposing shadow of the Superdome, intending to loop around it and then past, on toward help—somewhere help. But she found herself trapped in a perpetual circle: befuddled, she couldn't figure out how or where to break free of the building's draw and, as dehydration's confusion settled over her, she swiftly forgot why she should want to. Hunger, thirst, exhaustion: a hallucinogenic brew. In her counterclockwise plodding around the perimeter's concourse, in the eerie quiet of dead night, she slowly sensed the Superdome stalking her. No matter where she went, it hovered just a few steps away on her left-hand side. She cast her eyes toward it a few times, then averted her gaze, not wanting the structure to know she was on to it, the building's refusal to quit following her becoming evermore alarming. She picked up her pace, tried to run, but her feet could only shuffle along, never fully disconnecting from the sidewalk. The building was fast making headway in its pursuit of her; she could not shake its tail!

"Always fight back!" Mrs. Armstrong hollered. "Always!" She blew her whistle for emphasis. Rosy couldn't see her, what with the darkness and all, but she could smell her: Mrs. Armstrong's sweaty gym funk built up through six consecutive PE classes, 8 a.m. to 3 p.m. daily, sweating it out with her class through modules on hoops, or volleyball, or self-defense.

"Are you listening to me?" the phys ed teacher barked, materializing before Rosy in her coach's jersey, ALHS Pythians monogrammed in pale blue over her heart. "Buck 'em up! Buck 'em up, Pythian!" she shouted, characteristically turning the school mascot's chant into a personal directive, then bent toward Rosy till their noses virtually touched. "If you can't outrun him, then turn on him and fight back!" At that, Mrs. Armstrong grabbed Rosy's shoulders and pushed her toward the Superdome. "Catch your assailant off guard. Confront him. It's your best chance of surviving an attack." Rosy, always responsive to coaching, nodded her head. Mrs. Armstrong blew her whistle again: "Go!"

Rosy ran at the Superdome, both arms locked straight in front of her, screaming "Get away from me!" as she slammed into the wall and pushed hard to knock it off-balance.

"Don't give up! Don't give up!" Mrs. Armstrong encouraged.

Rosy kept pushing, with all she had in her. She would not let up. It took a moment, but she soon felt the building sway beneath her thrust. *There we go,* she thought, overwhelmed with relief as she turned to thank the teacher who had vanished into the night.

Then she passed out cold on the concrete.

She revived approximately twelve hours later, under a woolen blanket, when someone grabbed her right ankle and began dragging her along the concourse.

As she bumped on her back down the pavement, she had no idea where she was. Blind beneath the navy wool, still drowsy, dehydrated and disoriented, she could hear voices and engine noises and footsteps, but they came in muted snippets, a disconnected soundtrack. In her haze, she permitted herself to be towed, surprised, more than anything, to be moving along so incongruously. She only protested when her skin started to scrape, elbows and top-of-back scuffed on the sandpapery surface, hair tugged from its roots. Suddenly both indignant and curious, she yanked the blanket off her face, heaved against the counter-force at her foot, and sat straight up.

"Holy fucking shit—"

"Mary mother of God—"

Two men in camouflage cursed and leapt backward away from her, toppling a lawn chair they balanced between them. One of them tangled his legs in the chair's aluminum frame when he startled and wound up splayed on the ground beside Rosy, while a third soldier loosed his grip on her ankle and recoiled, screaming. He stumbled backward, shrieking like a B-movie actress, laughable but for the fact that he simultaneously cocked his rifle and aimed it at the pile of people on the ground before him.

Both soldiers at Rosy's side began cursing anew:

"What the fuck—"

"Drop your goddamn weapon!"

Still, the ashen-faced soldier framed them in his sights and screamed. The guardsman on the ground didn't move, but the guardsman standing at Rosy's side stepped slowly toward his comrade, hands up and fingers splayed, speaking loudly but calmly over the screams. "Drop your weapon, man. Drop it. It's just me and Darnell and … and … and a little misunderstanding we got going on here." He grabbed the barrel of the rifle in his outstretched left hand, directing it toward the ground, and patted his comrade's shoulder with his right. Finally the screaming stopped. "There you go, man. Calm the hell on down. You just got yourself spooked. Nobody's needing to get shot cuz of that." In the quiet, all three men turned and stared at Rosy.

"Christ almighty," exclaimed the screamer. Having relinquished his weapon, he melted into a catcher's squat, head in hands, blond hair sprouting between splayed fingers, shaking first his head, then his whole body. "I think I need to change my pants," he muttered.

"You sure enough do," one of the black guys said. "Look at you. You shaking like a hound dog trying to shit out a peach pit." At that, the white boy lifted his face and laughed—wracking convulsions of nervous laughter that made the other two laugh also, though they still kept a wary eye on him, as just a moment ago he'd seemed ready to kill someone.

Rosy waited until the guy at her feet calmed a mite before asking, "What's going on here?"

"We was moving the dead bodies," the soldier beside her replied as he stood.

"What dead bodies?" she asked.

"Yours!" the three said in unison.

"And his," the rifle requisitioner said. He nodded toward the body on the ground under the tipped-over lawn chair, blanket dislodged to reveal a milky fixed gaze above a wide-open, toothless mouth.

"Somebody check him," the screamer advised. "Make sure he's

dead!" His comrades stared at him, dumbfounded. The dead man lay on the ground in the same seated position he'd rigored into before tumbling out of the upended chair.

"Guess you could shoot him to see if he reacts," the leader said, handing back the rifle with a mischievous grin. "Why don't y'all finish moving him? I'ma stay with the girl."

The gunman took his weapon sheepishly. "Who would've thought a National Guardsman would have to carry a rifle on a hurricane relief mission just to keep from getting shot at by his fellow Americans?" he wondered aloud. "I can't fucking believe this shit. This is a disgrace," he insisted as he helped hoist the dead body back into the chair and walked off with it.

The soldier who stayed behind settled himself on the ground beside Rosy.

With a smile, he extended his hand and introduced himself. From the many pockets concealed within his uniform, he extracted three water bottles, a Snickers bar, two vacuum-packed spaghetti-with-meat-sauce MREs, and a half-eaten shrimp po-boy wrapped in foil. "Ain't dressed. Just got mayonnaise," he said by way of apology as he laid the picnic on the blanket that still covered Rosy's lap.

"I don't need nothing on it," she mumbled, already tearing into the French bread with such fervor that crumbs sprayed the soldier's face, making him look like a leopard in reverse: yellow spots on black skin. But he just smiled and dusted himself off.

They talked through her situation while she ate, the food making her lucid and conversant. He had an easy manner and a thoughtful gaze—more soulful giraffe than hungry leopard, she realized as she watched him—and because he immediately returned her mother's jewelry box, which he'd found lying beside her body, she judged him to be trustworthy. Moreover, he assuaged her fear and her guilt with reassurances that Cilla had gotten lucky, being arrested, for she'd be fed and guarded and transported to Texas, where they'd surely see she was ill and not evil and move her to a clean, modern hospital where her worst worry would be whether or not she'd seen all the movies showing on HBO on any given day. "Your mama'll be okay till you can figure a way to go get her, which is a helluva lot more'n I can say for most of the folks here," he said. "But before you can do something for *her*, you gotta get yourself outta here and rustle up someplace to stay—"

"—and the resources I'll need to come back for her," Rosy interjected. At that, she turned her face from him, tucked her head, and squeezed her eyes shut. "There's nothing left." She exhaled loudly, an ironic *humph*. "There wasn't hardly nothing to start with," she said, her voice cracking. "And now I've got nobody."

"Everybody's got somebody," he said. "What about your mama's family?"

She shook her head. "My mother was a foster child. She's got one foster sister we're close to—my aunt, north of here, in Alexandria—but she's worse off than we are."

"Not no more," he said gently. "But what about your daddy?"

"He's dead," she replied, eyes still downcast.

"*His* family?"

"They can't help me. I've never even met them."

He refused to give up. "What kinda talk is that … 'they can't help me' … just cuz you ain't never met them? I ain't never met you neither, and I'm sitting here helping you, ain't I?"

Though he meant just to bolster her spirits, he suddenly realized the larger truth in his statement, and it energized him. "Girl, you don't know! Y'all got the whole world's attention! Ain't gonna last long, but least for the next few weeks everybody with half a heart's gonna be looking for a way to help the poor black folk of New Orleans. See? Ain't no better time to gamble on finding your missing family. They your wild card! They your chance to get lucky!"

Rosy raised her face and looked at him, hope clouded by skepticism. He looked earnest, though. He wasn't joking.

"You know where your daddy's people stay?" he asked.

She opened Cilla's jewelry box and withdrew her father's obituary, then passed it to the soldier, index finger tapping the

Ellen Urbani

"survived by" section at the bottom of the page. "Tuscaloosa."

"Okay then," he said. "You got yourself a plan. First we gotta get you outta this here city. Once you outta here, then head on up toward your aunt in Alexandria, where's least you can get cleaned up and rest a spell. Then Tuscaloosa. You find your daddy's family; they'll help you. I guarantee it. Given these here circumstances, ain't no way not to and still show they faces in church on Sunday. You feeling me? They gonna help you! And when they do, you can go on and help your mama."

Rosy retracted the yellowing newsprint from his hands. "But this was almost twenty years ago," she said. "What reason do we have to think they're still there?"

He shrugged. "What reason not to?" He paused. "Besides, darling, this be the South! Who you know done ever left it?"

She looked slightly less dubious, so he kept coaxing. "Fly this on up the flagpole with me; let's see who salutes." That did it; she smiled in cahoots with him.

Rosy had herself a plan after all.

HER SOLDIER CONNECTED ROSY with a group of tourists who'd stopped to ask directions to the Crescent City Connection Bridge. They were moving in the opposite direction from her next goal, Alexandria, but word had it that the Highway 90 bridge to Gretna was the only viable route out of the city for those on foot, so he urged her on. "Get on outta here, get your bearings, then figure out a way to get yourself on up to Alexandria," he said.

Several hundred strong, the peregrinating group originally consisted of paramedics in town for an EMS conference and other travelers en route from the impromptu police command center at Harrah's on Canal Street. Locked out of their hotels, having collectively lost $25,000 when the buses they hired to drive them out of town were instead requisitioned by the military, they were advised by a New Orleans police commander to abandon their makeshift camp outside police headquarters and walk to the Pontchartrain

Expressway. "From there, cross the bridge to the West Bank of the Mississippi," he said. "The police have buses lined up over there to take you outta the city." His words prompted the crowd to cheer, and the group set forth straightaway. Wary of the misinformation abounding, however, a few skeptics among them halted the migration and asked the commander to confirm his words as fact. He stated, emphatically, "I swear to you that the buses are there."

By the time they circled the Superdome and began the arduous climb up the U.S. 90 ramp onto the Pontchartrain Expressway, their numbers had tripled, with Rosy and other local refugees inspired to escape with them to Gretna along the nearly four-mile route.

They walked in a rainstorm. Many opened their mouths and lapped at the droplets, their first water in days. Rosy had more energy than most, thanks to the soldier's food and water bottles. She pushed an elderly woman in a wheelchair who, in turn, carried another woman's newborn on her lap. People occasionally bumped each other, for some outpaced others, but nobody spoke much. Feet trudged, rain splattered, hands intermittently hit the pavement or slapped on bare skin as strangers reached to catch fellow marchers mid-fall. Only rarely did a groan or a "pardon" break the determined hush.

After the boisterous bedlam of the Superdome, the quiet walk should have struck Rosy as refreshing. But no. Their ranks felt eerily familiar to her; she'd seen this before. Gaunt, exhausted, dejected people marching across the TV and movie screens of her youth: Africans onto slave ships, Jews into boxcars, Cherokees toward the Oklahoman wilderness. *Lambs to slaughter,* she thought, but quickly endeavored to talk herself out of it. No need for melodrama. Things were bad, but she was on a high road in the United States, about to cross a bridge toward help as promised by the police and the National Guard, moving of her own accord, deprived of no freedom. So while there existed some similarities, perhaps, to those other diasporic horrors, she reassured herself with this: *I'm not a Jew or an African or a Cherokee. I'm an American in the twenty-first century. I'm fine.* And she forced a small smile.

She had long since mastered the art of "It could be worse."

"Ain't nothing so bad it can't be worse," Cilla said anytime something terrible happened. A nail through the foot beat a nail through the eye, bipolar disorder beat schizophrenia, a dead father beat an abusive one, being trapped in a flood plain beat being trapped *under* a flood plain. All true enough, but such rationalizations always reminded Rosy that something worse could be lurking out there, perhaps imminent.

During those days following the nail impalement, as her five-year-old foot healed, this line of reasoning first imposed itself on her, and she became increasingly wary. Still young enough to believe everything her mother said, yet too young to understand the nuance of language, she took Cilla seriously. If a nail went through her foot, it could just as easily have gone through her eye instead, and she began moving hesitantly, on alert for accidents that hadn't yet happened, waiting to be pierced about the face. Within a week, she had developed a full-blown hysterical aversion to nails. Coincidentally, during that same week, she had brought home from kindergarten her first fully recognizable drawing of a person: all appendages in the right places, facial features correctly aligned. Proud of her achievement, Cilla splurged on a frame and hung it above their bed. As her mother worked, Rosy cowered in the farthest corner of the bedroom, watching in horror as Cilla hammered the nail into the wall with the heel of her shoe.

"What you think? You like it?" Cilla asked.

Rosy didn't speak. Just shook her head.

Cilla looked back at the picture. "What's wrong? Ain't crooked, is it?" She angled her body as far back from the artwork as possible, gaining a new perspective and tapping gently on one edge of the frame.

"Don't look all catawampus to me," Cilla concluded.

Rosy scrambled out of the bedroom after her mother and spent the rest of the evening attempting to postpone her return: she dallied in the tub; asked for a second story to be told to her; plied her mother for an additional hug, glass of water, snack. Finally forced to confront bedtime, she balked, going boneless when Cilla tried to goad her into the bedroom, requiring her mother to heft her full forty-two pounds up onto the mattress without assistance. Once there, she bucked back out of Cilla's grip.

"Christ almighty, girl! You madder than a wet hen in a tote sack!" Cilla hollered, manhandling Rosy beneath the bedclothes. "I'll whup your butt, you don't settle down!" She squeezed the flailing child's shoulders rather too hard, doubly infuriated by Rosy's atrocious behavior and her own lack of self control. "Stop it *now!*" Cilla screeched.

Finally Rosy abandoned her protest and simply cried herself to sleep with her head tucked under the pillow for protection once Cilla cut out the lights. She slept peacefully enough until shortly before dawn, when the nail in the wall shot out through her drawing's eyeball with an almighty *zing*. Directly behind it, at least thirty other nails—brads and tacks and drywall screws—propelled themselves from the hole in the wall to hover in the air above her dreamy self. They grouped over the bed like swarming wasps, pokers primed, and made a V-shaped beeline for her eyelids. She awoke in terror and sat bolt upright in bed, arms shielding her face, screaming, "My eyes, my eyes!"

Shocked from slumber, Cilla fell flat out onto the floor. Despite loud and repeated assurances that she was having a nightmare, Cilla could not convince Rosy to quit screaming or lower her arms from her face until she carried her into the living room and curled up with her in the rocker, whose gentle back and forth lulled them both to sleep, arms wrapped fast around each other.

The next night proved a repeat of the same. "Argh!" Cilla screamed as they wrestled at the bedroom threshold. "What in the name of God done gone and got into you?"

Rosy crouched on the floor and pointed at the picture: "The nail."

"What about it?"

"It's fixing to poke me in the eye."

Cilla turned and looked at the artwork. "No nail can't poke you," she said. "There be a picture hanging in front."

"It might could get me in the night," Rosy insisted. "It gonna jump out and stick in my eye."

Cilla planted her hands firmly on her hips. "Get on up outta there and get in that bed!" This nonsense exasperated her. Another ploy to postpone bedtime, like Rosy's insatiable thirst and her boneless routine. "You ain't gonna get no nail stuck in your eye!"

"You said I could."

"Whatcha mean? I ain't never said no such thing!"

"Yes you did."

"No I didn't."

"Yes you did."

"When, then? When did I say that?"

"When the nail went in my foot, you said it coulda gone in my eye."

Cilla paused. Hmm. She had her there. "Well, I didn't mean it *would*," Cilla explained. "I was just saying, ain't so bad in your foot as if it'd gone through your eye."

Rosy's lips quivered as she said again, "It could go through my eye."

Cilla stared at her for a moment, then held up a finger as if to say *wait here* as she exited the room. She returned a moment later, jumped onto the bed, lifted down the artwork, and pried the nail out with a fork. Then she walked to the open window and cast the nail into the night.

"Better?" Cilla asked.

"Better," Rosy said, climbing between the bedclothes.

And so it was, until sometime in the middle of the night, when she woke with a start to the wild *zing* of the nail as it zoomed in through the window and back into her foot. Cilla had to cut on the lights and contort her, toes to nose, to prove that no nail had assaulted her. She wanted to vacate the bedroom again, but Cilla insisted they stay put. "It's nothing more'n a dream," Cilla reminded her. "It could be worse. Coulda been that …" But she let her words die off, realizing this is how the problem started in the first place. Instead, she snuggled her teary daughter up against her body. "I'll sing to you." As she sang, she stroked Rosy's hair and shielded her from dream-borne projectiles with her body.

> Hush, little baby, don't say a word.
> Daddy's gonna buy you a mockingbird.
>
> If that mockingbird don't sing,
> Daddy's gonna buy you a diamond ring.

Without forethought, having long ago internalized a proclivity for levity amidst the inane, she altered the third verse: "If a nail sticks in your eye, Daddy's gonna buy you a pizza pie."

Rosy burst out laughing. "More!" she exclaimed.

"If a nail goes up your nose, Daddy'll suck it out with the vacuum hose."

That got them both laughing. With some fits and starts as she fished for rhymes, Cilla continued playing to her rapt audience.

> If a nail knots in your hair,
> Daddy'll knock it out with the leg of a chair.
>
> If a nail pokes you in the ear,
> Daddy'll beat it up so you'll have no fear.
>
> If a nail sticks in your heart,
> Daddy'll scare it off with a big loud fart!

When she sensed Rosy's breathing alter, a deep, slow step-down into slumber, Cilla concluded:

> If a nail jams in your knee,
> Daddy's gonna ship it to Tennessee.
>
> In Tennessee they'll melt it down,
> and Daddy'll bring you back a princess crown.

Out of those accidental lyrics, a lifelong coping mechanism was born. Some weeks later, when a schoolmate called Rosy a baby and pushed her off the monkey bars, she stormed to the side of the playground where she defended herself with a low, deliberate hum. The same song, the same concept, only this time she sang out, "If you won't lemme come play, my daddy'll whup your butt and wreck your day!" With those words, she imagined her father striding across the playground, snagging the offender by the ear, and giving him a good wallop right there in front of everyone. From that simple inception, it grew. Lyrical imaginings of a man who didn't exist became the tool of her vengeance, which expanded in time to the simple, quiet contemplation of her father as avenger— her backup and protector.

Sans the ditty of her childhood, Rosy matured into a youth with a guardian angel. Her father's imagined visage strode with her into hospital rooms and police stations and he came, over the years, to assume for her all the visceral traits of an actual father: a scent, an emanating warmth, a manner of laughing off the complications of the most vexing situations with a breathy rumble and a crooked smile. He gave Rosy courage to tackle every mess her mother landed them in—the commitment papers, the apologies, the neighbors' stares and schoolmates' taunts—because she never had to do it alone.

"Now there's a kid mature beyond her years," a doctor would say.

"That's one self-possessed child," a psychiatrist would utter.

"That girl's got more nerve than Carter's got liver pills," the officers would nod in agreement.

No one ever knew to give credit to the man none of them could see, but whom Rosy could sense as real as any corporeal personage, standing beside her and staring down the strangers who otherwise might have determined for her and her mother a different sort of life. Because he showed up so regularly in her imaginings, she never held him accountable for not showing up for real; she forgave him for killing himself before ever setting eyes on her because he was otherwise such a stable, reliable parent.

She hadn't thought about him in days, though, not since Katrina hit. Hadn't had the luxury of thinking when there was hardly even time to react: get above the floodwaters, get to Maya's attic, get onto the roof, get into a boat, get food, get help. But in the plodding pace of imminent escape, with buses waiting and a family to track down—a family with no right or reason to spurn her now—her mind turned to her father again. His steady hand pressed to the small of her back, urging her on, and his voice lured her across the span: *Come on, Rosy. Come on. I'm right over here. I'm right on the other side of this bridge.*

The farther she walked, the more concrete Rosy's divinations became. After eighteen years, fantasy and reality began to converge. She was, in fact, walking toward him, not just his family. In her mind, he was out there, drawing her in.

It's not that she didn't know he was dead. Knowledge had nothing to do with it. It's that she'd sometimes seen hope win out over truth. Over the years, there had been a few events that fueled her persistent, though well-disguised, belief in the impossible. Days spent hungry as a child—weeks of Ramen noodles and watered-down juice—then a sack of groceries appeared on the porch. A new school bag full of supplies—pencils and notebooks and school shoes—materialized one August on the front steps. During a particularly desperate patch, when they got so far behind on the rent the sheriff came and posted an eviction notice on the door, an envelope replaced it the next day, stuffed full of enough cash to cover what they owed plus the next month's rent, too. And then, in the spring of her senior year, when the faculty chose her to be the Alfred Lawless High School representative to the statewide mock congress, and she cried herself to sleep knowing she'd have to turn down the opportunity for lack of funds for an adequate wardrobe, she awoke the next day to discover three smart dresses in her favorite hues hanging from the overhead hook on the front porch, skirts rustling in the breeze.

Cilla loved to search for answers to these Samaritan puzzles, and Maya enjoyed speculating along with her, always ending with the ever hopeful, "It could be anyone!" Such universal possibility provided a toehold for Rosy's lifelong yearnings. If it could have been anyone, it could have been him.

And then, suddenly, on the bridge to Gretna, there he was.

Rosy had been walking with her eyes to the ground, her body extended full-out—straight-armed leverage to hoist the woman and the baby and the wheelchair over the crest of the bridge entrance—but once the terrain leveled out and she raised her eyes, she saw him. He wore a Jefferson Parish sheriff's deputy uniform and stood with legs shoulder-length apart in the middle of the road. Perfect posture: chest out, chin up, cocooned in confidence. His fingers, wrapped around the shotgun barrel, mirrored hers wrapped around the wheelchair push-bar, thin and delicate and long. He stood tall, as she'd always imagined him to be, her own height a perfect stair-step between his and her mother's. His hair curled around his ears in tidy burls ... but those ears! Big, detached lobes, just like hers, and, from habit, her hand reached to rub the divot on the edge of her right ear; unable to see the matching divot on his from this distance but knowing it would be there, like in the photo in the newspaper in her mother's jewelry box.

She let go of the wheelchair and raced around it, shoving past the few people who stood between them, calling, "Dad!" as she pushed her way forward.

He took no notice of her, for he was arguing with a paramedic from San Francisco, a man unfamiliar with the politics of parishes and East Bank/West Bank prejudices, who, looking dumbfounded, kept saying, "I don't understand why we can't cross the bridge!"

"Dad!" she yelled at the deputy who nightly thrilled to such a cry from his toddlers—a little boy, two, and a little girl, four— when he burst through the kitchen door at the end of his workday and they leapt into his arms. He even answered occasionally to the endearment from other children, most recently a young boy stranded on the swing next to his kids at the park, who called out to him, "Somebody's dad, could you please gimme a push?" He laughed about it later that night with his wife, as they recounted their day in bed, tickled by the nameless child's faith in the universal role such a title dictated he assume.

"Dad!" Rosy cried, breaking through the hordes, edging ever closer to him, but still he did not turn to her.

Instead, the deputy shut down further questions from the paramedic with this cocky assertion: "The West Bank is not gonna become New Orleans; there will be no Superdomes in our city!"

That's when Rosy reached him. She fell on him, more than anything else, toppled by relief and the heady euphoria of fantasy realized, arms encircling his leg, her cheek pressed to his thigh. As she smiled up at him she said again, softly this time, "Dad!" and he—startled, unbalanced—reacted by kicking at her, knocking her to the ground as the crowd surged forward. With arm outstretched, she wrapped her fingers around his shoe, the only part of him she could still reach, so as to keep them together, touching, but he kicked her off again and, with the heel of his shoe, ground her hand into the asphalt.

Under other circumstances, the mob might have collectively assumed an eighteen-year-old woman clamoring for paternal attention from a twenty-five-year-old officer was a nutcase and therefore lent him their sympathies, but once Rosy hit the pavement, he became the public embodiment of police brutality. Invectives flew, bodies pressed in, fists raised, and control fissured.

He reacted again, doing what he could to seal the crack in the crowd's composure: racked his shotgun and exploded it over their heads.

In the stunned silence that followed, as backup raced to the scene to form the blue line that would drive the refugees back into the flooded city, she looked up at the young man and said, "But Dad, it's me, Rosy."

In response, he turned the barrel of the shotgun toward her face, finger on the trigger, and growled, "Get the fuck offa my bridge!"

XII. ROSE

"I forgive you, Mother."

THE ADDRESS ON THE florist's business card that had been salvaged from Rosy's pocket led Rose not to a flower shop, as she had expected, but to a private home. The just-finished Colonial anchored a new development where houses germinated in various states of construction: a few completed, a dozen or so under roof, others partially framed and due for Tyvek. Building supplies that had surely been stacked neatly at one time now littered the area, all thanks to Katrina. Nails and glass shards and chinks of concrete proliferated, plentiful as the budding grass might have been had not the seed been washed away, and two-by-fours sprouted from the strangest places: the parking strip, the shingled sides of completed buildings, and the cab of a track excavator stranded on its side in an otherwise pristine foundation. Down the middle of the as-yet unpaved main road, a bundle of pink fiberglass insulation had unrolled itself, a watered-down red carpet leading nowhere.

The asphalt driveway leading away from the address sloped slightly downhill, into a cesspool of collected storm water. Rose parked the car as close as possible, half a block away, but then sat immobile, sure she had the wrong address. Hard to reconcile the image she had of Jennifer Goldberg, the professional businesswoman and Rosy's savior, with the unassuming mom squatting on the doorstep beside two little boys. The three of them raced battery-powered speedboats through the stagnant moat around their house, high-fiving each other when the winning boat cleared the water, flew through the air, and landed upright in a vacant lot across the street. Rose laughed as the woman outfitted in a bandanna and Crocs leapfrogged across the water, bouncing like a child herself from one strategically placed paint can to another, the children cheering her on. *Must be nice for them to have such a great mom around,* she speculated as she restarted the car's engine, intending to head back into town to confirm her directions somewhere, certain she had the wrong house, the wrong woman.

"Hiya!" the woman called to her as she drew closer, waving with one hand, muddy toy boat secure in the other. "Can I help you?"

Rose shook her head. "I'm fine."

The woman looked her over. She pressed: "I was just about to pull together some lunch. If you're hungry, but not picky, you're welcome to join us."

Such intimacies from a stranger made Rose flinch. The woman took notice.

"If you've come looking for somebody, everyone else is gone," she said by way of explanation, "so you're alone and I could use the company. Come on in. Nobody's a stranger at times like this!"

And that is how Rose knew she had found Jennifer Goldberg after all.

※

HER QUEST, IF NOT her responsibilities, ended, for all practical purposes, in Jennifer Goldberg's disordered home. It smelled like a mortuary in there, befitting the resolution of the hunt for a dead girl. Amid the chaos of an entry piled floor-to-ceiling with boxes, granite countertops plastered with catalogues and juice rings and piles of fossilized bubblegum, and a hardwood floor peppered with crushed Cheerios and other foodstuffs, thousands upon thousands of flowers festered in makeshift vases or hung upside down from the cabinetry and light fixtures.

Pale pink Alstroemeria, loosely packed in industrial buckets lining the living room walls, had actually held up fairly well—still upright and plump these two-and-a-half weeks post-picking—and Cymbidium orchids in blush and celadon lined bookshelves and anchored tables with undiminished flair. Cut orchids live forever, and Jennifer had endeavored to take advantage of their resilience. She'd ripped through many a storage box to find her antique cut-glass vases to shelter them in, opulent Asian buds oozing from cobalt Depression glass. Her good intentions could not entirely forestall death, however. White lilies, crammed into beer and beach buckets clustered in shady corners, had a brownish postmortem stain, the petals' edges curled in on themselves as if sleeping.

As Jennifer led Rose deeper into her home, their footfalls ground a carpet of dropped leaves, step by crushing step, to dust.

Remember, O man, that thou art dust, and unto dust thou shall return.

Having confessed a full three times that day to her role in Rosy's death—in early morning to the Natchez nurse, in mid-morning to the ER housekeeper, and these four hours later to Rosy's Gretna bridge savior—Rose looked upon the dusty residue and imagined a priestly thumb blackened, smudging her forehead with an ashy cross, branding her penitent.

Repent, and hear the good news.

Jennifer took the news better than the others: without openly weeping, without injurious judgment. "Accidents happen," she said tenderly, having already absorbed Katrina's legacy: Destruction comes from all quarters. Even blue skies can rain down hell. Responsibility should not be assumed by the victims, for self-blame only compounds the mourning.

Ashes to ashes. Dust to dust.

Rose killed another blossom beneath her foot. As she felt its body momentarily resist her weight before disintegrating, she intuited deeper meaning in the liturgist's words. Searching out confessors, prostrating herself before them, acknowledging her sin over and over and over again would not rewrite the conclusion. Death is equally irreversible and unavoidable.

For I know my transgressions, and my sin is always before me.

At the end of the day, no matter whom she found, no matter whom she told, Rosy would still be dead.

Jennifer steered Rose into her kitchen. To navigate passage, the women had to duck under and around noosed roses suspended by the stems, their dehydrating heads angling toward the floor. Pink roses monopolized the underside of the cabinetry, while white ones dangled from the archways on either side of the room. But the lavender-hued beauties turned the open space into a maze, strung as they were from every overhead light fixture, rendering the kitchen impassable without an artful dodge-and-duck maneuver.

"Watch out for Barbra," Jennifer noted, plucking a petrified petal from Rose's ponytail as she maneuvered between the bundles with a quizzical backward glance.

"Barbra?"

"These purple ones are called Barbra Streisand roses. Don't ask me why." But, unprompted, she immediately began listing characteristics. "It's a strong, adaptable variety with really shapely blossoms. And the fragrance is overwhelming; definitely not one to be ignored." It did sound as if she were describing a superstar. So the name made sense, but a kitchen littered with inverted blooms did not.

Rose wondered aloud, "Why ...?"

Jennifer shrugged. "Everything's dying anyway. Figured I'd salvage what I could. I'm drying roses in an effort to turn a $4,000 loss into potpourri."

They looked at each other silently for a moment, then burst out laughing at the incongruity: stranded, starving, and making potpourri. "My apologies for the state of things," Jennifer said, her laughter ceasing as she gesticulated around the room with a broad stroke that took in the mess of daily living and the anomaly of the botanical bloodbath. But Rose took no notice; she had closed her eyes, and breathed deeply.

"Are you okay?" Jennifer inquired.

"That smell …"

Though the blossoms themselves had putrefied, their sweet scent lingered—a strong, soulful presence in the stagnant air.

"It's Barbra, and the lilies," Jennifer said. "Pretty intoxicating, isn't it?"

"Mmm hmm. It reminds me of my mother's funeral." Rose opened her eyes and locked on to Jennifer's. "Beautiful, but sickening."

Jennifer leaned across the island and cupped her hands over the young girl's. As they bowed their heads to gaze upon their palms clasped prayerfully together, Rose realized this might be the closest thing to a funeral Rosy Howard would ever get.

Despite being forced into the business of mourning, the flowers had originally been cut to celebrate a wedding at the historic Van Benthuysen-Elms Mansion and Gardens on the Avenue.

"It was my big break," Jennifer said. She'd landed the job over a year ago, before she'd even set up shop in the area. It was her foot-in-the-door with the New Orleans gentry, the official launch of her transplanted floral design firm, so, despite the reports of bad weather, she kept her family in town for the sake of the opportunity. The day before the wedding, scheduled for Saturday, August 27, the bride rang from the road to call it all off. She'd decided to evacuate to Vegas, would reschedule a celebration when the storm passed and things got back to normal, looked forward to employing Jennifer's services again someday. "You've been such a delight to work with!" Jennifer said, mimicking her client. "Hope this doesn't cause you any problems. Not our fault, you know. Blame the hurricane!"

"I reckon florists' insurance doesn't cover hurricanes?" Rose asked.

"Hard to say. 'Acts of God' are, as you can imagine, open to interpretation. But it might have been covered if I'd *had* insurance. I've got the application around here somewhere—"

She began riffling through a pile of paperwork underneath a spatula and a crumpled napkin, unearthing blank immunization forms for her sons, a completed but unsubmitted school enrollment form, three take-out pizza menus, and a neighborhood welcome packet that spewed coupons into the air when she tossed the envelope aside. Lunging for the coupons, she tipped a vase, which saturated a torn-open sleeve of Saltines and rehydrated a slice of American cheese affixed to the countertop. In one deft move, she sopped up the entire mess and dumped it, towel and all, into the sink without missing a beat.

"—but where, exactly, the application went is anybody's guess. First I was drowning in boxes, then I was drowning in forms. Now, of course, we're drowning in flowers and trying not to drown, literally."

"You're new to Gretna?"

"Yeah. We just moved here a month ago. From Minnesota. Between unpacking, transferring the kids' school and medical records, changing all the legal stuff like driver's licenses and car registrations … ugh. I didn't get half a minute to deal with my own business stuff. Seemed like a major coup just to get those new business cards printed up. I figured I'd just ride out this first event and then I'd have time to get everything organized later. Some kind of timing, huh?"

"You mean, you got here—"

"—two weeks before Katrina did."

"Good heavens," Rose whispered. "Talk about making a bad move."

On that subject, she considered herself expert.

Despite an unaltered family structure and a daily routine more rote than flowing, Rose lacked any sense of place or permanency. Like a leaf set to swirl in an eddy upon otherwise still waters, her life consisted of regular, aimless motion. She and Gertrude lived nowhere for long. Their last apartment they'd occupied for four years, longer than they'd resided anywhere else, though she hardly noted that fact. Rose lived so certain of the impermanence of their lodgings that she never thought to create attachments to place or, by proxy, to people, and had long since learned to stop counting the months or years of stability lest she jinx them and return from school one day to empty rooms, packed bags, and a new door key.

They hopped from apartment to apartment, school to school, like a military family but with a difference: they never left town; they only meandered from one side of it to the other. In the middle of her junior year, a girl arrived from Panama who had been in Jordan before that, and somewhere down the line had called South Africa and Thailand home, following her father's Foreign Service postings. Before the homeroom bell rang on her first day, she'd whipped out a story about rats the size of dogs and how one fell from the rafters and bit her on the nose, necessitating a full series of rabies shots. Her retelling secured her a seat, come lunchtime, at the table reserved for the popular crowd. The next year, after she won the Homecoming Queen crown and departed for parts exotic a month later, students continued regaling each other with her tales of rooster-wattle stew and tsunami devastation. That girl knew how to work a crowd, something Rose much admired but never determined how to emulate. What stories had she to tell? The Dairy Queen on the east side of Tuscaloosa served the same victuals as that on the west; the tornado that hit her old school had hit the new one, too, and every single kid had borne witness. No one needed Rose to fill her in. Thus, she always suffered the indignity of being new without ever being a novelty.

"At one time or another, I was a student at every school in our district," she said to Jennifer's back, which was bent over a collection of boxes on the floor. "Doesn't lead to great popularity when the only ace up your sleeve is that you can belt out every rival's fight song from heart."

Consumed by her search, Jennifer murmured a distracted, "Huh?"

"We moved a lot," Rose summarized, with a shrug.

Jennifer's voice drowned Rose's out as she exclaimed, "Here it is! Lunch!" and she hoisted a box from the floor onto the counter.

Rose read aloud from the list of contents penned onto the side in black marker: "Michael's Room—costumes, raceway & trains, Piglet." She paused and smiled. "Piglet. Would that mean we'll be feasting on pork chops?"

"Are you kidding me?" Jennifer replied. "Michael would disown me! Piglet is his most treasured possession, hence the fact that this box has actually been unpacked when most of the rest are ... well, you saw them," she said, gesturing toward the tower of still-sealed boxes in the entryway. "Now this box doubles as the family larder. You can have your pick of any of these tasty entrees, compliments of Uncle Sam." She held up each MRE package. "Cheese and vegetable omelet, veggie burger with barbecue sauce, cheese tortellini, or pasta with vegetables in tomato sauce. Just so you know, that would be the full repertoire of vegetarian options: four! As if I needed yet another reason to rejoice in the fact that I never joined the military."

"So you're not in the military, but you suffer through military rations because you're ... what? ... a glutton for punishment?" Rose teased. Jennifer smiled broadly. "No, wait!" Rose said. "I know! You're not really a corn-fed Midwesterner, are you? You're cardboard-fed!"

"Actually, they're giving the MREs out at the bingo hall," Jennifer explained.

"Four in a row and you get war rations!" Rose continued the game. "Hit on two cards simultaneously and they add in an M-16!"

Jennifer giggled. "No, no," she said. "I'm serious. Every day now, during 'regular working hours,' you can choose from a fine selection of the best in dehydrated food America has to offer over at the bingo hall. And a beverage to go with it." She reached into the box and withdrew a handful of water bottles. "Your choice: water, water, or water?"

"Water, please."

"We really shouldn't poke fun," Jennifer said, growing pensive.

"It's saving our butts. None of the grocery stores are open. We'd be eating the shingles off the roof and calling it fiber were it not for this."

"Given the alternatives—roof shingles or Michael's pig—I'll take the tortellini."

"Tortellini it is." Using her hip, Jennifer pushed open the back door and carried four packets outside. Rose trailed behind, appraising her hostess as she knelt to activate the self-heating devices in the meal kits. The frayed edge of Jennifer's underwear briefs peeked out as she squatted, drawing her shirt up and her pants down. She had wide hips, and a mole on the exposed skin of her back. Her hair needed washing. Her hands were callused. Fully human.

"I have to admit, you're not what I expected," Rose said.

"No?"

"Rosy referred to you as her savior, and I guess I rather naively imagined someone completely larger-than-life. But you're just a regular mom, in a house full of boxes, working from home." Jennifer turned and looked at Rose with amused indignation, and Rose realized her tone and her words could easily cause offense. "I'm sorry," she said, shaking her hands in front of her as if to erase potential insult. "It's good! It's nice. You're real and normal. It's just that the real you is so different from what I'd expected." She shook her head and laughed at herself. "I guess I envisioned a cross between Joan of Arc and Wonder Woman. Stupid, huh?"

"It's certainly flattering, even though it's completely mistaken."

"But what you did, that was amazing."

Jennifer tightened her mouth, her eyes. "I'm not sure I understand what you think I did."

"Rosy told people you saved her offa the bridge."

Jennifer relaxed her face and shrugged. "Well, I guess that's all a matter of perspective. I *did* go up onto that bridge—something my husband has repeatedly referred to as irresponsible and interfering, and something that surely brands me a pariah as far as my new neighbors are concerned. But the 'savior' part—that you've got all wrong."

"Not according to Rosy. She swore you saved her."

"Like I said, I was on the bridge. But as for 'saving' Rosy, you really don't understand." Jennifer turned and faced her guest fully. "The truth is, I had nothing whatsoever to do with that."

※

BY THURSDAY, SEPTEMBER 1, the fourth day without electricity— thirteen days before Rose showed up unannounced at her home— Jennifer's fridge needed emptying. It stank of curdling dairy, though the hard cheddar seemed to have held up fairly well. Still, it couldn't go another day. Jennifer made nine cheese sandwiches and let that be her excuse for risking the trip into the ghostly town center. She couldn't stay in the house another minute: too many boxes everywhere and the kids going stir crazy. She'd been standing in the kitchen, holding a cast iron frying pan, trying to decide on a permanent home for it, when a sofa cushion struck her in the back and knocked her to the floor. "Sorry, Mom," seven-year-old Sammy said sheepishly as he reached to retrieve the pillow. "I was aiming for Michael." For a moment, Jennifer considered walloping him over the head with the metal pan, and that is how she knew it would be safer for them to venture out than to stay cooped up inside together any longer. She cut up the whole block of cheese, sandwiched it with the last of the lettuce and tomatoes, corralled her kids, and drove the veritable feast over to her husband, Adam, and his colleagues.

The Gretna Waterworks was a hopping place four days post-hurricane. Whereas many other city workers had fled their workplaces and evacuated the town, most of the hydraulics engineers felt both a moral and professional obligation to stay. Hurricanes are a water guy's thing. They'd been sleeping in three-hour shifts on the conference room floor, subsisting on Reese's Pieces and Cheetos from the cleaved-open vending machine, and the building emanated a bleary-eyed buzz. Jennifer had never seen her husband so amped, high on the complexities of one mathematical puzzle after another—computations to determine levee failure or survival, sewer maintenance or overflow, tap water contamination or purity. Katrina shone a spotlight on his computer job in a back office, morphing it overnight into a Zeusian position: on the power of his mind, a town would live or a town would die.

In the same breath, he thanked her for the food and chastised her for making the drive, worried for his family's safety, yet starving. A small crowd gathered to eat, sandwiches torn in near-perfect halves by Sammy and passed into the workmen's hands by his younger brother. Between bites and swallows, someone just back from a water-level check described the situation unfolding on the Crescent City Connection.

"About time the police did something," the crew supervisor murmured, a piece of lettuce dropping from his lips onto his shoe. He wiped his mouth on the back of his sleeve. "Those fricking refugees ain't nothing but trouble! Goddamn nig—" He glanced sideways at the two young boys; stopped himself. "Y'all shoulda seen the number they did on the mall yesterday."

Jennifer opened her mouth to retort, but Adam's look restrained her. Over the circle of heads bent to their food, he stared at her, unblinking, as if to say: *Not here. Not now.*

"Amen," one of the mechanics replied.

A few of the men looked up and fidgeted—shuffling their feet and staring over the heads of their colleagues—but no one else said anything.

Jennifer thrust her chin forward, defiance widening her eyes; a silent reply aimed at her husband, *This is intolerable. How can you just stand there?*

"I say, let them drown," the man continued. "We'd be better off!"

"Let them drown?" Jennifer parroted.

With that, Adam closed his eyes, shook his head, and assumed the resigned moue of a wearied, mismatched combatant. The boys' eyes widened.

"Really?" she asked. "Those are people you're talking about, you know. Human beings."

Everyone stopped chewing. One young man had a sandwich half in, half out of his mouth. His grin grew around the edges of the crust. He hacked off a big hunk. "Not *our* kind of people," he goaded.

She glared at him, and he grinned back, mocking her, while a few others sniggered.

"By that do you mean they're not a bunch of buffoons?" she asked. "Or did you mean to say they're not bigoted assholes?"

But for the *humph* the two boys made—half chuckle, half shocked gasp—the group grew immediately silent again, all eyes on Jennifer. Adam stepped forward with a conciliatory, "Okay, now—" just as the crew chief said, "I do believe it's time your family was leaving, though we thank you kindly for the sandwiches, ma'am."

Without another word, Jennifer spun and stormed out to the car, a child dragged along at the end of each hand. Adam caught up with her as she was buckling the kids into their boosters. "Jen, you've got to understand—"

"*I've* got to understand?" she roared. "Understand what? There's no way I'm ever going to understand that kind of attitude—nor do I see any reason why you should want me to!"

"—this is my *job*. I have to work here!"

She jumped into the driver's seat and slammed the door. Revving the engine, she threw the gear selector into reverse, but then sat for a moment holding the wheel without moving. Finally she took a deep breath and smiled. She turned to Adam and spoke with an exaggerated calm through the open window. "Okay, then," she said. "Go back to work."

It wasn't until she was halfway out of the lot, driving away with their two children in the backseat, that he realized her intent. "Don't you dare!" he called, running after her. "Jennifer! Jennifer! Stay off that bridge!"

With only a quick pit stop to fill a bag with food she pilfered from her pantry, a few rolls of toilet paper, and the three umbrellas propped inside the front door, she drove toward the river. She got lost a few times, being new to the area and moreso inhibited by the need to abandon the most direct route due to downed power lines, but she persisted. Riffing off their surroundings, she and the boys sang every water-inspired song they could think of to keep themselves occupied—"Row, Row, Row Your Boat," "My Bonnie Lies Over the Ocean," "Waterloo"—before switching to a rousing game of I Spy that revealed some uncommon sightings:

"I spy something tipped over. A truck!"

"I spy something on a roof. A shopping cart!"

"I spy something sharp. A broken window!"

It was fun until four-year-old Michael called out, "I spy something dead!" and they all turned to look at two bloated pit bulls chained to a tree that had toppled into a nearby house.

"Ugh," Sammy responded, spinning away in disgust. Across the street, a middle-aged man balanced atop a ladder, hand-lettering a sign onto the plywood nailed over his front windows. "I spy someone painting!" Sammy called out, and read aloud the spray-painted message the man posted on his house: "Thank you and God bless Chief Lawson & Gretna PD."

"What does that mean?" Sammy asked as Jennifer angled them onto the freeway abutting the man's property. The on-ramp dropped them onto the empty downstream span of the Crescent City Connection, where it crossed over the Mississippi en route to New Orleans. On any other day, 180,000 vehicles would have kept pace with them, but today a lone gull soared alongside, her soft-winged flutters sluicing the silence. As car and bird flew together through the abandoned toll station, a gunshot suddenly echoed from the twin span to their left. Jennifer and the boys turned in time to witness a blue line surge forward, the gull dive for cover, and people scatter in a black confetti shower back toward the relative safety of the flooded city.

Jennifer's pulse skyrocketed. Her grip tightened. *Oh, shit*, she thought. She hadn't considered the reality that she'd have to drive into New Orleans in order to effect the U-turn that would put her back on the separate portion of the bridge where the hungry evacuees congregated. For all her bravado, she didn't feel so secure in her rash reaction anymore. Suddenly didn't want to drive into a flooded city with her children; didn't want to be somewhere where guns got fired.

She took the first off-ramp onto Camp Street, then a series of immediate lefts. Intent on reversing her course, she didn't look up when turning from Julia Street onto Loyola Avenue, meaning she paid no heed to the National Guardsmen skirting the Superdome two blocks away, shouldering a shrouded bundle between them. Nor did she note the prisoners shuffling in ankle chains onto a city bus beside the Amtrak station as she cut off Loyola onto Calliope Street. Instead, Jennifer kept watch for signs marked "US-90 BR W" or "PONTCHARTRAIN EXPY" and, in just under two miles, had looped back onto the highway toward Gretna. There she queued up with departing city officials and military leadership not tasked with overnighting in New Orleans, as well as some lucky survivors with access to transportation. The police didn't stop automotive traffic, which they figured would keep moving on past Gretna after traversing the bridge; they only stopped foot traffic: those pedestrians who'd have no option but to congregate in their town if they made it across.

Though some people still massed on the bridge, most refugees had begun an aggrieved and frantic retreat back into New Orleans after being shot at by the police. Some, young men mostly, spilled out into the traffic lanes and surrounded cars, banging on drivers' windows with jealous entreaty, yanking on passenger door handles in an effort to hitch a ride. One ardent group, small in number yet refusing to be cowed, had staked claim to the center divide of the Pontchartrain Expressway, between the O'Keefe and Tchoupitoulas exits, where they'd begun constructing a makeshift encampment. They huddled together under a staked-out tarp, waving to passersby—some calling out for help, others singing spirituals; all intent on drawing attention to their plight.

Jennifer kept her eyes on the road and accelerated, determined to get home. She felt foolish. This melee had nothing in common with the line of grateful souls to whom she'd envisioned herself distributing food.

"Mom, look! Campers!" Michael hollered, pointing at the transient camp.

Tethered in his booster seat behind Jennifer, closest to the crowd, Sammy couldn't reach the automatic window button with his hand so, instead, he used his toe to lower the glass, allowing both boys to wave back and call out "Hello!" to the assemblage.

"Stop that right now!" Jennifer yelled. "Face forward in your seats and don't look at them!"

Her unaccustomed tone took them aback. "Why?" Michael asked. "Why can't we look at them? Look, they're coming over to say hi!"

She pressed on the driver's controls to raise the back window and stammered, "Because I don't ... it's not very ..."

Seeing his window begin to rise, Sammy pressed his toe against the button and fought to lower it. Stymied, realizing what her son was doing, Jennifer snaked her arm back between her seat and his door and pinched his ankle, screaming, "Sammy, stop it!" She knocked his foot off the control button and finished raising the window herself. "Leave the windows up," she yelled, "and don't look at those people because ... because ... because it's not polite to stare!"

She slowly maneuvered the car around the milling pedestrians. As they neared the bridge crossing, Sammy went quiet, glaring at the back of his mother's head, but Michael continued to sneak peeks outside. "Sammy," he pestered, reaching across the back seat for his brother's hand, his apprehensive gaze pinned to the window, "Sammy, why does everyone here look different than us?"

He might have kicked his mother, the way his question resounded in her chest, that child's full-bodied truth. Her foot heavier on the gas, anxious avoidance of the crowd, fear of the flooded city and the gunshot and the fracas, yes, but all of it overlaid with the larger disruption, the power flip. She'd never been a minority in a room, let alone a city, let alone a mob. Easy to be a champion of civil rights when black people aren't surrounding you, angry and riled and wanting something. Easy to pack crackers and toilet paper in a grocery sack in the back seat; another thing to roll down the window and hand them to a gang of unfamiliars.

Michael swung his feet, scraping the sack. "What are we going to do with this food we brought to share with the hungry people?"

Caught off guard, Jennifer replied swiftly, "No one seems to need it." She glanced over her shoulder at her little boy and padded her lie: "No one looks all that hungry. And besides, they're all walking around. There's nowhere to sit and eat."

Michael, ever attentive, considered her words. He didn't believe her and didn't even deign to say so. He just frowned his disappointment in her direction; even after she turned away, she could still feel him blighting her, and the sense of wicked vulnerability left her equal parts meek and ashamed.

She drove even faster.

She'd have cleared the bridge. She'd have ignored for weeks, maybe months, the business cards shrink-wrapped in the glove compartment. She'd have hopped paint cans across a moat to retrieve a boat on a far-future day without pausing, for the street would have been vacant, no stranger's car parked at the curb. And she'd have done nothing to be proud of in that moment had not the single lane of traffic suddenly halted beside the wall of officers spanning the foot of the bridge when an elderly black man threw his LeSabre into park and burst from it.

"This the wrong thing!" he shouted, shaking a fist furiously at the cops. Despite his shriveled skin and stooped back, he persisted when two freckled officers came at him. "This the wrong thing to do! Wrong, I say! This messed up!" Without a word, they each slid a hand under his armpits and lifted him back into his car. "Them people's just trying to get cross the bridge so to catch a ride and get theyselves to Texas!" When the cops slammed his door shut, trapping him inside, he reached around and opened the back door onto an empty seat. "Come on, y'all," he called to the crowd. "I'ma give all y'all a ride!" One officer slammed the back door shut, motioning to the old man to drive away, as the other raised a hand, a cease-and-desist gesture meant to halt the eager evacuees who moved to accept the driver's offer.

Jennifer reached for her door handle. It's one thing to suffer the wrath of one's children, or to speed blithely past a wrongdoing, but it is another thing entirely to sit idle and watch the elderly summon the courage you yourself have lost. She jumped out of the car. "Officers," she called out in a friendly tone, recouping her confidence in the presence of white men, coming at them as an ally in a sea of strangers. She'd trusted officers her whole life and, with the notable exception of this afternoon at the water bureau, she'd never had trouble persuading men to her point of view. She smiled her contagious smile, pink and plump-lipped; surely this misunderstanding could be set straight. "Officers," she said, sidling up between them, "come on. These are just people, walking across a bridge. Why not let them past?"

"Ma'am, this ain't none of your business. I recommend you get back in your car."

The LeSabre hadn't budged. Traffic backed up behind the two drivers who'd exited their cars and the crowd continued surging forward, despite warnings to stay back. So the officers acted. The one nearest the LeSabre wrenched open the driver's door, threw the car into gear, and yelled, "Get the fuck outta here," as the other took hold of Jennifer's upper arm and escorted her toward her vehicle.

"Get your hands off me!" Jennifer insisted. "I'm not trespassing. I'm not doing anything wrong. You have no right to—"

"Look," the officer interjected, "I can tell from your accent you're not from round here. Now, I don't know how they handle things wherever it is that you're from, but in these parts, we do whatever it takes to protect our citizens."

Righteous indignation always trumped personal discomfiture in Jennifer's world. Fear may have reigned inside the car, but once she jumped out all bets were off. Tossing her head in the direction of the crowd behind her, she asked, "You consider this 'protecting your citizens'?"

"These aren't our citizens," he said, prodding her forward. "Our citizens are on the other side of the bridge there. Folks like you and me."

She threw a hand against the car door, to keep him from opening it. "What exactly is that supposed to mean?"

"It means this is a hostile and threatening crowd, and you're gonna drive on outta here and let us do our job."

They stood face-to-face—her hand on the door, his hand on her arm. She broke his gaze to glance at the assembled riff-raff—more babes in arms than irate protesters; an overwhelming percentage of elderly; women outnumbering men; no one apparently armed, unless canes counted as weapons. She nodded in mock understanding. "So this is what you consider 'threatening'? A group of dehydrated, starved, exhausted people?" She leaned in close and whispered, "If that's the case, then it sounds to me like what you really need is a new police force."

He went stone-still but for the back edge of his jawbone pulsing in-out, in-out, as his teeth clenched down, released, bit back.

"Get in the car."

She held her ground. "But I brought food to give out. Surely that's not a crime?"

Still the jaw, in-out, in-out. But then a sly smile. "Not at all. Happy to take your food. My officers haven't eaten a thing all day. Now get in the car."

She might have persisted, content to ignore the horns blaring as drivers behind her implored her to move, but Sammy suddenly called out "Mom!" and she remembered her children. "Mom!" he called again, and the officer released her arm, battle won, a child's cry more persuasive than any weapon in his arsenal.

"Michael did something," Sammy said three times over the roaring engine as they peeled across the bridge, ever the older brother, looking for ways to win favor at the younger's expense.

She glanced at them in the rearview mirror. Her children were safe. Ignorable. She swiped sweat off her face, tears now, too. Breathed like an animal chased, fast in, hard and long out. Adam would kill her. Absolutely fucking kill her. And he should, too! All this, everyone in danger, her stupid temper run amok—for Christ's sake, her kids could have gotten shot!—to accomplish … what? Nothing. Not one single thing! *I can't live here,* she thought desperately. *I cannot live here! How can I raise my children in this place?*

"Mom," Sammy implored again, "Michael did something."

"Sammy, enough!" Jennifer said, exasperated. She adjusted the rearview mirror to look at him. "Are you hurt? Did Michael hurt you?" Sammy shook his head, no. "Then whatever he did, it's none of your business. So quit tattling!" As she readjusted the mirror, she caught a glimpse of Michael's reflection. He smiled broadly. He'd done something.

Goddammit.

"Michael, did you do something wrong?"

He considered his mother's question, then shook his head very deliberately back and forth, no.

"Yes he did!" Sammy insisted, but Jennifer raised her hand swiftly, an indication to shush.

She continued to split her attention between the road and Michael's reflection in the mirror.

"Are you sure you didn't do something wrong?"

He crossed his arms, nodded his head hard, once, and said, "I'm sure I didn't do something wrong."

Jennifer stared at his ardent image once more, dubious, but let it go. She had more important things to consider. She would contact the ACLU, that's what she'd do. It was a state bridge, for God's sake! How could they justifiably prevent the state's citizens—whose taxes had built the damn bridge!—from walking across it? Racist pricks! And that officer who'd grabbed her, she'd memorized his badge number; she'd report him.

"I know I did the right thing," Michael clarified.

It was the way he phrased it. Not denying wrongdoing now but admitting something had occurred. She tapped the mirror back in his direction and, glancing into it, asked, "What did you do that was so right?"

"I did a kindness."

That dear phrase of his! It made her smile and relax, finally. "Who'd you do a kindness for?" she asked, turning in her seat and reaching an arm back to fondle his knee, sweet boy.

He pointed proudly toward the floor beneath his feet.

"For her!"

AIR PERCOLATED IN A bubbly stream out of the pump-action rifle when Jennifer submerged it in the half-emptied bathtub of clean water that she'd been rationing for the past two-and-a-half weeks. "I'm gonna get you!" she threatened, to which the boys responded by pressing their naked bodies against the back of her legs, stomping their feet and screaming gleefully.

"Me first! Me first!" Sammy climbed onto the bathroom counter and into the sink, where she doused him with well-targeted, ticklish squirts from the enormous water gun.

"It's fun, it gets them clean, and it saves water," she said to Rose, who left the family to their improvised bedtime bath ritual and headed back downstairs to sweep the kitchen floor, hoping to repay Jennifer's hospitality with some elbow grease. She washed their dinner utensils with bottled water and used the damp rag to wipe meal residue off the counter, swathing in circles around the map Jennifer had drawn for her on the back of an overdue and increasingly irrelevant school enrollment form: directions leading back over the Crescent City Connection onto I-10 W, then up I-49 N to Macarthur Drive, where a bright purple house with cyan trim sat directly behind a Popeyes restaurant in Alexandria. The house where Jennifer had delivered Rosy thirteen days ago. The aunt's house.

"I'll go with you, tomorrow, if you want me to," Jennifer had said, a sentiment echoed by Mac when Rose called him while cleaning to let him know where she'd be spending the night. But, no, she assured them both. This task was hers alone to do.

Neither acquiesced easily.

"I know you've done this three times already today," Jennifer remarked, "but you haven't had to tell anyone who loved her yet. Her aunt's response will be a whole other thing, an overwhelming thing."

"I can handle it," Rose said.

"Not your job to handle," Mac said. "I could drive on over there and meet you in the morning, tell the aunt for you."

"I'll make it up there in half the time it would take you to get over there," Rose rebutted, holding her ground.

They both continued to press her. Jennifer said, "You need to know that people can react in crazy ways to bad news—"

Mac said, "Whatever she says or does, it's about her, not about you—"

"She's gonna hate me," Rose said, first to Jennifer, then to Mac. "How could she not? I'm prepared for her to hate me. But that hatred is mine to bear, not yours to bear for me."

"So that's your thing, is it? You've got to do everything alone?" Jennifer chastised, scooping the boys into her arms and carrying them upstairs for their makeshift bath.

Mac just hung up, frustrated. "Stupid stubborn kid," he murmured affectionately as he tossed the phone aside.

Rose carefully folded the map into her pocket with the other paper items Mac had given her two days ago—the phonebook page, the business card, and the restaurant receipt—then finished her kitchen tasks by replacing the cardboard larder box full of MREs by the back door. Overlaying the quartered lid flaps, she realigned the notation "MICHAEL'S ROOM" into legible script across the box top. The swirling coil on the tail of the *R* and the heavy belly of the *S* harkened to her own mother's hand, scrawled across a similar box on a high closet shelf in her Tuscaloosa bedroom. Hard to believe it was only yesterday that she had reached inside it.

For many childhood years, the box marked "ROSE'S ROOM" doubled as a toy chest at the foot of her bed, housing overflow stuffed animals when it wasn't pressed into cargo service during their moves between apartments. Perhaps wariness drove Rose's initial impulse not to unpack it after one such move—why do so when repacking might be called for in the not-so-distant future?—but then the sturdy cardboard proved a reliable constant despite vacillating circumstances, a micro-settlement for her most beloved possessions in an ever-changing macro-environment, and wariness quickly segued to a sense of security. Her plush proxies transitioned safely in the box—always well-protected, never homeless, perpetually guarded. She clutched it on her lap during the short car rides between temporary locales; it was the last item she carried from each vacated apartment, the first item she settled into the new. Set upon an unfamiliar floor, lid unfurled, the box erupted with friendly felted faces that helped her stake instant claim to yet another new space she would not now be required to face alone. The box spoke of home more than any apartment ever would, which is why she willingly fought her mother for it on the day Gertrude tried to pry it away from her.

At the crossroads between childhood and adolescence, balanced on the cusp of the vulnerable years, she and her mother came to blows one day over the box. Transporting it from yet another emptied bedroom into their chock-full car, she strode past her mother, who snaked her hand into the cross-hatched lid and snatched the box away with a dismissive, "Enough's enough, Rose. You don't need these things any more."

I'm protecting her, Gertrude thought, reaching for the box. *She's no child anymore.*

As they'd packed, brushing past each other wordlessly in the ferrying of essentials, stooping to empty closets or unplug lamps, Gertrude had observed Rose's ankles skitter across the room. Looking up, she realized the new school pants that had fit her daughter in September now floated inches off the floor. They stretched taut, too, around her widening hips. Gertrude stared. Rose had taken on curves! Bless her heart, she needed a bra. Makeup, too, soon. Some lipstick couldn't hurt; it'd be a good place to start. Sorting through her own collection—chunking two tubes into the trashcan for every one she kept, manufacturing an upbeat attitude about another new start in a new place by focusing on new cosmetics—Gertrude considered what color would suit Rose best. Something youthful. Maybe a gloss. She'd choose one, at Rite Aid, when she stopped for her weekly *People* magazine. Pilfer a subscription insert from inside the pages of *Seventeen*, too, and order it for Rose once they got settled at their new address. The plan made her feel progressive, encouraging, a doting mom. Which is why she reached for the box. Teenage girls collect posters and CDs and jewelry, not dolls and teddies and other stuffies. If Rose didn't start acting her age she'd have a hard time fitting in, would be a lonely outcast at her new school, which is the worst way to spend an adolescence. *I'm protecting her,* Gertrude thought, and reached to relieve Rose of the box's implications.

It wasn't just the way she said, "You don't need these things anymore," but the way she grabbed at the box with such disrespect. Just another something of Rose's to steal away.

"That's mine! Give it back!" Rose yelled, fingernails scratching grooves in the smooth sides of the cardboard as she fought for a handhold. She'd said nothing when Gertrude pulled all her slacks out of her dresser before she'd fully emptied it, insisting it was time for new pants; they'd go shopping directly. She'd stayed silent while her mother walked the Disney videos to the curb and left them to be picked over by passersby, because it's true she hadn't watched them in a while. And she'd even held her tongue when Gertrude answered her inquiry as to where her hair ties had gone by accusing her of hoarding like a chipmunk; in response to Rose's set-jaw glare, Gertrude noted her hair looked prettier down anyway, so what sense in keeping more than two elastics?

But enough was enough, indeed. Rose refused to cede the box.

"For the love of God, Rose, you could start an argument in an empty house!" Gertrude admonished, tugging harder. "Quit carrying on. This beat-up old box of toys is about as useful nowadays as an ashtray on a motorcycle!"

Rose's fingers bit into the sides of the box as she scrabbled for a handhold and wrenched the box back. Her mother couldn't take this, too! The box contained the story of her life; it had lived every day alongside her. The cardboard was supple and threadbare around the middle, where her arms had hugged it gently through each move and lifted it bedside each night. Like a decrepit house marked by peeling shingles and hollows carved into the porch floorboards leading to a ragged screen door, its antiquity commanded respect for having long sheltered the most precious of things: The panda bear she threw up on when she was seven and had an allergic reaction to penicillin. Tweety Bird, smudged in a fall to the pavement when Gertrude twirled her in the air outside Six Flags, the greasy wing tip a tangible imprint of joy. Her one-eyed bunny, Aladdin's monkey, the silky Siamese gifted to her at the only birthday party she'd ever had.

"Thief!" she cursed, resisting her mother's grasp on the box. She yanked at it in retaliation for every home Gertrude ever removed her from, for every friend she'd lost when Gertrude separated them, for every question of her history gone unanswered. She threw her whole body into the fight because the box and its contents were all she had, all she was. Hers! Hers entirely. Hers alone.

Gertrude loosed one hand and shoved against her daughter's shoulder. "Let go!"

"You let go!" Rose screamed, smacking her mother's hand away.

Gertrude, startled, lost her balance and went down, shouting, "This damn box matters to you more than I do!"

"If my things don't matter to you, then *I* don't matter to you!" Rose screamed as she, too, stumbled backward. The box, between them, ripped open. Three sides and the bottom went with Rose; one lid flap and its attached side went with Gertrude. Rose's life, in plush, chucked to the ground between them. Rose stared at the ruin, stunned. She swallowed a gasp and turned it, instead, into a malicious question. "Happy now?"

"Like a tornado in a trailer park!" Gertrude retorted as she stood, smoothed her skirt, and stormed toward the car.

"HAVE YOU SEEN PIGLET?"

Rose flinched. With one hand still resting on the box marked "MICHAEL'S ROOM," she reeled around and found Jennifer standing in the kitchen entry, shifting her weight nervously from foot to foot.

"Have you seen Piglet?" she repeated. "Michael's crying for him, and I can't find him anywhere upstairs."

"Oh. No. He's not in the kitchen."

"I've got to find him," Jennifer said, rushing toward the living room with an uncommon zeal. She flipped aside sofa cushions and pushed books around on the shelves. "He can't sleep without Piglet. I've got to—shit!" She smashed her shin on the edge of the coffee table and it began to bleed, but she ignored it. "You're sure he's not in the kitchen?"

"I could look in the cupboards."

"Yes, look in the cupboards. Look inside the pots in the cupboards! And, and, and look in the trashcan!" Jennifer bent in half, hair pooling on the floor, to appraise the underside of the counter stools, as if a stuffed toy regularly affixed itself there. Rising, she watched hopefully as Rose closed the last under-cupboard door. Nothing.

"How could it not be here? It's got to be here!" She looked around wildly. "You're sure you haven't seen it? It's pink! And has a tail shaped like a corkscrew. And the left ear's raw, missing all the fuzz, because he rubs it while he sucks his thumb. It's the only way he can relax, and if he can't relax he can't go to sleep, and he'll be lying up there all alone, awake and upset."

Rose listened indulgently while Jennifer described to her what a pig looks like, but finally put a hand on Jennifer's shoulder to still her. "Listen, Jennifer. Listen. I don't hear crying. Michael seems okay for now. And I'll help you. It'll all be fine. We're gonna find the pig eventually. Like you said, it has to be here somewhere."

Jennifer took a deep breath and closed her eyes. Two more

huge sighs before she looked at Rose and spoke again. "You know, as a parent, you make these arbitrary choices, and try to do what you think is best for your family, but you ache with worry: how will it be for your kids? I want this move to be fine for them. I want to make everything fine for them. I want to start by finding Piglet," and here she gave a timorous, one-sided grin, acknowledging her hysteria, "and then I want to find them some friends. But we don't know this culture, or these traditions. We're Jewish in a Catholic and Baptist stronghold, we don't have the right accent, we don't know a soul ..."

She paused. "I hadn't realized it'd be so ... different ... here. I hadn't realized *we'd* be so different. I'm scared to death my kids are going to wind up being ostracized—who'll want to play with them? Who'll swap treats with them at lunchtime?" Jennifer's voice resumed its frantic tone. "With all that's gone on"—she waved a hand in the air, referencing the larger, external disaster—"it might seem crazy, but I haven't been nearly so concerned about losing the house, losing the car. Those things all seem so replaceable. But as I watched those refugees walking across that bridge, it occurred to me that the worst part for me would be the aloneness. I think I could handle homelessness, if I had to, as long as I wasn't roaming around out there by myself. Even that girl, Rosy—she wasn't looking for a place to be, she was looking for people to be with."

Saying that, her voice cracked, and she covered her eyes with her hands for a moment. When she looked again at Rose, her eyes glistened with welled tears. "I'm sorry. I'm overwrought, and I'm rambling." She tried to make light. "I've gone from missing a stuffed animal to considering the possibility of homelessness. Clearly, the stress of all this is getting to me."

"It's okay," Rose said. "But let's start with what we can handle most easily. We'll find the pig first. We'll come up with a solution for homelessness after that," she joshed, smiling.

Jennifer smiled back. "Thank you."

Together they began looking behind and inside the pile of boxes in the entryway.

"I think half my problem is that I'm not sleeping," Jennifer said. "I just can't turn my mind off. And with everything that's happened, you know what I lie awake at night, tossing around sleepless, thinking about? My kids' first day of school. And the irony, of course, is that the schools aren't even open! But still, I just don't want them to be teased! I don't want them to be alone, to feel lonely. *This* is what I obsess over, in the middle of the night, trying to figure out what I can do to lessen that possibility." She pushed one stack of searched boxes aside to access the next. "You said you moved a lot, right? What was it like for you?"

Rose's mind spiraled right back to the memory of cradling her animals in the remnants of the fractured box as they drove toward ... what? ... their fourth, fifth apartment? Gertrude said not a word as they unpacked, and tucked herself into bed at the customary hour. The next morning she was up by six, as always, and went to work as if nothing at all had changed. "My mother was a pretty stoic woman," Rose responded. "Compared to you, it's like night and day. It's hard to imagine her being anywhere near as concerned as you are. She always said: 'Adapt. Make do. Quit complaining. Plenty have it worse off than you.' And that was it. My life mighta been a whole lot different had my mother put as much thought into our moves as you put into yours. I don't think she gave a moment's notice to how it affected me."

Jennifer slid another box aside and stared at Rose silently for a moment. "Oh, that's hard to imagine," she finally said. "I'll bet you have no idea what was really going on in her head. Or her heart, for that matter. Believe me when I say: sometimes the most loving thing a mother can do is find a way to shield her feelings from her children."

✹

GERTRUDE NEVER SLEPT AFTER a move. She would go to bed at the normal time, resolute in her maintenance of routine, her veneer of "fine-ness." But she'd just lie there, listening through the door or the wall as Rose bumbled about, setting up house. Because Rose's box spring squeaked, Gertrude always knew when she turned in—could tell by the pace of the *creak creak* when her flip-flopping ceased, when she slept. Just to be safe, she gave it another half hour or so before cracking open the door and crawling with feline stealth across the floor to Rose's bedside. She sometimes sat there for hours, peering at her sleeping daughter, practically purring. She liked, most of all, to listen to Rose's breathing—so calm, so serene—and only at night could she touch her hair with abandon, smoothing it across the pillowcase and marveling at the colors reflected in the nightlight's sheen. From one angle, yellow; from another, gold. The closer to it she drew, the creamier it seemed, a sweet white chocolate when she leaned in to breathe the sleepy scent of her daughter. During the day, Rose smelled like whatever she last ate, or of sweat, or of erasers or her teacher's perfume, but asleep she smelled exactly like herself, utterly unchanged from the first night of her life, like a puppy's hot belly, pungent and earthy. How Gertrude longed to scoop her child into her arms, pressed against her chest, where Rose's smell could waft up as it did from the infant sling, allowing her, if she stood perfectly still with her eyes closed and her ears covered, to inhale the scent of new life and imagine for whole minutes at a time that all was well.

But she did no such thing. She denied herself the indulgence of conspicuous coddling because it could do Rose no good. The world: tough. Children: cruel. And the past catches up eventually. Only the independent, the hardy, make it through unscathed: a lesson hard-won, not to be squandered simply to satisfy some base maternal urge. She could do that on the sly, slouched against a mattress, face cradled on a pillow of her daughter's hair, without burdening Rose during the daytime with the kind of copious affection that would only soften her skin and set her up for a fall. *I have to protect her, even from myself,* Gertrude thought, modulating each stroke of her fingertips through Rose's hair so as not to accidentally skim the girl's cheek and risk waking her.

Beside that cheek, never so far afield as to preclude detection in a drowsy, half-conscious hand sweep, rested a mama panda bear with a cub Velcroed to one paw. Gertrude gave the bears to Rose on the eve of their first move, after having spent half the previous night personalizing the duo by lamplight. She'd put much thought into choosing the thread with which she embroidered the mama bear's shirt—a rosy mauve that spoke of girlishness without being so pink as to recall the Malibu Barbie hue that Rose abhorred. With dainty precision stitches she sewed the sentiment "Home Is Where the Heart Is" over a pair of hearts interlocked above a cottage.

Raised without a mother, and despite having the most doting of dads, Gertrude always felt slightly adrift, vaguely homeless, as if it took a mother to craft a safe sense of place. Even an abundant childhood home could not quell her perception of emptiness. Never enough chairs filled at the table, never a soft hand to her fevered forehead, no decorative pillows on the beds to say, "You are special to me." Faced with her zillionth TV dinner, or a tampon for the first time, or a wedding dress she could not zip on her own, Gertrude religiously thought, *I'd give up everything I have for one day with my mother.* Trusting that her presence alone satisfied her own daughter's craving for security, she spirited them without compunction from one transient residence to another. She knew it wasn't the easiest thing, but she knew it could be worse, and Rose's seamless adjustments proved her right. They were together and that was enough.

"Home Is Where the Heart Is" proclaimed the bear, interpreting Gertrude's truth to her child day in and day out. She tucked the panda mama and baby family closer to Rose's body before concluding their midnight communions. "You are my heart," she whispered softly to her daughter, "and I'll never abandon you." Then she slunk away to her own room, to sleep alone, to rise at six, to keep their days steady, to uproot them again at a moment's notice should she be required to do so to protect her daughter, to keep their secret.

It almost came out, the first time, when Rose slapped a fellow kindergartner, forcing Gertrude to rush from work for a noontime meeting in the principal's office. "I'm not condoning fighting, you realize," Gertrude said in Rose's defense, "but it can't be all that uncommon among kindergartners. She apologized. I'll talk to her. I'm sure it won't happen again."

"That's all well and good," said the principal, patting Gertrude's hand the way she might a puppy's head, to mollify it. "But this is a bit of a special case. I've lived round here a long time, and know the history of this place inside and out. I recognize your name. I remember the story. This is Roger's daughter, yes?"

It had been almost six years since anyone put her together with him.

"I thought so," the principal continued. Despite Gertrude's silence, her rapid flush and reflexive swallowing spoke volumes. "Now, given his proclivities, I think we should all be especially alert for signs of acting out—depression, aggression—in your daughter."

Gertrude stood up so quickly her chair fell over. Purse clenched in hands bent to chest, knuckles whitening, she paused for a moment as if to say something, but finally turned and exited the office, speechless. She entered the kindergarten class equally mute, took Rose in hand, and ushered her directly out of the building. Within two days they were settled in a different apartment in a different academic district, as far away as possible from the other school while remaining within commuting distance of the Kinko's where Gertrude worked.

It took two years before it happened again.

Bending to the pressure that had built with each passing birthday, Gertrude acquiesced and hosted a party when Rose turned eight. Together they decorated all morning, Gertrude inflating dozens of balloons, Rose rubbing them furiously on her head until her hair stuck straight up and the walls danced with static-clung balloons of every color. They cut a sheet cake into the shape of a flower and baked cupcakes, frosted to look like bees. They strung streamers from corner to corner until the ceiling disappeared, and they laughed and they welcomed and they partied until one of Rose's classmates' mothers cornered Gertrude in the kitchen, as she dished up ice cream, and said, "I been thinking ever since I arrived that there's something so familiar about you, and it just now occurred to me. Ain't you Gertie Chiles, who married Roger Aikens? I believe I remember you from—"

"No," Gertrude said quickly. "I was born Gertrude Aikens. Never married. You've got me confused with someone else." She grabbed the ice cream container and left to serve it directly at the table, encouraging the children to eat quickly, and hustled everyone home while they were still swallowing the last spoonful. She spent the rest of the night perusing the paper for apartments to rent—apartments always, even when she might have afforded a house. Apartments attract transients, whereas houses breed neighborhoods, and neighborhoods breed familiarity.

Never another party after that, no loitering in locker rooms after swim class to chat with the other parents, no volunteering for the PTA. She raised Rose to be friendly, of course, in a pralines-for-the-postman-at-Christmas kind of way; nothing committal, ever ready to make a swift break should a flyer arrive from school announcing a father-daughter dinner or another such unbidden threat. To Rose, she told lies: a false increase in rent; a desire to cut the morning commute; a yen to be closer to or farther from a park, playground, shopping center, whatever. Lies and disruption in service to peace, in service to the only truth that ever mattered.

I have to protect her, Gertrude maintained as they flitted around for nearly all of her daughter's eighteen years virtually unnoticed, in what anyone else might have considered the most hospitable of Southern towns.

"LOOK HERE," ROSE SAID to Jennifer, holding open a box marked "TOWELS." Inside, tucked between the fluffy folds of white terrycloth, Piglet nestled down with a doll-baby's milk bottle and *Pooh's*

Little Instruction Book. "Told you we'd find him," she said, smiling, handing Piglet off to Jennifer, who was already on her feet and headed for the stairs.

Rose closed and restacked the entryway boxes they'd torn through in their search. Lifting a particularly heavy one, the bottom gave way, and she hastened it back onto the floor where she smoothed the packing tape back into place. Hand pressed to slippery tape on cardboard, the tactile memory spun her back to thoughts of her own box, reconstituted with duct tape after it tore in two. She'd stuffed her animals back into the box but didn't trust it as a toy chest anymore (too flimsy), yet neither would she relinquish the win to her mother. So she tucked it onto one closet shelf after another, where it lived out her adolescence as something more resembling a scrapbook. Over the years, she slid markers of her youth inside: the dean's list certificate, her high school diploma, the catalog from the "Alabama Folk Art" exhibit. She'd reached into it just yesterday before starting her journey, the taxi idling at dawn while she balanced atop a chair on the tips of her borrowed sneakers to squeeze her mother's Order of Service in with everything else she'd once loved or been proud of but had, by default, left behind. Somewhere in there, tumbled among the other memorabilia, rested her own well-worn copy of *Pooh's Little Instruction Book* that she'd tucked away when loftier fare began populating her bookshelves. Scooping the Milne book off the floor in Jennifer's foyer, she opened it randomly and read aloud to herself, "Before beginning a Hunt, it is wise to ask someone what you are looking for before you begin looking for it."

Asked yesterday morning what she was looking for, Rose would have replied that she was searching for Rosy's family, nothing more. Yet the process had so far led her to Amanda, Latonya, Jennifer, and, if she were truly honest, to some formerly unconsidered version of her own mother. The closer she got to Rosy's family, the more she seemed to crash headlong into contemplation of her own. Dead, Gertrude somehow seemed more alive. Burrowing into an armchair in Jennifer's living room, Rose reconsidered her earlier comment about her mother's indifference and Jennifer's attendant conviction that no mother could have been so callous.

To be sure, Gertrude was no Jennifer Goldberg. Never one to race boats in floodwaters, nor bathe in squirt-gun blasts. *And she certainly never tore a house apart to bring me peace*, Rose thought. But now she couldn't avoid wondering: could there not exist some middle ground between the ideal of Jennifer Goldberg, thrashing in her bed on behalf of her children, and the impervious sleep she'd always ascribed to her mother on those lonely nights when Gertrude retired early and shut her out?

Rose closed her eyes and pulled a throw across her body. Exhausted, she wilted but did not sleep, though she feigned it when she heard Jennifer come back downstairs and pause in the doorway. She lusted for stillness, for a few more moments free of anyone else's questions or concerns, and took guilty pleasure in Jennifer's retreating footsteps down the hall. Isolation granted no immunity from stress, but it did offer her a necessary, glorious, reprieve.

Reprieve!

She sat bolt upright and felt the way she had a few days back when, sobbing against her front door on the morning of September 11, she realized her mother might have once sobbed against the front door, too, in contrast to her youthful perception that Gertrude took pleasure in locking her out on schooldays. She could empathize for the first time with Gertrude's desire to retreat to her bedroom early in the evening on moving days, not necessarily to sleep—in fact, perhaps not to sleep at all—but just for brief reprieve after hours spent carrying boxes and unpacking and trying to resettle. A closed door equaled privacy, peace!, a few stolen moments alone; eyes shut could have stilled a throbbing brow or helped facilitate the illusion, however fleeting, that all was well.

It slowly dawned on Rose that the gravest sin might not have been Gertrude's feigned sleep—if that's, in fact, what she'd been doing on those nights—but her own childlike failure to perceive it as anything other than indifference. *Perhaps I've been blaming my mother for things I have no right to hold against her*, she realized.

In the morning, she would be leaving to seek out Rosy's aunt. But she now understood that what she most hoped to find was forgiveness from Rosy's family, something she could not authentically ask to receive if she refused to grant it. She knew what she was looking for; she knew the route there. Now she needed a bridge from Gretna to the task in Alexandria.

For I know my transgressions, and my sin is always before me.

"I forgive you, Mother," Rose whispered into the weighty Louisiana air. "I forgive you for not knowing what I needed most. I forgive you for failing to be my savior. And I forgive you, most of all, for never finding a way to be my Jennifer Goldberg."

XIII. Rosy

"You really think there's any way this day could get worse?"

HE STOPPED. AND THAT is why she got in.

Rosy didn't get the time—privilege or curse that it might have been—to reflect on her choice, to play it over and over in her head at night when she couldn't sleep, altering this detail or the other to change the course of events: a line at the gas tank that held him up and gave her time to climb into another vehicle; an untied shoelace she bent to tighten as he sped past, her thumb on her shoe, not in the air, so he missed her; another girl closer to his starting point thumbing for a ride, another girl to smile back at his youthful grin and grasp his hand and take her seat. No, she didn't have time to imagine all those scenarios, for she had fewer than forty-eight restless hours before death came. Instead, just this: her shoes were tied and her thumb was out and, when he pushed open the truck's cab door and welcomed her in, she looked at him and thought: *In all my life, I've never seen a more beautiful man.* Brad Pitt in *Thelma and Louise*; innocent rogue, perfect white teeth in a mischievous smile; eyes like a clear-sky day, sun-drenched and endless.

Clear skies, she thought. *It's about time.*

So in she climbed.

※

"You can't be hitching your way to Tuscaloosa tonight!" her aunt admonished when Rosy made to leave just hours after Jennifer dropped her off. "It be getting on to night, and ain't nothing open past dark in these here parts but hospitals and legs. Ain't safe for a girl on them streets at night!"

Rosy closed her mouth around the last spoonful of mashed potatoes and said, "It's not like the highways of America are full of serial killers stalking their next victim, you know. Believe it or not, lots of good folk know how to drive. Besides," she added, rolling the two remaining biscuits into a napkin to save for later, "you really think there's any way this day could get worse?"

"Always," her aunt replied, twenty years wiser.

Rosy walked the two miles back to the interstate, impervious to the darkening sky and the occasional catcalls slung in her direction from under the raised hood of a pickup and lobbed at her from a ramshackle porch. She swung her arms mightily, the fabric of her aunt's oversized shirt billowing in the wake of the breeze she built as she hurried down the streets. She'd originally intended to stay awhile, to catch up on sleep, to rest before moving on. But once she showered and ate she felt refreshed. More than that: possessed, really. Compelled toward Tuscaloosa by some inner alarm, tolling minutes, ticking seconds, prompting her to get up, move fast, lest she miss the connection. Beyond that, she felt invincible. She'd beaten that hurricane wave: floated on it, rowed across it, blasted through it. Gun to head, water rising, raised baton, death's emissaries—all foiled. She'd gotten out. A dark memory rose from the depths, and Rosy saw again the man bobbing on the cooler, felt his hand as it clamped around her wrist, slicing the water to topple her from the roof, separate her from her drowning mother, and though she banished his face, as she habitually did when he encroached on her thoughts, she did not turn her mind entirely away this time. She indulged the sensation of her body, surging. Her foot, connecting. The power, the pride, the relief! (Not past there, not on to the other more haunting emotions; a bit of self-censorship in the interest of self-service). Whatever was required, she could do. Had done. Would do again to save herself, her mother. That knowledge hastened her step. She had to get on the road to Tuscaloosa in order to free her mother; she knew that as surely as if it were part of a history she'd already read. She couldn't wait for daybreak. Tuscaloosa beckoned.

Interstate 49 skimmed Alexandria to the west and made a straight line north to Shreveport. So she sought to jump off it quickly, just south of town at the junction with U.S. 167, where the roadway skirted the Red River in a northeastern stretch toward Mississippi's border and Alabama's promised land. A sketchy route at best, littered with travelers' toss-offs—more throw cups and cigarette butts than plants in some places—but, to her way of thinking, it was all beautiful for its guaranteed freedom from inhibited passage. No roadblocks, no barricades, no insurmountable obstacles. She tripped over a lone tire while walking backward with her thumb to the sky, but it didn't keep her down. Easy enough to step around. Sometimes she pulled her hand in, turned around, walked forward with only backward glances. She had scruples, after all; wouldn't take a ride from just anybody. No beater cars, no lone men in pickup trucks. A family-filled minivan would be best; a couple in a sedan, fine; truckers good.

She'd never forgotten the trucker who carried her and Cilla to Disney World eight years ago. He'd been the best part of that godforsaken trip. She'd slept through most of the journey, but had one glorious wide-awake hour at daybreak on the Florida Turnpike during which he'd let her steer, honk at passersby, operate the CB. "Let's raise us somebody," he'd said, and she replied that her mama raised her just fine, which made him laugh to no end. "On the radio," he replied, and showed her how to use the buttons to talk, to locate a clear channel.

"Breaker, breaker," Rosy barked into the handset in her childish voice, raising charges of "ankle biter" and "radio runt" that her driver defended her against, introducing her to a bit of CB lingo in the process.

"Good job, Ace," he'd congratulated her when she bored of the CB and replaced the set. They then shared a Coke from his cooler, and he handed her a stick of Juicy Fruit gum from his pants pocket that she gnawed on till long after he'd driven off, gnawed on till the boy in line at Disney's entrance knocked her to the ground and it popped out of her mouth. "You're welcome in my rig anytime, Ace," he'd said by way of goodbye, and from that next moment—standing on the sidewalk in pajamas with a raving woman at the gates of a theme park, hundreds of miles from home—it all got worse. Everything. Her whole life. Sometimes, reviewing another set of commitment papers, scrubbing another layer of Cilla's manically-applied hair dye off the bathroom floor, she wondered what might have been different had her trucker heard her cries on the street in Orlando, stopped, opened the door, and pulled her back in? What better life might she have had, contained in the insulated nest of his truck's cab?

She heard an engine rumble bearing down behind her, turned, put out her hand. Air brakes squealed. Eighteen wheels slowed on the asphalt, then dropped down onto the shoulder. Rosy lowered her thumb and ran toward the thrown-open passenger door. Less than fifteen minutes hitching it on I-49, and she was sheltered in a modern-day upgrade of the safe space she'd been daydreaming about for almost a decade.

"Where to?" the young man asked, and when she told him he said he'd be going right through Tuscaloosa, could drop her at her destination's doorstep, so she settled in for the long drive with uncharacteristic giddiness, high on her own good fortune. Their repartee of the next few hours got off to an auspicious if somewhat salacious start as they roared past a piano and organ shop on the outskirts of Alexandria with a billboard boasting, "It's never too late to get your hands on a good organ!" That started them laughing and they hardly stopped, swapping stories designed to keep the mood merry. The combined distraction of frivolous words and his fabulous profile did Rosy good and, as they rode, she angled her body farther and farther to the left, sneakers tucked under her right side, head lolling against the pleather at an angle that allowed her to gaze at her companion with abandon. Though race might have otherwise kept them apart, in the privacy of the truck their common age and class made them peers enough. He was as country as cornflakes; the sort of sandy-haired Southern boy who pitched varsity ball for Brother Martin or Holy Cross, a poor boy raised on po-boys who loved his mama, raised a coon dog or two, and had a Copenhagen ring burnished into the backside of every pair of blue jeans. But oh, those dimpled cheeks! Cleft chin, long lashes curled back on themselves … just looking at him lifted her mood, and he cottoned to the attention, accustomed though it was. That kind of beauty expected to be gazed upon.

Going on two hours out, just shy of Natchez, they pooled their accumulated resources and spread a motley picnic on the seat between them—the leftover buttermilks she'd brought, a few cold French fries, a Snickers bar. He kept one hand on the steering wheel, in perfect control, while lifting a snack to his mouth. She caught herself leaning forward, unbalanced, to watch those gleaming teeth cut into the dough, full lips massaging each other as he chewed, until—*thwamp!*—a bump in the roadway knocked her knees against the dash. "You okay?" he asked, trying to suppress a grin, but she erupted in giggles herself, such a fit that she choked on a caramel-coated peanut and caught herself up in a coughing binge. *Sure enough,* she thought, *that coulda been Maya's hand!*—a customary thwamp upside the head designed to knock some sense into her and chastise her all at once.

"You be stuck on that boy like hair on a biscuit!" Maya would have teased. And oh, she'd have been right!

"You sure you're okay?" he asked, laughing at Rosy as she chortled and snarfed. She kept nodding, yes, yes, between sips of water, so finally he quit asking, lowered the windows, cut on the radio, and crooned along with Phil Vassar's "I'll Take That as a Yes." The boy's voice wasn't good, but it was hearty as he sang about the teasing game of romance and the mundane chores of dinner out and roses and lit candles that lead to the reward of foot rubs and hot tubs and …

"Sing with me!" he taunted, encouraging her just to hum along when she said she didn't know the words, turning to her more than he had to, which she liked. He winked at her, as the lyrics dictated, alluding to French kisses on bear rugs, and she couldn't quite discern whether he was just singing along with the country star or whether he meant to ask straight-up if she liked it, did she wanna try it?

The cab vibrated in time with the banjo and bass twang and his tanned hands drummed the wheel, every fourth cymbal beat struck with a taut forearm at three o'clock. He held the truck steady despite snaking around in his seat, whole body engaged in the dance, leading with his chin, lips pursed, shoulders engaged.

When the song got to the part about touching, and promises of a sleepless night, he winked at Rosy again, then threw his head back, accenting the words of the chorus with ooohs and throaty grunts. Let his left knee fall aside, spread his thighs, pulsed to the beat by squeezing his ass; she watched the muscles contract beneath his jeans. Oh, cocky thing, he knew how to use that body! She began to move, too, up on her knees, arms stretched overhead, palms thrumming the roof.

"Do you like it?" he asked.

"Yes! Yes! Yes!" Rosy yelled in response, arms wide open, head tossed back, cool night air thrashing her clothes.

"Whoo-ee!" he howled, egging her on. They sang the last lines together, at the top of their lungs, words jumbling together about glances and gestures implying consent, with no inhibitions.

Spent, they looked at each other and laughed uproariously as the rhythm quieted. Rosy fell back against the seat, all smile. "Girl, you're hotter'n a billy goat's ass in a pepper patch!" he cheered, extending his right hand to her, which she grasped in her left and squeezed, pulling it toward her for a second before releasing it, then leaning her whole upper body out the window. Wind beating her, eyes closed, she disappeared into the dark and the noise, road flying past, thinking what joy it was just to have fun again. She stayed out there till her face stung.

Back inside, she found him talking on the CB, confirming there were no nightcrawlers near the park.

"Nah," said the voice on the other end. "You're clear. Enjoy that little bit."

"Ten four," he said, hanging up, then turned his attention back to her. "I gotta pee something awful," he said. "Mind if we stop? I shoulda pulled off back there in Natchez, but I was having too much fun."

"I gotta go, too," she admitted. "Is there a gas station nearby?"

"Nah, nothing along this stretch for a hundred miles." He angled the rig off the thoroughfare, onto an access road along a deserted stretch of Old Highway 84 where the railroad tracks cut off into an empty field, just south of Natchez State Park and east of Cranfield, just far enough out that the nearby town's lights weren't yet visible to her.

He shut the engine down and handed her a napkin out of the McDonald's bag on the floor. "Best I've got," he said apologetically as he jumped to the ground beside her. "Look, you stay up here by the truck. It'll be safer. I'ma run out into the field, give you a little privacy. Yell to me when you're done. I won't turn back till I hear you call out."

"Thanks," she said, then watched him saunter into the vacant field, a touch bowlegged, like a rough stock cowboy. She walked a few feet toward the rear of the truck and squatted beside a tire, keeping her eyes on his back, thrilling to the thought of his hand reaching into his pants, touching himself, fingers around cock. The thought swelled her, and when she wiped she was warm and slippery. She pulled up her pants, then watched him hitch his and pause in anticipation of her voice. She called to him and he loped toward the truck, their eyes locked together, a tandem pee suddenly a sensual thing. He opened the passenger door and, as if to reach for a handhold, she laid her palm deliberately atop his, traced her thumb along the side of his forefinger, then lifted her left foot onto the running board to hop in. In response, he pressed his free hand up under her raised thigh and cradled her ass in his palm, his fingertips just skimming her crotch.

Electric. With that one graze he made her equal parts thoughtless and hungry.

It had been more than two years since anyone had touched her there. Two years since she'd given up on sex after debasing herself under the blanket with the two football players, two years spent sacrificing daily in service to her academic goals, two years toiling to keep tabs on her mother's moods and meds while trying to tend to herself, two years suppressing all her immediate physical yearnings and channeling that energy toward future success. So, when the hand of the man who was whisking her to safety slid under her thigh, she decided she'd earned this liberty, had every right to indulge this craving, and, with a shudder, relaxed into his arms.

🪰

AFTER HAVING ALREADY DRAGGED her children across the Crescent City Connection once that morning, Jennifer didn't want to subject them to the six-hour round-trip drive from Gretna to Alexandria to deliver Rosy to her aunt's house. Which meant she had to go back to the water bureau with a favor to ask and quite a bit of explaining to do. Anticipating a row, Jennifer parked the car at the far end of the parking lot. No way to keep the kids from seeing, but at least she could prevent their hearing. Then she walked inside, coaxed her husband out onto the front steps away from his colleagues, and confessed what she'd done and who she had in the car.

From the passenger seat, having turned to observe them out the rear side window of the vehicle, Rosy watched the interplay of the couple on the steps.

Jennifer reached for Adam's hand, looped her forefinger around his pinkie in a conciliatory tug, then started to speak.

He paused, wrenched his hand away, took a defiant step

backward. Rotated to look at the car, bent forward, squinted, confirmed what she said, what she'd done. Clenched both fists, pounded the air.

She flinched. Opened her mouth, gestured toward the car with an open hand.

He crossed his hands in the air between them, threw his arms wide.

She closed her mouth. Stood stone still.

He pointed at the car. (*Those are our children!*) Thrust his hands at her face, palms skyward, rocking his hands, arms, whole body, up ... down ... toward her ... away. Imploring. Fists again, beating his temples, reeling in a circle from her, back upon her. Arms raised—

I should distract the kids, Rosy thought. She'd seen this plenty of times, on the street, in school halls, on *Jerry Springer*: arms raised, signaling the moment when the punch got thrown or the slap landed or the two parties stormed in opposite directions while screaming invectives. "Kids!" she yelled, hoping to turn them from the scene, but they kept staring, and when she followed their gaze she saw something entirely unexpected happen.

He rolled his head back, withdrew his hands from the air, and smoothed them firmly over his balding pate. He looked at the car. He looked at his wife. Then he reached an arm around her shoulders, pulled her to him, held her there, speaking into her ear, brushing the hair off her cheek. Then he walked with her toward the car.

Like nothing ever had, it took Rosy's breath away. *There it is,* she thought: *love.* This was the first she'd ever seen it in real life. No wild kiss beneath a sunset, no grand declarations on a tarmac; just a legitimately angry man, wiping his fury off his body, letting it go, putting an arm around a woman, and moving to help her.

Jennifer lifted the kids out of the car, folded the portable DVD player and some videos into Sammy's arms. Her husband came to Rosy's window.

"Hello," he said. "I'm Adam. Are you okay?"

"Yes," she said. "Though I apologize for all the trouble."

"You're no trouble," he said earnestly, and began to feel around in his pockets, coming up empty-handed. "I'm sorry. I'd give you some cash, to help, but I don't have anything on me. Everything's shut down around here."

Rosy waved her hands, said, "No, really, y'all are doing enough. I couldn't begin to ask you for anything more."

"Well, Jen'll get you to your aunt's house, and I'll write down our name and contact information. We're happy to help you however we can." He leaned through the open window and rummaged for a pen in the hollow in the dash. "Jen," he called, "is there a pen in here?"

"Glove compartment!" she yelled out, hugging the boys goodbye.

Opening the glove compartment, he found the stack of Jennifer's new business cards, still shrink-wrapped. "Even better," he said, tearing the edge with his teeth, taking the top card and folding it into Rosy's hand. "Guard this, so you know how to reach us," he said. "This isn't an empty promise. As soon as the phones are working again, call us. Let us know where you are and how you are. We'll help you however we can."

She slid the business card into her back pocket. Jennifer jumped into the driver's seat; the boys each strung a finger through their father's belt loop. Adam reached across Rosy, took Jennifer's hand. "Drive safe," he told her. "We'll be fine. See you tonight."

"Love you," Jennifer said, releasing his hand.

"Love you more," he replied. Then he nodded to Rosy, scooped up the boys, one in each arm, and backed away from the car as his wife eased it forward.

Last thing Rosy heard, as they turned out of the drive, was one of the children, arms tight around his father's neck, exclaiming, "I love *you* more!"

"No, *I* love *you* more!" rang out Adam's joyful response.

※

I LOVE YOU MORE, I love you more, I love you more … the refrain carried Rosy through the day. Wheels turning on the freeway echoed the rhythm of the words, air rushing past windows sang it out, bass notes on the radio kept the beat, I love you more. In the still field by the railroad tracks outside Natchez, crickets whistled their soprano trill, I love you more; the bullfrogs croaked a harmonious baritone, I love you more.

"Mmmm," moaned the young trucker as Rosy leaned her back against his chest, and the music stopped. One hand squeezed her ass, the other grasped a breast. All of a sudden, this didn't feel like romance. This wasn't love. This was a stranger on the side of the road with his grease-stained hands on her body.

"I'm sorry," she said, lifting her foot off the running board, pushing his hands away, turning to face him. "It's been a long day. I'm not really myself. Can we just get going?"

"Sure, we can get going," he said, friendly and comforting. He moved a strong hand to her shoulder, spread his fingers across her upper back, the way Adam had moved to hug Jennifer to him before leading her to the car, and Rosy almost succumbed again to the clear-sky eyes locked on hers and the pressure of his warm touch. Oh, to trust someone to lead her through the last of this day!

"Thanks—" she began, but his hand shifted. On his face nothing moved, every feature frozen just as it had been a quarter-second before, but still, everything changed. Those blue-sky eyes clouded from light to dark, sinking ever deeper, to the darkest place, beyond abyss. Her mind skittered just ahead of the swelling fear, all disjointed observation, so that she gazed on him and thought of the Mariana Trench. Eight tons of pressure per square inch, scalding vents, set to explode. As near to hell as this world gets, those eyes. And swimming just below, she saw a hinge-jawed creature lurking in the depths, all hooked teeth to spear prey—his smile, alive with bioluminescence, drawing her in with its false light. *He's a viperfish,* Rosy realized in that strange, elongated moment. *Whatever made me think he was pretty?*

His fingernails bit into the skin under her armpit and she flinched at the pain. Not full-blown fear yet, just surprise floating on the surface. Pure, stupid surprise. Bagged catch, jerking against the first startling prick of the hook, oblivious to fate, mouthing the lure that will reel it in. He jammed his free hand into the waistband of her pants and yanked her back against him.

"Ain't no need to rush," he drawled.

"Let go of me," she said and tried to step back, pulling hard, but he held tight. No matter how fiercely or in which direction she wrenched herself, she couldn't alter his grip. The upper half of her body he held immobile, her shoulders clamped in the embrace of his well-muscled arm.

He started to laugh. Stuck, she followed his tack and stopped straining. "Okay, you win," she said, forcing a smile. "Uncle! Now come on, cut it out. Let's just get back in the truck and forget this ever happened."

"Screw that," he said, tightening his grip around her shoulders, on her pants. "Nobody gets a free ride round here." And, that fast, he popped loose her jeans button with his thumb, flicked his wrist, tore the zipper.

She went for his eyes. Had heard that somewhere—"Go for the eyes!"—but he caught her halfway there. He moved faster than she, switched his grip, cemented both her wrists together, shoved her toward the ground. He pressed hard to break her wrists but the pain, instead of felling her, unleashed a hoarded memory: "Fight back! Catch your assailant off guard! Confront him! Don't give up!" She swung one leg wide, her dead weight pulling him further onto her, and cut him hard across the ankle with her heel as they toppled. He put out a hand to break his fall, lost his grip on her. She rolled from him and kicked but he was up, steel-toed cowboy boot flying toward her face. Arms up, instinctively, absorbing blows.

> "The victim exhibits extensive defensive wounds on her hands and forearms," the coroner dictated into the recorder that balanced on the cold metal table beside the Jane Doe's tagged toe. "Multiple triangular abrasions of unknown origin."

He knotted a hand in her hair, another at the back of her pants.

"You bitch," he yelled, lifting her off the ground, hurling her through the air. Her head ricocheted off the wheel well. She landed on her side in the gravel. Couldn't see, couldn't breathe, inhaling something wet, choking it back out. Hand to face, covered in goo, finger sliding in over her right eyebrow, touching bone.

> "There are severe non-lethal lacerations along the right hemispheric supraorbital ridge and zygomatic arch. Both anterior surface injuries present with ragged edges, indicating a crushing force." The medical terminology gifted the coroner emotional remove. The corpse had a supraorbital ridge, not a forehead split on mud-splattered metal. A zygomatic arch, not a cheek. "The apical wound measures exactly 4 cm, the inferior 2.85 cm." The coroner united the injuries in every sentence, made them concurrent, sparing himself any inkling of the terror and pain involved if one came first, the other later. But the cheek came later.

Rosy's assailant lifted her with one hand clamped around her neck. He smashed her over and over against the exterior wall of the truck, held her pinned up there, six, seven feet high. "You stupid, stupid bitch." Rosy clung to his wrist with both her hands, pushing back against him as she fought for air. His power: an uncompromising thing. When he squeezed, it cut off all her oxygen and he laughed at her response: the desperate scratching of her nails on his hand, the little bunny kicks not touching him, feet sliding on-over-against the metal rig, no footholds, little mewling noises. After a few seconds he'd relax, watch her suck in air, then resume strangling her to see the replay.

Finally he lowered her a foot or two, turned her head, pressed his lips against her left ear—the one without the river of blood flowing into it—and murmured quietly, as if into the ear of a lover: "I could kill you if I wanted to. Do you know that? Do you?" His hand started to shake, his arm, his whole upper body. She felt the alarming strength, understood it. He meant to kill her. His body yearned to kill her. It took every ounce of control he had not to do it yet. He moved his hands, one to either side of her head, a vise cinched so hard her teeth bit into the soft flesh inside her cheeks, his thumbs pressed into her eye sockets. "I could kill you right now. I could crush your bones," he said. "Say it!"

"You could kill me," she whispered, utterly convinced, and simultaneously flooded with an uncommon gratitude, insanely grateful for his struggle, for the mind that held his hands at bay. "You could kill me," she repeated, her voice raspy, cracking. *What to do?* she wondered. *What to do?*

Then she knew. In a lucid nanosecond—blinded by his thumbs in her eyes, deaf with his palms pressed to her ears—her mind took flight. *I'm killing myself,* she realized. *To hell with that fight-back shit. To resist is to die.* To live, she must talk to the piece of him that didn't want to kill her yet, convince him he was right, cede to him the control he wanted. With her fingers, she began to stroke the back of the hands that noosed her, butterfly kisses. Fingertips caressing his skin. She cried as she pet him. "I'm sorry. I'm so sorry I hurt you," she said. The harder she cried, the more he stilled. Soon her limbs weren't rattling, just dangling. He eased his thumbs from her eyeballs. "Please forgive me for making this happen," Rosy pleaded. She ran one hand down his forearm, massaging the bare skin, pliant as a paramour. He lowered her feet to the ground.

"Tell me you want it," he said.

"I want it," she replied.

"Tell me you want me."

"I want you," she repeated.

"No," he growled, squeezing her face again, cracking the incipient scabs where Cilla's nails had raked her during their underwater struggle. "Beg me for it."

"Please take me," Rosy sobbed. "Please. I'm so sorry. I was wrong. I was bad. I want you, I do!"

He grabbed the back of her head, yanked her hair so her neck arched up, and she gasped, taking his tongue into her mouth. She didn't flinch, eyes focused beyond him, taking it all in. Nowhere to run. Field: dark. Road: too far. He'd catch her. Nothing on the ground to use as a weapon; he'd beat her down. His mouth ground into her so hard her gums tore under the pressure of his teeth. She winced; he laughed. His laughter forced its way into her, ricocheting off the back of her throat, racing down her esophagus, pushing itself into her belly, but she didn't notice. She left her body to him in order to hide from him in her mind—eyes and spirit and all intentions aimed in the direction of the passenger door right beside her, still open. Light inside. *Where are the keys?* With the keys she could get in, lock him out, drive away. *Where are the keys?* Not in his hands. Either in the ignition or in his pockets. She wrapped her arms around him and hugged him closer, straining toward his buttocks. He smacked his hands over hers, pressed hard against her, slid her hands around to the front of him. She touched every pocket as he drew her hands forward. No keys on him. They must still be in the ignition.

She had a chance.

NOW!

Rosy smashed a knee into his balls, and when he buckled in pain she clamped her hands into a ten-fingered white-knuckled fist, best she could do, and clubbed him on the back of the head. Leapt from under him as he fell, foot on running board, up into cab, reaching for door, pull! pull!, two hands on door handle yanking closed, shirt billowing, aunt's oversized unbuttoned blouse hanging beneath her knees, shirttails flapping, illuminated white flag whipping into his hand so he jerked and she fell and the rock knocked her out.

Ragged edged 2.85 cm crush injury to the victim's zygomatic arch.

SHE CAME TO GASPING, scratching at the dirt as for a handhold, a rooftop to grab before the blackness swallowed her. There was a hawk not fifteen feet from her, tamping at the earth, screeching away, defending his turf. In cahoots with the cooling night temperatures, his protests roused her. It took her a minute to get her bearings. Once aware, she spun in a wild circle, looking for her assailant. The terrified bird flew off, and she collapsed back to the ground, alone. Face in the dirt, she sobbed for a long, long time. Lay in ache. Finally reached down and wriggled her pants back up over her thighs, as far as she could get them without hoisting them so far that they cut into her, too. And then she stumbled back toward the main road.

Car after car passed while she crouched in the scrub brush alongside the roadway, chewing on her fingernails, making them bleed, petrified. She couldn't keep walking, but she couldn't reach out, either. She'd done that once already tonight, and look. *Move!* she urged herself every time approaching headlights splintered the camouflage and speckled her skin, and she meant to, she did!, but the wheels spinning on the asphalt revived the memory of his voice, "Where to?" and she curled into a ball until the drone disappeared.

The longer she bled, the weaker she became. She knew it, could feel the energy seeping out of her into the dirt. She needed help, needed water; nothing left, not even for tears.

Unexpectedly, it is her mother who saved her.

In the past, scared and uncertain, thoughts of her father had always bolstered her spirits. Whenever Cilla broke down, forcing Rosy to care for her mother and herself, she conjured up her father and he saw her through. She felt strong and fierce and fearless in his presence. He'd never let her down. Until now. Tonight she'd needed a father, not an imaginary friend. She'd needed a defender, not a delusion. At precisely the moment when she could have used him most she didn't think of him even once, because he was useless to her. Always had been, she now realized. Always had been. What she'd felt all those times was false bravado; he was not her courage, but her failure. Her courage came from a resource pool he never stocked, from a woman who broke down but came back, time and time again: the mother who had been there beside her in the bed every night; the woman anchoring the only other chair at the table, her tattooed hand holding Rosy's through it all. Flawed, oh so flawed, flawed to such a degree that she'd cursed her and wished her gone a hundred times over, but now—hiding beside a highway, horrified by the consequences of seeking help—it was Cilla to whom she flew with her mind and heart.

Inside Cilla's jewelry box—the box Rosy had sheltered for days and safeguarded at her aunt's home only hours before—rested a tattered piece of legal paper, folded into a neat rectangle. On that paper, in a script that faltered as it progressed down the page, Cilla had written the same phrase, over and over. Rosy had uncreased the paper many times over the years, and in the cool Mississippi night, eyes closed to the threat of yet another passing car, she allowed her mind to uncrease it again, calling back the words from memory. She could see her mother, bent over a desk, slipping into the clutch of mania and writing to hold on, the pen careening off the page but still in her hand, valiant effort. Her own sanity close to faltering, Rosy spoke Cilla's words aloud as a prayer for them both: "Let me not pray to be sheltered from dangers, but to be fearless in facing them. Let me not beg for the stilling of my pain, but for the heart to conquer it." She repeated the phrases, rolling them off her tongue, but not releasing them. She clung to the words as to a mantra: "Let me not pray to be sheltered from dangers, but to be fearless in facing them. Let me not beg for the stilling of my pain, but for the heart to conquer it."

The distant thrum of an engine whistled from the east. She quaked with terror at the thought of flagging down the vehicle; she knew too well the ramifications of such blind faith, but she knew, too, that she had no other option than to give faith another chance. So with the same resolve that kept Cilla writing on that long-ago day, Rosy stood. Unbent herself like a new fawn rising, tenderly guarding each limb, setting her feet down awkwardly, but determinedly. Along with the sound of the approaching wheels that spit out stones as they rolled toward her, the image of him rose before her. He reached a hand to her from the cab, coaxing her in, "Where to?" but she fought to silence his words. Repeated, instead, those of her mother. Louder, and with authority: "Let me not pray to be sheltered from dangers, but to be fearless in facing them. Let me not beg for the stilling of my pain, but for the heart to conquer it." She actively stared down the recollection of his hand reaching for her, replacing it with the vision of another hand that had reached toward her that day, with a card and a promise: *We will help you.*

As the headlights reached her, she withdrew from her pocket Jennifer Goldberg's business card. It had not been lost in the struggle, not even sullied. One last time, she invoked her mother's words: "Let me not pray to be sheltered from dangers, but to be fearless in facing them. Let me not beg for the stilling of my pain, but for the heart to conquer it." Then, clutching the name of the woman who had already saved her once that day, she staggered out of the bushes and onto the road, waving her hands into the darkness bravely, exactly as her mother had raised her to do.

THE PHONE RANG JUST before midnight and, though he was sleeping, he had the receiver in hand before the second ring. They'd been expecting her call, since her contractions had been building all day. "Go to sleep," their daughter had urged a few hours back. "We'll call you when it's time."

"It's time!" she called, en route to Natchez Community Hospital. So they grabbed the bag filled with video camera, some granola bars, the receiving blanket they'd carried their own daughter home in thirty-two years earlier, and bounded into the car. Half an hour, at worst, Cranfield to Natchez; a straight shot down US-84 and they'd be there. The wife prattled on and on in her excitement. "Y'all will see I'm right. Yes siree! It's a girl, I know it. She carried high the whole time. Even there at the end, it was like she was holding a basketball right out in the front of her. And her face, I'm telling you, how round it got tells me it's a girl for sure! I just hope they're over that Sabine business. Sabine! Really, have you ever heard of any such name? I tell you, every time they says it all I can think of is those Pontipee brothers dancing round that barn, singing about 'Sobbing Women,' and while I'm always grateful for a reason to think about Howard Keel—"

"I'm telling you, Hester, there ain't nobody else thinking about *Seven Brides for Seven Brothers* when they hear the name Sabine."

"Well, what's everybody else thinking about then?"

"They're thinking about a Roman kidnapping called 'The Rape of the Sabine Women.'"

"Well holy shit, Daniel, that's worse! You want your grand-daughter associated with a rape? I'll have a talk with her about— Watch out! There's a deer!"

He hit the brakes so hard the car began to skid, spinning sideways onto the shoulder. He ran to the girl. Took off his shirt, draped it around her waist, lifted her tractable body and held it safely against him.

"What the … was she hit?" his wife asked.

"She wasn't hit," he said.

"What happened to her, then?"

"She wasn't hit."

They lifted a blanket from the trunk, laid her across it on the back seat. The wife patted the girl's arm gently as they drove. The husband patted his wife's knee and tried not to look back.

They carried her together into the ER, Hester supporting the girl's head and cooing to her, Daniel cradling her in his arms. They placed her on the gurney, wrapped in his shirt. Refused to leave until the nurse shooed them from the room.

In the maternity ward, Hester washed her hands, and her husband slipped out of his soiled clothes and into hospital scrubs. Beneath the disposable green fabric in which he posed for the last photograph with his daughter before she became a parent herself, a rivulet of the stranger's blood trickled around his ribs, pooled at his waist, and dried into a crackly, itchy mess in his pubic hair. It was still there in the morning, after Sabine was born and they rushed back downstairs to check on the girl.

But they got there too late. She was already gone.

XIV. ROSE

*"This phonebook page is the only thing
that still doesn't make any sense to me."*

ROSE STOOD STARING AT the front door of the little purple house
in Alexandria for a very, very long time. Then she knocked too
fiercely, hand as weapon driven by will: Little pig, little pig, let me
come in. She walloped the door soundly, to counter her true desire,
which was to slink away with her destructive news undelivered.
The larger part of her hoped the aunt didn't hear, wasn't home.
Might somehow avoid the wolf at the door.

The knob turned. The door opened.

A short woman with a tight afro smiled out, a toddler balanced
on her left hip, her African-print muumuu belted by the child's
chubby legs. "Morning!" the woman said over the sounds of children playing. A squeal, some laughter.

All Rose could think was, *Everyone seems so happy.* Scared of
ruining it all, she just stood there, mute. She confused the lady.

"Something you needing, hon?" the woman prompted.

Rose realized that if she opened her mouth she'd burst into

tears. Shit. She should have let Mac do this after all! She extended her right hand to introduce herself, to offer a polite handshake, but she started trembling so badly she immediately withdrew it, crossed her arms over her chest, and clamped her shaking hands under her armpits. But no!, that made her look defensive!, and her mother always said never to cross your arms when introducing yourself to a stranger; you look standoffish. So she uncrossed her arms. But what to do with them? Can't reach out for a handshake again, hands trembling too violently now. She raised her right hand to her mouth, as if to pull out some words, and clamped her left hand over her right forearm, to still the movement. She wound up hugging herself.

"Is you okay?"

She shook her head slowly, back and forth: *No, I'm not.*

The woman put down her child and shooed him inside, then reached out and rubbed Rose's upper arm gently. "Does you need help, hon?"

This wasn't fair, the woman now comforting her, what with the information Rose had to share but couldn't find the gumption to blurt out. She took two deep breaths, steadied herself, and managed, "My name is Rose Ai—" before a wail from deep inside the house cut her off.

"'Scuse me," the woman said, turning away but leaving the door open. As Rose watched the woman scoop up and comfort another little boy nursing a stubbed toe, she crossed her arms again, squeezing herself for fortification. When the aunt returned, Rose clasped her hands together at hip level. Friendlier, but still employed in the business of holding herself together.

"Sorry about that. You done said you name's Rose?"

"Yes, ma'am. I've come with news about your niece, Rosy Howard." There.

"Oh, thank you, Jesus!" the woman gushed. She relaxed against the jamb, hand to breast. "I been so worried! She supposed to have called me once she made it to Tuscaloosa, and I kept on telling myself, 'She just got busy, no news is good news'—you know that's what they says—but oh, I been so scared of opening the door one morning to find an officer standing out there looking just as grim as could be ..."

She quieted. She stared at Rose, who looked just as grim as could be. Then she straightened, a hand on either side of the doorframe, watching Rose's eyes well with tears.

"What kinda news you brung me?"

All Rose said was, "Rosy's dead," and the aunt collapsed to the ground, melted into a writhing, wailing mess of orange and red geometric print. A passel of children came running, confused and distraught, looking for an explanation. Rose thought she should do something but was too scared to reach out and touch the woman, afraid of being rebuffed, so she tried instead to soothe the children. She climbed over the woman, who took no notice of her—nothing but screams, pounding of floor, inhuman noises—and shuffled the little ones back into the house.

There were seven of them. All toddlers. All different colors. All discombobulated. "You're not all brothers and sisters?" Rose asked. No, they shook their heads. One little girl giggled at the thought and everyone relaxed a bit.

"She ain't our mama. She our auntie," one said.

"She watch over us," said another.

"What's wrong with her?" the boy with the stubbed toe asked.

"She's sad," Rose answered as the woman's noise weakened to a choking sob. "She's *very* sad, but she'll be okay. Don't worry. What makes *you* feel better when you're sad?"

Ice cream, said one. A movie, said another.

So it is that Rose dished up seven bowls of chocolate ice cream and settled the houseful of children in front of the TV, nestled together on a pile of sofa cushions. The upbeat chorus of *Barney & Friends* sang from the far side of the room as she settled herself on the floor beside the crying woman. Thirty minutes passed before Rosy's aunt lifted her face from the floor and turned toward Rose.

"Can I make you a pot of coffee?" Rose asked softly. The woman padded along behind Rose into her own kitchen, where Rose busied herself rummaging through the cupboards for grounds and sugar, boiling water, pouring two cups, which she saucered and blew and carried to the table. Sunlight spilled through a single window into the tiny room dwarfed by ancient, rumbling appliances. The hiccoughing fridge and the stuttering stove were the only conversation as the clock tick-tocked off more minutes. Both women sat, unflinching, in nature's spotlight, unable to meet the other's gaze. By and by, the aunt took a sip from her cup, then frowned and pushed it aside. She rose and returned with a tumbler of ice, into which she poured equal parts soda water and Herbsaint. Taking a long draw, she refilled the glass and held tightly to it as she spoke.

"My name's Carmeline," she said, "but most folks just calls me Lini. Now go on and tell me, please." Then she listened without interrupting, without stirring or taking her eyes off her hands that clenched the glass, while Rose summarized everything she had done and learned since the accident twelve days earlier. When she finished, they sat silently again. Finally, Lini downed her whole glass in one long draw, refilled it, and turned to Rose. "Why're you here? Why'd you go to all this trouble to find me?" Not accusatory, just inquiring.

Rose spoke tentatively, having anticipated the question yet unsure how the answer would be received. "I didn't want her family not to know what happened. I didn't want her just to disappear." She paused, but then pressed on. "That happened to me. My father, he disappeared. I know what it's like, and I couldn't let that happen to someone else."

Lini nodded. "Rosy never knew her daddy. He died before she was born."

Perplexed, Rose asked, "But wasn't she traveling to Tuscaloosa to find him?"

"To find his kin. She needed help for her mama, thought maybe they'd help her."

"Her mother …?"

"Her mama's name is Cilla," Lini said. She suddenly wanted this girl to know Rosy's story, needed her to know who her niece had been and what righteous motive had put her in that disastrous position on the road in Tuscaloosa. But she found it easier to talk around Rosy than about her. "Cilla got arrested in New Orleans, on down by the Superdome. But it weren't nothing she done, nothing deliberate. She got that manic-depressive disease, makes her do stuff that ain't her fault. When it come on her, she ain't in her right mind. It started when she was just a young'un, but it got right awful after Bubba died."

"Bubba ...?"

"My brother. Was three years older'n Cilla and me. We met Cilla when we all got sent to the same foster home—right awful place, but no matter. We had our share of fun, the three of us." At this memory, Lini finally smiled, briefly. "Cilla was so sweet on him, and he sure enough fancied her. After he died, she got the sickness real bad, got herself kicked outta one foster family after another, but we kept in touch all the same. By then we was like sisters. She the only family I got. And I hers. Hell, the whole reason she done moved on back to New Orleans from Tuscaloosa once she got herself pregnant with Rosy was on account of me being down there then. She took up housecleaning with me, but once I come up here and took up minding children I started trying to talk her into going to one of those cooking schools. She been talking about it of late, what with Rosy going off to college." Lini quieted at the mention of Rosy's name. Her voice cracked when she said, "Cilla been joking about how they'd be going to school together."

Rose wondered aloud if Lini knew what had become of Cilla since her arrest.

"Wish I knew," she replied. "I been hoping Rosy got some help and was busy tracking her mama down. I kept imagining maybe they'd just come walking on up my stoop one day, hand-in-hand like always." She brushed aside a tear.

"I heard they evacuated out the people left in and round the Superdome. Supposedly they bused them out of New Orleans and on down to Houston," Rose offered, wanting desperately to be helpful. "Surely in the past two weeks somebody realized she's sick. So even if she wound up in the criminal system at first, she probably got transferred to a psychiatric facility at some point. There can't be too many psychiatric hospitals in Houston, so I can't imagine she'll be too hard to find."

Lini didn't look relieved as Rose had hoped she might. She looked distraught and overwhelmed.

"Don't worry," Rose said. "I'll help you find her. We can track her down."

Lini stared at her uninvited guest for a long moment. *This girl didn't kill Rosy,* Lini reminded herself. *She was just the passenger. It was an accident. Don't hate her for something she didn't do. She could've just stayed away; didn't have to come here and own up to this.*

"You a good girl," Lini said, as much to herself as to Rose.

Rose lowered her gaze and shook her head. "You don't have to say that."

"I ain't gotta say nothing. But it's true." She paused. "And while you gotta know I sure enough appreciates your offer of help, finding Cilla's the least of our problems. They gonna be hospital bills, and legal bills, and—"

Rose interrupted her. "There's money," she said.

Lini's lips curved in an ironic smile; not mean, just resigned. It seemed to say: unless you've lived it, you can't understand. Then she spoke. "Not in this family. Not the kinda money that'll fix this kinda mess."

"Yes, actually. There is, now." Rose explained about the auto insurance, the wrongful-death payout awaiting her discovery of Rosy's next-of-kin. Cilla's inheritance.

As Lini listened, the implications of the news this girl had brought and laid across her threshold slowly dawned on her: Rosy's death would kill Cilla, and yet it would also be what saved her. Rosy had, in fact, found the help she'd sought and, though she hadn't lived to see it, that help had still come through. It balanced anxiously on the edge of an aluminum chair, knees mere inches from Lini's under the kitchen table, alabaster palms clasped together in entreaty upon the checkered tablecloth.

Lini placed the tips of her fingers on the curve of Rose's knee and patted gently. "Well, okay," she said, as much to convince herself as her guest. "Well, okay." She nodded her head a few times, and though she withdrew her hand she offered Rose a genuine smile and these words of forgiveness: "Whether Rosy ever knowed it or not, maybe you is just what she was looking for all along."

Then she laughed. "I can just picture Rosy right now, smiling down on us from heaven, full up on the love of the Lord her Savior and the satisfaction of knowing that she done a good thing, that she done finally found at least a tiny little piece of what all she been after."

✤

LINI PUSHED CILLA'S JEWELRY box across the table and set it in front of Rose, who watched as she lifted the lid, as if opening her family's life to her visitor.

The floral communion in Jennifer Goldberg's kitchen had struck Rose as a funeral, but now she thought, *This is Rosy's wake, the celebration of her life.*

"Only two things got saved outta that house the morning Katrina hit—this box and a pair of sneakers—and through everything that done happened afterwards, Rosy managed to hold onto both of them."

Rose uncrossed her legs and pulled her feet up onto the edge of her chair. Crisscrossing her arms over her shins, she squeezed the shoes between her flexed toes and her fingers, and tucked her chin into the valley between her knees. Then, before she could talk herself out of the impulse to admit it, she whispered, "I'm wearing her shoes."

Lini dropped her eyes to Rose's feet. The shoes were dirty, covered in dust and splattered with brown spots. The soles were worn down. Yet Rose rolled the frazzled laces between her thumb and forefinger as if they were strings of pearls passed down through generations.

Seeing the skepticism written in the crease of Lini's forehead, she volunteered: "I don't know why. Can't explain it. But I can't take them off."

Weird, Lini thought. Everything about this was weird. Yet it wasn't wrong. She couldn't shake the sense of liking this girl despite the gruesome nature of their connection. "Well, it sure do put a personal spin on the idea of not judging someone till you done walked a mile in they shoes," she said.

Rose nodded. "That it does."

Lini pulled her chair around the corner of the table, closer to Rose, so they could explore Cilla's box together. Lini pushed the interred objects around with her index finger, digging toward the bottom, and came up with a photograph of a cluster of black women in what looked to be a restaurant kitchen. "That's Cilla," she said, "before Rosy was born. She worked in the kitchen of one of those sorority houses at the university." She peeked at the back of the picture. "Kappa Alpha Theta it says."

"The Theta house," Rose translated.

"You know it?"

"You can't live in Tuscaloosa and not. You know how it is."

Lini did. She needn't have ever set foot in a college classroom to know that Greeks held sway all through the South. She passed the picture to Rose and reached for something else.

"Look at this!" she said, a mix of surprise and awe. She grasped two ticket stubs. "I saw this movie with Cilla," she exclaimed, holding aloft the *Flashdance* stub, "at the Joy on Canal Street! And we done watched *Grease* least a hundred times together on the TV over the years. If my memory serves, Cilla's grandmother took her to see it at the drive-in over in Metairie." She thought for a minute. "The Airline. Ain't there no more: they done turned it into a grocery. But I remember her talking about it—how her grandmother kept leaning over to cover her ears every time Rizzo opened her mouth, and how they had to buy a PIC coil at the concession to keep away the mosquitoes. We got us mosquitoes round here big enough to swallow a chicken, don't you know!"

Rose laughed, thrilled with Lini's stories.

"Bubba done squirreled away some of his earnings one year and bought us the *Grease* album and matching T-shirts for Christmas, and we took to dancing round for hours on end, singing at the top of our lungs." She started to hum and sway with the memory, first her shoulders, then head and torso. Sotto voce, she sang the refrain of the title song.

In the pause between stanzas, Rose mimicked the interjecting trumpet staccato by tapping on the table and humming "Dunh duh, dunh duh, da dum." They sang the final stanza together.

"You know the song!" Lini exclaimed, merriment crinkling at the corners of her eyes.

Rose nodded. "My mother was a big John Travolta fan. I used to catch her singing that song sometimes, when she was busy doing something else and not paying attention. She'd always quit the minute I caught her, but I heard it often enough that I picked it up."

"Cilla's a real singer," Lini said. "And Rosy too, when she wanna be." At mention of Rosy, Lini became somber once more and altered her tense. "She had her mama's voice."

To occupy the silence that fell between them, Lini turned again to the box. She lifted out a Valentine with the words "Will you be mine?" written in an adolescent boy's hectic script; a mass card was folded inside. "This was my brother's," she said, pausing to peruse the prayer printed on the back side.

"May I?" Rose asked, gesturing toward the box. Lini nodded, so Rose reached in among the personal treasures. She lifted out a handful of dried flowers and set them on the table, not wanting to damage them as she rooted around inside. Next she retrieved a quartered piece of unlined paper that, unfolded, revealed a recipe for blackened catfish. It reminded her of the phonebook page she had on her, folded around Jennifer's business card. Sliding her fingers into her back pants pocket, she retrieved the paper, smoothed out the creases, and waited until Lini set her brother's mass card down before offering it to her.

"They found this on your niece the day she died," Rose said, "along with a business card belonging to Jennifer Goldberg, the woman who drove her up here from Gretna. This phonebook page is the only thing that still doesn't make any sense to me. I'm assuming there must be a name on there of somebody Rosy wanted to contact. Maybe you can figure it out?"

Lini took it and began scanning the names while Rose turned back to the box. Beneath an elementary sketch of a person—signed "Rosy, age 5" in what must have been Cilla's hand—she uncovered a woodcarving resting in a corner. It was a dragonfly, so intricately limned it could have been an entomologist's specimen. She recognized the design immediately: it matched the tattoo inked onto the underside of Rosy's right hand.

Prior to seeing those black lines etched on the dead girl's palm, an image she knew she would never shake, Rose had only ever associated dragonflies with her mother. Gertrude had dragonfly earrings and a dragonfly brooch. Dragonflies flitted across her bookmarks and her hand towels, hung in suncatcher form on the sliding glass door, swayed in the breeze from potted patio plants, and took wing in framed cross-stitches from the living room to the bedroom and back again. Gertrude not only liked the form of the insect; over Rose's objections, she insisted it had greater purpose in her life.

Gertrude believed the dragonfly was her spirit animal.

Not that long ago, in preparation for a semester packed with art and literature classes—including one titled "Creative Perspectives in Indigenous American Belief Systems"—Rose had checked out a library book on Native American animal medicine. She never would've thought to share the book with Gertrude; she didn't share any of her books with her mother, who'd never expressed an interest in them. But when, absorbed in her reading, she failed to heed her mother's third call for help carrying in the groceries, Gertrude finally huffed, "Hell's bells! What're you doing?"

"I'm trying to decide if I'm a deer or a salamander," Rose responded without so much as lifting her head from the pages.

"Why would you wanna be an animal?" Gertrude asked. "I've always said: give nature some space and it won't kill you."

"It's an assignment—to identify a totem, a spirit animal."

Gertrude bent to put the milk and the eggs in the fridge. "Well, don't be the salamander," she called out. "I don't like nothing that ain't got feet."

This objection struck Rose as so absurd it broke her concentration. She walked into the kitchen, stared down at her mother over the open fridge door, and said, "Salamanders have feet."

"Really?" Gertrude thought about that for a minute as she unwrapped a rectangle of butter and plopped it onto the tray. "Well, I guess you're right, but they're so low to the ground, all slithery and slimy like a snake. Don't be that."

"You want my totem to be a deer by default?"

"Go ahead and read to me what it says about the deer."

Rose read aloud:

> Deer carries the message of purity of purpose, of walking in the light to dispel shadows. Deer knows the work that it must do, and goes about that work with no fanfare and no need for personal glory or recognition. Nothing can cause Deer to change its path. Deer steps over roadblocks or goes around them; it will not be turned from its mission. There are no shadows about Deer—no ulterior motives, no hidden agendas, no lies or misrepresentations. Deer carries a strong and focused message, but with a gentle touch, and takes a quiet and powerful path toward completion of any task it has undertaken.

"Well there!" Gertrude pronounced. "That's you—quiet, powerful, focused. Now come on and focus on helping me get these groceries put away, please."

Rose watched her mother heave a bag onto the counter and sort the contents into separate piles for the pantry, the fruit bowl, and the refrigerator. She started flipping through the pages again, scanning the headings, until Gertrude lost patience. "For God's sake, don't just stand there like a cow at a new gate! Get moving!"

Rose slammed the book on the countertop. "You're a badger."

"I'm not a badger," Gertrude said while aligning the soup cans—the Campbell's in one row, the Progresso in another—in the overhead cupboard. "I don't even know a thing about badgers."

"Trust me, you're a badger!" Rose said.

"No I'm not. I'm a dragonfly."

"No. You may *like* dragonflies, but that doesn't mean you *are* a dragonfly. You're a badger."

"Read to me what it says about dragonflies, please."

"I—"

"Just read it!"

Rose belabored the process of flipping pages, sighed, and then read:

> Dragonfly teaches us how to combine emotion and rational thought. Dragonfly is a voracious predator, eating away at anything that is out of control. Dragonfly people come to swift conclusions and new insights that propel them into new ways of being and doing. Dragonfly chooses for itself what it is going to believe in and focus on, and then uses its strength to take action that will change current circumstances for the better. However, Dragonfly can also be flighty and carefree, symbolizing swiftness and activity. Dragonfly is, above all, a temporary being, forever morphing into light, toward joy.

"That's me," Gertrude said.

Rose stared at her mother, gape-mouthed. "'Forever morphing into light, toward joy'? That's *so* not you!"

Gertrude stared back, offended.

Rose grinned. "It's not a criticism, but come on … that's *not* who you are!" She glanced at the page again. "'Flighty and carefree'? *You?*"

Gertrude scooped up the toiletries and walked toward the bathroom. "Well thank you kindly, Billy Sunday," she said, effecting a quick curtsy to mock her daughter's imperious tone. "I used to could be that way."

"'Used to could' doesn't count, Madam Badger," Rose said as she returned to the couch with her book. "But I'll tell you what: if dragonfly decides to make a repeat appearance in your life someday, you be sure to lemme know. I'm sure I'd find her very fascinating!"

On only one occasion had Gertrude come close to exposing her younger, more carefree self to her daughter. She and Rose were standing under a bower of tin roses in the Birmingham Museum of Art, on opening night of the "Alabama Folk Art" exhibit. She had splurged on tickets as a holiday gift for her eighteen-year-old daughter and had been rewarded with a joyful, intimate evening together. As Rose studied a sculpture of recycled cans fashioned into rose blossoms, she'd asked, "Why'd you name me Rose?"

Without thinking, Gertrude had answered, "It was my favorite flower, once," and then, deciding it was time to disclose the truth, added, "It was your father's favorite flower, too."

She always knew that someday she'd have to introduce the subject of Rose's father to her. Every once in a while during her childhood, Rose would leaf through their photo album and carry it over to Gertrude, asking her to identify the people in the picture on the first page. "That's my friend Carol," Gertrude would say as she pointed at the now-unfamiliar faces, "and this is her boyfriend whose name I can't remember. This person here is your father, and that's me ..." But it never progressed past that point. Rose never asked the questions whose premise caused Gertrude's chest to tighten whenever she watched her daughter lift the album off the bookshelf, the questions she'd kept a step ahead of by moving them from neighborhood to neighborhood, apartment to apartment, all through Rose's youth. But Rose would be starting college soon, and her sequestering would end. She would meet people, they'd talk; things would eventually get said. And knowing Rose, she'd wind up mad at her mother for letting the truth broadside her. So, despite her instinct to avoid unpleasantness, to overcome her emotions by exercising control control control, Gertrude had turned to Rose under the hot glare of the spotlights and initiated the unraveling of her daughter's life story with the statement, "It was your father's favorite flower, too."

But then the gallery lights went out. Three quick flicks to clear the rooms, a museum docent directing them to the exit, the brief reprieve only making it worse for her because it gave Gertrude time to think, to wonder: *Where to start?* She wound up so rattled that, for the first time ever, she forgot where she'd parked the car.

It took them a while to find it, settle in, separate from the crowd of vehicles jammed at the lot exit and hit a steady sixty miles per hour on the freeway, and by the time she finally turned to Rose and said, "There's something I need to tell you," Rose was already asleep, curled against the door with her feet on the dash, a thin line of drool oozing slowly from lips to chin.

She told Rose anyway, for practice, while her daughter dozed. Told her how she and Roger met in a high school Home Ec class that he—two years her senior—was auditing, short one liberal-art credit for graduation in a roster otherwise packed with AP physics and calculus and macroeconomics. He'd have aced the class had he slept right through it. Bored out of his mind, he sat in the seat behind her, cracking more knuckles in his fingers than could possibly exist, until she turned, cupped her hand over his, and said, "You're a distraction." And he had been every day after, up to and including the day the condom broke and the line appeared on the stick and he did what good manners dictate he do. They moved into a tiny apartment while all her friends were moving into dorms. It wasn't the life either of them expected, but she'd been happy anyway. Distracted by happiness. Flighty and carefree.

She'd wanted dragonflies everywhere: painted along the top of the wall in the bedroom nook where they tucked the crib they bought in her second trimester, embroidered onto the crib's bumper, ironed onto the onesies that lay in wait, dancing from the mobile in the corner where the baby's head would rest. Gertrude painted, embroidered, ironed. Roger crafted. Always secretive about his artistic work, he'd huddled in the late-night hours over his tools while she slept, though she'd sneaked peeks at his progress after he left for class in the mornings. Delighted with the dainty designs he carved, she especially thrilled to the ornament on which he'd etched the words "You are my heart" across the back. It made her smile whenever she held it, and she'd whisper, as if he were there to hear, "Yes I am," before returning it to his art box.

When Roger hung the dragonfly mobile over the crib, sans the inscribed piece, she said nothing; to do so would have exposed her as a snoop. Instead, she waited, sure it would come to her on some special date, as a birthday or holiday or shower gift, the missing piece reclaimed to make a perfect whole. But each of those days passed and, as they did, he became increasingly distant until the point she finally realized: *It's never coming. Not for the baby, not for me.*

So she followed him one day, conspicuous on campus with her bulge, hiding just off Colonial Drive in the shadow of the stadium, embarrassing herself. She only did it once; once was enough. Even before the phone call confirming his ultimate abandonment, she knew. And if she knew, then others had to know, too; Tuscaloosa is a small town. Beyond the Tide, ain't nothing so interesting as other people's business.

More than eighteen years later, putting away her grocery purchases, replacing the neatly cinched tube of toothpaste with a fresh one in her well-ordered bathroom, the echo of Rose's rebuke ringing in her ears—"You may *like* dragonflies, but that doesn't mean you *are* a dragonfly. That's *so* not you!"—Gertrude thought, *Oh, the things you don't know.* So yes, that element of her young self that had once been morphing into light, toward joy, that aspect was long dead. But with its death, the rest grew stronger.

> Dragonfly is a voracious predator, eating away at
> anything in life that is out of control. … Dragonfly
> always has the power to choose what it is going to
> believe in and focus on, and always has the power
> to take action of some sort that will help change
> current circumstances for the better.

After the horrific phone call, Gertrude decided just to let that other bit of information she'd witnessed while crouched behind a car in the alley behind the sorority house melt away. Hadn't considered the implications for almost two decades. Things ended badly enough without *that*, too. But over the years she came to realize that someday the truth would find its way free. The whole truth. Which is why she'd decided to capitalize on that intimate moment at the museum and toss a crumb to her adult child: "It was your father's favorite flower, too." But then Rose never followed the trail as she was supposed to; instead, she fell asleep in the car. Gertrude considered shaking her awake as they drove home from the museum that January eve to make her listen. She even reached toward Rose's shoulder to jostle her out of her slumber, but retracted her hand at the last minute.

What point in disturbing her peace? she thought. *I have all the time in the world to tell her.*

><

ROSE RAN HER FINGERS lightly over the dragonfly as she lifted it out of Cilla's jewelry box, admiring the craftsmanship and marveling at the depth of love and care it would take to create such an intricate thing. No larger than a silver dollar, the artisan had captured every detail in raised wooden relief—the swirls that wove through the parchment wings, the flinty antennae, a bevy of stars flickering off the end of the tail. Her fingertips took in every raised edge, including the markings on the back, and she was about to turn it over when Lini gasped.

"'Scuse me," Lini said, reaching under Rose's hands to retrieve a folded square of newsprint from the box. She unfurled it and rested it atop the phonebook page she'd been scanning, eyes close to the fine print, looking first at the name on the news sheet, then comparing it to the names on the torn-out page Rosy had pilfered from the Tuscaloosa phonebook. "Well, I'll be goddamned," Lini said. She turned her attention back to the notice cut from *The Tuscaloosa News*, dated Friday, January 2, 1987, and skimmed it. Lini'd been there on the day Cilla clipped it out, folded it, and tucked it into her jewelry box more than eighteen years ago. She had, in fact, been the one to root through the dumpster in the parking lot to find the days-old paper after Cilla's phone call on Monday, January 5, when she'd rushed up to Tuscaloosa from New Orleans to be by her side. After spending the holiday break nursing the flu compounded by morning sickness, Cilla had gone to the sorority house to help prep it for the influx of returning students only to discover the house staff all agog over the news that one of their houseboys had jumped from Denny Chimes on New Year's Day. The obituary didn't say anything about the manner of death other than that he fell, on campus. It didn't describe the scene at the foot of the tower, still roped off the next week, still stained with blood. And it certainly didn't say why he did it, though Cilla always forgave him the impulse: a pregnant black mistress, a pregnant white wife.

"Well, I'll be goddamned," Lini repeated. "She done found him. Right here," she said, laying the list of names and phone numbers, Afshore through Allen, face-up on the table, running her finger halfway down the page. "This is who she was looking for! It's her daddy's name! Well, can't be him, of course, him being dead for near nineteen years now. But maybe it's his father, or his brother."

Rose dropped the dragonfly and leaned over Lini's shoulder. "Who? Where?"

"Right here," Lini said, pointing at G. & R. Aikens...........(205) 348-9223. "R. Aikens. That's her daddy's name. I wonder who the G. is?" In her surprise, she kept folding time back on itself, at one moment recognizing that a dead man wouldn't still be listed in a phone book all these years later, and yet, in the next, reacting as if perhaps he were. "Maybe G. Aikens is the wife, or his mother?"

Rose didn't understand Lini's question. "Yes," she said, "she's my mother."

Lini kept her finger on the listing, but turned with a puzzled look to Rose. "Hmm? Whatcha mean?"

"G. Aikens," Rose said, placing her own finger next to Lini's, tapping the name. "Gertrude Aikens. That's my mother."

Lini glanced at the name, then back at Rose, utterly perplexed. "You know them? You know the Aikens folks?"

"I *am* the Aikens folks," Rose explained. "That's me, R. Aikens. I'm Rose Aikens."

"No, honey," Lini insisted, not yet understanding. "That R. stands for Roger Aikens." In her surprise and confusion she compressed time again, brought a dead man back to life momentarily, swapping 2005 for 1987.

Rose looked at the listing again, as if, perhaps, she'd misread something. Then she lifted her eyes to Lini and recited the phone number from heart. "See?" she insisted. "It's my number. It's me. *I'm* R. Aikens." Then she paused, eyes shifting to the side, bent on recapturing a thread she hadn't grasped at first. The name, so infrequently spoken, took a minute or so to sink in. When she finally made the connection, she snatched her hand from the page and flinched in her seat.

Lini's face, too, began to change, though not as swiftly.

"You said Roger Aikens," Rose prodded.

"Yes."

"Who's Roger Aikens to you?"

"He's Rosy's daddy, hon."

Rose gasped. "No he's not! He's *my* father!"

Jaw set, eyes afire, determined stare ... finally, Lini figured it out. The girl looked just like him. "Holy shit," she whispered, more like a prayer than a curse. She barely breathed the words: "You're the other one." Lifting the newsprint out of her lap, she laid it before Rose, her hand covering the text, pointing at the photograph.

Jaw set, eyes afire, determined stare: Rose saw herself in him. Everything but the ears; she had her mother's dainty ears, but in all other ways she was her father's child, right down to the freckles dancing across the bridges of their noses. She stared down at the man's face and harkened back to her mother's photo album, the one on the shelf in the living room of the home they'd shared together. This same man appeared in their book, in a single picture on the first page, next to a woman Gertrude insisted was her own young self but whom Rose could never connect with the mother she knew.

"I don't understand," she said in a tremulous voice.

Lini spoke slowly, emphasizing every word. "You say Roger Aikens is your daddy, right?" Rose nodded numbly. "Well, this is Roger Aikens," she said, patting the newsprint photo. "And this man, in the picture, this is Rosy's daddy."

Rose looked again at the man who looked like her, the father of the girl whose history she'd been chasing, the father of the girl her mother killed.

"But you said her father's dead," Rose whispered.

Lini lifted her hand from the newsprint and rested it on Rose's shoulder, rubbing ever so softly as she gestured toward the words with a barely perceptible thrust of her chin.

The Tuscaloosa News
OBITUARIES
Friday, January 2, 1987

Roger Allen Aikens
TUSCALOOSA – Roger Allen Aikens, age 20, of Tuscaloosa, died January 1, 1987, from injuries sustained in a fall on the University of Alabama campus where he was a junior majoring in biology. Graveside services will be held at 11 a.m. Saturday at Evergreen Cemetery with Tuscaloosa Memorial Chapel Funeral Home directing.

An excellent student, Roger made the President's List during each collegiate semester and recently received notice of early-acceptance to the School of Medicine at the University of Alabama at Birmingham. He was nominated to "Who's Who in American High Schools" as well as "Who's Who in American Colleges and Universities." In addition to his academic studies, Roger was a member of Phi Beta Kappa honor society, volunteered in the disaster services division of the American Red Cross, managed the campus Subway restaurant, was an on-call intake coordinator at the Indian River Mental Health Center on weekends, and served as a houseboy at the Kappa Alpha Theta sorority house. Additionally, for the past three years, he worked summers as a counselor at Camp ASCCA (Alabama Special Camp for Children and Adults) serving those with intellectual and physical disabilities.

Pallbearers will be family members Michael and Randall Aikens, along with the executive officers of Phi Beta Kappa honor society: Sam Shifton, Collin Ruel, Ben Schaeffer, and Kyle Burns.

Survivors include his parents, Michael and Faye Aikens; younger brother, Randall Aikens; wife of five months, Gertrude Chiles Aikens; and their unborn child.

In lieu of flowers, the family requests that donations be made to the American Red Cross Disaster Relief Fund.

EPILOGUE

ON SATURDAY, SEPTEMBER 17, 2005, Rose arrived in Houston to claim the woman who was not her mother, but her sister's mother; her father's lover. Not stranger, not blood. But somehow hers.

As Rose suspected, it had been easy enough to locate Cilla. Three quick calls from Lini's kitchen and they'd found her in the short-term inpatient unit at the University of Texas Harris County Psychiatric Center. Well-medicated, stable. Held pending the posting of bail and release to anyone willing to sign off as her legal guardian while her case progressed through the system.

Lini stayed in Alexandria, bound to her young charges, exhausted, too, from the intervening two days during which she'd spent long hours on the phone, consoling Cilla, who hunkered in an empty nurse's cubby, head bent to desk, handset stained with salty residue, listening to every detail of her daughter's death, over and over, and of the girl who'd come to deliver the news. "Tell me again," Cilla begged, "why she came looking for us. Tell me again how she looked when ..." and Lini would start over, from the beginning, describing the look on Rose's face when she opened the door, the way Rose fingered the shoelaces while she talked, how

Rose had recognized the dragonfly the minute she saw it as a match to the image on Rosy's palm.

While Lini and Cilla talked, Rose spent those two days wandering Alexandria, waiting for word from Lini that she could leave for Houston, that Cilla was prepared to receive her. As she meandered around the town, killing time, she came upon a story that intrigued her. A tour guide at the St. Francis Xavier Cathedral wove the tale, nonchalantly, into his spiel, part of the history of the structure. It had been built in 1834 and was left standing thirty years later during the Civil War when the Union Army burned every other structure in Alexandria to the ground, save a few homes owned by friends of General Sherman. The destructive fire squad had marched to the church, traversed the front steps, raised high their torches, but there, barring the door, stood a shotgun-wielding bishop who turned his weapon upon them and ordered them back. That lone man's effort saved the edifice from extinction.

I want to be like that bishop, Rose thought, which is why she refused Mac's repeated entreaties to join her on this last leg of her journey. Somehow this web of women had become her storm shelter, her makeshift family, and if any part of it were to be salvaged she knew she needed to do it alone. Still, once she arrived in Houston and stood peering through the front doors of the psychiatric center—watching the metal gates open and close around incoming visitors, listening to the buzzers sound permission to pass from one hall to the next—she couldn't help but wonder: *Who am I, really? Am I the bishop, protecting what's sacred? Or am I the destroyer, set to raze this poor woman's world?*

The question led her to retract her hand from the door handle and reach for her cell phone. Mac answered before the second ring, an allegiance that still struck her as a most remarkable thing. "I'm scared," she said, standing on the landing, staring in from outside the locked glass doors of the asylum.

"In my line of work, you see a whole lotta bad stuff," he said. "But if you're lucky, you get to see a lotta good stuff, too. Every once in a while, you even get to see something heroic." He paused.

"Now you listen to me, cuz it's the God's honest truth. Outta everything I done seen over the years, what you're about to do is the most courageous thing I've ever witnessed."

Rose's eyes filled, and she whispered, "I don't feel very courageous."

"You don't have to feel it to be it." Then he walked her through everything she might experience inside—the forms to sign, the permission to waive, the guard posts to pass—just as he had walked her through the experience in the Natchez ER four days earlier. He ended by reminding her, "If you need me, I'm right here. No further'n a phone call away."

With that, she pocketed the phone, squared her shoulders, and disappeared inside the building.

CILLA APPROACHED ROSE FROM a side hall, giving herself a whole thirty feet to steal upon the girl unnoticed.

"Consider all your possible feelings ahead of time," the psychiatrist had insisted earlier that morning, and Cilla thought she had done so, listing them out and talking them through. Hatred and rage for this person who played a part in the death of her child. Jealousy and spite that one girl should live while the other died. Guilt and remorse that her own failings landed Rosy on that road, in that town. Gratitude. Suspicion. Fury. Heartbreak. Together, she and her doctor had determined how to deal with each and every one.

But then something else entirely happened. Not that the anger or the pain melted away, nothing so trite, but instead something unintended sprouted. As Cilla strode toward Rose, unnoticed, the girl suddenly clasped her hands under her chin and twisted them, and she was Roger! His arms twined just like that, like a pale pretzel, face-to-face with Cilla under an awning at the Northport craft fair—thirty minutes after their accidental meeting, fifteen minutes after she fell in love—as he described the feel of basswood surrendering to his skew chisel, as he pressed his chin upon his fingers until they cracked, as he asked if she'd like to see his own woodcarvings and betrayed his nerves with every *pop! pop! pop!* of his knuckles.

Twenty feet out and the girl began bending her fingers in half, sideways, as Cilla had only ever seen Rosy do, and she almost admonished aloud, "You're gonna break a finger!" which roused the sound of Rosy's laughter for her, sweet safe child sound, accompanied by the memory of Rosy's constant retort: "No, Mama, it's in my blood. My fingers were made to bend this way!"

Ten feet out and the girl's foot moved—in the shoe Cilla bought at the Payless on Canal Street, in the shoe she last saw Rosy tie onto her own foot—a slow circle on pointed toe, the way they all moved when anxious: Rosy shyly introducing herself to someone new, eyes down then raised, radiant smile spreading; Roger tickling Cilla's rib cage with his toe as they lay naked, rolling his ankle, eyes down then raised, wondering aloud, "What would you say if I told you I loved you?"

Standing beside the girl, staring down on the same freckles that danced across the nose of the toddler who'd once run with joy into her arms, looking into the face that once hovered over hers in a clover field by the dam, every other emotion yielded to a flood of relief.

Oh, thank God, Cilla thought, *there's a piece of them still alive!*

And in a sure, steady voice, she said, "Welcome, child," as she cupped her hand around Rose's chin, dark dragonfly to blushing cheek, and lifted her face. Into light, toward some unexpected measure of joy.

About Ellen Urbani

ELLEN URBANI IS THE AUTHOR of *Landfall* (2015, Forest Avenue Press), a work of contemporary historical fiction, and the memoir *When I Was Elena* (2006, The Permanent Press; a BookSense Notable selection). She has a bachelor's degree from the University of Alabama and a master's degree from Marylhurst University. Her writing has appeared in *The New York Times* and numerous anthologies, and has been widely excerpted. She's reviewed books for *The Oregonian*, served as a federal disaster/trauma specialist, and has lectured nationally on this topic. Her work has been profiled in the Oscar-qualified documentary film *Paint Me A Future*. A Southern expat now residing in Oregon, her pets will always be *dawgs* and her truest allegiance will always reside with the Crimson Tide.

Acknowledgments

WITH THANKS,

To my in-process readers, who urged me on and held me accountable: Jaci Urbani, Ann Goschke, Junean Grady, Diana Blake-Boon, Janice Kaminsky, Wendy Lawton, Julie Laut, and Katie Urbani. Your generosity is so very much appreciated.

To Ann and Doug Goschke, who sheltered this author in the most beneficent of ways—with support from both the heart and the checkbook, which helped keep a roof over my head while I made it happen.

To Martin and Judith Shepard who gave *Elena* a home, and me a new focus.

To Soapstone for a room of my own; the Oregon Writers Colony for use of the Colonyhouse; the boys of beach week (James Bernard Frost, Jeffrey Selin, and Brad Bortnem) for graciously letting a girl crash their party; and to the sharpest damn writers' group cohorts around for making me better than I'd have been without you: Kerry Cohen, Gigi Rosenberg, Katie Schneider, Jeffrey Selin, Ken Olsen, Michael Lewis Guerra, Yuvi Zalkow, Greg Robillard, Liz Prato, Tracy Burkholder, Jason Sandefur, and Merilee Karr.

To Laura Stanfill and Forest Avenue Press for a whole host of things—the title, the tightening, the chance—but most of all for loving Rose and Rosy as much as I do and for providing them, at long last, with a resting place. And with her, Gigi Little, who crafted a magical cover that I can only hope my words are worthy of; Phyllis Hatfield and Sharon Eldridge, who with well-bred Southern manners whipped my words into shape while leaving me charmed; Mary Bisbee-Beek, whose championing lifted us all to new heights; and Edee Lemonier, webmaster (and patient teacher) extraordinaire. One of these days, somewhere in the Pacific Northwest we all now call home, I'm determined to find us a joint where they make a right fine Southern biscuit and real sweet tea to wash it down with, and the chairs alongside mine at that table shall be reserved for you gals; peaches, all.

To the innumerable people who have lifted me up, nudged me along, or in some other way have made my journey more fruitful. Among them Stephanie Kallos; Sheri Fink; Timberly Marek; Sara Grady; Rene Denfeld; Ron Thibodeaux; Elissa Ward; Pat Conroy; Mark Suchomel and Jeff Tegge of Perseus Books Group; John Coyne of Peace Corps Worldwide; Dawn Stuart and Haley Kastner of Books in Common; the women of the Delta Omicron chapter of Kappa Alpha Theta; and Richard Pine, Eliza Rothstein, and the generous team at InkWell Management.

To my beautiful friends who carried me, over and over again, through the tortuous times. The tip of that iceberg: Wendy Lawton, my buoy; Cheryl Strayed, my compass; Julie Laut, my Jiminy; Jaci and Gabrielle Urbani, my roots; and Jennifer Greenberg, aka Jennifer Goldberg, who is every bit the savior I made her out to be.

To Clara, who grew from baby to toddler, and Elijah, who grew from toddler to child, during this process. Who—when I finished typing the last word of the original draft at 5:49 p.m. on Sunday, November 9, 2008—still needed to be fed, and bathed, and tucked into bed. Who reminded me that writing a book is just writing a book; it isn't love, it isn't purpose, it isn't what matters most at the end of the day.

And to Steve, the husband I adore, who has enriched and expanded my life's story beyond measure or imagining.

References

ALTHOUGH THIS BOOK IS a work of fiction, about invented main characters, I endeavored to cleave as closely as possible to the truth of the events surrounding Hurricane Katrina and the documented aftereffects. Doing so required a voluminous amount of research: I read countless articles in print and online; spoke to storm survivors, first responders, reconstruction workers; watched documentaries, interviews, televised newscasts; and culled memories from my personal experience as a citizen of the South. While I have attempted to accurately portray the essence of the time and place, it would not be possible for one person to summarize with authority the environmental, psychological, logistical, political and/or personal impact of a tragedy as vast as Hurricane Katrina. As such, I have not attempted to do so, and instead have pulled together only those resources necessary to tell the most honest fictional story I could muster. There is only one liberty I knowingly took with actual events. The jail to which Cilla is escorted from the Superdome on Wednesday, August 31, in *Landfall* was not actually erected until the following weekend—Saturday, September 3—and did not receive large numbers of detainees until Monday, September 5. With that exception, it operated as described herein.

The dialog between the main characters in the book is all invented. However, in places there are quotes from named sources who are not recurring characters in the story. In those cases, those quotes are from real people, quoted directly, in published—and public—sources. You will find this happens most frequently in Chapters X, XI, and XII, all of which refer to the events on the Crescent City Connection. I found the following resources most helpful in reconstructing that event in particular:

cbsnews.com/stories/2005/12/15/60minutes/main1129440.shtml

npr.org/templates/story/story.php?storyId=4855611

cjr.org/behind_the_news/what_happened_and_why_at_the_g.php

en.wikipedia.org/wiki/Gretna,_Louisiana

sptimes.com/2005/09/17/Worldandnation/Neighboring_town_deni.shtml

articles.latimes.com/2005/sep/16/nation/na-gretna16

socialistworker.org/2005-2/556/556_04_RealHeroes.shtml

In the immediate aftermath of the storm, there were chronic and often escalating reports of violence and civil unrest in New Orleans. Based on media reports, people inside *and* outside the city were of the opinion that the town had quickly devolved into a banana republic. While there were certainly acts of violence, looting, and the general consternation that accompanies any disastrous event, in hindsight it came to be determined that by and large the citizens of New Orleans behaved with much greater grace and respect than had been initially reported. Much of the confusion, it seems, came from panicked citizens and rescuers themselves, who, in the wake of significant trauma, understandably responded in emotive ways to conjecture, rumor, and hearsay. Unfortunately, in their distress, they sometimes transmitted inaccurate information to the media, which was then widely dispersed, further obscuring the truth. Because I was writing a story set in the immediate aftermath of the storm—when emotions were high and before misstatements and misperceptions regarding violence were clarified and debunked—I portrayed *Landfall*'s characters reacting *in the moment* to those initial rumors and reports. Inclusion of such responses in the book is not meant to imply that the acts of violence were eventually proven to be true. The *Times-Picayune* staff is to be credited for their coverage of the storm and its aftermath; their reportage and the following sources should help clarify outcomes and appraise the truth regarding reports of violence:

nytimes.com/2010/08/27/us/27racial.html?pagewanted=all&_r=0

seattletimes.com/html/nationworld/2002520986_ katmyth26.html

propublica.org/nola/story/nopd-order-to-shoot-looters-hurricane-katrina/

pulitzer.org/archives/7075
pulitzer.org/archives/7076
pulitzer.org/archives/7087

As for other resources, I used the following so extensively or specifically that I feel obliged to name them:

Chapter II: The "Urgent Weather Message" read in the newscast cites the full and actual text issued by the National Weather Service/New Orleans, Louisiana, on August 28, 2005, at 10:11 a.m.

Chapter XII: Powers, J. *Pooh's Little Instruction Book.* New York: Dutton Children's Books, 1995.

Chapter XIII: The quote Rosy cites, that Cilla wrote on a piece of paper—"Let me not pray to be sheltered from dangers, but to be fearless in facing them. Let me not beg for the stilling of my pain, but for the heart to conquer it"—is attributed to Rabindranath Tagore.

To all of these people and sources, I owe a debt of gratitude. Their hard work elevated mine.

– E.U.

READERS' GUIDE

*This guide is intended to augment your experience of
Ellen Urbani's* Landfall *by helping you understand
the events of Hurricane Katrina and the author's passion
for this story, while providing you with a taste of the
culture of the South—New Orleans, in particular. May
you enjoy and benefit from sharing this story and its
implications with those around you.*

*To invite Ellen Urbani to call in to your next book
club event, use the contact form at ellenurbani.com.*

Questions for Discussion / 296

Enhance Your Book Club Experience / 298

Recommended Reading / 300

Questions for Discussion

1. *Landfall* is set in the wake of Hurricane Katrina, which wreaked havoc on the southern United States in late August 2005. At that time, it was considered the greatest environmental disaster in U.S. history. The book also reflects on another monumental disaster of the same generation: 9/11. How did linking the two events augment or change your understanding of the characters' experiences?

2. Gertrude and her daughter Rose appear to be a couple when first introduced. What effect does this sleight of hand have? Where else in the novel did you find yourself needing to adjust your preconceived notions?

3. The author has written from the perspectives of women whose races and/or cultures differ dramatically from her own. Do the voices feel authentically rendered to you? Why or why not?

4. In the cooler scene, Rosy makes a harrowing split-second choice in an effort to save her mother's life. Did you think better or worse of her after reading that passage? In what other ways do characters throughout the book make terrible mistakes, but with the best of intentions? How do you judge them?

6. For Rose, the Gee's Bend quilts are the highlight of the Alabama Folk Art exhibit at the Birmingham Museum of Art. The quilts are described as "resistance pieces, the spirit of Harriet Powers turned indignant." Do you believe that common folk, performing an everyday task, can find themselves players in, or symbols of, a resistance movement? If so, what other examples of this phenomenon can you think of in the last century?

7. When considering how to ride out the storm, Cilla remarks, "Ain't no Red Cross shelters round here. Oh, no. They don't come to New Orleans. They everywhere else, but not New Orleans!" However, the American Red Cross's decision not to immediately set up aid stations in the city was complex and complicated by

numerous external factors outside of Cilla's personal experience. In what other ways does *Landfall* highlight the manner in which individuals' misperceptions interfere with their ability to access help or make a genuine connection with others?

8. The text is full of regionalisms and vernacular common to Alabamians and New Orleanians. Did this endear or frustrate you? Of the colloquialisms, are there any that stood out as your favorites?

9. Of the four main characters—Rosy, Cilla, Rose, Gertrude—who would you want to invite into your world and embrace as a friend?

10. *Landfall* is full of characters who are tightly bound to one another, but also to the things they've acquired. Which objects helped move the plot forward? Do you believe possessions might have more or less import in the lives of the impoverished or disenfranchised? In a natural disaster, what would you hope carry away with you from your home, and why?

11. The incident on the Crescent City Connection is detailed as if it is an Op-Ed column. How does transmitting that information in article form work differently than if it had been conveyed through a scene?

12. *Landfall* contains numerous references to racial tensions in the South. Most of these observations are made by Rose, the young white girl, who seems more attuned to racial issues than does her African American counterpart, Rosy. Why do you think this is?

13. There is a significant plot twist near the end of the book. Looking back, are you able to identify clues and allusions to the truth scattered throughout the text? If so, how did your personal perceptions, prejudices, and assumptions lead you to miss (or catch) those clues along the way? Can you identify real-life examples—either personal or historical—when one person's misinterpretation of facts resulted in a significant misconstruing of reality?

ENHANCE YOUR
BOOK CLUB EXPERIENCE

GET THE LAY OF the land. Acquaint yourselves with maps of the city of New Orleans, which has a rich and fascinating neighborhood and parish history. The interactive map graphic by *The Times-Picayune* staff artist Dan Swenson makes understanding the levee breaches and their localized impact much simpler. It can be found at: nola.com/katrina/graphics/flashflood.swf.

WATCH A FILM TOGETHER. Spike Lee crafted two much-lauded documentaries in the wake of Katrina. The first, *When the Levees Broke: A Requiem in Four Acts*, was released a year after the storm and features the true stories of New Orleans residents who survived the disaster. The second, *If God Is Willing and da Creek Don't Rise*, is a follow-up to the first film, and came out on the fifth anniversary of the storm.

LITERATURE IS ONLY ONE form of art; reading together, and then translating your experience into another medium, may be a fun challenge. Grandma Moses enjoyed embroidery before she took up painting late in life. Embroidery and needlework kits featuring her artwork are available online, as are kits for quilting in the style of the women of Gee's Bend. If you're more of an art observer than an art maker, check to see if there are local folk art festivals and plan to go together, like Cilla, Rose, and Roger all did.

CONSIDER RAISING FUNDS OR donating to an organization involved in ongoing reconstruction efforts. Choose one that best aligns with your politics and beliefs, or check out these three noteworthy nonprofits:

Common Ground Relief (commongroundrelief.org): headquartered in the Lower Ninth Ward, runs numerous programs ranging from new home construction to wetlands restoration and community education.

Rebuilding Together New Orleans (rtno.org/about-us): focuses on the total renovation and rebuilding of storm-damaged homes in order to allow the urban poor to return to their own properties.

Habitat for Humanity – New Orleans Area (habitat-nola. org): NOAHH has built hundreds of homes in Orleans, Jefferson, St. Bernard, and Plaquemines Parishes, and spearheaded The Musicians' Village (www.nolamusiciansvillage.org), conceived by Harry Connick Jr. and Branford Marsalis, which consists of seventy-two single-family homes for New Orleans musicians displaced by Hurricane Katrina.

DISCUSS THE BOOK OVER dinner. Cajun and Creole cooking traditions are rich with flavor and history. On the author's website, ellenurbani.com, you will find recipes for the dishes Cilla was most famous for, including gumbo, jambalaya, and shrimp étouffée. You'll also find the recipe for Rose's Praline Pecans that she left in the mailbox for the postman every Christmas. Or consider ordering in some down-home goodness from these purveyors, who will ship right to your door:

Alabama's Dreamland Bar-B-Que is best known for their ribs. Better to eat them while tailgating at Bryant-Denny Stadium in anticipation of a Bama win, but your dining room will do in a pinch.

Café du Monde is an original coffee stand that still operates from Decatur Street in New Orleans French Market. They'll ship their pastry mixes to you, so with a bit of water you can pass yourself off as a tried-and-true Louisiana chef. Choose from Mardi Gras King Cakes or their quintessential specialty: beignets. Don't forget to get some chicory coffee to pair with your treats.

Who wants to read about a hurricane without a Hurricane in hand? **Pat O'Brien's** signature drink mix, the Hurricane, famous the world over, will surely spike some fun, and they'll even send you the proper glasses in which to serve your libations.

LISTEN TO THE SOUNDS of the South over that dinner you're ing to make for your book group. At ellenurbani.com, you'll f four playlists sure to have you reaching for a harmonica: cl New Orleans songs, songs about Alabama, quintessential m the South, and songs cited in *Landfall.*

Recommended Reading

If you'd like to know more about Hurricane Katrina and its effect on the people of the South—not just New Orleans, but all of Louisiana, Mississippi, and the Gulf Coast—you may appreciate these works by other authors:

FICTION

Salvage the Bones, by Jesmyn Ward (National Book Award winner)
Beneath a Meth Moon, by Jacqueline Woodson (young adult)
City of Refuge, by Tom Piazza
Zane and the Hurricane: A Story of Katrina by Rodman Philbrick (middle grade)

NONFICTION

The Great Deluge: Hurricane Katrina, New Orleans, and the Mississippi Gulf Coast by Douglas Brinkley
Do You Know What It Means to Miss New Orleans, edited by David and Bruce Rutledge (essay collection)
Zeitoun, by Dave Eggers
Five Days at Memorial, by Pulitzer Prize winner Sheri Fink
Beyond Katrina: A Meditation on the Mississippi Gulf Coast, by Pulitzer Prize winner Natasha Trethewey
Breach of Faith: Hurricane Katrina and the Near Death of a Great American City, by Pulitzer Prize winner Jeb Horne
Two Bobbies: A True Story of Hurricane Katrina, Friendship, and Survival by authors Kirby Larson and Mary Nethery and illustrator Jean Cassels (picture book)

GRAPHIC NOVEL

AD: New Orleans After the Deluge, by Josh Neufeld (nonfiction)

POETRY

Mourning Katrina: A Poetic Response to Tragedy, edited by Joanne V. Gabbin, as part of the Mourning Katrina National Writing Project at James Madison University
Blood Dazzler, by Patricia Smith